If You Want
to Make God Laugh

ALSO BY BIANCA MARAIS

Hum If You Don't Know the Words

If You Want to Make God Laugh

BIANCA MARAIS

G. P. Putnam's Sons

NEW YORK

PUTNAM
— EST. 1838 —

G. P. PUTNAM'S SONS
Publishers Since 1838
An imprint of Penguin Random House LLC
penguinrandomhouse.com

LIBRARY OF CONGRESS CATALOGING-IN-PUBLICATION DATA
Names: Marais, Bianca, author.
Title: If you want to make god laugh / Bianca Marais.
Description: New York: G. P. Putnam's Sons, 2019.
Identifiers: LCCN 2018052506| ISBN 9780735219311 (hardback) |
ISBN 9780735219328 (epub)
Subjects: LCSH: Apartheid—South Africa—Fiction. | South
Africa—History—1961-1994—Fiction. | South Africa—History—
Soweto Uprising, 1976—Fiction. | BISAC: FICTION / Family Life. | FICTION /
Family Life. | FICTION / Literary. | FICTION / Coming of Age. |
GSAFD: Christian fiction.
Classification: LCC PR9199.4.M3414 I3 2019 | DDC 813/.6—dc23
LC record available at https://lccn.loc.gov/2018052506
p.   cm.

International edition ISBN: 9780593085820

Printed in the United States of America
1   3   5   7   9   10   8   6   4   2

Book design by Francesca Belanger

For Poodle

*(Please forgive me for what I did to Sodom and Gomorrah.
You can't win 'em all but at least you got "orc" and "Faloolah.")*

If You Want
to Make God Laugh

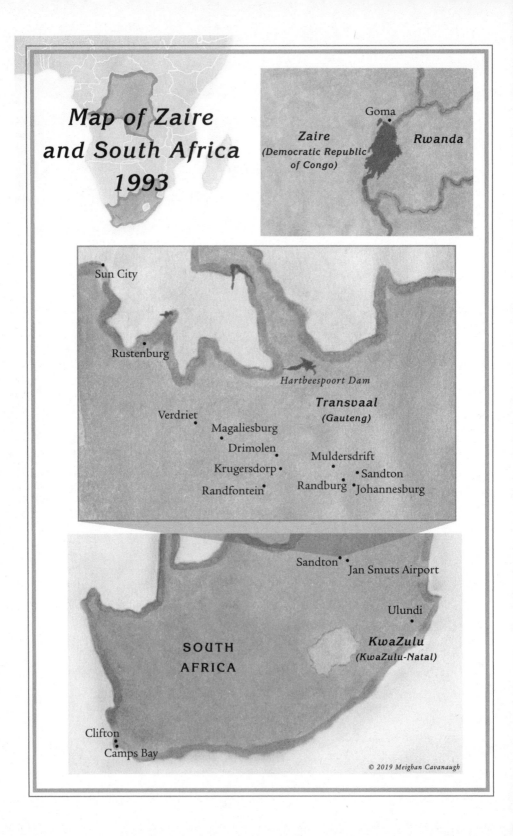

Map of Zaire and South Africa 1993

Zaire (Democratic Republic of Congo)

Goma

Rwanda

Sun City

Rustenburg

Hartbeespoort Dam

Transvaal (Gauteng)

Verdriet

Magaliesburg

Drimolen

Muldersdrift

Krugersdorp

Sandton

Randfontein

Randburg

Johannesburg

Sandton

Jan Smuts Airport

Ulundi

SOUTH AFRICA

KwaZulu (KwaZulu-Natal)

Clifton

Camps Bay

© 2019 Meighan Cavanaugh

CHAPTER ONE

Zodwa

✦

21 November 1993
Sterkfontein, Transvaal, South Africa

A thread of smoke snakes up into the cloudless sky and serves as Zodwa's compass needle. She trails it until the sandy path dips suddenly, revealing a squat hut nestled in the grassland below. A woman sits waiting at the threshold. She's hunched over like a question mark, her headdress of white beads partially obscuring her face. A leopard skin is draped over her shoulders and the sight of it reassures Zodwa; the gold-and-black-spotted pelt *ibhayi* signifies the *nyanga* is a healer of great power.

The woman chews tobacco, which she spits out when Zodwa reaches her. "What took you so long?" she gripes, rising up on arthritic knees.

"How did you know I was coming?" Zodwa herself hadn't known she'd be making the journey until the early hours of that morning.

"The ancestors told me." The *nyanga* holds out her palm.

Zodwa reaches into her bra and withdraws a few crumpled notes. They are everything she has. "How much will it be?"

The *nyanga*'s knobbly hand shoots out and snatches it all away before Zodwa can protest. She disappears into the gloom and beckons for Zodwa to follow. Inside, it looks like a regular

1

hut with its circular walls, thatch roof, and dung floor, but Zodwa knows it's imbued with the spirits of the clan members who have gone before; the *ndumba* is a sacred place.

The healer motions for Zodwa to sit on the floor. "How many years do you have, child?"

"I'm seventeen," Zodwa replies. "Almost eighteen." She knows she looks younger and blames it on her rounded cheekbones, which lend her face a childish quality.

The healer's eyes inspect Zodwa from head to toe and Zodwa flushes, knowing that the old woman disapproves. Her pleated black skirt is hemmed to just below her knees, but still it's too short for traditional wear. The white blouse is a fraction too tight, but this is because Zodwa has outgrown it, not out of choice.

The *nyanga* holds up a gourd. "*Undlela zimhlophe*," she explains before swallowing its contents. She limps to her mat and kneels down.

It's past midday and the powerful root has to be consumed on an empty stomach so that it can induce the lucid and prophetic dreams that will help her hear the ancestors' voices. The old woman must be hungry. Zodwa's hungry too, though not because she's been fasting. Her hunger isn't the temporary kind that will soon be satiated; it's the gnawing kind that takes up residence in a stomach that has been empty for too long. It's a hunger born of poverty.

The *nyanga* begins groaning while rocking back and forth. The smell of *impepho* burning saturates the air, and the sage fills Zodwa's lungs with every breath she takes, dulling her senses with its hypnotic scent. The hut, darkened and warm, reminds her of home. At least, the home she'd lived in with her grandmother in KwaZulu before she joined her mother in the sqatter camp earlier in the year.

Her grandmother had been reluctant, at first, to relinquish Zodwa to Leleti and considering everything that had happened, Zodwa couldn't blame her. Her *gogo* had lost her only son, Zodwa's father, to a mining accident in the City of Gold, and then Zodwa's eighteen-year-old brother, Dumisa, disappeared less than a year after leaving for Johannesburg when Zodwa was seven.

"Be very careful, my child," Zodwa's *gogo* had cautioned her before she left the village for the township. "Bad things happen in the city. Its gods are very hungry and must be appeased. Don't become one of the sacrifices made to it.

"You must study hard, *mzukulu wami*," her grandmother had continued. "You must be brave but do not try to be as brave as your brother was. If your light shines too bright, someone will always seek to extinguish it. And do not give in to temptations. The city makes girls forget their virtue and modesty. It makes them behave in wanton ways. Remember, my child, that a good bride price comes from respect."

Zodwa had tried to follow her *gogo*'s advice, she really had, but the township had awakened something in her. It was as if the city's electricity had jump-started her body, and no matter how much she tried to keep her thoughts pure, they simply wouldn't cooperate.

There will be no good *lobolo* now. There will be no bride price at all since no offer of marriage has come.

Zodwa's thoughts are interrupted by the *nyanga* rising from her place on the floor. The old woman winces as she stands up on stiff knees and shuffles over to where Zodwa sits.

Her voice is hoarse. "The *amadlozi* are angry with you."

It is what Zodwa most feared hearing. No one wants to incite the wrath of the ancestors. "Because of the baby?"

The old woman shoots Zodwa a shrewd look. "It is not the baby the ancestors speak of."

Zodwa hangs her head, the familiar shame slithering its way up her spine.

"What did you dream the last time you slept?" the healer asks.

It isn't difficult to answer, as the nightmare has stayed with Zodwa all day. "I dreamt I was being chased."

"By what?"

Zodwa shivers inwardly. "Two white owls. Their wingspan stretched across the sky, blocking out the sun."

The healer's frown deepens. "And then what happened?"

"I thought they were going to kill me, but it wasn't me they wanted."

"What then?"

"The baby. They snatched it from me and flew away."

The *nyanga* nods and sighs. "It is as the ancestors have said. You wage a war with yourself by following the wrong path. You have only yourself to blame that you are now expecting this child who will bring you even greater misery."

"What can I do?"

"About the baby . . . only you can decide." The *nyanga* shrugs. "I can give you herbs to try to take care of it. About the other matter . . . the ancestors say that you must walk the path that is intended for you. Only then will you find peace."

Zodwa can't think of that now. Any peace she could wish for in that regard would only follow a termination of her pregnancy, which is the more urgent of her problems. "I will take the herbs."

"It may already be too late." The *nyanga*'s face is inscrutable as she turns and hobbles to the table laid out with dozens of pots and baskets.

She moves assuredly between them, picking sprigs from some and roots from others, as she sets about making her infusion, adding water to a three-legged cast-iron pot and emptying the ingredients into it, before setting it over the coals in the middle of the room. Stirring it occasionally, she brings the mixture to a boil and then removes it, straining the liquid through a cloth.

"Drink," she says, handing Zodwa a gourd filled with an acrid-smelling brew.

Everything makes Zodwa nauseous these days but the concoction is especially vile. She struggles to drink it, gagging a few times and almost bringing it up.

When she's swallowed the last drop and wiped her mouth, the *nyanga* takes the gourd back. "Now we wait."

CHAPTER TWO

Delilah

✳

22 April 1994

Goma, Zaire

The letter that changed everything arrived as Xavier and I were coaxing the generator back to life after the power had gone out again. Considering that the orphanage housed more than two hundred children, the lack of electricity for lighting and heating was bad enough, but not being able to pump water out of the borehole was a potential crisis.

Everyone's nerves were already on edge after the plane carrying the Rwandan and Burundian presidents was shot down two weeks before. Thousands of Rwandans were fleeing for their lives, the Tutsis streaming across the border into Zaire. We were all on full alert and had to be ready to make a run for it if the Rwandan military sent incursions across the border. It seemed more and more likely that it would.

As it was, the generator was useless without fuel, every last drop of which had been poured into the Land Rovers' tanks in case we needed to evacuate. I'd had to siphon off some of it for the machine but the cantankerous beast was still refusing to accept the offering and start.

I looked to the horizon at the sun that would soon be setting. Xavier couldn't work in the dark, so there wasn't much time left. I was about to start sieving leftover sunflower oil through a sock, to serve as lubricant in case Xavier needed it, when I heard my name being called.

I turned to see Doctor grinning wildly and running at me while waving something in his hand. Everyone stepped back as he made his way through the playground. He was like Moses parting the Red Sea. "Granny! Granny!" he shouted.

That's how all the children naturally addressed anyone over forty and, being closer to sixty, I more than qualified. When I was much younger and starting out as an aid worker across the border, I'd been called "Mother." It had felt like a slap in the face to be named that, as if they were mocking me for my childless state, which of course they weren't. All those countries and missions later, after all the thousands of children I'd tended, I'd finally grown used to it.

As Doctor ran at me, I should have chided him for his recklessness around the machinery but I didn't. His joy at being alive was so pure that I found myself favoring him, even granting him amnesty from the rules all the others were expected to live by. My partiality for the boy wasn't solely based on his positive outlook on life; I'd delivered him five years before.

Despite having had no child-birthing training, I'd stepped in when all the other midwives had refused to help his HIV-positive mother, back when HIV was so rare that it was considered more black magic than a disease. His mother had gone into labor a few weeks premature after almost being stoned to death as she was chased from her village. I'd refused to allow her to go through another ordeal alone.

Coached over satellite telephone by a Doctors Without Borders obstetrician, I'd kitted up in a makeshift kind of hazmat suit before helping bring Doctor into the world. We were lucky. Despite his mother's health issues, it had been a textbook birth.

She'd cradled him to her chest for an hour afterward, too weak to sit up but too fierce to allow me to take him from her. She held him while I held her, my gloved hand over her bare one, which was resting on his scrawny buttocks.

"He will be a great man, this one," she said, smiling weakly. "I name him Doctor." It was the highest honor she could think to bestow on him. It depressed me, given that the medical profession had been able to do nothing for her.

I'd often wondered since then if a child could be inoculated in the womb against the horror of the world through the power of its mother's love; if that love could infuse joy into a child even when her presence couldn't. God knows, if ever there was a woman who wanted to live to raise her child, who'd fought like a hellion just so that he could be born, it was she. She told me it was because he was the only thing in her life that was truly hers.

"I have a letter for you, Granny," Doctor now said, smiling proudly as he handed the envelope across.

He was painfully thin and out of breath from the short sprint. Breathing should never sound that way. As though lungs are blades and air is something solid to be chopped up. Still, Doctor had lived three years longer than any of us had expected and he accepted his condition stoically.

"Thank you, Doctor. You've done a good job getting it to me," I said solemnly as I reached out and squeezed his shoulder. He beamed at the contact. "Could you put it in my pocket?" I asked, indicating my dirty hands and turning so he could tuck the envelope into the back of my trousers.

It was after midnight when Xavier and I finally parted ways, exhausted yet triumphant. The generator was running again.

Disaster had been staved off for another day. Seeking refuge in my room, I made my way to the narrow bed and lifted the mosquito net to sit on the cotton sheet I'd paid such an exorbitant price for.

The view from there was of my makeshift wardrobe, which consisted of a pole balanced between two columns of raised cinder blocks. The few items of clothing I owned were hung up while my empty rucksack sat propped in a corner of the room. Amelia, the UN aid coordinator, would've had a fit if she'd seen it, since we'd been given strict instructions to be ready to evacuate at a moment's notice.

Where did you flee to, though, when you were already in purgatory and surrounded by hell on all sides? And how was running an option when it would mean saving yourself while abandoning hundreds of defenseless children?

I lit the candle on my bedside table, pushing away thoughts of the threat across the border just as the light pushed away the darkness, and bent down to undo the laces of my boots. We usually wore flip-flops because of the heat, but they'd been banned that week because it was impossible to run in them. Boots made your feet sweat, but they wouldn't trip you up or twist your ankle if you needed to sprint to safety.

Once I'd kicked off my shoes, I pulled the wrinkled envelope from my pocket. I held a candle up to the postmark, careful not to let the flame lick at the paper. The letter had originated in Johannesburg, though the date was too smudged to read. There was no return address, but I suddenly recognized the handwriting even though I hadn't seen it in many years.

My pulse quickened as I set the candle holder down and slipped my finger under the envelope's flap. I wriggled it until the seal tore and found a single sheet of onionskin paper inside.

9
.

When I unfolded it, a Polaroid fluttered to the floor. I bent to pick it up and when I flipped it over, the face I beheld made my heart stutter. Setting the photo aside, I held the page to the light.

Dearest Delilah,

    I pray that this letter finds its way safely into your hands. Please forgive me for being both the bearer of bad news, and for having to convey it in this impersonal manner.

The page trembled in my grasp as impossible words marched across its landscape: *Father Daniel . . . rectory . . . robbery . . . Joburg General Hospital . . . coma . . . fighting for his life . . .* I had to read it three times before I understood its full import. The past was beckoning and I had no choice but to answer its siren call.

I would leave as soon as possible.

CHAPTER THREE

Ruth

❖

22 April 1994
Clifton, Cape Town, South Africa

I have to use my forearm to clear the mist from the bathroom mirror because my hands are both full: one holds a wineglass and the other, a razor. I've already swallowed the tablets, so at least I don't have to clutch the pill bottle as well. Thank God for small mercies.

"So much for traveling light when you die." Muttering around the cigarette propped between my lips, I giggle when I catch sight of my blurry reflection. The smoke's tip end is in my mouth while the lit filter smolders comically. Once my gaze lifts from my mouth, I stop laughing. My mascara's badly smudged and has bled into the cracks around my eyes. I look like a raccoon in drag.

I sigh, setting the glass and razor down. Aging is a bitch. Looking in the mirror and seeing a melting gargoyle face that absolutely isn't yours is a bitch too. In fact, life in general is a bitch.

Plucking the useless smoke from my mouth, I spit out flakes of tobacco. Once I've set it the right way around, I close the bath taps and then head back to the kitchen to get my lighter and top up my glass. It's on the marble counter next to two mostly empty wine bottles and the phone, which I've left off the hook. I'm reminded to check the clock to see how much time has passed

11
·

since I made the call. There are probably about fifteen minutes left, but the pills are making me foggy, so I can't be sure.

I light the smoke and inhale deeply. My eyes are drawn to the enlarged and framed magazine cover of myself from thirty years ago that hangs prominently in the lounge. It should console me that I once looked like that naked, beautiful girl staring defiantly back at me—a python draped around her neck, covering her breasts—but it doesn't. She doesn't feel like a part of me at all, just someone younger and wilder that I used to know.

Tearing my gaze away from her, I distract myself with the view. It's spectacular. The wraparound glass doors perfectly frame the twinkling lights of Camps Bay to the east, while the infinity pool just in front of the patio creates the illusion that you could swim right out of our home into the ocean.

Well, I say "our home" but really, it's Vince's. I should never have signed that damn prenup. Hell, I was the one who suggested it in the first place. Stupid love makes you do stupid things. In my defense, I didn't need his money when we got married. That's not what we were about. But I've made a few bad decisions since then and I'm not quite as independent as I once was. To be perfectly blunt, this is the worst possible time to lose everything.

Stubbing the cigarette out, I press play on the CD I'd cued up earlier, and then drain what's left of the Kanonkop Pinotage into my glass. I prop the note to Vince against the empty bottle where he can't miss it, and head back to the bathroom with a candelabra. Once the candles are lit (musk-scented to add to the drama), there isn't much left to do except fix myself up as best I can.

I remove the dark smudges and reapply my mascara and signature red Dior lipstick. My final decision is whether I should be naked in the tub or not. Naked would create more of an impact but the old body isn't what it used to be. I want to remind Vince what he'll be losing, not send him running for the hills.

Deciding that killer cleavage is a girl's best friend, I keep my La Perla lace bra and panties on, reclaim my wineglass and the razor, and then step into the bath. Setting everything down on the side of the tub, I sink into the water. Air Supply is crooning "Without You" loudly from the hidden speakers. It's the song I want playing when Vince finds me. I've set it to automatically replay, as I can't be sure exactly what time he'll arrive.

Things are getting woozy and I blink a few times to see better. The bath needs some blood for effect, but I really don't want to have to cut myself too badly or bleed out too much, so I'll only do that at the last minute. Even the sight of my own period used to make me queasy, before the onset of menopause.

I sink lower into the water just to ease the strain on my back and take a sip of wine, careful not to let the bathwater flood over the rim and into the glass. Diluting award-winning wine would be sacrilege. Sweat runs down my forehead and pools into my eyes. Still no sign of Vince, but he'll come. Of course he'll come.

What if he doesn't come?

I bat away the thought and close my eyes for a second. The water rises up to just below my nose. It's a pleasant sensation that tickles.

CHAPTER FOUR

Zodwa

21 November 1993
Sterkfontein, Transvaal, South Africa

An hour after Zodwa drinks the infusion, the cramps begin. They start like ripples on a pond. Soon they expand into swells that rock her from side to side. When the pain peaks, it spills over into whitecaps, frothing until Zodwa kneels on the dung floor clutching at her belly.

No. No. No.

Her bowels loosen and Zodwa groans as she grabs at the bucket the *nyanga* left next to her. The scent of sage is no longer comforting. It has become the smell of suffering and it offends Zodwa even more than the stench of her own waste.

Perhaps this is her punishment for trying to bend the Lord's will to her own. She knows her mother would strongly disapprove of her being here trying to play God. When the cramps finally subside, Zodwa's groans give way to whimpers. She lies curled up, shivering and spent, and watches as the *nyanga* rises from her place at the fire and limps over to her. She roughly spreads Zodwa's thighs and then reaches down between them. Her fingers come away clean.

"No blood. The baby will not leave. It has fought this battle and won. May you be stronger to win the other struggle. Now leave, child. You have made this old woman tired."

14

There's no money left to pay for a taxi home like she'd planned, so Zodwa will have to make the journey on foot. Considering her weakened state, she knows it will take much longer than the five hours it took to get here.

She takes the first staggering steps from the hut, squinting in the sunlight. Her senses heightened, Zodwa thinks she can hear the wildflowers and insects along the pathway speaking to her. The cosmos's pink and white petals bob in the breeze, nodding their agreement with the ancestors that she is, indeed, a disappointment.

This, despite the fact that she tried so hard to do everything right: working diligently in class and studying by candlelight late into the night; giving a wide berth to the boys who congregated at street corners in packs; turning down offers of liquor and other distractions; being an obedient daughter and granddaughter; being a good friend.

A good friend.

Zodwa can no longer ward off thoughts of Thembeka, who she's been avoiding since discovering her pregnancy. Thembeka: her best friend. Thembeka, whose boyfriend's child Zodwa is now carrying. As difficult as breaking the news to her family will be, telling Thembeka will be infinitely worse.

The prophesied misery is already beginning.

CHAPTER FIVE

Delilah

∴

25 *April 1994*

Goma, Zaire

My departure from Goma in Zaire was a noisy and frenetic affair as children surged around me, pulling me in to the current of their exuberance even as I tried to wrench myself free.

Michel latched on to my leg even as little Sonia begged to be picked up. Xavier, my colleague and closest friend at the orphanage, marched ahead of me, his rigid spine and brisk steps condemning me with everything he wouldn't say. Wasn't I the woman who'd told him just weeks before that she wouldn't evacuate even if we were given those orders? And yet there I was, jumping ship without so much as a word of explanation.

Doctor was nowhere to be found. I'd searched everywhere for the child that morning so I could say a proper farewell. The boy, already no stranger to abandonment, had decided he wouldn't give me the opportunity. I didn't blame him. Even as I took my leave, I knew it was the worst possible time to go.

Considering what was happening across the border in Rwanda, my help at the orphanage was needed then more than ever before. The mass murder of the Tutsis was leaving thousands of their children orphaned, and the pervasive use of rape as a weapon of war by both the militia and Hutu civilians would create even more unwanted babies that would need to be taken care of. But staying was no longer an option.

When I'd called the Johannesburg General Hospital ICU after getting the letter about Daniel, the nurse who answered my inquiry came back with a question of her own. "Are you a family member?"

I'd swallowed past the lump in my throat. "No, I'm just a friend."

Even that was a lie. There was a time when I could have been so much more to him but I'd run away, trying to put as much distance between us as possible, fleeing both the church's condemnation and my own shame at what I'd done.

"I'm sorry, but I can only disclose information to family."

"Could you please just tell me if he's okay? I'm calling from Zaire and am about to leave for Johannesburg to see him. I just need to know he's okay. Please."

She'd softened at the obvious desperation in my voice. "All I can divulge is that he's still in a critical condition."

At least he was still alive. I hadn't been sure he would be, considering the letter revealing his condition was two weeks old. There was still hope if I could just get to him in time.

The guilt that followed me out the orphanage gates still bogged me down hours later when Xavier dropped me off at Goma International Airport. He was a big man, in both height and girth, and he usually wore a big smile, an outward reflection of the optimism that drove him, but just then he looked forlorn.

"Xavier . . ." I said, trailing off as we faced each other.

I wanted so much for him to understand why I needed to leave, but there was no simple way to explain how almost forty years ago, I'd fallen in love with a priest and committed a terrible sin while in the process of taking my vows to become a nun. Excommunication had followed, and I'd agreed to leave the Catholic Church quietly in order to spare Daniel the shame.

For despite how much I'd loved him—despite the fact that he may have wanted me to remain a part of his life and to hell with the consequences—I knew if I insisted on staying that he'd eventually come to despise me for it. Choosing to love him from afar was the hardest thing I'd ever had to do. Sometimes what we deem a sacrifice worth making is one that comes with a price too high to expect another to pay.

There was no encapsulating a lifetime of heartbreak into a simple explanation and so I merely patted Xavier awkwardly on the arm, apologized, and then turned to leave.

When the plane took off a few hours later, the sunlight glinted off Lake Kivu. I watched as Mount Nyiragongo's volcanic peak became a harmless speck on the horizon. It was only once we landed in Kinshasa, and I waited to board my connecting flight to Johannesburg, that I finally began to feel some of the guilt lift.

"I'm coming, Daniel," I whispered. "I'm coming. Hold on."

CHAPTER SIX

Ruth

❊

23 April 1994
Groote Schuur Hospital,
Cape Town, South Africa

I wake up in a hospital bed, which is all wrong. The clinical smell of it, the beeping machines and squeaking shoes on linoleum, the hideous cotton gown: all wrong.

The only thing that's right is Vince.

He's asleep in the chair next to me looking immeasurably sad. God, how hard I fell for that basset hound face with its noble jowls and soulful brown eyes, its five-o'clock shadow and incongruently dimpled cheeks. How I love it still even though it's been so firmly set against me lately, hardened by disappointment and disapproval.

Vince must feel my gaze on him because he suddenly opens his eyes. "Ruth." It isn't so much an utterance of my name as a statement of defeat.

I smile to take the sting out of it. "Hey, baby," I whisper. My throat hurts and I can't figure out why until I remember the stomach pump and induced vomiting.

Vince rubs his eyes, his giant hands briefly covering his face. His Armani suit's all wrinkled and his silk tie is slack around his neck, a hangman's noose. Gray chest hair peeks out through the loosened top two buttons.

"Where am I?"

"Groote Schuur Hospital," he says.

"You look like shit." I smile. "You could at least have made an effort before you came a' callin'." I'm hoping for a laugh because that has always been our thing.

Not anymore. Not even a smile. "You almost died," he says.

"No," I scoff, too tired and weak to keep up the ruse. Of course, I didn't almost die. I'd had absolutely no intention of dying. I just wanted to get his attention, that's all. "I only took two Rohypnols." Considering the number of pharmaceuticals I have in my handbag and the bathroom cabinet at any given time, I could have killed myself a few times over if I'd really wanted to.

"You passed out in the bath and almost drowned," he says flatly. "I got to you just in time to pull you out."

That gives me pause. Death is a complication of my suicide attempt that I didn't foresee.

I study Vince's face to try to read what he's thinking, what he's feeling. He used to be an open book and as he sits there, he gives me one last glimpse into his inner workings and I know. My plan hasn't worked. I can see it in his eyes and the way he's crossed his arms tightly across his heart. I know this stance. It's his defensive posture, and I hate when he uses it against me, as if I'm a threat he has to protect himself against. When did I become the enemy?

I clear my throat. "Still leaving me, huh?"

I've never seen my stoic husband cry, not once in the twelve years we've been together. His tears are his answer.

I nod once, accepting defeat.

CHAPTER SEVEN

Zodwa

❋

24 April 1994
Big Hope Informal Settlement,
Magaliesburg, South Africa

The dog whimpers in its sleep, thrashing out with scrambling hind legs. It wakes Zodwa before dawn and sets the baby off hiccupping in the womb. Uncomfortable as she is, and as much as she wants to swat the dog away, Zodwa tries not to move in case it bothers her mother. They share a mattress on the floor of the shack, and as Zodwa's belly has grown, so has Leleti's irritation with everything she does.

Zodwa lies awake listening to the squatter camp's nighttime chorus, which is as much a companion as her mother's labored breathing. The shacks in the Big Hope Informal Settlement are erected almost on top of each other, their walls offering no insulation against the cold, and sound travels unobstructed through the corrugated tin. Music, laughter, conversation, cursing, the sound of babies crying, and noises that could either be of sex or violence, or both, drift in and out like uninvited guests.

When Leleti finally wakes to a distant cock's crowing, she gets up and lights the burner on the paraffin stove. Zodwa wrestles her way up, wraps herself in a blanket, and walks to the communal privy to empty her bladder. She has to be careful in the dark not to stumble into the pile of stones that her mother

21

adds to daily; knocking the shrine over would be an unforgivable offense.

It's cold outside, but the chill means the stench rising from the long drop isn't that bad. During the day, the heat bakes the human waste to a near boil so that the stink of it, coupled with the frenzied flies buzzing around, makes her light-headed. It was even worse in the earlier months of her pregnancy.

Upon Zodwa's return, Leleti finishes her morning scripture reading and closes her Bible. The candlelight is forgiving but despite the soft glow it radiates, Leleti looks much older than forty-seven. Having given birth to Zodwa when she was twenty-nine, Leleti's the oldest of Zodwa's friends' parents. Still, she'd always looked youthful, until her health deteriorated so rapidly that the weight fell off of her, leaving her skin looking like an oversized garment. Her hair, cut into a short afro, hasn't grayed at all but her eyes are lined with worry and exhaustion.

She wordlessly hands Zodwa a mug of black tea and a stale slice of bread smeared with apricot jam, as the big dog rises from the bed and pads its way over to her. Leleti passes it a slice of polony, making it wait and take it nicely.

"Good dog, Shadow," Leleti says, smiling, and Zodwa feels the usual resentment bubbling up.

It's ridiculous that they have this *hinja* as a pet. They're the laughingstock of the township, at least of those who aren't terrified of the dog. Who gives meat to a dog when they can't even afford meat for themselves? Still, Leleti loves the black beast and won't hear a word against it, claiming it's twice as loyal as any person she's ever known.

Leleti herself doesn't have anything to eat. She claims she'll have the children's leftovers when she's at her job as a maid in Rustenburg more than sixty kilometers away. She has to be in the kitchen at 7:00 a.m. on weekdays so she can make the children's breakfast before they leave for school. It means she has to wake up at 4:00 a.m. ahead of a long commute. Her madam has repeatedly warned Leleti that if she comes in late, they'll hire a maid who's prepared to live on the property and is more accessible to them. With today being a Sunday, Leleti can leave two hours later.

"Have you gotten Wednesday off to vote?" Zodwa asks to break the silence.

Leleti shakes her head.

"It's an important day for our people and you should—"

"You think I don't know that?" Leleti shoots back. "You think that it's for fun that I do this job that you're too good for?"

"I've never said I'm too good for it—"

"I'm telling you that you're too good to be a maid. And don't tell me how important Wednesday is! It's the day I've been waiting my whole life for, but food is also important. Money is important. Who do you think brings that home?" Leleti shakes her head and then starts coughing, the outburst setting her off.

Zodwa hands her mother a handkerchief. As Leleti coughs into it, each racking spasm rocking her whole body, Zodwa looks away so that she doesn't have to see the blood splatter darkening the fabric. She wonders how Leleti has managed to hide her sickness from her madam for this long. How much longer will she be able to do so?

The fit finally passes and the pacing dog settles down. When Leleti resumes speaking, her tone has lost all of its bite. "The hopes I had for you, my child. The hopes we all had for you. After your brother . . ." She trails off.

Leleti doesn't need to finish the sentence; Zodwa knows exactly what her mother is thinking.

23
·

When Dumisa left for Johannesburg more than a decade before, his future looked about as bright as a black man's possibly could during apartheid. He'd completed his last year of schooling in KwaZulu with top marks and secured a position as a junior administrator at Baragwanath Hospital in Soweto. The family rejoiced at the news.

There would be no manual labor for Zodwa's brother. Dumisa would be the first man in the family who would go to work in a suit and tie, using his brain rather than his muscles, and as he prospered, he would pull his family up behind him as a reward for all the sacrifices they'd made.

That had been the plan and for the first while, everything had gone better than expected. Dumisa sent money home every month and soon could even afford to buy a secondhand car due to a promotion. His letters were filled with descriptions of the things he'd bought, the house he was saving for, and the many gifts he was setting aside for the family. He was the embodiment of the country's hope for their black sons, and he was living the kind of life the rest of them had never dared to dream of.

But all that changed once Dumisa was recruited by the Inkatha Freedom Party Youth Brigade in Soweto. Within months of joining the resistance movement, he mysteriously vanished like so many anti-apartheid activists before him. The last person to have seen him alive reported seeing Dumisa being tortured by the security police for refusing to betray his comrades. The man spoke of his bravery and honor, and after that Dumisa was hailed a hero for his efforts on behalf of his people.

Leleti would have preferred a living son who was realizing his potential than one who'd died to advance the cause of the masses. Since her son's body was never recovered, Leleti refused to accept that he was dead. There was no final resting place for him—no grave site where Leleti could find peace—and so she kept searching for him even as she built a shrine to him, adding a stone to a pile for every day that he was gone.

After Dumisa disappeared, it fell to Zodwa to live out the dreams everyone had had for her brother, but instead of stepping out from under his shadow into her own light, Zodwa has cast a deeper darkness upon herself and her family, one of her own making and impossible to escape: shame. For while teenage pregnancies are nearly commonplace in the township, they're not something that happen to Khumalos.

Leleti shakes her head now. "What is the use of freedom if you are not going to grab the opportunities that I fought for—the opportunities that Dumisa fought for—so you could have a future? You may as well be a maid if having babies is the best you can imagine for yourself."

Zodwa hangs her head.

"And for what, my child?" Leleti asks. "Where is the father of the baby? There is no man here who loves you." Her voice breaks. "The good Lord knows that you do not even want this child."

It's the first time her mother has said such a thing and it pains Zodwa to hear the terrible hurt in her voice. She wants to reach out to her, to show Leleti a display of the love she feels for her—an indication of how sorry she is that she's disappointed her—but her mother's scorn has built this wall between them. No gesture that Zodwa can think of could knock it down, not even the truth.

Especially not the truth.

25
·

CHAPTER EIGHT

Delilah

❋

26 April 1994
Johannesburg General Hospital
Johannesburg, South Africa

H ello," I greeted the ICU nurse. "I'm here to see Father Daniel, the priest. He was brought in just over two weeks ago with a gunshot wound. This is the soonest I could get here," I said, aware that I was babbling but unable to do anything to stop myself. "I've actually come straight from the airport."

"Oh no. You weren't caught up in the bomb blast, were you?" she asked, an expression of concern on her kind face.

"What bomb blast?"

"A car bomb went off at Jan Smuts two hours ago. I heard about it on the news," she said, nodding at her little radio.

"Two hours ago? That must have been just after I landed."

"Well then, I'd say your guardian angels are working extra hard today. What's your name, dearie?"

"It's Delilah. Delilah Ferguson. I'm not a family member, if that's what you want to check," I said, peering over the counter to see if there was an official visitors list, "but I know he'd want to see me, which is why I rushed back from Zaire as soon as I heard the news. Please could you let me in? Just for a moment. I promise not to stay long."

"I'm afraid that won't be possible, Mrs. Ferguson."

"Here's the thing. I'm going to be honest with you," I said, preparing to bare my soul to a complete stranger and tell her the details of how Daniel and I were connected in the hope that it would make her more sympathetic to my plight. "He—"

"I'm not trying to be difficult, hon. There's only one visitor allowed at a time and another priest is with him now keeping vigil in case the last rites are required."

The last rites.

"He's that bad? There's no chance at all that he'll come out of the coma?"

"Miracles have been known to happen," she said, absently fingering the cross around her neck. "But, yes. He's still in a critical condition and has yet to regain consciousness." She nodded behind her at a window cut into the wall allowing visitors a view of the ICU.

All the beds beyond were occupied, and there were almost a dozen patients hooked up to all different kinds of life-saving equipment. Only one had the curtain drawn around it, though it stopped short of enclosing the space completely.

Through the open sliver, I could see a priest standing next to the bed.

He was slightly stooped with age and his head was bowed in prayer. He clutched a Bible in his hands, but even as I watched, he set it down and then reached over, drawing the patient's hand into his own, weaving his rosary beads between both their fingers so that they were bound together.

The tableau struck me so fiercely that I felt a stab of pain in my chest. As much as my religion had once been a part of me, as much as it had once defined me, I was no longer a part of that world like Daniel was, the world of faith and God and the church. I'd been cast out and was now an impostor whose lost

27

CHAPTER NINE

Ruth

◦

25 April 1994

Clifton, Cape Town, South Africa

I'm busy packing when Vince walks into the bedroom. His eyes are bruised with lack of sleep. "I went to the hospital to pick you up but they said you'd checked out early."

"Yes, well. You checked out of the marriage early, so consider us even."

"Ruth." He groans. He looks awkward just standing there a few feet into the doorway, like he's been marooned in currents he no longer knows how to navigate. He anchors himself by putting his hands into his pockets. "You don't need to move out right away, you know. There's no rush."

"I know when I'm not wanted." Even as I say it, I'm aware that I sound like my mother: martyrish. "Just give me an hour to finish packing and I'll be out of your hair."

"Can I ask where you're planning to go?"

"No."

The truth is that I don't know just yet. My options are severely limited. I once had four rental properties but only one remains, the proceeds from the sale of the other three poured into bad investments that I hoped would replenish the dwindling coffers. I've always had money but have never been very good at managing it. Of course, Vince knows nothing about any of this. It's a point of pride that I've never needed his money. Until now, that is.

Ten months remain on the lease of the last remaining property, an apartment in Camps Bay, so selling it or moving into it aren't options right now, and though I have plenty of acquaintances, I don't have the kinds of friends who'd take me in, nor the kind who I'd want to see me tossed to the curb like this.

I've been hoping for a sign, something to point me in the right direction, but the universe is mute at the moment; it's probably as dumbfounded by my predicament as I am.

"Look," Vince continues, "why don't you stay until you can find something more permanent? I'll move into one of the guest bedrooms until then, make myself scarce."

That's just the thing. I don't want him to make himself scarce. I couldn't bear living in the same house, knowing he's in another bedroom because he won't share ours.

"No, but thank you. I've made plans." I don't look at him while I'm saying it. I concentrate on folding up a few blouses and my silk kimono to stop myself from throwing myself into his arms and begging him to reconsider. Well, that, and beating the shit out of him for abandoning me like this.

He comes to sit on the bed, and the suitcase dips along with the weight of him. I turn and head back to my dressing room just to put some distance between us.

Vince's voice is muffled when it comes from behind me and his tone is falsely cheery. "Listen, there's another option that I'd like you to consider. I spoke to the doctor, the one who treated you at the hospital, and he wanted me to talk to you about checking yourself into a treatment facility."

"Rehab?" I laugh. "Forget it." Been there, done that. Didn't stick. "I don't need rehab."

"Not rehab." Vince clears his throat. "A mental health facility."

I can't have heard right. I clutch the negligee I'm folding and march back into the room. "A mental health facility?"

He nods, looking nervous.

"You mean a loony bin? You think I belong in a loony bin?"

"It's not a loony bin. It's a facility for people—"

"Who are crazy," I scoff.

"—who are emotionally fragile and need a bit of time to regroup." Vince talks over me.

"For God's sake. I'm not 'emotionally fragile.'" It would sound more convincing if my voice didn't crack like I'm about to fall apart.

"You tried to commit suicide, Ruth."

"No, I didn't!" I shout, gratified to see him wince. "The whole thing was staged, and yes, it was a stupid thing to do, but someone should fight for this marriage, since you so clearly don't give a shit about it."

Vince runs his hands through his hair. "My therapist said you'd do this. Become manipulative and direct blame at me to try and move it away from yourself." His eyes leave my face, alighting on one object and then another as he avoids catching my gaze.

"Your therapist? You're seeing a therapist?" I can't help it, I laugh.

"Therapy has helped me with a lot of my issues and I think seeing a professional will help you too. There's so much from your past that you've never worked through—"

"What's that got to do with any of this?"

"I think that's why you drink, Ruth. To drown your feelings about all that, and perhaps if you spoke about it—"

"Then what?" I snort. "I'd magically go back in time and

31

everything would work out? Please, it's ancient history and no good can come from wallowing in it. And you don't need a reason to drink beyond having a raging thirst."

The phone next to the bed suddenly trills and I dive to pick it up, desperate for a distraction. The man's voice on the other end is excited, and I listen with growing relief as he imparts his news.

When I replace the receiver, Vince carries on as though the conversation hadn't been interrupted. "Please consider it. I mean, you have the time—"

"I'm afraid that's where you're wrong," I say with grim satisfaction.

The call from the estate agent couldn't have come at a better time. I've been trying to sell my childhood home for the past few years but until now there haven't been any takers. The property was left to me when Ma died, and though I never lived on it again after eloping on my twenty-first birthday, I couldn't bear to part with it for sentimental reasons. Thirty years after Ma's death, those reasons aren't as clear as they once were. Also, it's amazing how sentimentality goes out the window when misfortune knocks at the door.

The universe has come through for me without a moment left to spare; I have my sign and know exactly where I need to be.

CHAPTER TEN

Zodwa

❂

27 April 1994
Magaliesburg, Transvaal, South Africa

D awn announces itself with a blush on the horizon just as Zodwa reaches the high school's perimeter. She's tried not to think too much about all that she's missing out on beyond those gates but being at the threshold brings it all back: the classes at which she excelled; the friends who admired her and the teachers who were proud of her; the inconsequential chatter about boys and fashion amid the serious political discussions and heated debates.

Zodwa casts aside thoughts of what might have been and joins the voting line snaking out the school gates. A *gogo* stands in front of her; she's gnarled like an ancient branch and hunches over her *knobkerrie* walking stick, which seems to be the only thing keeping her up. Her eyes are clouded with cataracts but still they shine with excitement. Through their intermittent chatting in the queue as dawn ripens into day, Zodwa discovers that the old woman is ninety-four years old and lives in a village half an hour away.

"The people from the white church in Fouriesburg came this morning to fetch us. *Yoh*, they had such nice vans, like taxis but white-people taxis, that even had heaters." She hugs herself, savoring the warmth of the memory, as she smiles a gap-toothed smile. The wrinkles around her eyes deepen into crevices.

After four hours of shuffling forward in tiny increments, Zodwa sees the old woman beginning to exhibit signs of strain. "*Gogo*, we must find you a chair."

"No, my child, we must find *you* a chair." The old woman laughs, nodding at Zodwa's heavily pregnant belly. "Besides," the *gogo* says, attempting a lively two-step shuffle, "I want to stand so I can jive a bit. Today is the first time in all my nearly hundred years that I will get to vote for one of my people to be president. Today is the day to dance." She throws her head back and laughs, toppling forward in the process.

"Are you all right, *gogo*?" Zodwa says as she reaches out just in time to steady her.

The woman looks dazed but still she smiles. "Jiving is difficult at my age. My blood pressure is not what it used to be and I didn't take my tablets for the past few days. Too expensive."

That helps make Zodwa's mind up. "Come, *gogo*. Come with me. We will speak to someone who will take you to the front of the line or let you sit in the shade while you wait."

With some cajoling, the old woman steps out of the line and starts walking toward the school gates with Zodwa. Despite the long wait and the predawn chill that has been burned away and replaced by biting heat, the mass of people waiting to vote are in good spirits.

If there is one thing we know how to do, it is to wait. We have had decades' and decades' worth of experience doing it.

It's something her mother has told her many times.

Though their people are used to waiting, standing single file in lines isn't something they do well. Groups gather and break into song. The deep baritone strains of the apartheid protest song "Shosholoza" rises and falls throughout the morning.

A gum-boot dancer nearby entertains the crowd, kicking up dust as he stomps his way through the mining dance, his black rubber boots providing the percussion, while an enterprising teenage boy makes his way along the line selling roasted *mielies* and Styrofoam cups filled with lukewarm Coke. The police step in to separate African National Congress and Inkatha Freedom Party supporters after a skirmish breaks out between them. They're hauled off to the dreaded Hippos, the armored South African Police trucks.

Zodwa recognizes a few faces in the queue and issues greetings as they walk along. Her smile freezes when she sees them up ahead: Thembeka and Mongezi; her ex–best friend standing with the father of Zodwa's child. The fact that they're still a couple hurts more than Zodwa can express.

Before Zodwa can dip her head to pretend that she hasn't seen them, Mongezi turns and catches sight of her. Quickly checking that Thembeka is otherwise occupied, he turns back to Zodwa and winks. Something inside of her cracks; it's like the lightning bolt that slices through a block of ice when it's dropped into a warm drink. She can almost hear the fissure as it cleaves through her.

Zodwa turns from him. She resists the temptation to speed up, as there is no way the *gogo* could keep up. When they finally reach the front of the queue, Zodwa spots someone wearing the blue Independent Electoral Commission bib. It's only when the person turns around that Zodwa realizes it's Beauty Mbali, a township neighbor and her mother's best friend. The woman hugs Zodwa when she catches sight of her. She's in her element today as an IEC volunteer, something she never thought she'd live to do, and it makes Zodwa happy to see the huge smile on her face.

"Where is your mother, child?" Mama Beauty asks.

Zodwa doesn't want to get Leleti in trouble with her zealously political friend, so she pretends not to hear the question. "Excuse me, Mama Beauty, but *ugogo* is ninety-four years old and she has been standing in the line for more than four hours. The heat is making her light-headed. Would it be possible to let her vote now?"

Mama Beauty looks past Zodwa's belly to the tiny woman behind it. "*Sawubona, gogo,*" she greets her. "*Unjani?*"

"Good morning, my child," the woman replies. "I am so well today. I am the best I have ever been because today is the day I vote."

Mama Beauty laughs. In her sixties herself, she is hardly a child except to someone so much older. "Then let us not delay any longer, *gogo*. Let us take you now so you can make your mark."

She leads them up the stairs past the queue into a blessedly cool classroom whose tables and chairs have been neatly stacked against the walls. "Can I have your identity books, please?"

"Identity book?" the old lady asks, her smile fading, and Zodwa's spirits drop. "But I don't have an ID book."

"The temporary voting card will be fine instead," Mama Beauty replies.

The *gogo*'s look of bewilderment grows. "I don't know what that is. I've never had a birth certificate and so I couldn't apply for any of these things."

"But, *gogo*," Mama Beauty says gently, "without proper documents, how do we know who you are?"

The *gogo*'s smile returns as she touches her chest. "My dear, I can tell you who I am. I'm Eunice Dlamini and I was born on New Year's Day in the year 1900. I may not have a birth certificate, but I know my own history. I know who I am." Her face turns serious. "I'm ready now. I have been waiting my whole life and I will not wait any longer. Tell me, where do I write my name and put my cross? I want my God to watch me as I do this."

Mama Beauty's expression is pinched. It clearly pains her to say, "I am so sorry, *gogo*, but without an ID or a voting card, you cannot vote."

The *gogo*'s smile falters and then dies on trembling lips as it slowly dawns on her that all of her struggles and suffering—the ninety-four years that she's lived as a nonentity in the country of her birth—have all been for nothing.

She will not get to vote this day or any day. She will never leave her mark.

As Zodwa clutches the old woman's hand and Mama Beauty leans in to comfort her, a white-hot rage flares up inside Zodwa. The baby kicks out in protest.

Now you know, Zodwa says to her unborn child. *Now you know what to expect from this world.*

CHAPTER ELEVEN

Delilah

27 April 1994

Verdriet, Magaliesburg, South Africa

It was a shock to find myself by the wild fig tree that stood sentry at the entrance to the farm. I couldn't remember getting there, couldn't remember anything at all beyond running from the hospital and getting into my rental car. I must have driven around for hours because darkness had fallen without my noticing it.

I considered turning around and making my way back the eighty kilometers to the hotel I'd booked near the hospital, but I was so bone-tired that it seemed a miracle I'd made it here without incident.

When I pulled up to the old gate hanging off rickety hinges, I had to get out to swing it open, and then again to close it behind me once I was through. Rounding the bend, I was greeted by the rusted windmill that looked as decrepit as it had when I'd left almost forty years before. A waning gibbous moon backlit its enormous blades, and the moonlight reflected off the dam, casting eerie shadows in the thatch grass.

The farmhouse hadn't changed. It was still painted the same muddy brown I remembered, and the paint was chipping and peeling from the fascia boards and drainpipes. Though I couldn't see them in the dark, I knew the avocado orchards stretched out behind the house, and that beyond them, the Magaliesberg mountains rose up in the distance. They were giant waves on an otherwise calm sea, the only thing breaking the monotony of a landscape made up of seemingly nothing but earth and sky.

When I came to a stop in front of it, I eyed the darkened house warily. The farmstead was called Verdriet. It meant "grief" in Afrikaans and if that didn't sum up everything there was to know about it, then I didn't know what did. My Afrikaner grandfather had named it just before parceling it off and bestowing it to his daughter and her new Scottish husband as a wedding gift. My mother had said it was a prophecy; my father believed it to be *oupa*'s curse.

I left the headlights on and opened the car door. My shadow loomed large as I slowly walked up the stairs. The illumination made finding the old concrete statue of the angel easier. I hefted it to the side, tipping the base, and there it was in the wedge that had been chiseled out specifically for it: the key my father told me would always be waiting for me in case I ever decided to come home. At the time, I hadn't known if the gesture was a taunt, my father's way of predicting that I would fail at something he so strongly disapproved of, or if it came from a sincere place.

Dislodging the key, I blew the cobwebs and dust off and fit it into the door's lock. It yielded immediately like it had been expecting me. After I locked the car, I hitched my rucksack over my arm and went back up the stairs, shouldering my way into the house.

It was dark inside and smelled strangely of stale cigarette smoke. Closing the door with my foot, I automatically turned right, knowing the light switch lay against the wall two steps in that direction. When I flicked it on, the fluorescent lights hummed awake, revealing an odd scene in the lounge.

A woman lay stretched out on the couch, head resting on a throw cushion and one arm flung up over her head. She was wearing a red negligee with a bodice made almost entirely of lace, which exposed, rather than covered, her large breasts. Empty wine bottles and an overflowing ashtray cluttered the table in front of her. Two candles had burned down completely, leaving puddles of wax. The woman snored softly, completely oblivious to the lights that had been switched on and the noise I'd made getting inside.

It took me longer than it should have to realize who she was.

In my defense, it had been almost four decades since I'd last laid eyes on her. And seeing her there was unexpected; the last I'd heard, she was living with her third or fourth husband in Cape Town somewhere. Rumors of other things before then had also made their way to me, but they were so outlandish that I hadn't known if I could believe them.

"Ruth?" I whispered, not wanting to startle her. When she didn't so much as twitch in response, I said her name louder. Still no reaction. I walked over to the couch and shook her arm, repeating her name until she finally woke up.

"Wha—?" She blinked myopically up at me and then narrowed her eyes, a look of bewilderment on her face. "Ma?" she asked stupidly.

She blinked a few times more and then struggled into a sitting position, not taking her eyes off me the entire time. Finally, my sister's expression cleared.

"Dee? Is that you?" she asked. "My God, you look old."

CHAPTER TWELVE

Ruth

❋

27 April 1994
Verdriet, Magaliesburg, South Africa

Dee scares the bejesus out of me, looming over me looking so much like Ma that it's like being visited by a ghost who's been dead for more than thirty years.

Her short gray hair stands up in greasy spikes and her face, completely devoid of makeup, has streaks of either sweat or tears that have carved their way down her cheeks. She's wrinkled and stern; it's like being visited by an avenging angel, and I wonder if I'm having a nightmare.

"Get up and go to bed, Ruth," she instructs, and it's such a banal and typical-of-Dee thing to say that I know it's not a dream.

Still, just because it's not a dream doesn't mean her sudden appearance isn't an omen.

I have always believed in signs. Dee used to as well but since her signs came from the man upstairs, she didn't view them as signs at all; rather just her listening to God telling her what to do. Sounds like most of my relationships with men, now that I come to think of it, so I really shouldn't point any fingers. People in glass houses and all that.

She said it was God who told her to leave our childhood home when she was seventeen so that she could fulfill his wish for her to become a nun. I thought it was more likely that it was the hunky priest, Father Somebody or Other, who charmed her so completely that she abandoned our mother's Dutch Reformed Church for the Catholic faith.

I remember her blushing scarlet when I suggested as much, insisting that he'd had nothing to do with it but of course that was nonsense. He was so gorgeous that I might have joined the church for him if he'd ever given me the time of day. That puppy dog sweetheart of hers, Riaan van Tonder, broke down and cried the night before she left. I know because I followed Dee when she snuck out of the house to meet him in the avocado orchard.

I was there, too, the day Dee became a novice and the whole thing gave me the absolute creeps. Dee wore Ma's wedding dress, which should have been kept for me since I was the eldest. Luckily, it was way too conservative and not my style at all, so it was only the principle of it that bothered me. The dress was tight on Dee because she'd put on weight sitting around all day praying rather than working on the farm. Her getting fat was karma for her being given something that was rightfully mine.

She and the other pustules (which is what I called them even though Dee insisted it was "postulants") walked down the aisle like blushing brides, veils over their heads, because they were supposedly taking vows to marry Christ. Ma even squirreled money away for months so that she could afford to buy Dee a gold band for her "wedding" ring.

Watching my sister stand in a row with the other young women so that they could all marry Christ was chilling. I didn't know anything about cults then, but if I had that's exactly what I would have likened it to. I remember thinking that God was a terrible polygamist and I hoped like hell that he'd leave Dee jilted at the altar.

42

We were all shocked when Dee dropped out of the convent just a few months later. She never revealed in her letter what made her quit, all she said was that God had changed his mind about her vocation.

After we got the news, Ma waited impatiently for Dee to come home and explain herself.

Instead, we received a letter from her in Rwanda saying that God had decided that she should head farther north to become an aid worker. I couldn't understand why a scorned woman would take orders from her ex and didn't think God should get away with that kind of behavior just because he was the Almighty.

We expected Dee to come visit us over her holidays but we never saw her again. Not when Da was so sick nor for his funeral, though I suppose that was to be expected. What I didn't expect was for her to ignore Ma's pleas six years later when she was dying and begged Dee to come and see her. It struck me as a terribly vindictive thing to do, not to grant a dying woman her last wish to see her favorite daughter, and not at all in keeping with the piety Dee projected.

God knows that her praying was always the showy kind, on her knees on the polished floor, lips moving fervently with her hands clasped together clutching her rosary beads as if they were a lifeline to keep her from drowning. I tried it a few times myself but I never heard back from Him.

I know the seventeen-year-old Dee would've flat-out dismissed my belief that I've been having a lifelong conversation with the universe just as profound as the one she's been having with God. She didn't believe in any kind of spirituality that wasn't dressed up as organized religion—with all of its rituals and vestments and judgments—and she definitely wouldn't have understood the universe's subtlety.

The universe speaks in clues and signs, gentle nudges and hints, rather than pontifications and proverbs, commandments and condemnations. I have trusted its signs all my life, which is why I listened when it seemed like it wanted me back here.

As I stumble to bed under Dee's disapproving gaze, I can't help but wonder why fate has brought us back together like this. I guess I'll find out soon enough.

CHAPTER THIRTEEN

Zodwa

✶

27 April 1994
Big Hope Informal Settlement,
Magaliesburg, South Africa

As the raindrops begin to clatter on the tin roof, Zodwa flinches, dropping her book onto her lap. The fluttering pages blow out the candle, plunging the shack into darkness.

After more than a year at the squatter camp, Zodwa still hasn't gotten used to it: the panic when those first few discordant taps find their rhythm and become a steady drumbeat heralding disaster. The shacks near the riverbed were washed away by flash floods in January. She'll never forget the woman's wailing when they retrieved her two-year-old's bloated body a kilometer downstream a day later.

The worst of their problems if the shack floods is the thin foam mattress stinking from the damp and the floor that stays caked with mud for days at a time. It makes Zodwa feel like an insect who lives burrowed in wet soil rather than a human being trying to eke out a life in the tiny patch of land they've claimed as their own.

Even the concept of ownership is an illusion. They may have erected their shack there but it isn't their property. They, like so many thousands of other people, squat without formal permission to do so, living as much in fear of the bulldozers as of the shack fires that occasionally flare up and tear through the camp. The government and the police pose as much a threat as the elements.

Zodwa is relieved when the raindrops die away, and has just struck a match to relight the candle when her mother suddenly sits up as a fit of coughing seizes her. The dog, who's sleeping curled up between Leleti's legs, gets up too.

Leleti has lost so much weight in the past few weeks that she's all edges. When Zodwa reaches out to place a hand on her mother's knee, the sharpness of it feels like a rebuke. "Mama. What can I do?"

Leleti waits for the coughing fit to pass before wheezing her reply. "Nothing, my child, but thank you. Try to get some rest." The dog whines in response to her voice and licks her hand.

"I can't sleep. Let me help you. I'll go and wet the cloth so that you can hold it against your face," Zodwa says, beginning to rise.

Her mother indicates the pot full of water next to her, the cloth floating uselessly inside it. It's stained with blood that seeps out in ribbons, painting the water in swirls of pink. "It makes no difference."

Finally, the assault subsides and Leleti lies back down, the dog settling with her. Zodwa just thinks her mother has fallen asleep when she speaks. "You should go home."

"I am home, Mama."

"No, back to Ulundi. In KwaZulu. Back to the village."

"I want to stay here with you."

"I am sick with this coughing disease, Zodwa. It is not getting better and I cannot take care of you or the baby." Leleti continues, "You will need help to look after it when I am no longer here."

"Do not speak like that. You will get better."

"This is no place for you. I should have left you there with your grandmother. She said it was a mistake to bring you but I was selfish wanting you with me."

Zodwa can't help but think back to the day they were re-united in the township just over fifteen months before. Leleti had sat for hours on the side of the road in the blistering heat, waiting for the taxi that would finally discharge her daughter.

"My child," Leleti had said, her frown of concern turning to relief when Zodwa finally stepped from one of the dozens of minivans that had pulled up. "Look what a beautiful woman you have become." After almost twelve years apart, Leleti was a stranger to Zodwa.

"Thank you, Mama." Zodwa felt shy under Leleti's gaze. As much as she'd yearned for her mother after she'd left, she now fervently longed for her *gogo* who'd stepped into that role so neatly that her real mother had become a kind of myth others only spoke about. Yet there she was in front of her, a flesh-and-blood woman who was clearly sick, though Zodwa didn't yet know with what.

"You have made me so proud," Leleti had said, cupping Zodwa's face. "Just like Dumisa. And you will go on to even greater things. I know it."

It shames Zodwa to think how badly she has let her mother down.

"You would have finished school if you'd stayed in KwaZulu. This," Leleti says, nodding at Zodwa's belly, "would not have happened there. I have just enough money to send you back. If you leave tomorrow, you will get there before the baby comes."

"No, Mama. We will use the money to take you to a doctor so you can get medicine."

"Doctors are not for people like us."

Leleti speaks the truth. Just days before, Leleti's friend Mama Beauty came over with two plastic bags filled with baby things. Some of the clothes hadn't even been worn yet but still smelled of fabric softener because the whites apparently washed everything straight after purchasing it, regardless of whether their babies ever used it or not.

Mama Beauty was the only black person Zodwa knew who had a white friend, a younger woman named Robin who would drive out to the squatter camp regularly to visit her. From what Zodwa could tell, Mama Beauty had worked for Robin's family as a maid before she'd retired.

Apparently the white woman, Robin, appealed to Mama Beauty regularly to move in with her in Johannesburg, but she refused the offer, wanting to stay near her sons, who both worked in the platinum mines in Rustenburg. Zodwa knew there was an older daughter, Nomsa, who'd gone missing in the 1980s, because that was the basis of Mama Beauty and Leleti's friendship: they'd bonded over the fact that each of them was searching for a child who'd disappeared during the worst of the apartheid era's atrocities.

Mama Beauty was kind to Zodwa, sourcing maternity clothes and baby things for her, while sharing information about a world that Zodwa would otherwise never have known about, like how white women went for regular blood tests and checkups while pregnant, and how they took pills that pregnant women were supposed to have.

There have been no doctor's visits or tests for Zodwa. It was only the cessation of her period and the tenderness of her breasts that had confirmed she was pregnant. The nearest clinic is half a day's walk away and when her mother forced her to go,

Zodwa arrived at a long queue that barely moved. After waiting for hours and still not being seen, Zodwa set out for home and never tried to return again. There seemed to be little point.

"You will get better, Mama. You just need to rest. I will go speak to your madam and ask if you can take a week off—"

"I was fired today. I no longer have a job." Leleti's voice is hollow.

"Why? You even went in when you could've taken the day off to vote."

"Look at me, my child. I cannot clean a house properly. I am surprised it took this long for her to let me go."

Apparently, the madam had paid Leleti only what she owed her for that month. It's all the money they have and Leleti wants to use it to send Zodwa back to the KwaZulu homeland. They sit in silence for a while, each lost in her own thoughts. With only enough money for one of them to travel home, and no prospects for earning more, they will both have to stay.

"At least tell me who the father of the baby is," Leleti says after a pause. "He is the father of the child and he must give you money to help you."

"Mama, he won't—"

"He will! I will go speak with him. I've been praying on it and it's the Lord's will that I shame him until he pays."

"No, Mama."

"Just tell me who he is! What self-respecting man will refuse to look after his own child? Stop this nonsense and tell me who—"

"I was raped, Mama!" Zodwa is so shocked by the admission that she claps a hand over her mouth. She looks at her mother, frightened by the horror on her face.

They have spoken more in the past half an hour than they have in the past few months. Zodwa has wished so much for them to get back to the closeness they used to share, but now that she's confided the words that have been building up inside her for so long, they feel more like weapons.

Leleti's face crumples then. "My child, who did this to you? Who?"

Zodwa shakes her head and is surprised by the emotion that constricts her throat.

Leleti pulls Zodwa to her chest and begins whimpering. "Lord Jesus, tell me it isn't so. Tell me this isn't what happened to my beautiful child."

Zodwa allows herself to be rocked as her mother cries. She can't help but think that sometimes it's easier to stagger under the weight of our heaviest burdens with our heads bowed down, just so we don't have to witness the pain that our suffering causes those who love us most.

"I'm sorry, my child. I am so sorry." Leleti's crying is punctuated at intervals by apologies and self-recrimination. "I should have protected you from this . . . Forgive me, my child . . . I will make it right. Forgive me. Forgive me."

Her mother's tears drip onto Zodwa's cheeks, and she wants so much to contradict Leleti and tell her that she isn't to blame but she can't explain any further, not without losing the tenderness her mother feels for her.

You could not have protected me, Mama. I was raped because I loved the wrong person. I still do.

CHAPTER FOURTEEN

Ruth

❖

28 April 1994
Verdriet, Magaliesburg, South Africa

I thought I dreamt you," I say after shuffling through to the kitchen, where Dee's making a god-awful racket and generally being very inconsiderate of the throbbing in my temples. "Though it felt more like a nightmare than a dream, to be honest."

She pours coffee and hands it to me. "Here, this should help."

"Help what?"

"The headache and nausea you probably woke up with."

"I don't get headaches and nausea. I get raging hangovers."

The comment is meant to break the ice a bit but Dee doesn't thaw at all. "Sorry there's no milk or sugar for it but the cupboards are completely bare. How can you live like this?"

"I only just arrived from Cape Town yesterday, a few hours before you did," I say in my defense. "It's not like I'm Mother Hubbard."

"Well, in that case you should have realized there wouldn't be any provisions and gone shopping before you arrived."

"There wasn't time."

"There was time to stop at the liquor store." Dee eyes the empty bottles standing next to the bin. "The only things in the fridge are wine and tonic water."

"You could just as easily have stopped at the shops, Dee. I don't see all your provisions stocking the cupboards." She flushes but doesn't explain why she didn't do any shopping. Typical of her. Hypercritical of everyone else, but God help you if any of that criticism is directed at her. "At least we know one of us has her priorities straight. And thank you for the reminder about the tonic," I say airily, getting up to fetch a ciggie and the ingredients for some hair of the dog.

"Do you really need a drink just after waking up?" Dee rinses an ashtray and plunks it down in front of me.

"Mosquitoes are the biggest killers in Africa. They claim more lives than hippos. This is just good sense. You should have one too."

"There's no malaria in the foothills of the Magaliesberg mountains. You know that."

"You can't be too careful." I add an extra tot of gin for good measure.

"It's the quinine in the tonic that's the mosquito deterrent, anyway. Not the gin."

"Oh well, it's not like I can take the gin out now, can I? Ma could say what she liked about the Brits, but they brought G and Ts to Africa, so they couldn't have been all that bad. Are you sure you don't want one?"

"Yes."

"Suit yourself," I say, and then mutter under my breath, "Someone woke up on the wrong side of the bed this morning."

Dee's attack comes seemingly out of nowhere. I thought we were bantering but clearly not. My sister is as sensitive as she ever was. "Why are you here, Ruth? Another failed marriage or are you recovering from the most recent round of plastic surgery?"

I won't let her get away with that. "Why are *you* here, Dee? Wait, don't tell me. There's someone who really needs you in Zaire or Rwanda or fucking Timbuktu, and so you thought you'd leave because isn't that what you've always done best?"

Dee flinches but doesn't rise to the bait. "I've retired, actually."

"Retired? Well, I hope you don't expect to stay here."

"Why not? It's as much my home as it is yours."

That's what she thinks. "I'm selling it."

"What?"

"That's why I'm here. We've had an offer on the farm that I'm in the process of accepting."

"You can't do that!"

"Oh, but I can. You signed over your power of attorney to me decades ago, remember? When you left me alone to deal with everything by myself, all that pesky paperwork included?" I hate that I sound hurt. To hell with her.

"I'll rescind the power of attorney. You can't sell the farm."

"We'll just have to see about that," I say, taking my drink and sweeping out of the room, cigarette smoke and my silk kimono trailing behind me.

CHAPTER FIFTEEN

Delilah

❉

28 April 1994

Verdriet, Magaliesburg, South Africa

There wasn't a time that I could recall being free of Ruth's torment.

With her being older than me by ten months but born in the same year, we were considered "Irish twins," though no one ever called us that in front of our Scottish father, Angus. Their restraint may have been because he had an unpredictable mean streak, or it could've been because they simply didn't know the term. Our town was a small farming community populated mainly by Afrikaners who were suspicious of anyone who was an outsider or read anything other than farming periodicals and the Bible.

The fact that my parents had produced two children so quickly may have been misconstrued as them having some affection for each other, but they didn't. Their marriage was one long war punctuated by regular skirmishes, and the only battle Ma ever won was naming Ruth.

My father had wanted to name her Donalda, after his own mother, but my mother had insisted on naming her for a biblical character, someone the child could aspire to. It was probably the sight of that thatch of red hair on Ruth's newborn head that scared her and made her refuse to back down. My mother knew that a daughter who took after her father in both looks and temperament would be too much for her to handle. She probably hoped that naming Ruth after an obedient woman might bestow a sobering effect.

It didn't.

Da got his revenge against Ma on the day I was born when he was sent to the registry office with instructions to write "Naomi" on my birth certificate. Because she'd won the battle of naming Ruth, my mother thought she'd win again.

She was wrong.

"Yeh wan' a bloody biblical name, woman? I'll give yeh a biblical name!"

And that's how I came to be named Delilah.

It was our father's idea of a joke, especially since I'd been born on Christmas Day, our Lord's birthday. And how ironic it was too: the Ruth of the family being wild and agnostic, and the Delilah being pliant and religious. I like to think that was my own way of rebelling against him and getting revenge on behalf of our mother, turning it around so that the laugh was on him.

Every day of my parents' union that I can remember bearing witness to was bloody, and growing up on a battlefield took its toll. "God help you, Delilah, but you'll understand when you're older," my mother told me one day when I sat glowering as she made my father's breakfast. She had a fresh bruise on her cheek that sickened me. "This is what marital relations between a man and woman are like." She shrugged as though there was nothing to be done but to accept it.

The more Da drank, the more belligerent he became, listing Ma's many shortcomings and the myriad ways in which she'd failed him. The community wryly twisted the farm's name, Verdriet, changing it to Dronkverdriet, which was the Afrikaans word for depression brought on by drunkenness. Da's lack of success with the farm was Ma's fault because she'd taken a shipbuilder and a man of the sea and forced him to become someone who labored in the dirt. His failings as a husband were her fault too because she emasculated him. How was a man supposed to be a man when his wife didn't respect him?

Of course, I wanted no part of that then. If that's what love could do to you—for I had to assume that they did love each other once—then I wanted nothing to do with it. Yet even while I rejected that kind of love, I still yearned for a great love, an exalted one that transcended earthly desires. Thus began my love affair with God and the church, which I stupidly thought would inoculate me against the messiness of human emotions.

It didn't.

If anything, all it did was facilitate my ruin, for it was through the church that I fell in love with a priest, and it was that infatuation that was the catalyst for everything that came afterward. I thought at the time that I'd done a good job of hiding my feelings for him, but there was no hiding them from Ruth. She sniffed them out and tormented me relentlessly.

Ruth, the ruthless.

That's how she was then and it's how she still was. It was a quality, like her alcoholism, that she must have gotten from Da.

After our conversation about selling the farm, I knew I had to get out of the house or run the risk of throttling Ruth's cosmetically enhanced neck. Besides, we needed supplies and she clearly wouldn't be going shopping for anything more substantial than lemons for her gin and tonics.

Before I left for the shops, it took me ten minutes to build up the courage to call the ICU, and I let out a quavering breath when I was told Daniel's condition remained critical and that nothing had changed. I tried to push away thoughts of him as I got into the car, fueling myself instead with anger and murderous thoughts directed at Ruth.

Though I'd driven the roads to the farm the night before, nothing looked familiar as I backtracked in the light of day. On the way to town, I passed a sprawling mass of shacks that stretched out as far as the eye could see. They covered acres of what used to be farmland. I'd kept up with South African news and knew it was one of the squatter camps that people euphemistically preferred to call "informal settlements." Cities attracted thousands upon thousands of black laborers but had nowhere to house them, and so the camps were springing up all over the place.

I found a grocery store in town and after doing my shopping, I joined the long queues for the tills. My cart was half-full but other shoppers had two or three trolleys filled with nonperishable goods. I couldn't understand why a weekday would be so busy and I asked the white cashier about it when I finally reached her. "What's going on today? Some kind of sale or something I'm not aware of?"

She was wearing a National Party T-shirt with State President F. W. de Klerk's face on it to show her support of the apartheid government. "No, everyone's just stockpiling," the woman replied in Afrikaans, which I then switched to as well. Though Ruth and I had been sent to study at an English school by our father, the entire farming community, as well as Ma, had been Afrikaans and so we were fluent in both languages.

"Stockpiling? For what?"

"For when Nelson Mandela becomes president and the civil war begins."

I thought she was joking but she looked dead serious. "Civil war?"

"Yes, the blacks have been threatening for years to come after all the whites as revenge for apartheid. None of us will be safe anymore. Women especially. Can you imagine anything worse than being raped by a filthy *kaffir*?"

As I drove back to the farm five minutes later, my mind was still reeling from what she'd said. Passing the squatter camp, I was forced to stop when the light turned red. Signs were posted at various points across the intersection warning drivers to be on the lookout since it was a prime hijacking location. I locked the doors.

While waiting for the light to change, I took in the chaotic scene around me. Minivan taxis were stopping, loading up passengers and then pulling out again haphazardly, kicking up dust. Pedestrians chatted in groups or stood with their hands out, the splay of their fingers indicating where they were headed. Hawkers shouted out their wares as guinea fowl and goats roamed the side of the road.

Everyone was black and a vast majority of the people were sporting Nelson Mandela's popular green, yellow, and black African National Congress colors. Considering that the ban on his party had only been lifted in 1990, the support for it was impressive. The only white faces in the throng were those in their cars like I was, their doors locked but their faces still betraying their anxiety. Could the cashier at the Spar have been right? Was there reason to be scared?

She'd probably lived in the town her whole life whereas I'd only just returned to a country that was as wholly changed as I was. How could I profess to know my country as a prodigal daughter returning after all that time?

I was startled by a black face that suddenly loomed at my side window. Knuckles rapped against the glass and I flinched. The light had turned green and I accelerated, looking into my rearview mirror to ensure that I was putting distance between myself and the man who'd approached me. That's why I didn't see the pothole in time to swerve. There was a loud bang followed by a jolt. I felt what had happened by the sluggishness of the steering: I'd damaged one of the tires. There was nothing to be done for it but to pull over onto the shoulder of the road.

CHAPTER SIXTEEN

Zodwa

✳

28 April 1994
Big Hope Informal Settlement,
Magaliesburg, South Africa

Zodwa locks the shack, tucking the key into her bra. On her way out, she passes the meager vegetable garden she's been trying to grow, as well as the shrine her mother built to Dumisa. Three thousand, five hundred, and eleven. That's how many stones now lie heaped in a pile; one for every day since Dumisa has been gone. Zodwa touches it briefly, the mass as solid as Dumisa's absence, and thinks about all the time she and Leleti have spent searching for him.

Their first outing together after Zodwa arrived in the township was meant to be for buying school supplies. They could have just gone to the shopping center around the corner, which is why Zodwa was confused when Leleti made them catch a minivan taxi into Johannesburg.

"Don't you want to see the city?" Leleti asked when Zodwa inquired about their destination.

Zodwa did but also knew that the taxi fare there was more than they could afford. It was only once Leleti consulted instructions written on the back of a pamphlet to get them to a block of flats in Hillbrow that Zodwa realized her mother's true agenda: she wanted to interrogate an ex–Inkatha Freedom

Party Youth Brigade member for any information he might have about her son and his role in the Zulu youth movement's anti-apartheid struggle. The trip had been fruitless—they hadn't even gotten the schoolbag she needed—and it marked the first of many such trips mother and daughter would take, some by themselves and others with people like Mama Beauty, fellow seekers whose hearts had similarly been broken.

As Zodwa now makes her way down the lane between shacks toward the main road, she's assaulted from all sides by music blasting from boom boxes, radios, and car speakers. Bob Marley, Whitney Houston, Lionel Richie, and Michael Jackson compete with Miriam Makeba, Rebecca Malope, Yvonne Chaka Chaka, and Brenda Fassie to be heard. Eddy Grant's anti-apartheid song, "Gimme Hope Jo'anna," throbs from the shack closest to the tap as marijuana smoke drifts out, mingling with the woodsmoke from cooking fires.

Everyone is in celebration mode. Yellow, green, and black signs have been appropriated from lampposts and strung up along fence posts. *Mandela for President. The People's Choice! Vote ANC!* People spill out of shacks and into the lanes. Some are draped in ANC flags, and some are clutching beer bottles while others hold gourds of sorghum beer, *umqombothi*, or cartons of fermented *mahewu*.

"Here, sister," a neighbor says, passing Zodwa a bottle of Black Label. "Drink this. Beer is good for the baby. It will make him big and strong."

Zodwa smiles and thanks him for the offering. She wishes instead that he would give her some of the sheep's head that he's roasting on a grill over a drum. The smell of the meat makes her stomach rumble.

"Viva, Mandela! Viva, freedom!" The cries ring out from all sides.

She keeps walking, skirting the shack that stands all by itself on a corner. It's the only one in the squatter camp that doesn't have three or more other shacks pressed up against it. The woman who lives inside it, Gertie, is rumored to have the killing sickness, *ingculaza*, or AIDS as the whites call it. As bad as Zodwa's luck has been of late, at least she's not an untouchable like Gertie, who's wasted away, gone from being over a hundred kilos to looking like a skeleton the last time Zodwa saw her.

The sun is setting as Zodwa steps from the muddy, littered lane into the main road, and it lights up the clouds in the pinks of cosmos flowers, and the greens and purples of cabbage leaves. It sometimes amazes Zodwa that beauty can exist in a place like the township. With all its shacks thrown together from things the white man has found no use for, or hasn't been vigilant enough to guard, it's a festering pile of scrap metal. And yet as unsightly as it is, as fragmented and desperate and temporary, all it takes is seeing it in the reflection of dusk's forgiving gaze to realize that the discarded can be beautiful.

Zodwa heads for the spaza shop, counting her change to ensure she has enough. She doesn't know where Leleti has been all day. Her mother left before sunrise but no longer has a job to go to and no one in their right mind would hire her looking the way she does. Zodwa wants to surprise Leleti with a meal when she gets home. She's leaving the shop with a small bag of Iwisa when a commotion across the road catches her attention. A car is pulled up on the verge. Its presence bothers the taxi drivers, who hoot and wave emphatic arms out of windows to express their displeasure. A white woman sits inside it, ignoring the newspaper seller who is rapping on her window and motioning for her to wind it down so he can talk to her.

"I want to help you," he says, while pantomiming changing a tire. He calls to other men in the vicinity, asking them to assist so they can get the crazy *mlungu* back on the road and out of the way.

As more men approach the car, the woman appears to grow more fearful. She stares at the gathering crowd with widened eyes and Zodwa shakes her head at the woman's stupidity. There's a group of people wanting to help her, but her fear of the black savage doesn't allow her to see that. Finally, something appears to get through to the woman, who tentatively winds the window down and begins talking to the newspaper seller. Within a minute, she nods and pops the boot open, and the men spring into action, getting to work on taking out the spare tire to change it for her.

The woman gets out of the car and steps to the side, her arms wrapped around herself as she watches one of the men jack the car up. After a moment, she begins engaging with them, and whatever they say to her makes her smile. Zodwa is just about to turn and leave when she spots her mother and Mama Beauty getting out of a taxi that has pulled up.

They start to cross the road when Leleti turns and notices the commotion. Her mother does a double take when she sees the woman and something in her expression changes. She waves Mama Beauty on and turns to walk toward the car, a tentative smile on her face.

Zodwa is surprised when her mother addresses the white woman. They chat for a minute and then Zodwa watches in disbelief as Leleti throws herself into the stranger's arms, embracing her as though they are long-lost friends. Their voices rise up into the night but Zodwa can't hear the actual words over the sound of the traffic. What she can see is her mother smiling and laughing, wiping away tears as she holds the woman at arm's length before pulling her back, time and again, into an even tighter embrace than before.

After a few moments of conversing, the woman reaches into the car's boot and removes a few plastic bags. She holds them out to Leleti. When Leleti refuses them, the woman takes Leleti's hand, holding it up and pressing it to her own heart before forcing the bags on her. The encounter is abruptly ended when the tire change is completed and the taxi drivers begin furiously motioning for the woman to move out of the way.

The woman gives the newspaper seller some money. As she pulls away, she winds down her window and waves and smiles at Leleti. "Goodbye, Precious! It was so wonderful seeing you!" *Precious.* It's Leleti's English name.

Leleti waves and smiles back, an expression of wonder on her face. Zodwa doesn't know if it's because of the windfall of groceries or the effect seeing the woman has had on her.

Zodwa smiles timidly as she greets her mother after she's crossed the road. "Hello, Mama. Where were you today?"

"With Beauty in Soweto."

Zodwa is taken aback. "Soweto? Why?"

"We were making inquiries about Nomsa and Dumisa."

"Mama . . ." Zodwa shakes her head. That Leleti has traveled so far in her weakened state is worrying. At least she was with Mama Beauty, who would have looked out for her.

"What? I need to know what happened to him before I die."

"Mama, you're not going to . . ." Zodwa trails off when she

sees the expression on her mother's face. "Who was that you were with now?"

"Someone I used to work for very long ago when we were both just girls. The good Lord brought us together then and still He works His wonders today."

Zodwa doesn't share her mother's faith. From what she can tell, it's a quirk of fate or a spin of the wheel that decides who must suffer and who will be spared. Still, it's more comforting believing that than thinking God chooses which of His lambs to torture and which to reward. If Zodwa's rape and Leleti's suffering were God's will rather than something random, how much worse would that be? Still, she knows better than to say as much.

"You were hugging her," Zodwa says accusingly.

Leleti smiles in admission.

"I thought you said all white people were demons."

"Not that one," Leleti says. "That one is God's child."

"What did she give you?"

"Groceries. Have I not always told you that the Lord provides?"

As the laneway narrows, Zodwa is forced to trail a few steps behind her mother. She wants to remark that it was the white woman who provided and not God, which makes it charity rather than a blessing, but that is a sacrilege her mother would never allow.

Zodwa's curiosity about the woman may not be sated but at least her hunger will soon be.

Praise God.

CHAPTER SEVENTEEN

Ruth

❉

5 May 1994
Verdriet, Magaliesburg, South Africa

Dee walks into the lounge and eyes the cardboard box next to me. "What are you doing?"

"Packing up ahead of selling the farm. What does it look like?"

"You're wasting your time. I'm on my way to a lawyer now to revoke the power of attorney. We won't be selling."

I ignore her and just keep on sorting through Ma's giant *kist* of mementos.

"Ruth, did you hear me?"

I hum a few bars from Elton John's "The Bitch Is Back" but, of course, Dee doesn't get the reference. She's never had any use for music unless it was the background to some Bible verse wrapped up as a hymn.

"Ruth? I'm talking to you. Could you please listen?"

I open a photograph album and turn the pages. "Do you know," I muse, "there was a time when I really wanted to hear from you. All those times I wrote to you telling you how much we needed you, how much I needed you . . . pouring my heart out, begging you to come home and help me . . . But you were silent then, sending a very clear message of how little we meant

66
·

to you, and now after all this time I find I don't much care what you have to say anymore."

"The farm was left to both of us," Dee insists stubbornly, though she has the grace not to meet my eye.

"Then all the debt was left to both of us as well. Except, again, where were you for that? Not here. Not paying the bills. Not pouring money into the farm just to keep it afloat. Not paying Sarie and Stompie a monthly salary to take care of the property."

"I'll pay you back for all of that."

"With what?" I laugh. "Look at you. You look like a homeless person. All you have in the world is a rucksack filled with shitty, threadbare clothes. You're like those squatters at the camp down the road. Trying to claim something that isn't yours."

"I have savings, Ruth, and the farm is half mine."

I shrug.

My indifference seems to be what sets her off. "And at least I wasn't taking off my clothes, parading around like a whore for money. At least I was earning it the hard way."

I look at her, surprised.

"Yes, I heard about what you were up to," Dee says. "I know what you were."

"So, you kept up with all the gossip about me, just not with me personally?" I smile though it takes some effort. To hell with her and her precious sanctimony. "I'm ashamed of nothing. I earned an honest living, though not an entirely legal one, and it paid the bills. If I wasn't out there working my butt off, expos-ing my tits and ass"—I carry on speaking as she flinches—"then you wouldn't even have this farm to come back to. It would have been repossessed years ago. So, how about thanking me instead of judging me?"

"I'm still seeing my lawyer."

"Be my guest. I'll see mine too." I may not have that much money left but I know people in high places. They're almost as helpful as those in low ones.

She slams the door on her way out and I wait ten minutes before getting up and propping it open again to get a breeze through the lounge. It's hot and I'm sweaty, and silk probably isn't the most practical fabric to do manual labor in. Also, quite honestly, the packing is boring. I've been doing it more to get on Dee's nerves than to get anything productive done.

I'm so desperate for distraction that I almost consider actually talking to Vince when he calls for the second time in a week. I regret giving him the number. Clean breaks are so much easier than protracted ones. Besides, it hurts to hear his voice.

"Ruth, can you talk this time?" I'd told him I was on my way out the last time he called. "You didn't phone me back."

"If you want your car, you can come and get it yourself." I *might* have stolen his convertible BMW M3 just to rankle him since I know it's his pride and joy.

He laughs. "You haven't taken a baseball bat to it, have you?"

"Don't give me ideas, buster." God, I miss these wry back-and-forths.

"I don't care about the car, Ruth. You can keep the bloody thing for all I care." It's disappointing to hear him say that. I was hoping that his wanting to retrieve the car would make him come after me. What happened to good old-fashioned materialism? "I just wanted to see how you're doing and to ask you to give Bill a call sometime this week, please."

Bill is his lawyer. "Filing for divorce this soon? Jesus, you don't waste any time, do you?" I feel such a stab of pain I wonder if I might be having a heart attack.

"No. Nothing like that. I just want to make sure that we get the maintenance sorted out while we're . . . separated . . . and figuring things out."

Typical Vince. Generous to a fault. "I don't need maintenance, thank you."

"Ruth, according to the prenup—"

"Fuck the prenup. I've never wanted nor needed your money, Daddy Warbucks. Now, if there's nothing else, I need to go."

"I was wondering if you've given any further thought to the treatment facility we spoke about?"

In response, I hang up the phone in his ear and get back to clearing the cupboards. When I find Ma's old knitting basket on the top shelf of the storage cupboard, I yank the needles out, not prepared for the unfinished baby's bootie they still cling to. I'm not prepared for the hot flood of tears either.

What little foot with its dimpled, tiny toes my mother was knitting it for, I have no idea. Probably one of our many fertile cousins. All I know is that if I were thirty years younger, I'd take the discovery of the blue bootie as a sign. Since it can't be a sign, it has to be the universe mocking me. It seems to be doing that a lot lately. Still, the air crackles like it knows something. I wish it would share its secret.

CHAPTER EIGHTEEN

Delilah

❋

I n my past three attempts to go back to the hospital, I'd only gotten as far as town before turning around and heading back to the house in defeat. I told myself it was because Daniel was still in a coma and wouldn't know I was there anyway, but really it was the image of the priest at his bedside; how he'd looked so assured in his right to be there; how he'd claimed Daniel in a way I never could.

It was late afternoon and Ruth still hadn't risen. Based on the noise from the radio, which had served as accompaniment for her drunken singing until well after midnight, she'd clearly been on a bender. I'd tried to get her to shut up and go to sleep, but the bedroom door was locked and my banging on it had only made her sing louder.

Half-filled cardboard boxes were scattered all over the place though she didn't seem to be making any progress with them. Ruth clearly still had the attention span of a goldfish. I was tempted to unpack the boxes, mostly to annoy her but also to give myself some distraction, but with her power of attorney revoked after my visit to the lawyer the day before, Ruth couldn't sell the farm without my permission. And since I

wasn't going to give it, I looked forward to watching her unpack everything herself. Especially after she found the nota-
rized document I'd propped against her gin bottle where she
couldn't possibly miss it.

When the telephone trilled half an hour later, I considered
leaving it so the noise would wake Ruth, but after six rings, I
couldn't stand it anymore and picked up. "Hello?"

"Ruth?"

"No, it's Delilah."

There was a long pause. "You sound just like her. I thought
she was playing the fool."

"No. Who am I speaking to?"

"Her husband, Vincent."

"She hasn't gotten up yet but I can call her for you if you like?"

"No!" he virtually shouted before lowering his voice. "She
probably won't want to talk to me anyway." Before I could ask
why, he continued with, "So, you're the long-lost sister. I always
thought she'd made you up."

"That's me," I said. "Not made up."

"It just seemed so improbable that a family would have two
sisters called Ruth and Delilah. Aren't you a nun?"

"No, I left the convent when I was still a novice."

"Still, from what Ruth says, you're very different."

"Like shooting stars and mason jars," I murmured, remembering.

"What?"

"It's something our father used to say. That we were as different as shooting stars and mason jars. Ruth was the shooting
star, of course."

"Huh," he said. It was clearly the first time he'd heard the anecdote. That Ruth hadn't bragged about it to him vindicated her somehow. "So, how is Ruth?" he asked, changing the subject. "Really, I mean."

"Well . . ." I glanced at her closed bedroom door, not quite sure how to answer that. Why was he asking me, anyway?

"Look, I'm only asking because I'm worried about her."

"There's really nothing to worry about," I said tartly. If anyone could win their own battles, Ruth could. "She's absolutely fine." In perfect fighting shape, in fact.

He sighed and went quiet for a bit before blurting out, "She almost died a few weeks ago. Did she tell you that?"

"No." That was a surprise. "What happened?"

"She tried to commit suicide. Well, she says she didn't mean to actually commit suicide but I found her in the bath with a razor next to her. She'd taken pills and passed out. She almost drowned."

I was so taken aback that I didn't know what to say.

"Look," he continued. "I probably shouldn't have told you that but you need to know her frame of mind." He sighed again. "Anyway, please just keep an eye out for her. Ruth likes to put on a good show, but I worry about what's going on underneath sometimes."

I said goodbye, mulling over what he'd said. It didn't seem plausible. The Ruth I knew loved herself way too much to ever purposefully harm herself, so I was more inclined to believe her version of events than his. Still, it gave me pause and I couldn't quiet the niggling voice that wondered just how wounded my sister was.

I was relieved when Sarie came into the kitchen a few minutes later, as it offered a welcome distraction from worrying about Ruth. I invited her to join me at the dining room table and while she resisted at first, she gave in after I insisted. She'd been our family's maid as far back as I could remember, and my mother had never allowed the help to sit or eat inside. Some habits apparently died hard.

Sarie was in her seventies and, although tinier than I remembered, having shrunken into herself in the way old people do, she still had arms that were ropy with muscle from a lifetime of manual labor. A multicolored *doek* covered her head but gray hair sprouted from underneath the front of it. Her eyes shone as they peered at me from behind thick glasses.

"*Miesie*," she said, "*dis so lekker om jou weer te sien*." Missus, it's so good to see you again.

"Don't call me *miesie*, Sarie. You're older than I am. I'm the one who should be calling you that. Please call me Delilah."

"*Ag nee, miesie*." She laughed. "I can't do that even though things are all *deurmekaar* now that apartheid has ended. White people are acting crazy. Just the other day, Maria told me that her madam, *Mevrou* van der Merwe, told her to come for tea. Poor Maria thought the madam wanted her to come in and make the tea, so there she was in her apron and slippers, but the madam was all dressed up to serve Maria cake."

"No!"

"Yes!" Sarie slapped her thigh, laughing as though it was the funniest thing she'd ever heard. "Forty years Maria has worked for the madam and now the madam wants to wait on her and have a visit? It seems like in the new South Africa, white people want to have black friends just to prove they're not racist, but the only black people they know are their maids and gardeners. This is all Mandela's fault."

We both laughed and then she caught me up on farm news and town gossip. Ruth had been paying Sarie and her husband,

Stompie, to continue to take care of the property after Ma died and Sarie was grateful for it. "Where else could we get work at our age?" She went on to tell me how Ruth had also paid for Stompie to have hip replacement surgery a few years ago, and that she'd put two of their grandchildren through school.

I was surprised by Ruth's altruism and, to change the subject, I filled Sarie in on the encounter I'd had with Precious the week before. Even as I did so, I was aware of skimming over the details, leaving out my ridiculous overreaction to the perceived danger. I was ashamed of how I'd allowed the general level of hysteria in the country to affect me.

"Precious doesn't come to visit anymore," Sarie griped after I'd shared my news. "Not since her daughter moved from Kwa-Zulu to be with her. Precious expected great things from her but . . ." She sighed heavily and lowered her voice. "It wasn't to be. No one can break your heart like your own children." She was clearly hinting at some scandal that I refused to be drawn into.

We'd both known Precious since she was orphaned at seven months. Ruth and I were ten when Precious came to live with Sarie and Stompie, who were distant relatives who'd agreed to take her in. It wasn't just out of benevolence; extra hands were always needed on a farm and a little girl would grow into a kitchen maid.

The baby's presence gave Ruth and me something new to bicker over since, of course, it never occurred to us to share her. Ruth almost always won the fights to play with Precious, which bothered me at first, until I realized the reality of a baby wasn't nearly as appealing as the idea of it. Somehow, this never deterred Ruth, who, even though she normally had a short attention span, would spend hours dressing the baby up in outfits

Ma had knitted for our dolls. Not even the baby's vomiting and pooping could put my sister off.

While my interest in Precious waned early on, it was rekindled when she turned three and started following me around, parroting everything I said. She soaked up the world around her, becoming bloated with knowledge like a little intellectual tick, and the more conversant Precious became, the quicker Ruth lost interest in her and the more engaged I found myself becoming.

Precious was a quick and eager learner, remembering words I taught her like *Jesus, Bible, Lord,* and *savior.* It was this zealousness for religion that made Ma tolerate her; Precious would otherwise have been relegated to the kitchen since Ma discouraged any kind of relationship with a black person, be it a child or otherwise.

This casual sense of racism—an innate belief that as whites, we were far superior to blacks—appeared to be the only thing Ruth had ever inherited from Ma. While Ruth liked the infant Precious (squealing that black babies were the cutest), she never engaged with any of the other black people on the farm beyond issuing instructions, and certainly never fostered any kind of friendship with them.

It seemed contradictory, given the revelation of Ruth's helping Sarie's family financially, but it wasn't. Being a charitable benefactor and being a friend were two totally different things. The first kind of relationship suited Ruth's view of the world: that black people were dependent on whites to survive. It wasn't selfless giving; it was a generosity that reinforced Ruth's belief in her own supremacy. I'd seen it time and again at the various aid organizations I'd worked for across Africa: white saviors who swooped in with the sole intention of saving black people from themselves.

It was the one thing about me that Ma disapproved of. That, despite the teachings of the church and the politics of the time, I didn't believe in white supremacy or the division of the races. It wasn't a political statement I was making back then. It was just that Sarie was kind to me and showed me love, and so I naturally returned the consideration and affection.

When I left for the convent, Precious, then seven, was heartbroken. My attention had singled her out and probably made her feel as special as her adoration had made me feel. Sometimes all we need is to be seen in order to blossom. Just be seen, nothing more.

"How did she recognize you after all this time?" Sarie now marveled. "She hasn't laid eyes on you since you were seventeen."

"She said I look just like Ma." I laughed. "She thought I was a ghost." Considering Ruth had thought I was our dead mother when she first saw me, I supposed there was an uncanny resemblance.

I was surprised when Sarie changed the subject. "Did your friend find you, by the way?"

"What friend?"

"The one who came here just over a month ago looking for you. I told him you hadn't lived here since you were a girl and that the family was all long gone. He was very disappointed."

"Did he tell you his name?"

"I don't think so. I don't remember."

"Do you remember what he looked like?"

Sarie shook her head. "That was the week my glasses broke, before I was able to get a new pair. All I know is that he was tall and he spoke English. His hair was white here," she said, indicating temples that had grayed.

I'd had a fantasy throughout my life that one day I'd open the door to find Daniel standing there, wanting me to be a part of his life and to hell with all the reasons I'd had for leaving him. For a moment, just a moment, I allowed myself to believe that the fantasy had come true, that he'd come in search of me after all those years.

But I know better than anyone how the heart can play the most terrible tricks on the mind. It's a traitorous beast that can't be trusted at the best of times, but even less so when it's so utterly broken.

CHAPTER NINETEEN

Zodwa

* * *

10 May 1994
Big Hope Informal Settlement,
Magaliesburg, South Africa

The celebration of Nelson Mandela's victory is electric. It animates the squatter camp so wholly that for a few hours it's transformed from a scrap heap of human and metal debris into a living, breathing thing. Life calls a refrain and the township, itself, responds.

When Mandela was released from prison more than four years before, hope was born. Everyone knew, though, that hope was a fickle thing; it would allow you to warm your hands against it one minute, only to flare up and burn you to a husk the next, which is why people were cautious with it. But on this day, the day on which millions of dreams have impossibly come true, hope has ignited into joy.

Zodwa feels it. The township is celebrating and there will be no sleep for anyone that night because who would want to sleep through such a moment? The ANC has won. A black man is president. History is being made, and to be a black person who has lived through apartheid and come out of it the victor is a blessed, blessed thing.

The festivities are so loud that Zodwa's cries cannot compete. As contraction after contraction rages through her, she grips the foam bed and waits for the pain to consume her. Leleti sits next to her, wiping the sweat from Zodwa's brow and stuffing a cloth between her jaws to clamp down on every time her belly tightens. Their roles have been reversed, and it is now Leleti's turn to watch as pain racks her daughter's body, helpless to do anything to keep it at bay.

Even as Zodwa pants fiercely, the baby struggling to be free of her, she recognizes her mother's frailty. Leleti has aged ten years in the past week and Zodwa knows it's as much her confession about the rape as it is her mother's worsening illness. Leleti positions herself between Zodwa's knees and instructs, "Push now. Push, my child."

The dog whines and paces, and Zodwa pushes until she is sure she will die from the pushing. Her mother fades in and out of focus until it's no longer Leleti between Zodwa's thighs, but Mongezi.

She sees his face, hovering just above her, contorted with both fury and triumph just as it was on that fateful day so many months ago. Zodwa couldn't move under the weight of him and struggled to breathe around his rough cheek, which was pressed down hard against her mouth and nose. She bites through the pain now just as she wishes she had bitten through his cheek then.

"Push," Leleti wheezes, and Zodwa does until something finally releases like a dam wall breaking, after which she slips blessedly into unconsciousness.

When she wakes, a baby is suckling at her breast. Leleti's dog stands close enough to Zodwa that she can feel its hot breath on her face.

"Born free," her mother whispers from next to her, her tone one of hushed awe. "Your son is born free."

Your son.

Zodwa cries steadily though she feels nothing at all beyond the sensation of being drained of milk and tears. She thinks of Thembeka, the object of her desire, and how this child is the price she had to pay for that, the punishment that was meted out to her for loving a girl. Her son's penis feels like a cruel joke, just another reminder that men run the world and will never allow themselves to become obsolete.

When Zodwa feels her mother lifting the baby from her breast a short while later, she opens her eyes drowsily. Leleti looks steady on her feet, her one hand cupping the baby's head while the other is wrapping around his thighs as she presses him against her. The last thing Zodwa sees before her mother turns away from her is the birthmark on her son's left buttock.

Africa, she thinks. *It looks like Africa.*

She closes her eyes then and allows the dog's whining to be a lullaby that carries her gently to sleep.

CHAPTER TWENTY

Ruth

❖

10 May 1994
Verdriet, Magaliesburg, South Africa

Dee fiddles with the bunny ears above the television, trying for better reception, but Ma's ancient black-and-white Telefunken remains obstinate.

"This thing is as old as Methuselah," I say, walking up behind it and smacking it for good measure. Dee opens her mouth to object but I point at the screen, which has lost a few degrees of fuzziness. "It worked. You're welcome."

She doesn't thank me but I wasn't expecting her to. She's gone ahead and reinstituted her power of attorney, and I'm waiting to hear back from my lawyers to see what kind of case I have considering her absence for all those years.

What it boils down to is that neither of us has anywhere else to go and so we're stuck with each other for now. The bickering, at least, has been kept to a minimum but only because Dee locks herself away in her room most of the time. In all honesty, though, I prefer the sniping to the silence. I'm so bored and desperate for company that I'm even prepared to try to extend an olive branch for one night, if for no other reason than olives go well with martinis, and martinis are always a good idea. Also, talking to Dee will stop me from calling Vince, something I'm way too tempted to do.

"What are you watching?" I ask.

"The news."

"God, why?"

"I want to see Nelson Mandela's inauguration address."

"Well, if I'm going to be forced to watch it with you, I'm going to need a drink," I say, heading to the fridge.

"Of course you are," she mutters.

"You want something?"

"No."

"Come on, live a little! Surely it wouldn't kill you to celebrate the 'new South Africa.' One drink?" I cajole. "To toast the new president."

Dee considers it and then, to my surprise, nods. "Okay. One drink."

I pour myself a vodka martini and Dee a glass of wine as the news jingle plays and the newscaster begins intoning about the day's events. It's that Cruywagen fellow, the one who looks like a ventriloquist dummy after too many face-lifts. That's the thing about plastic surgery: you have to know when to stop. Hell, that's the secret to just about everything in life, isn't it?

"Here you go." I hand the glass to Dee, who immediately shushes me.

Nelson Mandela's flat, monotonous voice blasts from the TV's tinny speakers. He sounds so calm amid the hysteria that his presidency has incited that I can't help but be soothed by it.

"We understand it, still, that there is no easy road to freedom. We know it well that none of us acting alone can achieve success. We must therefore act together as a united people, for national reconciliation, for nation building, for the birth of a new world. Let there be justice for all."

The inauguration crowd roars in approval and I swear Dee wipes a tear away. She takes a quick sip of her wine and I lean forward with my hand extended. "Cheers," I say, and we clink glasses.

"Cheers."

She turns the volume of the television down and we sit in silence. Some silences can be comfortable, I suppose, but this isn't one of them. I light a cigarette and lean back into the couch, closing my eyes. "Do you think he means what he says?" I ask, nodding at the television. "All that stuff about reconciliation?"

"Yes, I do."

"But is all that 'Kumbaya' stuff even possible? I mean, if I was Mandela, I'd be really, really pissed off about all those years in prison. I'd want revenge against the people who did that to me."

"Lucky you're not him then."

That's when I hear an eerie, high-pitched noise coming from outside. "Did you hear that?"

Dee cocks her head and listens for a moment.

I feel a sliver of alarm. "I really think we should get better security. I've been hearing that the crime here has been getting out of hand. Just another reason why we should sell," I can't help adding.

There's a noise outside again, one we've both heard because Dee's head snaps in the same direction. It's piercing and sinister, like cats mating.

Dee gets up and heads for the door.

"Wait! Don't open that. We have no idea what it is."

"We have to," Dee says, reaching for the handle.

"Jesus, wait!" I run to the bedroom and take Da's old Winchester rifle off the wall before rushing back. Sarie mentioned an increase in farm attacks, and two women alone on a rural property would be easy targets.

"Is that even loaded?" Dee asks dubiously. It dates back to the Anglo-Boer War.

"No idea but it may be enough to scare someone off."

I'm standing behind Dee with the rifle when she slowly unlocks the door and then pulls it open. I look over her shoulder but can't see anything. There's no one on the veranda. "Must just be horny cats," I say, trying to pull Dee back. The sooner we can close and lock the door, the better.

But Dee won't step back. She's staring down at something and I have to nudge her aside to get a better look. When I spot it, I know the booze isn't making me see things because Dee can see it too.

It's a big black dog. And it's guarding something.

CHAPTER TWENTY-ONE

Delilah

❋

10–11 *May 1994*
Verdriet, Magaliesburg, South Africa

O h my God," Ruth exclaimed, trying to push past.

The large dog rose up on its haunches in response, the hair on its back raised as it gave a low warning growl, and Ruth froze next to me. The creature was black as tar and looked like a cross between a Rottweiler and a Labrador. It licked its lips, eyeing Ruth warily, before settling itself back down again next to the crying bundle.

I turned from the dog to the little wriggling creature on our doorstep. "It's a baby," I said stupidly.

"No shit, Sherlock," Ruth whispered, staring at it in awe.

I bent down slowly and held my hand out, palm down, for the dog to sniff. It did so cautiously, and then, seemingly deciding that I didn't pose any threat, it stood up and shook itself before pacing to the edge of the veranda, where it stared off into the darkness, whining softly.

Ruth stepped back inside to put the rifle down and when she returned, she reached out to the bundle with trembling hands, scooping it up as though she was afraid it was an illusion that, when touched, would dissolve into nothing but smoke. The dog rushed to her side but didn't show any further signs of aggression.

I stepped past Ruth to go outside. Two plastic bags had been placed to the side of the door and I shot a quick glance inside them. They were filled with what looked like baby things and didn't appear to contain anything sinister. I craned my head around the veranda and the parts of the garden I could see.

"Hello?" I called out into the darkness. The sounds of crickets and of cars whooshing by on the main road were all that answered. Behind me, the dog whined plaintively, but the baby had thankfully fallen silent. "Is anyone there?"

"Oh, for God's sake, Dee! Stop calling out like that. No one's going to answer you."

"How do you know?"

"It's not like he was left here accidentally."

"He?" I eyed the pink woolen blanket that the baby was swaddled in. "Looks like a girl to me."

"It's a boy," she said firmly.

"But it has a pink blanket."

"Trust me. It's a boy," Ruth repeated.

She walked inside to the couch and gently laid the baby down. I trailed behind her with the plastic bags. As Ruth unwrapped the blanket, the dog trotted to her side, where it sat next to the child, who'd begun to mewl. The dog licked the baby's cheek and it stopped fussing.

"Don't let it do that," I said.

"What?"

"Cover it in dog slobber."

"The dog's soothing him," she said. "See? He's stopped crying."

The baby was wearing a mint-green Babygro that had fasteners all down the front. Ruth rubbed her hands together to warm them before reaching down and undoing each snap. She pulled the baby's legs free of the cotton leggings and then undid the safety pin of the cloth nappy.

"Aha!" she cried. "A penis! I told you so!"

I walked over and looked down at the baby, who was, indeed, a boy. "How did you know that?" I asked incredulously. "Do you have some kind of penis sensor?" I was only half joking.

Ruth shrugged. "I saw a sign the other day."

"A sign?"

"Yes, a blue bootie attached to one of Ma's knitting needles."

"So what? What did that have to do with this baby?"

"I told you. It was a sign pointing to the arrival of a boy. I just didn't understand it at the time. Now I do."

There she went spouting that psychic nonsense again. "Well, the odds were in your favor," I said. "It could only be a boy or a girl. You had a fifty percent chance of being right."

"As did you, but you were wrong." And then she laughed. "Will you look at that? He has a birthmark on his butt that looks just like Africa."

I peered over and had a look. "Looks more like a cauliflower to me." I noticed that the baby was still covered with a thin layer of vernix—the white substance babies are born with—and that the piece of thread that had been used to tie off the umbilical cord looked a bit grubby. It was unlikely that the baby had been born in a hospital.

The dog padded over to Ruth and put its head on her knee, sniffing the baby as if to make sure she hadn't hurt it. Something about the creature niggled at me.

"Is it just me," Ruth asked, "or does this dog look almost like the one you used to have when we were kids? What was his name again?"

I smiled despite myself. Of course, that was it. Ruth was

right. "Shadow," I replied. And then the strangest thing happened. The dog's ears perked up in response and it turned to me as though I'd called its name.

Ruth laughed. "It certainly seems to think it's Shadow. Maybe it's a ghost come back to haunt you."

"Don't be ridiculous," I said, walking to the telephone. "I'll make the call. You sit with him and keep him calm."

"What call?"

"To the police."

"The police? Why on earth do you want to call them?"

"A baby has just been left on our doorstep, Ruth. Of course we need to report it."

"No!" She said it so forcefully that she startled the baby, who started crying again. "We're not calling the police."

"Abandoning a baby is a crime. Whoever did this needs to be found and held accountable—"

"It's not like his mother left him at a garbage dump or in a field somewhere. She left him on our doorstep where she knew he would be safe."

"The baby needs to be taken into custody—"

"Listen to you! 'Taken into custody.' He's not a criminal. He didn't do anything wrong."

"For God's sake. Will you please stop interrupting me? I was going to say he needs to be taken into custody so that he can be transferred to a place of safety."

"And then what?"

"First, they'll look for his mother—"

"Oh, please! How will they ever find her? It would be an impossible task! And even if they do by some miracle, it doesn't matter, really, because she clearly can't care for him since she left him here."

88

"Believe me when I tell you that most women who give up their children regret it immensely."

"Then it makes more sense to keep him here. That way she'll know where to find him if she changes her mind."

"We can't just keep him, Ruth. He needs to be processed into the system."

"Which means what, exactly?"

"He'll go to a children's sanctuary—"

"You mean orphanage!" Ruth snapped. "Stop trying to sugarcoat it, Delilah." She took a deep breath. "Look, I say we let the poor child have one night of peace and decide what to do in the morning."

With that, she turned her back on me and returned to the couch, where she sat down and placed the baby on her lap before reaching for my wineglass and taking a long sip. There would be no rationalizing with her, not just because of the drama of the evening, which Ruth was clearly enjoying, but also because she'd been drinking.

Instead, I marched over and snatched the glass from her. "No drinking while you're looking after the baby. Or else I'll definitely be making that call." I glared at her, daring her to challenge me. She pulled a face but let me take the glass without any resistance.

I went through the plastic bags, pulling out a bottle and a tin of formula. "This looks like it's for older babies but no shops nearby will be open at this time. It will just have to do until tomorrow."

"Will you make it up while—"

"No, this is all on you. You want to keep him for the night, you take care of him. And the dog too. I'm going to bed," I said.

The baby's sudden appearance felt ominous, as though my

past was following me into my present, whispering that it couldn't so easily be forgotten. I'd just left hundreds of orphans behind in Goma even though they desperately needed me, and the guilt I carried was already a constant reminder of that. I didn't need another abandoned baby in my life.

He'd started screaming at three a.m. and hadn't stopped since. Not even a pillow pulled over my head could drown out the noise. I'd considered coming to their aid but since Ruth clearly saw herself as some maternal fairy godmother, I'd decided against it. I didn't know why she'd responded to the child as strongly as she had—if it was just another example of her white savior complex or if something else was at play—but the sooner she was stripped of those notions, the better.

When I came through to the lounge the next morning, I found Ruth exactly where I'd left her: sitting on the couch with the baby swaddled in her arms and the dog lying next to her. Her eyes were bloodshot but, for once, it wasn't from alcohol. Judging by the sound of things, they'd both had a rough night.

"Oh good, you're up," Ruth said. She looked so happy to see me that I had to turn away and busy myself with making coffee.

I wished she wasn't there. I was used to my morning ritual of calling the ICU in peace. It would have to wait now. "Have you been up with him all night?"

"I managed to put him down for a few hours after you went to bed, but then he woke up in the early hours and nothing I've done has been able to soothe him. I don't think the formula agrees with him," she said while standing up and ambling over. "He vomited most of it up. He must be starving by now." As I turned to face her, she tried to pass the baby across to me. "Hold him while I dash to the loo and take a quick shower. I need to

get to the shops to get him the right formula and proper supplies."

"Ruth, we need to call—"

"We can't hand a starving child across to the authorities, can
we? Jesus, where's your compassion?" Her expression was one of
such judgment that I couldn't find words to reply. Instead, I
turned back to the sink, washed my hands, and then took the
baby from her.

His cry was reaching that quavering, heartbreaking note
that only newborns can produce as he gasped for air. Not knowing what else to do, I stuck my finger in the baby's mouth to try
to soothe him.

He latched on immediately, sucking so ferociously that it
almost undid me.

CHAPTER TWENTY-TWO

Zodwa

11 May 1994
Big Hope Informal Settlement,
Magaliesburg, South Africa

When Zodwa awakens, it's to the strange sensation of her organs shifting back into their natural positions. She rolls over and the motion aggravates the tenderness in her swollen breasts and groin.

That's when she remembers the baby.

She uses her elbows to prop herself up and looks around the shack. The baby is nowhere to be seen. Neither is Leleti. Her mother must have taken him away so that she could rest.

Zodwa lies back down again and closes her eyes. The present is too painful a place to inhabit, but the past is a well-worn path she can choose to walk whenever she wants. That's where she seeks refuge now, in those moments prior to her life splitting into a "before" and "after."

She conjures up the image of how Thembeka looked on the day they first met and it's an instant balm to her pain. She was so beautiful, with her high forehead and rounded cheekbones, with her wide smile exposing pink gums and glistening white teeth. Her eyes were a lighter shade than Zodwa's, more rust than brown, and though they had a sleepy quality to them, they twinkled with mischief.

What she felt for Thembeka then was love at first sight and guilt at first sight; it was shame and fear and joy at first sight.

How clearly Zodwa can see it all now: how everything began and ended the very second she laid eyes on Thembeka. How strange that a person can look back on her life and see all the tiny decisions and actions—even the moments of inertia in which nothing appeared to be happening at all—all the trailing comets of them hurtling forward like fireworks, not into nothingness or insignificance, but toward a future moment, a split second, in which everything came together in an explosion of certainty and unity so that you could only gasp: *Oh! So that's where it was all leading to.*

There are so many bright memories with Thembeka to choose from, and Zodwa hops between them like a magpie, picking out the shiniest ones with which to distract herself. She sees Thembeka, soon after they met, on the day Zodwa was teaching her how to balance a bucket of water on her head.

"You city girls think you know everything," Zodwa teased. "And while knowing how to catch a taxi to Pretoria has its uses, knowing how to carry water while still keeping your hands free to carry firewood is even more important."

Thembeka laughed but still she tried it, yelping in pride when the bucket didn't immediately topple off.

"Okay, now walk," Zodwa encouraged.

After four shuffling steps, the bucket tilted sharply and before Thembeka could get her hands up to steady it, it tumbled down, soaking both her and Zodwa in the process. They fell against each other, weak with hilarity, and Zodwa felt Thembeka's heart beating against her palm for the very first time.

The second time was just before the rape, when she and Thembeka were sitting on the bed in Thembeka's shack doing their homework. A long piece of plyboard was balanced on their knees, serving as their makeshift desk, and a textbook was laid out before them.

Zodwa finished all the exercises on the page and took a break while Thembeka copied the last two sums down. As Zodwa waited for Thembeka to finish, she pulled a small tin of Vaseline from her shirt pocket, opened the lid, and dipped her finger inside before spreading the shiny substance over her lips.

The motion of her finger was so meditative that she got lost in a trance, spreading more Vaseline on than she normally would. When she snapped out of it and turned to Thembeka, she found her friend watching her, her eyes fixed on Zodwa's mouth.

"I want some too," Thembeka said.

Zodwa held the open tin out to Thembeka but before her friend could take it from her, Zodwa accidentally dropped it. She instinctively reached out to grab it, trapping the tin between her hand and Thembeka's chest. Zodwa flushed at the sensation of the swell of Thembeka's breast against her palm, the steady heartbeat counting off the seconds of contact, and snatched her hand away so that the tin fell and got lost between them.

Thembeka merely laughed and then shook her head. "It's okay. I don't need the tin." She leaned in with exquisite slowness, gently touching her lips to Zodwa's. Zodwa closed her eyes, hardly daring to breathe as she savored the sensation of Thembeka's mouth pressed against her own.

Is this a kiss? Are we kissing?

A dog barked from somewhere down the lane and a metal spoon grated against a pot's surface in a shack nearby. The scent of frying onions competed with the smell of Vaseline and the talcum powder Thembeka used. Zodwa's entire universe expanded and then contracted, and if ever there was a perfect moment in her life, then that was surely it.

"There," Thembeka said. "You put too much on. That's better." She smiled at Zodwa, holding her gaze for a few moments as she smacked her lips together before returning to her homework.

It was such a tiny moment, just a few seconds, but it was so intimate that Zodwa couldn't imagine that it could be anything else than a coded gesture. It was enough to make Zodwa work up the courage two days later to write a letter declaring her feelings, which definitely weren't the platonic kind but rather were fevered and all-consuming.

It was this letter that Thembeka's boyfriend, Mongezi, somehow managed to intercept before Thembeka could read it. And that was the beginning of everything unraveling, the moment when Mongezi decided that Zodwa should be taught a lesson about the kind of desires women should and shouldn't have.

Zodwa wonders if there could ever have been a happy ending for a love so unnatural that it angered the ancestors enough to curse her.

CHAPTER TWENTY-THREE

Ruth

❋

11 May 1994
Verdriet, Magaliesburg, South Africa

When I get home from the shops, I'm laden down with bags of feeding bottles, teats, multiple brands of formula, dummies, disposable nappies, bum cream, lotions, wipes, and various other baby paraphernalia including a bassinet and a tiny bathtub.

Jesus, babies are materialistic little buggers.

The dog rushes out to greet me and follows me back and forth during the three trips it takes between the house and car to get everything inside. Where are Dee and the baby? I don't want to call out—if the baby's fallen asleep, it's an absolute miracle—so I tiptoe to the door of Dee's room and peer in through the crack.

Dee is sitting on her bed with the baby clutched to her chest. Tears stream down her cheeks.

"Dee?" I whisper. "What's wrong?"

"Nothing." She gets up wearily, wiping the tears away, before passing the baby to me. He wakes immediately and begins mewling, and I watch as Dee heads for the bathroom, where she closes herself in.

"Dee?" I call but she's already started running bathwater,

which probably drowns me and the baby out. God, to think Ma called me the drama queen. I roll my eyes at Dee's theatrics. Keeping the baby for one night rather than handing it in to the authorities is hardly something to blubber over.

I turn my attention to the poor mite, who is clearly crazed with hunger. There are a lot of instructions for sterilizing the bottles and teats, which are mostly helpful, but I'm also grateful for all my years of secretly watching TV shows and movies that featured babies. I always considered it my guilty pleasure, but it's amazing how much you can learn about burping, feeding, and changing nappies by watching someone else do it.

I'm trying to do everything one-handed as I hold the little guy against my chest, but it's almost impossible and I give up and put him down on the couch. The bassinet will need to be properly set up before he can use it, so I put together a makeshift nest by placing the baby between four pillows arranged in a square. He's so tiny that he barely moves even while he's bringing the place down with his screaming.

"Watch the baby," I instruct the dog, who dutifully sits down next to him.

"Almost done. Your food is almost ready," I croon from the kitchen. The baby's face is scrunched up in fury and his pouty lips are pulled back from his gums. I hope that the sound of my voice is doing something to soothe him, even though all signs point to the opposite.

The dog licks the baby's hand and his crying goes down a few decibels.

"Good dog."

When I've finally mixed the formula in the bottle and let it cool to the right temperature, checking it on my inner arm to be sure, I rush it over to the baby and pick him up. Holding him in the crook of my arm, I put the bottle to his lips and squirt a drop of liquid onto them.

The baby's lips immediately close over the teat as he snuffles and begins sucking with such zeal that I'm scared he'll choke. "Slow down, little fella. Take it easy. There's plenty more where that came from." He's clearly skeptical because he keeps taking great big gulps. Most of the formula pours from his mouth, down his chubby cheeks and into the multiple little fat rolls of his neck.

We finally get into a steady rhythm and his cries die away. His face is like that of a wise old man and a cherub combined, like he knows the answers to life's mysteries, but also enjoys hanging out on clouds with harps to balance out all that heavy stuff. As he sucks, the creases in his brow smooth and his eyes close. He's blissed out and I did that. I made that happen. I wish so much that Vince were here to be a part of this. That he could see how luminous the little tyke is and how well we fit together.

I didn't need a head doctor, Vince. This is all I needed. Just this.

I swallow back an unexpected rush of emotion that takes me back to all those times I visited parks and sat on benches, not even attempting to disguise my mission by hiding behind a newspaper or a book. I can only imagine the raw hunger that must have been written on my face as I stared longingly at babies in prams and toddlers running around on sturdy legs.

I'd look at the crook of my arm and wonder what it was for if not to hold a baby. My breasts, which stirred men into a frenzy of lust at night, felt ornamental and frivolous during the day. What was the point of them if not to nourish a child?

When I started having fantasies about walking past a pram, picking a baby up, and just carrying on walking, I knew it was time to stop going to parks to torture myself.

It's funny how our dreams change over time, how lofty they are at the beginning and how quickly we're prepared to lower our expectations when it becomes clear we've been aiming too high. I'd first dreamed of beautiful babies that looked like the perfect combination of me and whatever man I was with at the time: blue eyes, red hair, freckles; green eyes, blond hair, dimples. Now, all these years and disappointments later, this baby who looks nothing like me feels like an embarrassment of riches, too much to dare hope for.

The dog whines suddenly, pulling me from my reverie, and I'm grateful to have the distraction from old memories that should no longer have the power to wound. It's sitting staring at us and I'm just wondering if it's a boy or a girl (since my penis sensor apparently doesn't extend to dogs) when it cocks its leg open and flashes me. She's a girl. I laugh as she opens her leg even wider and starts licking herself.

"Quite the Jezebel, aren't you?" And just like that, she's named.

When the baby has finally finished the bottle, I lift him and hold him over my shoulder to burp him. After only a few pats, he gives the most satisfying belch and then vomits down my back. "Charming. Thanks for that."

I put him back down on the couch and he's asleep almost immediately. I kiss his forehead, which smells of milk and impossible dreams that finally come true. A hiccupping sob from the bathroom brings me back to reality. I know the sound is amplified by the tiles and bathwater, but it's still alarming. Good grief, it seems I have two babies I need to look after.

Knocking on the bathroom door, I call out, "Dee?"

"Go away."

She sounds like she has a cold, so I can only imagine the amount of crying she's done. This can't be about not turning the baby in last night. Something else must be wrong. "Are you okay?"

"Leave me alone."

Thinking back to my own misadventures a few weeks ago, I know the bathroom is a good place to make bad decisions. I had no intention of going through with my staged suicide attempt, but I have absolutely no idea what's going through my sister's head. She's more a stranger to me now than she ever was.

"I'm coming in, okay?" She says something but I can't make out what it is. The handle turns in my hand. At least she didn't lock herself in.

"What the hell are you doing?" Dee is in the process of climbing out of the bath, one foot on the bath mat and the other still in the water. Her face is a picture of dismay.

"Just checking you're okay. Sounds like the world is ending in here."

"God, Ruth," she mutters as she tries reaching for the towel draped over the toilet lid, but it's too late. I've already seen what she doesn't want me to see.

My sister has jagged white stretch marks that crisscross her stomach and breasts. My breath catches. I know those marks. They're rites of passage I've coveted all my life. It doesn't seem possible and yet it has to be. "Who . . . when . . ." I have so many questions but I'm not able to get any of them out in a way that makes sense.

Dee yanks the towel and wraps it around herself as though it's armor that can protect her.

"You're a mother?" I ask. She doesn't answer but her face crumples in response. "Oh my God, you are. You had a baby."

"Yes," she whispers. "Daniel."

CHAPTER TWENTY-FOUR

Delilah

❊

11 May 1994
Verdriet, Magaliesburg, South Africa

It was Father Thomas who discovered my pregnancy and sounded the alarm when I was seven months along. I'd managed to hide it from myself for five of them, refusing to believe that my period drying up and my stomach and breasts swelling could mean I was carrying a child. Instead, I saw the symptoms as a physical manifestation of my guilt.

Hiding it from the rest of the nuns wasn't easy, but also not as difficult as it should have been; a convent, after all, is more focused on the soul than the body. We wore loose habits and were encouraged to always keep our eyes directed at the floor so that nothing could distract us from our communion with God. No one ever saw me naked except for the novice, Sister Marguerite, who helped me change from my street clothes into my convent garb on the day I arrived. While her eyes had lingered on my body, and it looked like she wanted to say something, she kept quiet about whatever suspicions she may have had.

The day my secret was discovered, I was in Father Thomas's office because it was a visiting Sunday and my parents, so busy on the farm, were unable to come out and see me. Since he was the priest who'd recruited me to the faith, the one who'd overseen my conversion to Catholicism, the Reverend Mother considered him a friend of the family.

"Ah, Sister Mary Teresa," he said as I entered his office, calling me by my new name, the one I'd chosen for myself when I'd been received as a novice. "It's good to see you." He held his arms out to me as he walked around his desk, but I pretended not to see the gesture, just as I had the past three months, as I hurried to sit down before he could embrace me.

"Good evening, Father." I sank into the chair a moment before he reached me. Another close call.

He dropped his hands to the sides of the chair and swooped down to give me a chaste peck on the temple instead. Even that, I recoiled from. "How are you, my child?"

"I'm well, Father."

As he returned to his spot behind the desk, I chattered nervously about my week, what I was learning in Latin class, and the general goings-on in the convent. Where I'd once felt safe in his presence, I no longer did. It was just a matter of time before my true nature was discovered and I was kicked out, which was exactly what I deserved.

A half an hour passed in this way, Father Thomas asking me questions and me answering to the best of my ability. His opinion of me had always mattered greatly—how could it not when I'd been so desperately in love with him—and so I was careful not to do or say anything that might make him think less of me. When it was time for me to leave, he rose and walked around to my side of the desk.

The pregnancy made me awkward and slow, and so I'd only just managed to leverage myself out of the chair when he reached me. Before I could turn, he stepped forward and enveloped me in a hug. I will never forget the expression on his face, the way it changed from one of affection to confusion and then horror, when he realized what my swollen belly pressed against him meant. I still burn with shame to recall it.

There were accusations and recriminations from all sides, and the fact that I wouldn't reveal the name of the father only made it worse. The scandal was so big that not even the convent rules about silence could contain it. The other nuns' whispers followed me everywhere I went.

"How old is she?"

"Only seventeen. Still a child herself."

"Well, what did everyone expect? She's only been a Catholic for a few years."

"I heard she grew up as part of the Dutch Reformed Church. Barbaric people."

One or two of the younger nuns looked at me with something akin to sympathy, and Sister Marguerite reached out one day to quickly squeeze my hand, but the rest of the sisters turned against me completely, comforting Father Thomas and the Reverend Mother.

"Don't be too hard on yourselves for not seeing the Jezebel she is."

"Her own mother took her for the virginity test just before she joined the convent."

"Who could expect her to use her last week of freedom to rid herself of her virtue?"

It was Father Thomas who suggested to the Reverend Mother that while they had no choice but to excommunicate me, they should keep the baby and raise it in the convent. "This child deserves a chance at a good life. Let us not punish it for its mother's sins," he said. "She has let us down terribly, and no one feels more disappointed in her behavior and deceit than I, but surely this innocent child should not suffer for that?"

The Reverend Mother was moved enough by his mercy to agree to such an unusual arrangement.

The birth was a difficult one. I was in labor for close to forty-six hours. Two older nuns served as my midwives and seemed to rejoice in each second of my agony.

"This is God's punishment for your sin," the one reminded me as I panted through a haze of pain.

"You're lucky Father Thomas is saving your baby from the fate of the orphanage."

"Can you imagine the stigma of a fallen nun as a mother hanging over the poor child? Can you imagine the terrible shame?"

The pain gouged a chasm between me and the baby as the minutes stretched into hours, each contraction bringing it closer to the world but taking it farther from me. When the baby was finally born, I was left so weak that it felt as though it had drained all the life out of me.

"It's a boy," I was told.

"Praise the Lord. Less likely that he will have his mother's weak character."

"Yes, indeed. He will be raised by true women of God and instilled with Father Thomas's moral fiber."

"Please," I whispered. "Please can I hold him?"

"I think not."

"Please. Just for a moment. To say goodbye."

"Give her the child." It was the Reverend Mother, who'd come to check on my progress.

She was a kind woman, a true Christian, and I was grateful for her timely intervention. I don't remember if I thanked her for her mercy. All I remember was my son's face as he was reluctantly handed across to me. It was contracted into a rictus of disapproval, as though he too found our predicament distasteful.

"Forgive me, my son. Forgive me for what I am about to do," I whispered into the tiny helix of his ear as I stroked his silky hair. I was crying freely by then, my tears spilling over onto his perfect face.

"Would you like to name him?" the Reverend Mother asked. "Before you have to leave?"

I nodded, grateful that abandonment wasn't the only legacy I'd be leaving my son with. "I'd like to call him Daniel."

"'God is my judge.' It's a good name."

I chose it exactly for its meaning. Having been judged harshly by both myself and the church, I never wanted Daniel to be accountable to anyone but God.

The Reverend Mother held out her arms for him. "It's time, my dear."

My grip around Daniel tightened. "Just a moment more, please."

I leaned down to kiss him on his forehead, anointing him not with oil, but with a mother's love that I hoped would protect him from the worst that life might throw at him. Of course, it hadn't, but then I'd been thinking of sadness and despair, not bullets fired from close range.

What a cruel twist of fate that the first time I saw my son was just after I'd given him life, and the next was almost thirty-nine years later when he was fighting so hard to cling to it. I could never have foreseen that, nor that it would be Father Thomas—the very man I'd so desperately loved and who'd cast me out—who'd be the priest praying at my son's bedside, standing between us once again.

CHAPTER TWENTY-FIVE

Ruth

11 May 1994
Verdriet, Magaliesburg, South Africa

The baby is asleep between us on the couch as Dee stammers her way through the story. She's gotten back into her pajamas even though it's almost midday and she pulls her ratty old gown tightly around herself.

She's too thin, but then she's always been lean whereas I'm voluptuous.

Voluptuous.

The word conjures an image like a magician pulling a rabbit out of a hat: Dee in her wedding dress during her novice reception ceremony. How stupid I was. She wasn't fat, she was pregnant.

The thought enrages me, as does the knowledge that she gave the child up. "Why didn't you just leave the convent and come home with the baby?"

"You say it like it would have been the easiest thing in the world. It was 1955, Ruth. Unwed Catholic mothers weren't allowed to keep their babies then. Their little 'bastards' were sent to orphanages, and those who weren't lucky enough to be adopted were raised in terrible conditions." She gazes off, eyes unfocused, and then startles me with a humorless laugh. "And could you imagine what that would have done to Ma? My leaving to become a nun and coming back unmarried with a baby when I was eighteen? God, it would have killed her." She closes her eyes and shakes her head. "Letting them keep Daniel and raise him was the best solution for everyone. I did what was best for him."

Jezebel suddenly gets up from where she's lying on the floor and pads over to the baby to nuzzle his face. He squints and looks like he's going to wake up. "Jezebel, no!" Dee flinches as though I've slapped her. "What? I don't want her waking him."

"You've named the dog Jezebel?"

"Yes, so what? Does it offend your sensibilities? It's just a funny name." I don't let her get a word in. I'm not in a mood for a lecture about respecting the Bible, not today of all days when my holier-than-thou sister has been revealed to be nothing but a hypocrite. "So, how did you get the church to not tell Ma and Da?"

She sighs. "They agreed to keep it quiet if I left without a fuss and took up the position with the aid organization they'd found for me. They didn't want the scandal and were happy to spare the family one in the process."

"But, Jesus . . . Going to work in orphanages after you'd just given up your own child?" I want to ask how hardened you have to be to be able to do that—to be around all those motherless babies after just abandoning your own—and not have a complete breakdown.

Dee's voice is devoid of emotion when she replies. "It was meant to be a punishment, Ruth, and I accepted it as such. Doing penance is an integral part of faith, but I wouldn't expect you to know the first thing about it."

I mean to say something biting in response but surprise

myself with, "I used to watch you when you prayed sometimes, you know. When we were kids. You'd close your eyes and get all still like the *bushveld* does before a thunderstorm."

Dee smiles wistfully. "I used to imagine that I was gathering up the four corners of the room and wrapping it around me like a blanket to hide me away from the world."

"My favorite part was always when the furrows of your forehead would smooth out. Your mouth would turn up and you'd nod once, and that's when I had to look away because I knew your eyes would open in a second or two and you'd be cross if I was staring at you."

"I thought you hated my praying."

"I just hated being left out." The confession feels too personal and so I quickly add, "Do you still pray?"

She shakes her head and I'm not surprised. The sister who has come back is not the sister who left. I suppose it's understandable considering everything but for some reason, it makes me sad.

"Are you going to tell me who the father is?"

Dee winces as if I've insulted her by suggesting her baby was the result of a sexual dalliance with a man, but it wasn't a divine conception, I can promise you that. Still, it's probably a stupid question. I saw her with Riaan van Tonder in the avocado orchard the night before she left and things looked pretty hot and intimate between them. I'd just assumed it was nothing more than heavy petting, but clearly my teenage sister was wilder and more interesting than I ever gave her credit for. Hell, even I was positively virginal when she left home. Okay, one or two blocks west of virginal, but not so far off that it wasn't within walking distance.

"So, what happened to Daniel?" I ask when it becomes clear that Dee won't be answering my question about his paternity. "Where's he now?"

Her voice cracks. "He's fighting for his life in hospital."

I wasn't expecting that. "What happened?"

"He grew up and became a priest, and then he was shot during a break-in at the rectory a little over a month ago. He's been in a coma ever since."

"I'm so sorry." And I am. Shit, if I had the money to move him to a private hospital with better neurologists, I'd give it to her though it's probably this generosity of spirit that's contributed to my current financial predicament. Vince always said my heart was like a clown car: always room for one more.

"Thank you." She stands up, wipes a tear away, and walks to her room. She turns back when she gets to the threshold and looks at the baby. "You now know everything, which is why I'm sure you understand why it's too much having him here."

"But . . . you managed to be around all those other orphaned children for so long without it getting to you, maybe you'll get used to—"

"No, Ruth, I'm done with punishing myself like that. My days of doing penance are over. I can't be around him. The baby needs to go."

CHAPTER TWENTY-SIX

Zodwa

12 May 1994
Big Hope Informal Settlement,
Magaliesburg, South Africa

When Zodwa rises again, Leleti is back and she's lying next to her. It was her mother's coughing that woke Zodwa but she feels well rested and clear-headed for the first time in as long as she can remember. It's as though she's coming out of a fugue state, one in which everything felt numb and distant, and has gone from feeling nothing at all to feeling too much.

I have a son.

The thought makes Zodwa smile. She sits up and rubs her eyes. Something feels wet against her chest and she looks down to find the front of her nightgown saturated. Milk leaks from her aching breasts. She's ready to nourish her son willingly now and looks around for him, suddenly desperate to hold him.

When she can't find him, Zodwa assumes he's cradled next to Leleti, who's lying on her side. She leans across her mother to peer over her shoulder, surprised to discover there's nothing there. Looking around the shack, she notices that the bags of baby things that she stuffed under the table are also gone. The dog is nowhere to be seen either.

Zodwa feels a jolt of alarm as she jostles Leleti awake. "Mama." Her mother is hot to the touch.

111

Leleti rolls over, her eyes glazed with fever. The pillow is stained red. She groans and then closes her eyes again.

"Mama, wake up."

Leleti's eyes open again and seek Zodwa's, though when they meet, it feels as if Leleti is looking right through her.

"Where's the baby?"

The corners of Leleti's mouth twitch upward. "Dumisa, my son, is that you?"

Dread washes over Zodwa. Her mother is clearly delirious, and who knows what a person in her state might have done.

"No. It's me, Zodwa. Your daughter," Zodwa says, shaking her gently. "Where is my baby, Mama?"

"Baby?" The ghost of a smile disappears.

"Yes, the baby. Don't you remember? Where is he? Where is my son?"

Leleti's eyes widen in what appears to be a moment of clarity. She opens her mouth to answer, and Zodwa strains forward to hear what her mother will say.

"I took . . . I took him . . ." She stumbles over the words.

"You took the baby?" Zodwa prompts, trying to keep her voice calm despite her rising panic. "You took him where?"

"He . . . he . . . is gone."

"Gone? Gone where, Mama? What did you do with him?"

"I did it for . . . you," Leleti answers. "And for him."

"What? What did you do?"

Leleti seems to consider the question, but before she can answer, her eyes roll back as she begins convulsing.

CHAPTER TWENTY-SEVEN

Ruth

✦

12 May 1994
New Beginnings Baby Sanctuary,
Rustenburg, South Africa

There's been no swaying Dee about the baby. She's called the police and arranged a time for us to meet with social services to hand him over today.

"How dare you do that without discussing it with me first?" I'm on my hands and knees bent over the little plastic bath that's placed in the tub. The baby is on the changing mattress on the floor next to me.

"For God's sake, Ruth. You don't even know what you're doing. You shouldn't be bathing him yet. Not until the umbilical cord falls off."

"Oh really? And just how am I supposed to keep him clean?"

"By dipping cotton wool in warm water and running it over him."

Oh.

I feel a bit stupid considering I have my elbow dipped in the bathwater trying to figure out if it's the right temperature. Trying to save face, I say, "I knew that. I was planning to wrap his stomach in ClingWrap to keep the umbilical cord dry. Besides, babies love baths, everyone knows that. It reminds them of being back in the womb."

She shakes her head and mutters, "All you're doing is proving my point that you're not equipped to care for this child."

"It's not like he's come with an instruction manual," I snap. "And I could learn, couldn't I? I could get a book, or how's this for a really crazy idea? Instead of you doing nothing but criticizing me all the time, you could actually help me look after Angus since you know so much about bloody babies!"

"Angus?"

I feel my cheeks color. "We can't just keep calling the poor little thing 'he' and 'it,' so I named him after Da." Dee's face contracts into such a scowl that I feel some of my bravado evaporating. It probably wasn't the best idea considering Dee's feelings for our father but since I never got to name a son for him, it felt like the least I could do.

"You've honestly named a black child Angus?" She shakes her head like it's the stupidest thing she's ever heard.

"What's wrong with it? I know you had issues with Da but—"

"That's beside the point. Has it not occurred to you that this child has his own culture? His own people and a whole history that has nothing to do with us? You should have given some consideration to that, or at least tried to respect it, by naming him something more appropriate."

"How the hell am I supposed to know what culture he's from?"

"He's damn well not descended from a redheaded Scottish drunkard, I can tell you that much!" She shakes her head and crosses her arms. "You know, I really don't understand you at all."

"Well, of course you don't, but what the hell is that supposed to mean?"

"Your infatuation with this baby doesn't make any sense. You know he's black, right?"

"I have eyes, Dee. I'm not blind."

"Well, you've never been color-blind, that's for sure."

"You're calling me racist?"

"If the shoe fits . . ." Before I can reply in my defense, she adds, "We either go and voluntarily hand him over today or they'll come here and get him. You decide."

Her words strike a chord and I retaliate without thinking. "Just because you gave your baby up doesn't mean you can force me to give up mine."

Dee's face drains of all color. "This is not your baby, Ruth. You might do well to try and remember that." With that, she turns and leaves.

The meeting with social services is at an orphanage half an hour away. We don't have a car seat for a newborn and so Dee is buckled up into the backseat holding Angus while I drive. I've put the roof up to protect him from the wind, but the window of the passenger seat is open and Jezebel has her head hanging out.

The directions lead us to a large face-brick building hunkered down in the surrounding earth, as squat as a mound of cow shit and just as offensive. A forlorn playground takes up most of the outside space, which would traditionally be called a garden, though a garden by its very nature implies the presence of grass and trees, neither of which I can see anywhere on the property. It's called the New Beginnings Baby Sanctuary.

"Well, isn't this lovely?" I say dryly as we pull up and park. "Give Angus to me and you can lead the way since these are more your people than mine."

"I'm not going in."

"What? For God's sake, you're the one who set this up. I'm

not going in by myself." I turn around in my seat to glare at her. Dee resolutely avoids my gaze. She looks like she's on the verge of tears again, which almost pushes me over the edge. She's forcing me to hand Angus across and yet she's the one crying? I get out of the car and pull my seat forward so she can pass Angus to me. Jezebel steps forward to jump out with us.

"Stay, Jez." She whines in response but obeys.

As I stand in the parking lot, taking it all in, I know I'm stalling for time. When I finally shake off the paralysis, I head to the entrance and go inside. A black woman is waiting in the reception area. She has a cherubic face and graying hair that she wears in a short afro.

She immediately reminds me of someone but it takes me a moment to figure out who. "Hello. Has anyone ever told you you look like you could be—"

"Archbishop Desmond Tutu's sister?"

"I take it that's a yes," I say.

She laughs. "Many, many times. But there's unfortunately no relation that I know of. Are you Mrs. Richardson?"

"Yes, I am."

"I'm Lindiwe Nkosi, the social worker. The police liaison called to say they're running late," she says. "I'll give you a tour of our facility while we wait."

We walk along a corridor and as we near a yellow door, I hear the muted sound of a baby crying from inside. It's alarming because it's so pathetic, more whimper than wail. The door has a sign that says *Do Not Enter*. They may as well wave a red flag at me.

Lindiwe keeps walking but I stop. "What's in here?"

She clucks and says, "You don't want to go in there."

"Why not? Isn't this a part of your facility?" If she's trying to hide something, I want to see it. "I thought we were doing a tour."

"Yes, but there are only two babies in here. Come, let's go to the angel sanctuary where all the rest of the children are."

"But I want to see the babies in here."

"It's actually a quarantined area. Only qualified nurses are allowed inside." When it becomes clear that I'm not going to move, she sighs loudly and says, "Okay, fine, but the baby isn't allowed inside with you. And you'll need to wear a mask and gloves."

I'm nervous now but don't want to back down considering the fuss I've made. She reaches for a cubby next to the door and pulls out a surgical face mask and latex gloves. "Here, put them on," she says.

I don't know what I was expecting when I go inside, but it's not the antiseptic smell of a hospital. Three incubators line the walls and as I look around at them, I notice the ominously still bundles inside two of them. Tubes of fluids creep like vines around oxygen tanks and other kinds of lifesaving equipment that you'd expect to find in a geriatric ward at a hospital, not in the pediatric ward in an orphanage.

I step toward the nearest incubator and bend over to peer inside, slowly and quietly so as not to wake the sleeping newborn, which is what I judge the shape inside it to be. I am wrong. Two black sunken eyes stare back at me, the pitiful creature looking unlike any baby I've ever seen. Its cheekbones jut out obscenely on a too-large head, and I realize I've never thought of babies as having cheekbones until now. It's not a feature of their skull that should be visible.

Where's the angelic face and chubby cheeks? This child looks like an alien and is undoubtedly terminally ill. I step back, revolted at the sight of it and even more revolted at myself for my response. I sway as I struggle to control my mutinous thoughts and reach out to balance myself. Within a second, a nurse is next to me, stabilizing me. She too is wearing a face mask and gloves.

"It's very sad, hey?" she says kindly, nodding at the shriveled child. "His name is Themba, it means 'hope.' He's two years old and has been very sick. We are surprised he has even lived this long. There isn't anything we can do for him except manage his pain and wait for him to pass." She shrugs as if this is a perfectly reasonable course of action.

"What's wrong with him?"

"AIDS."

AIDS. That at least explains the latex gloves and the air of sickness that permeates every inch of the room. But it doesn't explain much more. "But AIDS is a gay men's disease." Everything I've read about it says so. "How can a baby have AIDS?"

"It's no longer a homosexual disease," she says. "Women are very susceptible to it, and anything they're at risk of getting, they're likely to pass on to their unborn children."

Jesus, talk about a double whammy.

"I think I'd like to go outside now," I say, and she nods.

Once I'm back in the corridor, I rip off the mask and gloves while taking great big gulps of air.

"I told you that you didn't want to go in there," Lindiwe says. "Don't worry, as you can see, we keep the dying ones far away from the living. Come, let's go see the others."

I take Angus from her and struggle to regain my equilibrium as I follow her down another corridor. I can hear what sounds like a raging battlefield coming from the other end of it and it's getting louder with every step.

"It is now bath and feeding time. They are very busy."

She takes a sudden right turn and then we are in another room, no closed door barring our way this time, no door at all, just an open doorway.

The first thing I notice is the chaos. The long and narrow room includes over two dozen shabby, mismatched cribs, six metal trestle tables, five high chairs, two rusting zinc bathtubs as well as piles and piles of sad, gray terry-cloth nappies, baby grows, and blankets.

Seven women, all equally sweaty and disheveled, tend to approximately two dozen babies, who range in age from a couple of months to about two years old. A definite assembly line has been set up. One woman lifts a baby from a crib, brings it over to a trestle table, undresses it, wipes its bum, and then passes it to one of the two women sitting on the floor in charge of the washtubs.

The baby is then dipped into the water by one of the washers, has a cloth rubbed over it a few times, and is then passed up to another woman at the next trestle table. Here the baby is patted dry, rubbed with a few creams and powders, has another nappy applied, and is then passed to the next woman, who dresses it.

Once this is achieved, the baby is either placed back into a crib and given a bottle to hold for self-feeding, or it's placed in a high chair, where it's quickly spoon-fed a vegetable-and-maize mush. The only babies who are crying are the ones who aren't being held.

I'm just marveling at the fact that Angus can sleep through all the noise when he stirs and wakes up. He starts crying and from the pitch of it, I know he's hungry.

"I just need to feed him," I say to Lindiwe.

She points me in the direction of another room. "That's the kitchen. You can mix his formula there."

When I come back, ready to feed Angus, another woman is standing next to Lindiwe. She's wearing a police uniform and introduces herself as Mandy, the social services liaison. "Mrs. Richardson, I'll need you to come with me to the office to give me your details and write a statement about how you found the baby. After that, you're free to go."

Free to go.

As if leaving Angus will be that easy.

Lindiwe, reading my mind, smiles reassuringly. "We'll take good care of him. Don't worry." She reaches out for him and I feel a rush of vertigo.

"Let me just feed him first," I say, stalling for a few more minutes.

"Mandy is unfortunately in a bit of a hurry. You go with her to make the statement and I'll feed him. He'll be fine."

And then she pries him free of my grasp. Without the reassuring warmth and weight of him anchoring me, I feel as insubstantial as a cloud, as though all I'm made up of is the cotton-candy fluff of yearning and despair. Don't tell me you can't hear a heart breaking. It sounds exactly like a baby that's been yours for two days being carried away, its quavering cries growing fainter as the world rushes in to close the gap between you.

Walking like a zombie on my way out, I can't help but think of how I've spent my whole life searching for signs only to find them in the most unusual of places. The most powerful ones came when I wasn't even looking for them.

One such sign came in the form of a song on the radio the night the universe suggested it might be time to leave my first husband, Doug. As I tore out of the yard in Doug's Ford Cortina with my dress ripped and my mouth bleeding, "You Always Hurt the One You Love" by the Mills Brothers filtered out from the speakers.

It was the same song I'd sung in the bar the night we met, and the same one we danced to a week later as he whispered in my ear that I was the most beautiful woman in the world. Of course, that was before he started hitting me. The thing about fists is that they have a way of robbing you of things—your beauty, your dignity, your sense of self-worth. The song reminded me that I wasn't that beautiful anymore.

You have him to thank for that, Ruthie, the universe whispered. *He took that from you. You know what to do.*

And I did.

Some signs have saved my life while others reminded me that I had a life worth saving. Reading them hasn't always been easy; a precious few are unambiguous; the rest are as ephemeral as smoke and as clear as mud. None has been quite as definitive as a baby left on my doorstep.

And yet I've just given him back; rejecting a literal gift from the gods.

CHAPTER TWENTY-EIGHT

Zodwa

◦

13 May 1994
Big Hope Informal Settlement,
Magaliesburg, South Africa

Leleti has had so many seizures in the past twenty-four hours that Zodwa has lost count of them. Zodwa hasn't slept at all and only managed to eat half a tin of cold baked beans during a brief respite between her mother's attacks. What keeps her going is needing to make Leleti better so she can find out where her baby is.

Zodwa shouldn't leave Leleti alone but she needs to empty the bucket that has served as their toilet. She also has to fetch clean water to wash the soiled bedding. The stench has become so overpowering that she worries it's contributing to Leleti's distress. She wonders briefly where Leleti's dog has disappeared to, as its presence would probably calm her. So much for loyalty.

Zodwa detours past Mama Beauty's shack and knocks on her door to ask her to stay with Leleti but no one is there. Zodwa is just wondering who else she might ask for help when Mama Beauty rounds the corner carrying shopping bags.

"My child," she exclaims, rushing to Zodwa. "I heard the news and am so sorry for your loss." Mama Beauty puts her bags down and envelops Zodwa in a hug.

Zodwa's thinking is so foggy from fatigue that she can barely make sense of what Mama Beauty is saying. "My loss?"

Mama Beauty clucks in sympathy. "I can see you are not handling it well but that is completely understandable. To lose a baby during birth after carrying it for nine months is a heartbreaking thing." Mama Beauty releases Zodwa, and her eyes are filled with such compassion that it almost brings an exhausted Zodwa to her knees.

She shakes her head to clear her mind so that she can focus on the task at hand. "I was just taking this to empty it." Zodwa nods at the bucket, which she's covered with newspaper. "Mama is very sick. I need to get back."

"Oh, I am sorry for keeping you! You go dispose of that, my child, and I will go see your mother."

They part ways, Mama Beauty's words playing in a loop through Zodwa's mind.

To lose a baby. To lose a baby. To lose a baby.

What did she mean by that?

The laneways between the shacks are narrow and Zodwa keeps getting jostled by the people streaming into and out of the squatter camp. It takes her longer than it normally would to reach the privy. She empties the bucket and then goes to wash it out, filling the water bucket in the process. Black smoke billows from somewhere nearby and Zodwa looks up at it, fearful of what it means.

A woman walking toward her sees Zodwa's concern. "Don't worry, *sisi*. It's a controlled fire. They're burning down Gertie's shack. It's the only way to rid it of the killing disease now that she's died."

Zodwa thanks her for the information and tries to keep moving, but the woman stands in her way.

"There are others who have the killing disease," she continues. "More and more every day. If we let them stay here, it will spread to all of us. What we need are more fires. That will teach them."

"Yes," Zodwa agrees so the woman will let her go.

When she gets back, she's made up her mind to ask Mama Beauty what she meant about losing a baby, but finds her on her haunches in their shack with her back to Zodwa. Leleti is rolled over, one arm flung out to the side.

Zodwa drops the bucket. The water splashes out, pooling into the dirt. "Mama?"

There is no reply from Leleti but Mama Beauty stands and turns to Zodwa. "My child," she says with trembling lips as she takes Zodwa's hand. "My child, I am so sorry." Her eyes are filled with tears.

Zodwa forces herself to pull her hand free as she takes one step forward and then another until she sees what her mother's friend is seeing. Leleti lies with her eyes wide open and foam crusted at her lips.

Zodwa drops to her knees, the moment so surreal that it feels as though she's hovering just below the shack's roof looking down on herself. What she sees is a selfish girl whose unnatural appetites have brought great suffering upon them, a daughter who made her mother's last months on this earth bitter with disappointment.

She wants more than anything to retrace her steps out of the shack and then to keep retracing them so they take her back to her grandmother's hut in KwaZulu, back to an idyllic childhood before brothers went missing and mothers contracted tuberculosis, and girls were correctively raped to cure them of their love of other girls.

She wants to go back to a time when her future was promising, a time before babies were born and then disappeared into the night, before being eighteen years old made her feel ancient with all the weariness she is weighted with.

Oh, Mama. Mama, no.

CHAPTER TWENTY-NINE

Delilah

·☀·

14 May 1994
Johannesburg General Hospital,
Johannesburg, South Africa

I had just stepped into the ICU waiting room when I saw him. Father Thomas was sitting in the corner reading his Bible, but he looked up as though he sensed my presence. I was frozen in the doorway when he caught sight of me.

I knew he was in his late seventies but he'd aged well in the way that handsome men sometimes do. Though he was completely gray, he still had a full head of hair that was cropped close to his skull. Wire-rim glasses framed his dark eyes, intensifying rather than diminishing the power of his gaze, which still had the capacity to unnerve me so thoroughly. Even after all that time, what I felt most strongly in his presence was shame.

"Delilah," he said, standing up. "It was you, after all. I thought I'd imagined it." So he'd recognized me when we caught sight of each other the last time I'd been here.

I couldn't help but marvel then at how a lifetime wasn't long enough to break the hold some people had on you. After all, I was only fifteen when I'd first laid eyes on Father Thomas and fallen so desperately in love with him.

It had been a Sunday and my mother wasn't joining me for church because she had to stay behind and help with the harvest. Da had insisted I stay to help too, but Ma had told me to go and that she'd deal with the fallout. On impulse, just before I reached my usual place of worship, I ducked into the nearby Catholic church for mass instead. Having learned that the Dutch Reformed Church only accepted men in the service of the Lord, I'd become disillusioned with the limitations of it, and having recently read about nuns, I wanted to find out more about Catholicism. Forgoing my own faith's devotions to sneak into those of another's was the most rebellious act I'd ever committed up to that point.

Father Thomas was standing in the pulpit that morning as I slipped into the back of the church a few minutes after mass had already begun. I was struck first by the breathtaking stained-glass windows depicting biblical scenes behind him, and then by him as the rainbow colors painted him with diffused light, lending him an aura of otherworldliness.

He spoke with a grave conviction, like a man truly possessed of the Holy Spirit, and radiated such majesty that it was impossible not to be entranced by him. Judging by the rapt faces of his congregants, most of whom were women, I knew I wasn't the first person to fall under his spell. Without a doubt, he was the most beautiful man I'd ever seen, and I fell as much in love with him that day as I did with the mesmerizing rituals of his faith.

And now, after all those years and everything that had happened in the interim—even after Father Thomas had served as my judge, jury, and executioner by taking my son from me, and then excommunicating me from the church—some specter of that feeling remained.

"Father," I said in acknowledgment. It was all I could manage under the circumstances.

"How did you know to come?"

The question threw me. "What do you mean? I got your letter."

"Letter?" He looked genuinely confused. "I didn't write you a letter."

I thought of the dozen missives that had arrived sporadically over the years and the handwriting that had become familiar because of them. I'd always just assumed he'd been the one sending them. If not he, then who?

Father Thomas tilted his head as he regarded me, as though I was a puzzle he'd long before given up on solving. He still wore that air of wounded disappointment that I'd found so difficult to bear in the last weeks of my pregnancy, as though I'd let him down in some unbearable way that he'd never recover from.

He took my elbow and led me toward the viewing window, nodding beyond the glass. I looked from his face to Daniel's bed. My view was unhindered by curtains this time, and I could make out Daniel's upper body hidden under a sheet and raised up a few degrees by the incline of the bed. He had bandages wrapped around his head and his face was swollen. I wouldn't have recognized him as the man from the last photo that I'd been sent. But then, without all those photos over the years, I never would have recognized him at all.

A nun was sitting beside Daniel's bed. She had her elbows propped up against his mattress with her forehead resting against her interlaced fingers. Her wimple hid most of her face, but I could see she was mouthing what looked like a feverish prayer as tears coursed down her cheeks.

"See that woman? That's Daniel's mother. She's been his mother ever since you left."

Even if he hadn't filled me in on their relationship, I would have guessed it. If ever there was a picture of maternal anguish, then she was it.

Father Thomas continued, "Your being here will just upset her. I know you think there's something here for you, but there isn't. There's nothing you can do for Daniel but you can do the right thing for her. The past is in the past. I beg you to put it behind you where it belongs and move on."

I wanted to tell him that he was wrong. The past wasn't a place you could just walk away from; it was something you carried with you your entire life, and year upon year as your arms got weaker, the burden just got heavier and harder to bear. But I wanted so much for him to be right because that meant I got to set it down—all that guilt and regret and shame—and leave it there.

This is yours now, I wanted to say. *You take it.*

"Go home, Delilah," he said.

And so I did, because beneath it all, even after everything I'd done, I was still a good girl who wanted to do the right thing and who listened when told what to do.

CHAPTER THIRTY

Ruth

·※·

14 May 1994
Verdriet, Magaliesburg, South Africa

I'm pouring another drink, my fifth or sixth of the day. It's been two days since I was forced to give the baby back and I find that booze takes the edge off the worst of my fury at Dee and some of the fury at myself. It doesn't help that I keep reaching for the phone wanting to call Vince because he's the person I always speak to when I'm most wounded. Remembering each time that I can't speak to him just makes me pour the drinks stronger.

"*Jirre*, man. Check out the *kwaai* BMW M3!"

The voice coming from the front yard startles me. I peek out the window to discover two men in camo gear getting out of a *bakkie* and walking toward Vince's convertible. By the looks of lust on their faces, the car is giving them major hard-ons. Blond, broad-chested, and taller than six foot, they both look like mirror images of Maynard Coetzee, the town's golden boy who I'd briefly had a fling with when I was seventeen. They have to be his sons.

"Killer mag wheels and spoiler. I wonder if it has a proper racing steering wheel," the one with the cap replies in Afrikaans as he leans in for a closer look.

"It does," I say, opening the front door and stepping outside, "but the car's just been cleaned, so try not to drool on it."

He spins around, snatching his hands back from the door, and smiles when he sees me. "Hello, *tannie.*" Being called "auntie" by someone who's in their thirties rankles me but I know they don't mean anything by it. "Is this your husband's car?" he asks without any hint of sarcasm or irony.

"No, it's mine," I brazenly lie. You're not going to win any poker tournaments if you're not good at bluffing.

"*Regtig?*" I nod and he carries on. "A small lady like you driving a big car like this? So, what's the fastest you've done in it?"

"Oh . . . " I think back to the dusty Karoo expanse on the way here. "About two hundred and twenty kilometers per hour."

He whistles appreciatively just as the one without a cap spits out, "*Kak,* man! There's no way."

I just shrug and smile mysteriously. "I'm Ruth, by the way. And you're which of the Coetzee brood, exactly?"

"I'm Klein Maynard and this is my brother, Henning," the one with the cap says. "*Klein*" is the way Afrikaners preface names they share with older members of their family; it means "small" and is their way of saying "junior."

"Lovely to meet you. I knew your father many moons ago." There's a smirk of recognition from both of them, so I know they've heard the stories or, at least, some bastardized version of them. "Would you like to come in for a drink? I don't have beer but I'm sure I could rustle up a brandy and Coke."

They thank me and follow me up the steps, sitting on chairs on the veranda after indicating that their boots are dirty and they don't want to trek mud inside. After I mix their drinks, pouring a double for myself, Jez follows me outside as I deliver them. She stops short of going near the men, her ears and tail lowered, and then she surprises me by baring her teeth and growling at them.

They laugh nervously and I apologize, scooting her back inside before closing the door behind me. Jez hasn't been herself since we handed the baby the over. It's like she's bereft without him. I know how she feels.

We sit and chat about the weather for a bit, and then talk turns to Hartbeespoort Dam, and how it's become a drawing card for rich people from Johannesburg looking to get away from the city for the weekend. Golf courses and resorts are springing up all over the place and it's bringing a lot of pleasure-seekers with money to our neck of the woods.

"Which is why we're prepared to up our offer," Klein Maynard says.

"Your offer?"

"For the farm. Since you turned us down." I'm taken aback. The estate agent told me it was some consortium who'd made the offer but didn't tell me who was behind it.

"We want to make you an offer you can't refuse," Henning says before Klein Maynard offers a million rand more.

The total figure makes my eyes water.

Damn Dee for making us turn it down. Damn her for making me give back the baby. Damn her to hell for all of it.

And it's in damning her that I somehow conjure her, like one of those demons in horror movies who appear when you mention their name, because there she suddenly is, pulling up in Da's old Chevy Impala. We watch as she parks behind their *bakkie* and gets out. Her eyes look swollen, as though she's been crying again, and I suddenly realize where she's been all morning: at the hospital visiting her son. I'm just wondering how to ask her if anything has changed without letting on too much in front of our guests, when she walks up the stairs and glares at them.

"This is my sister, Delilah Ferguson," I say by way of introduction and to cut through the awkwardness. "These boys are Klein Maynard and Henning Coetzee."

They stand and Klein Maynard removes his cap before reaching out to shake Dee's hand. She leaves him hanging.

"Entertaining AWB members now, are you?" she asks me acidly.

"I beg your pardon?" I have no idea what she's talking about. "What's the AWB?"

"It's the Afrikaner Weerstandsbeweging," she replies through gritted teeth. "An Afrikaner resistance movement."

Klein Maynard takes his hand back and shoves it in his pocket. "That's right. We're members," he says proudly, indicating their outfits, which I now realize aren't hunting camo but uniforms.

There is an insignia on each side of his chest: a red, white, and black one that looks like a variation of the Nazi symbol, and the Vierkleur insignia, a flag that was designed for the South African Republic that stopped existing a hundred years ago.

"These idiots are part of the group who could have killed me at the airport if I'd arrived half an hour later," Dee says, turning to me. "More than thirty of them were arrested in connection with all the bombings that have been happening across the country. You're fraternizing with terrorists."

"The ANC's chief terrorist is now president of the country, so it seemed to work out quite well for them," Klein Maynard says. "How many bombings weren't they responsible for back in the day? All we're doing is fighting back and defending what's ours. You'd better believe there's a civil war coming, the whites against the blacks, and you'd better hope people like us will protect *kaffir boeties* like you when they come for you in your sleep."

He glares at her menacingly and so I step between them. "Dee, why don't you go inside while I finish up with our guests over here?"

"Be careful," she says. "Like Ma always said, if you lie down with dogs, you're going to wake up with fleas."

"Come," Klein Maynard says to Henning, "let's go." He turns back to me. "The offer is valid for a day. Let me know what you decide."

They pull off in a cloud of dust and I watch openmouthed as they go. "What the hell was that about? One minute we're sitting like civilized people having drinks and the next you march up here and start attacking them."

"My God," she says. "Did you not hear a word I said?"

"It's not illegal to belong to the AWB, is it? They're perfectly within their rights to belong to whatever organization they want."

"They're militant racists, Ruth. Neo-Nazi white supremacists. Do you not see the hypocrisy of defending them when two days ago you wanted us to keep a black baby?"

It's my turn to glare at her. "I don't see what one has got to do with the other. And you're the one who made me give up that black baby, remember?"

"Not because he was black, Ruth." She shakes her head and starts walking away before she stops again. "What offer were they talking about?"

"They've upped their offer for the farm, and it's an extremely generous one, which we should consider—"

"They're the ones who want to buy it?" Dee snorts. "I already told you it's not happening but this just makes it easier to repeat myself. No!"

"Stop being so pigheaded about this. Five million rand is nothing to be sneezed at! We could split the profits and you could buy a mansion wherever you like and still have a lot of change left over."

"I don't need a mansion. Not everyone is as materialistic as you are. Do vile things have to personally affect you for you to give a shit?"

"What things?"

"Racism and white supremacy, for a start."

It's a stupid question because how can racism affect me personally? I ignore it and pose one of my own. "Don't you want to be able to be in a financial position to help Daniel? Move him to a better hospital or help with his recovery down the line—"

"Don't you dare. Don't you dare use my son to manipulate me. My God, how low are you willing to stoop to get your own way?"

As she storms off, I realize that I'm not going to get this farm sold. It seems like the universe really wants to keep me here and I think I know why. It's time to make the best of a bad situation.

CHAPTER THIRTY-ONE

Zodwa

❂

19 May 1994
Big Hope Informal Settlement,
Magaliesburg, South Africa

N one of the roads leading into the squatter camp are wide
enough to allow bringing the coffin directly to the shack
by vehicle, and having it carried there will require at least six
men and a lot of awkward maneuvering.

Instead, the *bakkie* stops on the sand verge on the side of the
main road. Cars speed by and kick up dust, their exhaust fumes
making Zodwa dizzy. The driver hops out, hat in hand, to offer
his condolences.

Leleti's basic pine coffin lies in the extra-long Venter trailer.
This is how she will be taken home to KwaZulu, where she will
be buried in the village graveyard alongside her husband, and
this is where Zodwa and Mama Beauty will say their goodbyes.

"Are you sure you don't want to go, my child?" Mama Beauty
asks. "I am happy to give you the money for the return journey."

The payment for the transport to take Leleti back home
came from the last of the money she'd gotten from her madam.
Thank God Leleti religiously contributed to the Burial Society
every month or else Zodwa wouldn't have been able to purchase
a coffin, simple or not. Mama Beauty knows that Zodwa can't
afford the transport for herself.

The driver addresses Mama Beauty. "She can ride there with me for no extra cost since she already paid for the remains to be taken home."

The remains.

That's what her mother is now. Remains, but of what? What remains when a small life ends too soon? At least there is a body that can be laid to rest and some closure to be had. Unlike with Dumisa all those years ago and now with the baby.

The baby.

Zodwa hasn't been able to sleep wondering what became of him. She goes over and over it in her mind, trying to under-stand how he could have been sickly enough to die so soon after birth when the only thing she remembers about him is the sheer force of his suckling. Besides, it doesn't align with what Leleti told Zodwa just before she had her first seizure.

If Zodwa was lost in a fog during her entire pregnancy and just after the birth, it's lifted now, burned away by the over-whelming sense of loss. When Leleti cut the umbilical cord, in-stead of severing Zodwa from her child, it's as though that moment sparked her journey back to him. She thinks with won-der of all those months when she felt nothing for the baby at all when now she feels so much.

"My child," Mama Beauty says, bringing Zodwa back into the moment. "Do you want to go with him?"

"Thank you, Mama Beauty, but no," Zodwa says, her mind made up.

She doesn't deserve the comfort of her family, nor the peace that will come from seeing her mother being laid to rest. There will be too many questions and the one person she's never been able to lie to is her grandmother. It's better to leave her hungry for the truth than to poison her with answers.

Besides, as Zodwa herself suspected, and as the local township healer confirmed, Zodwa is undoubtedly cursed.

"My child," the healer said the day after Leleti died. "To lose both your baby and your mother within days of each other . . . it is a fearful thing. An unnatural thing." She waved burning sage around the shack in an attempt to rid it of bad energy. "You have been cursed by powerful black magic for sure. I don't know what you have done to deserve such terrible things in your life, but you must go see the *sangoma* and get *muthi* to rid yourself of it. It is the only way."

The healer may not know what she's done but Zodwa knows. The *nyanga* she consulted six months ago knew too.

Zodwa thought she could outwit the ancestors and find peace by getting rid of the baby, but here she is with the baby gone, though not in the way she intended, and still peace eludes her. It's clear now that peace will never be hers as long as she loves a girl. Zodwa had honestly believed that she and Thembeka had a special connection, something profound that she hadn't just imagined, which is why she'd risked so much by writing that letter in the first place.

When she told Thembeka about the rape and pregnancy last Christmas, Zodwa knew it would hurt her friend, but she never doubted that Thembeka would believe her. She expected her to immediately end her relationship with Mongezi, and perhaps even encourage Zodwa to report the assault to the authorities.

She wasn't prepared for Thembeka's utter denial, that she'd rather believe Zodwa capable of such a terrible lie than believe that Mongezi had not only cheated on her but did so with such violence. Still, despite the betrayal, Zodwa has never stopped yearning for Thembeka, wishing with all her heart that they could find a way one day to be together.

And this is the price she has paid for angering the ancestors: both her mother and her child taken from her.

Zodwa can't return to KwaZulu with the curse still working its evil magic. She cannot put her grandmother and those she loves at risk. Not being there to lay her mother to rest will be a scandal she will have to learn to live with. Some evils are greater than others.

"Are you ready to say goodbye?" the man asks, and Zodwa nods though she isn't ready.

The man steps forward and opens the latches so that the trailer splits apart to reveal the pine coffin wedged inside. He removes the lid that hasn't yet been secured. That will only be done after the family has seen Leleti for themselves. The driver and Mama Beauty step aside to give Zodwa privacy, or as much privacy as she can be afforded as dozens of cars and trucks whiz by, pedestrians and goats dodging between them.

A dragonfly flits past Zodwa's cheek and zigzags to Leleti's face, stitching together the infinite space between daughter and mother, the living and the dead. The insect comes to rest on Leleti's lips, giving the illusion that she's making its wings move by the power of her breath. The dragonfly glints with a metallic green-and-blue sheen in the sunlight; it may be the most beautiful adornment Leleti has ever worn.

Zodwa closes her eyes to steady herself. When she opens them again, the insect is gone and so is the fleeting beauty it bestowed upon Leleti. Her mother's gaunt features are slack and almost unrecognizable. Whatever force animated Leleti and made her who she was has been extinguished in this world.

There is a universe of sorrow trapped in Zodwa's throat that she cannot find the words to express. But Leleti was never a person of words; she was always a woman of deeds, showing her love by putting food on the table no matter how much the work to earn it demeaned her, and searching for her missing son decades after everyone else had given up on him.

Zodwa leans forward and kisses Leleti on her forehead, tears clouding her vision as she does so. She allows herself a few parting words though she doesn't speak them aloud.

I will make you proud of me, Mama. I will make you proud. Just wait and see.

CHAPTER THIRTY-TWO

Delilah

❁

27 May 1994
Verdriet, Magaliesburg, South Africa

After turning down the Coetzees' offer on the farm, we'd woken up to find graffiti covering the garage door. *SLET* and *KAFFIR BOETIE* were spray-painted in red next to a giant AWB symbol.

"Gee," Ruth said, standing outside in her kimono, "I wonder which one of us is the slut and which one the *kaffir* lover?" She flicked her cigarette butt and turned. "You've made us a target. Happy now?"

We hadn't spoken a word to each other since.

Ruth had handed the baby over to the sanctuary just over two weeks before, and her drinking—which had already been worrisome—had just steadily gotten worse. On most days, she was drunk and belligerent by noon, which was a feat considering she usually only woke up at eleven. I thought Ruth would get over the baby more quickly, since I'd seen her form strong attachments time and time again and knew only too well how they all played out.

Regardless of whether the object of her affection was a person, an animal, or a material possession, Ruth would form an instant obsession that was always as brief as it was intense. She'd done it with countless boys whose love and attention she claimed she couldn't live without, only to dump them just as soon as they declared their devotion to her, and I recalled the time she begged our parents for months for a baby goat after seeing one at a livestock fair.

Da finally gave in and rode miles to another farm to swap one of our piglets for one of their kid goats. Ruth was over the moon when Da brought it home, naming her Faloolah, and ridiculously asking Da if she could sleep in our room. Of course, she'd lost interest in it before a week was up, claiming it stank and that it was out to get her. The goat's care fell to me after that.

Why would the baby be any different? Did he deserve to be abandoned twice so early in his short life? I thought the best strategy was pretending the baby hadn't existed so everything could go back to normal, or at least as much semblance of normal as Ruth and I could manage, but in those past instances, the difference was that Ruth had gotten what she wanted, possessed it, before losing interest. The baby remained out of her grasp and she seethed with resentment because of it.

It was awkward living that way but it couldn't possibly last for much longer. Now that I'd made it clear I wasn't going to approve the sale of the property, Ruth would have to return to Cape Town empty handed.

To stop myself from obsessing over Father Thomas's parting words, and to prevent myself from driving to the hospital to keep vigil in the parking lot, I'd taken to hiking the foothills around the farm with the dog as my companion. She needed more exercise than she was getting following Ruth from the liquor cabinet and back to her room a dozen times a day, and it was nice to have company. Plus, since she'd been branded a Jezebel just as I once had, I felt a kinship with her.

Jez and I would leave midmorning before Ruth woke up and

walk for miles, cutting across cattle paths, mapped-out trails, private properties, and sand roads; climbing over stiles or ducking under fences when they stood in our way. We occasionally encountered baboons and rhebok, scrub hares and dassies.

Jezebel quivered at the sight of them all, but she was an obedient dog who always stayed at my side. Whoever had trained her had done a good job. She hadn't given chase when we'd spotted a brown hyena the day before, allowing it to disappear with a casual grace, blending so perfectly into the landscape that I wondered if I'd imagined it.

That day, I planned to set out toward the valley with its quartzite boulders that gleamed pink in the sun and follow the river to the side of the gorge. I remembered magnificent views of cascading natural swimming pools from my childhood and was curious to see if the area had remained so unspoiled. I'd just let Jezebel out of Ruth's room and was lacing up my boots when there was a knock at the door.

Jezebel barked in response.

"Shh. Quiet, girl," I said as I reached for the handle.

The man on the doorstep stood in profile gazing off toward the road as he smoothed his hair back and straightened his shirt. When he turned and faced me, my heart galloped in recognition. Standing on my doorstep was Riaan van Tonder, my childhood sweetheart and the best friend I'd ever had.

Though his mop of curly hair was cut short and was now white instead of brown, the fifty-nine-year-old Riaan was instantly recognizable as the nineteen-year-old he'd been the last time I'd seen him. His hazel eyes were the exact same shade of autumn leaf I remembered, deepening from emerald to russet. Though they were bracketed by wrinkles, they were the same eyes that had beseeched me not to leave almost forty years ago.

Riaan reached out to shake my hand, clearing his throat as he did so. "Hello, Delilah."

That's all he said, just my name, but his voice caught as he said it, and I felt the scab I'd let grow over that particular wound crack a little in response.

I reached my hand out to match his formal greeting. "Riaan. What a surprise."

"I heard you were back but didn't believe it. I thought I'd come check for myself." His Afrikaans accent was stronger than I remembered.

"Yes, I am," I said stupidly. "Please, come in. Can I offer you some tea or coffee?"

"Coffee would be good, thank you."

I led him through the dining room and then back outside, pushing aside the sliding door to the patio, collecting my racing thoughts as I set about making the coffee. Jezebel hopped up onto a patio chair next to him, making him laugh.

"Your dog has been keeping me company," he said when I came back out and set a mug down in front of him. "How did you find one who looks just like Shadow?"

Riaan had loved that dog as much as I had. She'd always been just a step or two behind us when we were children, trailing us on all of our adventures.

"She found us, actually. And she's more Ruth's dog than mine."

Riaan took a sip of his coffee, closing his eyes to savor the patch of warmth he was sitting in. Winter was making itself felt and the houses were cold inside. Without double-glazed windows or central heating, a South African winter, mild as it was, could feel quite brutal. When he opened his eyes again, he looked out onto the garden. He didn't say anything but he

144

didn't have to. I knew what he was thinking, that Ma would have had a fit if she could've seen it.

The garden was the only part of the property that hadn't served a practical purpose back in the day, and it had been her domain, her pride and joy. The rest of the farm had been a working farm, but despite her fierce practicality, Ma insisted on having something of beauty to look at.

She refused to grow anything that was too finicky and she definitely wouldn't grow anything that wasn't indigenous to South Africa. Roses were judged to be the flowers of the British, and since they were the people who'd put Ma's ancestors in concentration camps, killing close to thirty thousand Afrikaners during the Second Boer War, she refused to touch them. Chrysanthemums, peonies, impatiens, begonias, and petunias were judged similarly to be too English.

Instead, she planted arum lilies and *Strelitzia*, which she called by its common name, bird-of-paradise. She was also partial to *vygies* in pinks and purples, and oranges and yellows, because they could grow in rocky areas and still flower spectacularly without much care.

"The garden needs some work," I said. "Stompie hasn't been able to manage it by himself, which is why it's so overgrown. It's on my list of things to work on."

"So, you're going to be staying?"

"Yes. I'm retiring here."

He nodded, but when he didn't say anything further, I rushed in to fill the silence. "Enough about me, tell me all about you."

"There isn't much to tell," he said. "We still run the farm but we've branched out from agriculture into game farming." His use of the word *we* could have referred to himself and a wife, or it could have encompassed his brothers, who all probably still had stakes in the family business.

What I really wanted to know was how life had treated him—if he'd gone on to marry, how many children they'd had, if he'd been happy—but he batted away my awkward attempts at steering the conversation in that direction. While he was guarded about his personal life, he chattered animatedly about the volunteer work he'd been doing with the Wits University scientists who'd been streaming into the Kromdraai, Gladysvale, and Sterkfontein areas over the past few years.

"At the Gladysvale caves, they've discovered the first hominid specimens, which are humanlike apes—our human ancestors, pretty much—that date back as far as 3.5 million years," he said. "The fossil sites here are producing more hominin fossils than anywhere else in the world."

His excitement took me back to our childhood—when I was seven and he was nine—and the time he'd crawled through a tiny opening into a limestone cave on their property. I remembered his feet disappearing into the black hole as he wriggled his way inside, and how his disembodied voice echoed to me from inside.

"Look," Riaan had said as he pulled himself free of the yawning blackness a while later, holding up something yellowish that looked like an upside-down rhino horn, only smaller. "I think it's a cat's tooth."

I had looked at it skeptically. It was much too big to be a cat's tooth and that he thought otherwise annoyed me. I said as much, pointing out that a cat's whole head was smaller than the thing he was holding up.

He'd laughed, which rankled me even more.

"No, not a house cat," he said. "A saber-toothed cat. They lived millions of years ago."

"With the dinosaurs?" I asked.

"I don't know," Riaan said. "But I'm going to find out." He'd always had an insatiable curiosity.

"Delilah?" Riaan smiled nervously then, bringing me back to the present. "Am I boring you?"

"Not at all. Sorry, I was just remembering how much you used to love all of that stuff."

Riaan flushed and then said, "I actually came here today to speak to you about the Coetzees."

The abrupt change of subject was disorienting. I had thought he might segue into questions about my unexpected home-coming, but if he had any, he'd done a good job of suppressing them.

"The Coetzees?"

"Yes. Rumor has it that you've gotten on their bad side, and judging by the graffiti I saw outside, I'd say the rumors are true."

"They're terrible people," I said. "And I refuse to pander to them." It suddenly occurred to me that with all the time that had passed, Riaan was as foreign to me as my countrymen were. Just because he hadn't been racist as a child didn't mean he hadn't grown up to be one of them. "Wait, you're not part of their group, are you?"

"Of course not," he said, looking affronted that I'd even ask. "But they're a powerful family in these parts, not people you want to offend."

"Then they should grow tougher hides so they aren't so easily offended."

"I heard they made an offer on the farm that you turned down. Sounds like Ruth was eager to accept it."

"Yes, but like I said, I'm retiring here. I'm not in the market to sell." I took a sip of my coffee, which had gotten cold. "I don't see what the big deal is, anyway. So they don't get our farm? So what? I'm sure there are plenty of other farms up for sale. Productive ones that will at least bring in an immediate income, unlike this one, which will need a lot of work."

"They're not looking for a productive farm, Delilah. They're looking to open a canned-lion-hunting operation and have bought all of the surrounding property to that end. Yours is the one in the middle that links them all. It's crucial that they have it for the breeding-and-hunting station they're planning."

"Canned-lion hunting? What's that?"

"It's a barbaric practice where lions are placed in caged areas for so-called hunts." He scoffed. "It's hardly a hunt since the animals have been raised in captivity and used in petting zoos. They have no fear of humans and then have nowhere to escape to beyond the confines of the enclosed compounds. They're sitting ducks for the kind of people who don't even have hunting licenses and generally don't know how to fire guns, but who still want a lion-head trophy."

"My God, that's terrible! They're effectively shooting tame, caged animals. I mean, how is that even legal?"

"It brings in tourism and big money." He shrugged sadly. "Never underestimate the power of the almighty dollar."

"Well, then I'm even happier that we rejected their offer!" I sat upright as something occurred to me. "Did Ruth know about this? The canned-lion-hunting thing?"

He shook his head to my relief. "No, they've kept it all very hush-hush and are hiding behind some consortium from what I understand. She wouldn't have known."

I was relieved but still couldn't help but wonder if it would have made a difference to her if she had. "So, this isn't a social call?" I tried for levity but it fell flat.

"I wanted to warn you what you've gotten yourself into," Riaan answered. "The Coetzees are not going to just let this rest, because they need this property too much. Please be on your guard"—he nodded his head in the direction of the house—"the both of you. You have no idea what these people are capable of."

CHAPTER THIRTY-THREE

Ruth

❋

27 May 1994
Verdriet, Magaliesburg, South Africa

I'm not a big coffee drinker. I prefer my morning beverages to be healthier options like orange or tomato juice. Laced, of course, with something fermented or distilled for a bit of kick. So the first shock of the day is the bitter sip of the coffee I made myself. The second is seeing Riaan van Tonder walking inside from the patio and heading for the main door.

He spots me at the same time I spot him and blushes scarlet. Not much of a poker player, that one; you could see his tells miles away. I wink a greeting, which makes him color even more before he stutters a greeting in return. Silly boy should have slept with me when he had his chance all those years ago. I would have made him forget about Dee, I promise you that.

"Let me know if you need help with removing the graffiti," he says to Dee before he's out the door.

"Did he come by to pay you all that backdated child support?" I ask to see what kind of reaction I'll get, and she rewards me by flushing. "Just kidding. Why was he here?"

"Sit down, Ruth. We need to talk."

"As Meat Loaf would say, 'you took the words right out of my mouth,' because we absolutely do need to talk. I'll stand, though, if it's all the same to you." She looks taken aback but sits down. "Would you like to begin, or should I?" When she doesn't say anything, I jump right in. "Okay, I'll start. I'm on my way to the orphanage to start proceedings to foster Angus."

"You can't possibly be serious?"

"I've never been more serious in my life."

"Okay, let's set aside the craziness of that for a minute. I told you—"

"Yes, I know, you can't be around the baby, but since you won't let me sell the farm and return to Cape Town with the proceeds, I'm now forced to stay."

"Who's forcing you to stay? If you're so hell-bent on this stupid scheme, why can't you take him back with you and leave me in peace?"

"I'm getting divorced—"

"Of course you are." She snorts. "What is this now? Divorce four?"

"Three, actually, and what can I say? The fellas like me."

"But still, why would you want to stay here? Why not take the baby and go back to Cape Town?"

"I'm a little strapped for cash at the moment, which is why I needed to sell the farm. No money from the sale means I have to stay here. So you know how to get rid of me, Dee. It's very easy. Just sign off on selling it."

"No," she says, jutting her jaw out.

"I don't see why you're being so stubborn about this. Why do you even want to stay? My God, you couldn't wait to get the hell out of here, remember?"

"How can you blame me for that, Ruth? After everything that happened here?"

"Oh, here we go again. Boo-hoo. Poor Delilah who was so hard done by. You weren't the only one who had a shitty childhood, you know."

"Oh, please. Everything was always so easy for you, Ruth."

"No, it wasn't."

"Yes, it was. Do you remember when we used to play 'the Princess and the Pea' game? You always used to know exactly where the pea was and I never did. You were always the real princess, just like in the story, and I was the perpetual peasant."

I laugh at the memory of it, something I haven't thought about in decades. "Oh God, Dee. You were so easy to fuck with."

"What do you mean?"

"I always repositioned the dressing-table mirror just before we played. I tilted it downward so I could see where you hid it. That's how I got it right every time."

"No!" Her face is such a picture of shock that I laugh.

"I can't believe you never figured it out. Or that you even remember that."

"Of course I remember it. It felt like the story of my life, the story of us. That I never quite measured up."

And suddenly I'm not laughing anymore. "But you were Ma's favorite. She adored you."

"And you were Da's. And everyone else's."

"I didn't really care about everyone else. I cared about Ma. And I had to work for it, you know," I say, "Da's love. It didn't just come naturally. I worked my ass off for it."

"And it protected you from him. He never lifted a hand to you."

I don't need to ask her what she means. I saw him hit her more than once. I could have protected her if she'd just let me, but no. Like Ma, she always had to run her mouth off at him, provoking him.

Dee shakes her head. "You didn't know him like you thought you did. He wasn't a good man."

"He wasn't that bad."

She holds up a hand to stop me. "I don't want to hear it."

"If you have so many bad memories here, then why stay? Why not just pack up and leave and start over?"

"I'm sick of leaving," Dee says. "Can't you understand that? This is my home and I'm staying, but you might want to re-think bringing the baby here."

"No. You already got your way with the farm, I'm not—"

"Ruth, just listen to me for a minute," she says, and then tells me about Riaan's warning and what the Coetzees are up to.

So that's why they're willing to pay so much for an unproduc-tive avocado farm. "You realize that we could use this as leverage, don't you?" I say. "Make them up their offer even more?" She glares at me and I shrug. "What? It was worth a try." I stand to go. "Now, please excuse me. I have an appointment at an orphan-age that I need to keep."

"You're going to go ahead with it? Trying to bring a black baby to a place that's being targeted by white supremacists?"

"Listen, I hate being bullied as much as you do, and I'm just as sick of running away from things as you are. Apparently, we're both taking a stand."

"But why this baby? Why now? If you wanted children so badly, why didn't you just have your own?"

"Some of us weren't given a choice in the matter despite how easy you think we've always had it." With that, I pick up my handbag and walk out the door.

CHAPTER THIRTY-FOUR

Zodwa

❋

27 May 1994
Krugersdorp Mortuary, South Africa

Zodwa has been waiting for two hours in the mortuary queue when she finally gets called. She's already been to two morgues and a funeral home in the Magaliesburg area, but none of them could help her. This is where all unclaimed bodies from the area are sent, she's been told. It depresses her to think that there would be so many waiting for their families to fetch them and lay them to rest.

Zodwa borrowed the money for taxi fare from the township to Krugersdorp from Mama Beauty but lied about what she needed it for. It's not that she doesn't need money for food, but this is more important than eating.

The woman assisting her is white and looks to be too old to be working. She peers at Zodwa out of thick spectacles.

"I'm here to inquire about a child that died . . . to see if his body was brought here," Zodwa says.

"A boy?"

"Yes."

"What was the date of his death and how old was he?" She's pulled out a form and is filling it in as Zodwa answers.

"Either the tenth or the eleventh of May, just after his birth. He would have been a day or two old."

"Did he have any distinguishing features?"

"Yes, a birthmark on his left buttock in the shape of Africa."

"And where was the body taken?"

The body. As though it's a bag of stones or something else lifeless and lacking value. Zodwa suddenly hates the woman for her objectivity even as she envies it. How wonderful it must be to constantly be exposed to so much suffering and to sit safely in the knowledge that it isn't yours.

She grits her teeth. "I don't know."

This gets a reaction out of the woman. She stops writing and looks up. "You don't know what happened to the body?"

"My baby," Zodwa says. "Not 'the body.' My baby." The woman blinks at her and Zodwa keeps talking for fear that she'll be cast out for insolence. "Please, madam. I don't even know if my baby actually died. He was fine after his birth and then . . ." Zodwa trails off, not wanting to speak ill of Leleti even after her death but needing to explain her predicament. "He was taken away and I never saw him again. I was told he died."

The woman sighs. "But you don't know where he was taken or if he really had . . . passed?"

"No."

"Can't you ask the person who took him?"

Zodwa shakes her head, startled by the tears. "She died as well."

To Zodwa's surprise, the woman clucks and sets down her pen. She reaches for Zodwa's hand and squeezes it gently. The gesture almost undoes her. "*Ag,* my child. It sounds like you've had a very rough time of it. Are you okay?"

Of all the places Zodwa might have expected to find comfort, it would never have been in this place with this woman. She nods but the tears undermine her answer.

"I'll look at our records but I don't recall a newborn being brought in then. I remember the babies, you see."

And suddenly Zodwa understands that what she mistook for lack of feeling was this woman's defense mechanism against feeling too much.

"Let me go see." The woman leaves Zodwa for ten minutes and when she returns, she shakes her head. "There were older babies but no newborn males brought in. Have you checked the orphanages near the camp?"

"No."

"Sometimes babies are taken there or they get abandoned and end up there. It's worth a try."

Zodwa closes her eyes and feels a spark of hope she never knew she was so desperately seeking.

Is it possible that Leleti took her baby to such a place? That she took her grandson away from her daughter because she thought he stood a better chance raised by strangers than by Zodwa?

I took him . . . He is gone . . . I did it for you and for him.

Zodwa grabs the woman's hand, squeezing it hard before turning away. Hope is a trail of bread crumbs that she will follow.

CHAPTER THIRTY-FIVE

Delilah

❋

4 June 1994
Johannesburg General Hospital,
Johannesburg, South Africa

The nurse sounded panicked when she heard my voice. "Delilah? I didn't think you were going to call today."

I called the ICU every day at 7:00 a.m. but had slept in late that morning since I'd been doing a lot of worrying about things I couldn't control: Daniel's condition; the baby, whose homecoming was being expedited since the orphanage was so overcrowded; and the constant hovering threat of the Coetzee family.

They'd upped their intimidation tactics by leaving poisoned wild animals on our doorstep every few days, and the last one had been eviscerated, its innards trailing down the stairs. I was edgy all the time and the slightest noise outside had me up and peering through the curtains. Exhausted from the lack of rest, I'd finally fallen into a fitful sleep in the predawn hours, only waking just before nine.

"Rachel? What's wrong? What's happened?" I'd been on a first-name basis with the ICU nurses for a while.

"It's Daniel," she said. "His organs all started shutting down last night. They're taking him off life support at eleven o'clock. I'm so sorry."

"I'm on my way."

Like during my first sojourn from the hospital to the farm, I didn't remember anything of the trip back beyond whispering, "Please, please, please, please." I repeated the entreaty over and over, the litany the closest I'd come to prayer in forty years.

I ran into the waiting room at 10:30 a.m., out of breath but steeled for the fight I knew was waiting for me. Father Thomas had appointed himself as Daniel's gatekeeper, but he wouldn't keep me from seeing my son. Not again, not when he was moments away from death. I was almost disappointed when I didn't see him there. At the nurses' station, Rachel looked up and spotted me.

"I made it in time," I said. "Please let me in to see him. I know it's only supposed to be one visitor at a time, but I'm sure you can make this one exception."

"Delilah." She shook her head.

"I'm his mother. I know I said I wasn't family, and maybe I'm not—at least not in the traditional sense, considering I gave him up when he was born—but I'm his biological mother. He needs his mother, Rachel. And I need him."

Her eyes were filled with tears. "I tried to call you, Delilah, but you'd already left. He passed away just after we spoke. I'm so, so sorry."

"No." I shook my head. "No." I turned away from her and made my way to the viewing glass like a sleepwalker.

The nun was there again and she was holding Daniel's hand, my Daniel, who would still have been alive for me to say my farewell if I'd just called the hospital at the time I usually did. It seemed an unbearable cruelty to have me be an hour too late, as though God was still punishing me for my transgression almost forty years before. Then, I'd run from Daniel when I should have stayed, and this time, I'd rushed to his side just as soon as I'd heard the news of the shooting. Still, I'd allowed myself to be kept from him.

I never knew until that moment when the opportunity was taken away from me, how desperately I'd needed to talk to him, to tell him how much I loved him and how not a day had gone by without my thinking of him. For four decades, I'd held imaginary conversations with him in which I'd crafted apologies and explanations, entreaties and justifications.

And now, I'd never get the chance to voice any of them.

The church had kept us apart all those years ago and now it was God Himself who'd stepped between us. There was nothing more final than that.

CHAPTER THIRTY-SIX

Zodwa

2–30 August 1994

Big Hope Informal Settlement,

Magaliesburg, South Africa

Zodwa makes her way along the laneways, hurriedly greeting people without stopping to chat. The first wave of workers leaving the squatter camp for their jobs in the city was already two hours ago. She's getting a later start to her working day than most, but then she finishes later than most too.

She's ten minutes late because she had an early appointment at another orphanage, this one slightly farther afield than the last. None of the children there matched the timeline of when her baby disappeared, but it's another place Zodwa can cross off her list.

"Hello, Mama Mashigo," Zodwa says when she walks through the door of the Good Times Drinking Establishment. "I'm sorry I'm late."

The *shebeen* queen, which is what the speakeasy owners are nicknamed, is sitting at her table in the corner tallying up the number of empty quart beer bottles she'll be returning for deposit refunds. She's perfectly put together, as she always is, wearing a matching dress and elaborate head wrap made out of blue *seshoeshoe*. A tall glass of Coke sits next to her. It's Zodwa's job to ensure that it's topped up all day, and that it has two cubes of ice floating in it at all times. Mama Mashigo may be a purveyor of alcohol but she never touches the stuff herself.

She glares at Zodwa and pointedly checks her watch but doesn't say anything. Zodwa knows she'll exact her revenge later by making Zodwa stay late and carry out the worst of the closing duties: cleaning up the vomit and broken bottles, and scrubbing out the bottoms of the cast-iron pots Mama Mashigo cooks *mogodu* and *pap* in.

Zodwa doesn't mind. It's a small price to pay for having a job.

When she began looking for one two months ago, she knew that venturing out of the township in search of work wasn't even a possibility because a job that far away would require money for daily transport, which Zodwa didn't have. Working in a shop or any kind of office required decent clothing as well, which she couldn't afford. Her only option for finding employment was in the township itself, but everyone she approached said there weren't any jobs available and that times were tough.

Zodwa knows that wasn't the truth. They just didn't want her bad mojo anywhere near their businesses. News travels quickly in the township, and the local healer isn't the only one who thinks Zodwa's cursed.

The *shebeen* queen was either too practical to believe in such things or she felt sorry for Zodwa, because she'd agreed to grant her a trial period after Zodwa had come to the *shebeen*, with eyes still swollen from grief, to ask if she had any positions available. She was put on a month's probation and after proving herself a hard worker, Mama Mashigo allowed her to stay on.

Zodwa spends six days a week at the Good Times Drinking Establishment, which is approximately the size of seven regular shacks laid end to end, and can seat up to a hundred people when necessary. It has a concrete floor and the tin walls on three sides are covered with pictures of African icons torn out of *Drum* magazine. The fourth wall comes up only halfway so that the customers can see and be seen, which is almost as important as the actual drinking.

Mama Mashigo has an illegal electricity hookup to the butcher shop that's almost a hundred meters away. The electricity allows her to run three fridges and two freezers, and also powers the superior sound system that sets her place apart from the other *shebeens*. *Kwaito* music is already blaring from the two speakers that are hung up in the corners of the room. Zodwa taps her feet to the rhythm, which helps her get through the day as she hustles for tips, serves drinks, and navigates the world of men.

There's nothing chivalrous about drunks in a *shebeen*. And though Mama Mashigo watches over her girls, she expects them to keep those men coming back no matter how much they bruise the girls' bums with their grabbing.

"The best way to stop yourself from being hassled is to get a boyfriend," Ntombi told her after her second day on the job. She's one of Mama Mashigo's best girls and makes the most money. "A *pantsula* boyfriend is the best kind to have because then no one wants to mess with his property."

Zodwa laughed the suggestion off. She refuses to be anyone's property.

But today, Mongezi and his friends stop by.

As they take their seats around a small table, ready to gamble with dice, he acts surprised to see Zodwa. "Look who it is," he says to his two friends, "my other girlfriend." His cohorts laugh stupidly as he wraps his arm around Zodwa's hips and pulls her closer to him. "This one just couldn't get enough of me. Don't tell Thembeka." He winks at them. "She'll get jealous."

The last time Mongezi used this flirtatious tone with Zodwa was on the day he raped her. It was one of those hot August days that made winter feel like a distant memory. At least the seasonal winds provided some relief, which is why Zodwa had left the shack door propped open while she did her homework. She remembers battling to concentrate because her thoughts were so filled with Thembeka.

A whole day had passed since she'd slipped the letter into her friend's school case. Thembeka should have found it by then but she hadn't been at school that day, so Zodwa had no way of knowing how she'd reacted to it. She was just wondering if she should go and seek Thembeka out when a shadow fell across the bed and she looked up to see Mongezi leaning in the doorway.

"Mongezi," she said. "What are you doing here? Is Thembeka with you?"

"Hello, baby girl," he said. "No, it's just me. She was sick today. Can you guess what caused it?"

He was acting strangely and Zodwa was beginning to feel uncomfortable. She was glad the door stood open.

"I asked you a question," Mongezi said, still smiling. "Can you guess what made her so sick?"

"No, what?"

"It was your letter."

A chill went down Zodwa's spine.

"Your disgusting letter telling her all your disgusting feelings for her. It made her sick to her stomach." He smiled as he said it. "It made me want to puke as well." Mongezi stepped inside and closed the door behind him.

Zodwa tried to swallow but her mouth was too dry. She tried to speak, but fear had paralyzed her.

"You think you're a man now? You think you have one of these?" He grabbed at his crotch as he advanced toward her and Zodwa could see how his member strained against his trousers. "Because only one of these can please a woman." He stepped forward and fell upon Zodwa before she could protest or scream for help.

"Please," she whispered. "Please."

"Yes, I know you want it but you don't have to beg for it. I'm going to give it to you so that you can see what you've been missing." He tugged down the zip of his school trousers and she could see he wasn't wearing any underwear. "This will fix you good."

After he'd meted out his punishment, Mongezi stood and pulled his trousers back up. "I was kidding about Thembeka. She didn't see the letter," he said as he closed his zip. "She was sick from something she ate. But if you try to speak to her again about your filthy lesbian feelings, I'll tell everyone about you. And then I won't be the only man in the township trying to fix you. Maybe you'll enjoy them as much as you enjoyed me."

Then he was gone, never to return, not even after Zodwa told Thembeka the truth about what he'd done. And now he's back, goading her. "Have you missed me, baby doll?" Mongezi asks to his friends' delight.

"No." Zodwa pulls away. Her fear rendered her defenseless that day and she refuses to allow it to paralyze her now again. "And I'm not your girlfriend."

"Oh really?" Mongezi challenges then, an evil glint in his eye. "Then whose girlfriend are you?"

He knows as well as Zodwa does that to be called out as a lesbian is the worst thing a black woman can be labeled. It's better, so much better, to be considered a loose woman—even one who sleeps with her best friend's boyfriend—than to be known as a woman who's attracted to other women.

If Mongezi shares her secret, if he tells his friends and the rest of the township what Zodwa is, she'll become both a pariah and a target for other men like him. Men who believe that there's only one way to cure women like Zodwa of their unnatural appetites. She wonders what's stopped him from telling anyone up until now and can only conclude that he enjoys lauding this power over her. That, and he's probably also worried that people might wonder about Thembeka's orientation and what she might have done to attract the attention of such a woman as Zodwa.

"I'm no one's girlfriend," she says softly.

And that's exactly the problem.

When Ace Boyi comes into the *shebeen* one day, bragging about the stolen goods he just off-loaded for a tidy sum, Zodwa pretends to be impressed by his small-time gangster status. Even though he isn't a real thug, he's still higher up in the pecking order than Mongezi, who doesn't have any gangster affiliations and is five years younger.

Becoming Ace's girlfriend means she will be off-limits to Mongezi. It will also prove him to be a liar if he tells anyone her secret since if Zodwa has a boyfriend, a real man like Ace, then it proves she can't be gay. It doesn't matter that her skin crawls every time Ace touches her. Or that she wants to cry the first time she lets him have sex with her. Pinned under him, she feels both sickened and relieved. Sickened that she's degrading herself like that. Relieved that she's finally doing something that's perceived as normal. Perhaps the more she does it, the easier it will become.

The first two weeks with Ace are the hardest. Pretending to like him. Pretending to be aroused when she's with him. He brings her gifts, luxuries like meat and toiletries, but instead of helping take the sting out of their relationship, it just makes Zodwa feel worse. Like she's a prostitute who's being paid for her services. And then he offers her a sip of his beer one night and she thinks, *Why not?*

She takes a few sips and they help make her feel detached, like things are happening to her rather than her being an active participant in her own degradation. And if a few sips can do that, then how much more can a bottle or two do? Feeling nothing is what Zodwa craves more than anything.

CHAPTER THIRTY-SEVEN

Ruth

❋

10 October 1994
Verdriet, Magaliesburg, South Africa

Five months after the baby first showed up on our doorstep, his room is ready and waiting. All it needs now is Mandla.

Mandla: That's the baby's official name as registered on his birth certificate. It means "strength" or "power" in Zulu, and it's also only one letter away from spelling "Mandela," the man who made history by becoming president on the day Mandla was born. The name was given to him as a kind of talisman by the black staff at the orphanage and I like it; it suits him.

The fostering process usually takes ages but since we're the ones whose care he was left in and the orphanage is so over-crowded, they're expediting it. Of course, a part of the process is trying to find his real mother in case he was either taken from her or in the event that she changes her mind and wants him back. They place adverts in the classifieds of various news-papers to that end for ninety days after an application to foster a child is made and then there's nothing left to do but wait.

Each day that goes by without someone claiming him is just another sign that he's meant to be mine.

As I lie awake each night, thankful that no one has re-sponded to the ads, I can't help but wonder about her, his mother. Where is she? What made her give him up? And, most important, what led her to our door out of all the doors in the world? How did she know that mine was the one that contained the most need?

I know Dee would scoff if I confided this belief to her. Well, the old Dee would have waved it off as sentimental nonsense and told me not to be ridiculous. The new one doesn't do much but sit out on the patio staring off into the distance.

She's been almost catatonic since Daniel died and nothing I do or say draws her out. It's completely understandable under the circumstances. I can't begin to imagine the guilt she's feeling. At least it means she hasn't put up any kind of fight about Mandla, but then she isn't putting up any kind of fight about anything, not even the onslaught from the Coetzees, which has just intensified since news of Mandla spread and set the town on fire.

The first people to call us were our cousins from Ma's side, who I haven't spoken to in decades. I had more fun with the calls than I should have.

"Oh, Cecile. You're still alive? How wonderful! Yes, I'm very well, thank you! Delilah is marvelous too . . . What's that? You heard I'm adopting a *kaffir* child? Oh no, you absolutely must have misheard . . . Yes, I can imagine how relieved you are to hear that . . . In point of fact, I'm fostering a black child . . .

"It's the new South Africa, Cecile. You can't say the word *kaffir* anymore. With the way you speak, I would almost be forgiven for thinking you're one of those racist *boers* who still has the old apartheid flag up rather than embracing the new rainbow nation one . . . Oh? You do? Hello, Cecile? Are you there? Hello?"

That's how most of those calls went, with only the slightest variations.

In between the ones I got from people I knew were the scary ones from anonymous callers, threatening to do harm to us or the baby. If I was willing to sell the farm before, I'm digging my heels in now just because I'm being bullied. The idiots have somehow made me side with Dee. I suppose there's a first for everything.

Today, the town sends in the big guns in the form of a holy man.

"Good day, *mevrou*. I'm *Dominee* Johannes Oosthuizen from the Dutch Reformed Church," he says when I open the door. "You won't know me, but you may remember my father, *Dominee* Hendrick Oosthuizen? I took over from him thirty years ago when he retired."

"Charmed, I'm sure. I'm Ruth Richardson, but then I think you already know that. Won't you come in?"

"Thank you." He steps over an ominous black bundle at the door's threshold and into the house, seemingly filling up every corner of it with his huge frame. Despite his age, which looks to be in the late sixties, Johannes Oosthuizen is a formidable man. At six foot two, and broad-shouldered in the way of rugby players and wrestlers, he looks like someone who uses intimidation to get his own way.

I offer him a seat on the couch where Jezebel usually sits, knowing that he'll leave with half of the fur she sheds on his clothes. It's a pity she's closed in with Dee in her room, as I'd like to subject him to the Jez test; I suspect she'd bare her teeth at him just like she did with the Coetzee brothers. She's a good judge of character, that dog. "Can I get you some tea and a rusk?" I ask since that's what Ma always served guests in the *voorkamer*.

Of course, her tea had been steeping in a pot on the stove for hours so that the whole house perpetually stank of rooibos, and her rusks were homemade from a recipe that had been handed down for generations. I serve him Ouma-brand rusks that Dee bought from the shops and make the tea by quickly dunking a tea bag into boiling water. Still, he's lucky to be shown any hospitality at all considering the purpose of his visit.

"What can I help you with, *dominee*?" I ask as I put the tea and rusk down on the table in front of him.

His eyes flicker to something behind me, probably just so he doesn't have to look at my defiant face, and I see them widen as he spots what's hanging on the lounge wall. It's my old magazine cover that I had Vince ship from Cape Town. It seems he either can't take his eyes off the snake draped over me or my naked body. Definitely one of the two.

"So, it's true what my father said," he says. "About you and the . . ." He trails off there, clearly at a loss to find a polite enough word that will encompass all the debauchery I personify, and then settles on "dancing."

"I was actually less of a dancer and more of a stripper," I say. "But how lovely that your father still remembers my show so many years after he sneaked in to see it."

He puffs himself up like a bullfrog. A large, menacing bullfrog. His father was an imposing bastard too. "He didn't sneak in. As a man of God, it was his duty to go and see for himself if the rumors were true."

"Hmm. Yes. And once he'd confirmed for himself that I was, in fact, dancing naked with a snake, you'd have to assume that he'd leave immediately."

He squirms.

"Or at least after a few minutes," I amend generously.

"He had to see for himself the degree of degradation—"

"You know that he stayed right until the very end?"

"It was his duty as a man of God to bear witness!" he splutters, and sloshes some tea into his lap. I hope it's burned his crotch.

"How strange that he didn't tell you and the rest of the congregation, during that particularly malicious sermon he gave about me, that he took my hand and put it on his penis to show me how very hard I'd made him. Perhaps he was proud that a man his age could still get it up." I laugh. "But that was how most of the men in this God-fearing town went about trying to make me see the error of my ways, so don't feel too bad, *dominee*. Your father wasn't the only one."

"You are a lying slut!" He stands so quickly that he knocks the table over.

"Ah, yes," I muse. "Isn't it funny how a bitch is a woman who won't sleep with you, but a slut is a woman who'll sleep with anyone else except you, which was your father's real issue with me, I suspect." I stand and walk to the door. "Now, is there anything else I can help you with before I ask you to leave?"

Suddenly remembering the mission he's been sent on, and clearly nervous that he'll be tossed out before he can fulfill it, the *dominee* straightens his tie and clears his throat. "I wanted to talk to you about this nonsense I've heard about you bringing a *kaffir* baby to come live with you in your home."

"What about it?"

"It's unnatural in the eyes of the Lord."

"Really? It offends the Lord that an orphaned child is going to find love and comfort within these walls?" He nods warily and begins to reply but I cut him off. "Well, you know what I think is unnatural in the eyes of the Lord? Hypocrisy. This whole damn town stinks of it. And you know what? You can

171
·

shove it up your sanctimonious asses." I walk to the door and open it for him. "Oh, and on the way out, could you please take that black bag with you? It has a poor decapitated animal inside it, one of many that your devout congregants have left for us, because apparently disgusting cruelty to animals, harassment, and intimidation are all natural in the eyes of the Lord."

I pick up the bag that I'd had Stompie put the poor civet into and hand it across to him. He instinctively reaches out for it.

"The baby won't be safe here," the *dominee* says, a note of desperation in his voice. "Who knows what might happen to him."

"Don't you dare threaten me," I say, pointing my finger at his face. He flinches and steps back, and I force a sickly sweet smile. "Now, please don't take this the wrong way, *dominee*, but you can all fuck right off."

And then I slam the door in his face.

CHAPTER THIRTY-EIGHT

Delilah

❄

10 October 1994
Verdriet, Magaliesburg, South Africa

N ow, please don't take this the wrong way, *dominee*, but you
can all fuck right off."

I couldn't help it, I laughed. It was the first time I'd done so
in months. I stepped away from my door where I'd been eavesdropping and sat down on the bed, rubbing Jez's back.

Four months after Daniel's passing, I still couldn't shake off
my malaise. I was in limbo, unable to grieve him properly and
yet also unable to move on. How did you mourn someone you'd
never known but had always loved? How did you let them go
when they'd never been yours?

I kept telling myself I had no right to any kind of grief at all—
that what I was mourning was what might have been if things
had been different—but still I felt as though his death had
gouged a hole in me. I could feel the wind whistling through it,
the sound so forlorn that it kept me awake at night as I stared
into the darkness.

Ruth had tried to make me go to Daniel's funeral after she'd
found me curled up in bed, staring at the last photograph I'd
received of him.

"He's so handsome," she'd said, taking the Polaroid from my
hands as she sat down on the bed next to me. "He looks like

173
•

you." I didn't see the resemblance. I thought he looked like his father. "Are you going to the funeral?" Ruth asked, handing the Polaroid back.

I shook my head.

"You could never tell anyone you were his mother when he was still alive. Surely now that he's passed on, and you're no longer in that secular life, you can go and talk to his friends and congregants. Tell them that you're his mother. I'm sure they'd love to talk to you about him and you can get to know him through them. Even claim him as your own."

Claim him. As if such a thing could ever be that easy.

"Okay," she continued through my silence. "At least think about going to visit Daniel's grave. Maybe get some closure. It couldn't hurt. And if you're not ready now, wait until you are."

"How will I know when I'm ready?" I whispered.

"You'll get a sign, of course."

Ruth thought it was callous of me not to go and lay my son to rest, but how could I, when Father Thomas would be there conducting the service? What kept me away was cowardice. Say what you wanted about Ruth, she wasn't a coward and didn't take crap from anyone. There was a lot about my sister that drove me crazy but I had to admire her courage. More than admire it, I was envious of it. Her audacity in standing up to the *dominee* was more than a mere act of defiance, it was completely taboo in the Afrikaner culture, which emphasized respect for male elders and community leaders above all else.

As little girls, Ruth and I were taught to always defer to the most senior white male at any gathering, and then to view the pecking order down from him according to age and social standing. It didn't matter if you didn't know the men at any given event, you had to go and greet them all, kissing them on the lips, before you were able to run off and play with the other children.

If a man wet his lips too much or opened his lips a fraction too wide—perhaps touched you in a way that made you feel uncomfortable or made you sit on his lap just a bit too long—that was no excuse to avoid him the next time. In fact, if you did, it was viewed as being extremely bad mannered, and there was no greater indictment of a child, or their parents, than declaring them to be lacking in manners. It was a girl's duty to grin and bear it. No matter what any man did, she absolutely wasn't to make a fuss.

It was a dysfunctional way to be raised and judging by how I'd allowed Father Thomas to treat me, first at the convent all those years ago and then recently at the hospital, it was a way of thinking that I hadn't grown out of. I had so many regrets since Daniel's passing, but not standing up to the priest and asserting myself was the greatest of them. I took vicarious pleasure in hearing Ruth rage against a system that had always made me feel so powerless.

Her sudden knock at my door startled me.

When she stepped inside, Jezebel immediately ran out of the room as though desperate to be free of me and my melancholy. "Riaan's here again to see you," Ruth said quietly. "Are you coming out?"

I shook my head.

"Are you sure? You've been cooped up for ages. A bit of company might do you a world of good."

"No, Ruth. I'm not up for visitors." My voice was scratchy from lack of use.

"Okay." She sighed. "Can't say I don't wish it was Vince knocking the door down every day. I'm tired of lying to the poor man and making excuses for you, though," she said before leaving.

I could hear her murmuring an explanation.

"Did I do something wrong?" Riaan asked. "Is she upset with me?" I felt a stab of guilt at that, that he'd think he was to blame for anything.

"No," Ruth said. "It's not you." After that, I could only make out fragments: "she's had some bad news . . . she lost someone close to her . . . isn't taking it well."

I was grateful to Ruth for her rare diplomacy as I got back into bed and closed my eyes.

CHAPTER THIRTY-NINE

Zodwa

❋

S tubble scratches against Zodwa's neck, rough like sand-paper. She turns over, wincing at the stab of pain in her forehead. On her back, staring up at the shack roof, she can smell the stale beer on Ace's breath.

He's lying on his side, snoring with his mouth wide open. She shrinks away from the stench of it, and her elbow connects with the empty Black Label bottles standing sentry next to the mattress on her makeshift bedside table, a milk crate loaded with books. Their clinking wakes Ace up and he grumbles as he glares at her. "Why are you making such a noise?"

"Sorry," Zodwa whispers. "Go back to sleep."

Zodwa checks to see if beer spilled on her books. Since she doesn't have a proper fixed address, she doesn't qualify for library membership, not even in the new South Africa. Instead, she begs and borrows textbooks from Mr. Tshabalala, her old high school English teacher who's taken pity on her, and then buys the others if Mama Beauty isn't able to source them for her.

Since Zodwa considers the books necessities, as essential as food and water, she doesn't feel guilty about the money spent on them. Besides the math, science, and biology textbooks, which she's studying from so that she can write her exams to finish high school, she also has *Narrative of the Life of Frederick Douglass, an American Slave, The Communist Manifesto*, and three books by Dr. Martin Luther King Jr.

The only fiction books Zodwa owns are *Waiting to Exhale* by Terry McMillan and *Beloved* by Toni Morrison. She's read both books multiple times and often looks at the author photographs to remind herself that black women are fit for more than labor, that they can have ideas and thoughts and dreams worthy enough to be committed to paper, compelling enough for strangers to read.

Assured that her books are fine, Zodwa checks her wristwatch and curses, stands up, and then curses again as her toes sink into mud. It must have rained during the night because the shack has partially flooded. Zodwa doesn't want to think about how drunk she must have been to have slept through the drumbeat of rain against the roof. She sighs and lights the primus stove to put the kettle on to boil. She missed the appointment she had at the children's sanctuary and now may even be late for work, but she can't leave without making Ace his usual breakfast: *kota* and sweet tea to wash it down with. Zodwa pulls the loaf of white bread toward her, cuts it in quarters, and then scoops the guts of it out.

She fills a quarter with some fried cabbage and then reaches for the Vienna sausages and chips left over from last night's meal. Waiting for the kettle to boil, Zodwa looks at the newspaper that had wrapped the sausages. It's a luxury she can't usually afford and so she skims through one at every opportunity. These pages aren't articles or anything interesting. They're just legal notices in the classifieds.

While she fills a tin mug with four teaspoons of sugar, she catches sight of the letters under the sugar canister. They're all from her grandmother, beseeching her to come home and explain herself, and they've all gone unanswered, though Zodwa goes to the building society to do banking as often as she can to send money home to her *gogo*. It helps assuage the guilt and she hopes it tells her grandmother what she can't: that she loves her even though she's lost; that she misses her even though shame keeps her away.

Once Ace's breakfast is made, Zodwa gently shakes him awake and leaves before he can pull her down onto him. The man's sexual appetite is insatiable. It's bad enough having sex with him when she's drunk and partially anesthetized to it. Doing it when she's hungover is its own kind of hell.

Zodwa heads out of the shack, finds another stone in the laneway, and adds it to her brother's shrine. As she touches the mass of rock, a vivid image comes to her of the very last time she saw Dumisa. He was impeccably dressed in their deceased father's best suit even though he would be walking for hours on dusty roads ahead of two days of travel to Johannesburg. Her brother maintained, like their father before him, that a man who looked sharp was one who garnered respect. A well-dressed man, even if forced to his knees, had dignity.

Dumisa had bent down so he was at eye level with Zodwa and she'd blinked as his hat cast a shadow across her face, briefly blocking out the sun. Everyone said he looked like their father but since Zodwa didn't remember him at all, she had to take their word for it. Dumisa wasn't only strong and handsome, he was also clever and successful. Being his sister bestowed a special kind of status on her that she feared would weaken in his absence.

As Dumisa removed his hat and tucked it under his arm, Zodwa wanted to wrap her arms around his neck and beg him not to go. No one who left ever came back, including their mother, who'd gone away to work in the city two years prior with promises that the arrangement was only temporary. Dumisa was Zodwa's protector and best friend. He was what made both the separation from their mother and their father's death bearable. She couldn't imagine a world in which he didn't bring her red lollipops from the shop in town, or one in which he didn't charm the white ladies at the church so he could dig through the charity bins for shoes that wouldn't be two sizes too big for her.

"You must be good, little sister, do you hear me?" Dumisa said.

Zodwa nodded, eyes cast down at his wing tips that shone even in the dirt.

"Look at me," he instructed gently, chucking her chin so that she met his gaze. "You are a Khumalo, just like me. We are a great people, proudly Zulu. We meet the eyes of the world. And if we do not like what we see when we go out into it, then what do we do?" he asked, repeating a refrain that Zodwa had heard many times.

"We change it."

"Yes, we change it. We make it better. Now is my time but one day it will be yours. When that time comes, make me proud, little sister."

Dumisa is another person that Zodwa has let down, which she prefers not to think about, but in keeping Leleti's ritual alive, she ensures that she starts every day thinking about her brother and mother whether she wants to or not. She's an orphan now since both of her parents are dead, but is there even a word for someone whose whole family is dead?

Yes, there is. Cursed.

But maybe her whole family isn't dead. She needs to go call the children's sanctuary again from the spaza shop pay phones to apologize and set up another appointment. This time, she'll keep it.

CHAPTER FORTY

Ruth

✻

2–17 December 1994

Verdriet, Magaliesburg, South Africa, and

Turffontein, Johannesburg, South Africa

I snatched up the phone when it rang. "Hello, Ruth speaking."

"Hello, Ruth. It's Lindiwe." I'm so relieved to hear the social worker's voice, I could cry.

"Please tell me there's good news." I don't want to be rude but I'm also not in the mood to make small talk. The fostering process has been dragging on, each phase stretching out longer than the one before, and if this is what an expedited process looks like, I don't want to see a slow one. I'm hoping for some finality now that all the medicals have been completed along with the other mounds of paperwork.

Lindiwe, to her credit, gets straight to the point. "Something has come up. I think you should come see me so we can talk about it."

"Oh? What is it?"

"As I said, I think it would be better for us to chat face-to-face," Lindiwe says.

"Okay, you're scaring me now. Please just tell me what it is or else I'll only imagine something worse."

Lindiwe sighs deeply and then clears her throat. "Okay. The thing is . . . I'm looking at Mandla's medicals . . ."

182

·

"Yes?"

"And . . . we have a problem."

"What kind of problem?"

"I'm sorry to tell you this, Ruth, but Mandla has tested positive for HIV."

"Oh my God."

No, please no.

We start the Saturday morning off in a tiny training room near Turffontein with scarred wooden tables and uncomfortable plastic chairs set up in a classic U-shape. The room doesn't have air-conditioning and it's sweltering in the December heat. I wrestle a tiny window open for fresh air.

I'm here out of desperation because I don't know where else to go or what else to do. All I know about HIV and AIDS is what I've been reading in the newspapers and they make it sound terrifying.

When I told Dee the news of Mandla's status, she cringed, looking horrified, and then said, "Well, that's that then."

"What?"

"At least you can now put an end to this fostering nonsense since you can't possibly still be considering going through with it."

It's exactly what I'd been thinking myself, that his status meant all choice had been taken from me, but her arrogant certainty made me cross my arms and challenge her: "Why not?"

"AIDS is a death sentence, Ruth. That child is going to die. It was a ridiculous scheme to begin with, but now . . ." She trailed off and then shook her head before adding, "As though you, of all people, would possibly be equipped to deal with it."

If her words were meant to dissuade me, they had the

opposite effect. Instead, they made me want to prove her wrong. And the only way I could do that was to seek out contradictory information, which is why I've signed up for this course.

A young woman with long brown hair strides in and pulls a binder from her bag. She looks like the kind of person who doesn't take shit from anyone and I like her immediately. "Good morning, everyone. My name's Courtney and I'll be your course facilitator." She walks around the room, thumping thick manuals onto desks. "This is the official course material but I have to warn you that it's exactly what you'd expect from a bunch of bureaucrats with fancy degrees who push pencils all day and write training programs about things they don't know the first thing about.

"These manuals are packed full of dense paragraphs with dry descriptions, and the language is so clinical and inaccessible that I wonder if this attempt at formal euphemism is meant to shield you from what awaits you instead of preparing you for it. Luckily, you have me to translate it for you. Now, let's go around the room so you can all introduce yourselves and tell us why you're here."

It turns out that although we're quite a mixed group, we share the common goal of wanting to learn how to care for HIV-positive people. More than half of the group are health-care professionals, with the rest, besides me, being volunteers. All of them are going out into the field to deal with unknown patients, mostly homosexual men. I'm the only one considering bringing an HIV-positive baby into my home and the only one for whom this is personal.

Courtney fiddles with the overhead projector and cues a slide. "Right, they say that the first rule of war is to know your enemy. So, here it is. Your first look at it. This is a 3-D rendering of the HIV virus. Don't be fooled by how innocuous it looks. It's a hateful little bastard."

The picture branded onto the screen shows what could be a ball of clay with dozens of bolts embedded in it. She's right, it doesn't look all that dangerous but I know better. I think back to the emaciated child with his spindly legs and sunken cheeks that I saw in the orphanage that day. Anything that could do that to a baby has to be completely without mercy.

Courtney gives us a moment to look at the slide and then launches into the syllabus. I struggle along with everyone else to keep up with her. Every half an hour or so, she marches to the whiteboard and adds a new term to the growing list. I copy them all down and size them up as I try to figure out who the biggest villains are: HIV, AIDS, TB, opportunistic infections, lesions, diarrhea, pneumonia, cryptococcal meningitis, toxoplasmosis, candidiasis, or Kaposi's sarcoma.

The terms swarm around my mind, as real to me as fire-breathing dragons and hobgoblins. They're the stuff of fantasy and nightmares.

"AIDS is no longer a homosexual disease limited to men, it's now predominantly a women's and children's disease. The number of recorded HIV infections in South Africa has grown by more than sixty percent in the past two years and that's just the recorded cases. With the huge stigma surrounding the disease, deaths are being attributed to TB and pneumonia on death certificates so that funeral parlors won't refuse to handle the bodies. I suspect the real figures are double the official ones. We're heading for a pandemic, there's no doubt about it."

The only man in the room, Julian, puts his hand up and then speaks before being called on. "So, what can we do to stop it? Everything we've talked about is how to manage secondary infections and palliative care. How can we stop this disease?" His question seems apt, considering men think everything can be fixed while women just try to make the best of bad situations.

"It's easy to stop," Courtney surprises us by saying, and the young man nods as if he suspected this all along. "Just make everyone in the world stop having sex. You can lead by example," she says to him with a wry smile.

Julian shakes his head. "What about a cure? Or an inoculation?"

"At the moment, studies are showing positive results in terms of something called AZT, which is helping to drastically reduce mother-to-child transmission. But once you are infected, there is no cure. The US is working hard on medication that HIV-positive people can take, called antiretroviral therapy, but it hasn't shown very good results just yet. They're trying their best but it will take time."

I raise my hand. "What's the life expectancy for a child who's born HIV positive?"

"Fifty percent of HIV-positive children will die before their second birthday," she says.

Mandla is already eight months old. That means he has just over a year left.

"Okay, that's it for the theory part of the course," Courtney says. "Let's look at some videos to help us prepare for what awaits."

She pulls a television and video machine on a trolley over from a side wall and pops a VHS cassette in. I take deep, steadying breaths and try to stop my hands from trembling as Courtney closes the curtains. We watch instructional videos, which thankfully include the caring for HIV-positive babies as well as adults, and are shown how to treat a severe rash brought on by days of diarrhea and how to prevent bedsores. We're also taught the correct way to administer medications through plastic syringes. Immediate vomiting means the medication hasn't gone down, so we'll have to do it again.

I scribble notes furiously, terrified that a slight lapse in concentration will result in my missing out on some technique that could one day save Mandla's life. And then we're told that even though HIV can't be transmitted through tears or mucus, we should wear medical gloves when touching HIV-positive people.

Just in case.

It's a jarring thought but one that makes the butterflies stop flitting against my rib cage. It's the only reassuring thing I've heard all day and I'm immediately depressed about what that says about me, that I want to put a latex barrier between myself and a baby that up until a week ago I wanted more desperately than I'd ever wanted anything. And I'm a person of voracious appetites, so that really says something.

When the course is over and everyone has packed up, I can't bring myself to move.

"Are you okay? You look a bit green," Courtney says as she ejects the cassette and shoves it into her bag along with the binder full of slides.

I want to tell her I'm fine but what comes out is, "I don't think I can do this. It's too much. It's not what I signed up for."

She stops fussing with her bag and leans against the desk next to me. "So, what did you sign up for?"

"A healthy baby. One who would cause a bit of a ruckus in the community because he's black, but nothing I couldn't deal with since God knows I've caused enough ruckuses in my life. What I wasn't expecting was for . . ."

"Him to be dying," she finishes for me, and I wince.

"Yes."

"Because, make no mistake, this diagnosis is a death sentence." She sighs and reaches into her bag for a pack of smokes and an ashtray. They're Dumonts, the long brown cigarettes that always make me think of cinnamon sticks. She taps the pack and two cigarettes eject on cue. "You want one?"

Damn right I do.

She lights up my smoke and then her own, taking a long, deep drag. After she exhales, she says, "This is about as real as shit will ever get. And I don't just mean for you, because you're all . . . you know . . ." She trails off as she waves her hand to take me in.

"All what?" I try not to bristle.

"Rich and white and privileged," she says matter-of-factly. She isn't trying to insult me. She's just stating the truth. "I don't know you, Ruth," she says. "I've just known many women like you. Women who didn't like getting old, so they made themselves younger. Women who didn't like being alone, so they made sure they weren't. Women who didn't like having nothing and so they got themselves everything."

"And what's wrong with that?"

"Nothing. Nothing at all. That's life, you know? But here's the thing. You're someone who's not used to being helpless, to not being the master of your own destiny. And that's the worst kind of person to be in the face of this." She pauses and then asks, "What's his name? This baby you thought you wanted so badly?"

"Mandla."

"Mandla." She breathes out a plume of smoke. "Don't take him unless you want him more than you have ever wanted anything in your life. Because here's the thing, Ruth. All that wealth, and your important connections, and your big, perfect tits, and your beauty-school charm? All of that means jack shit going forward." With that, she stubs out her smoke and holds the ashtray out for me to do the same.

I see her leave through the mist of my tears. I know she's right. I also know that sitting helplessly by and watching a child die is not something I can do.

CHAPTER FORTY-ONE

Zodwa

❋

17 *December 1994*
Big Hope Informal Settlement,
Magaliesburg, South Africa

W here are you going in such a hurry?" Ace asks, reaching out for Zodwa's leg and looping his arm around it. "Come back to bed, baby."

"I can't. I'm running late for an appointment." She extracts herself from his grasp and walks to the table, where she opens her purse and counts out the taxi fare.

"Another appointment?" Ace groans, falling back onto the mattress. "If I didn't know any better, I'd think you were seeing another man behind my back." He laughs to show he isn't serious. What woman would need someone else when she's already been serviced by Ace?

Certainly not Zodwa, who finds his attentions too much as it is. "You know there's no one else."

"Where are you going then? Who is this appointment with?" He reaches for his pants, which are lying in a heap on the floor, and extracts his cigarettes from a pocket.

Zodwa throws the box of matches to him before he can ask for them. "Someone my mother wanted to see about Dumisa."

Leleti kept a detailed journal of everyone she spoke to over the years in her quest to discover exactly what had happened to her son. Zodwa only discovered its existence when Mama Beauty told her about it soon after Leleti's death.

For some reason Leleti was never able to explain to Zodwa, she didn't believe the account of Cyril Malema, the man who claimed to have been the last person to see Dumisa alive, and so Leleti had been interviewing all of Dumisa's ex-comrades in the hope of shaking some kernel of truth loose from one of them. Each person Leleti saw was meticulously crossed off the list, and now only a few names remain.

Zodwa has made it her mission to track each of them down with Mama Beauty's help.

"And yesterday morning?" Ace asks, blowing a ring of smoke up at the roof. "Where did you go then?"

Zodwa can't tell him that she'd been to another orphanage where she'd handed a baby photo of Dumisa across to the social worker in case there was a chance her son looked like her brother at the same age.

"One boy here meets your description. He too has a birthmark but the file doesn't say where it is or what it looks like," the social worker had clucked in response. "I need to speak to them about being more fastidious in their record keeping."

Zodwa wasn't expecting that, that there was a chance her son might actually be there. After so many disappointments, that glimmer of hope felt all at once too much to bear. She'd followed the woman through a series of passages to the baby asleep in the crib, suddenly daring to believe that this might be it, the moment she finally found her son. And it was only then that it occurred to Zodwa that if she did, if her baby was still alive and she took him home, she'd be blatantly flouting Leleti's wishes.

What had her mother known about Zodwa that she herself

didn't? What had Leleti seen in her that was so flawed that she believed the baby to be better off without her?

She was sick and she wasn't thinking straight, Zodwa answered herself. *She was confused and upset about the rape. She was trying to spare me, not the baby.*

And then the social worker was taking the baby's clothing off and turning him on his side, and Zodwa floated free of herself, looking down at the child, who had a birthmark on his buttock.

But it was on the wrong side and not in the shape of Africa. Zodwa was too disappointed to cry.

"Hey," Ace says now, snapping his fingers at her. "I asked you a question. Where were you yesterday?"

"I was at the clinic," Zodwa lies.

"Which clinic?"

"The birth control one."

"*Hhayi ngeke,*" Ace says, voiced raised. "Don't think you're going to try to make me wear those condom things. Black men don't wear condoms. Our dicks are just too big." He smiles lasciviously before his expression turns serious. "Besides, I heard that's where the AIDS comes from."

"What?" Although Zodwa was lying about having been to the clinic, it's somewhere she plans to go soon. The last thing she needs is to fall pregnant again and Ace can't always be relied on to withdraw quickly enough.

"The AIDS. I heard that the whites put it in the condoms and then force the black man to wear it to make him sick. I'm not falling for that shit."

Zodwa shakes her head at his faulty logic. Ace refuses to eat meat that isn't cooked well-done for the same reason: he heard that's how you get AIDS. She says goodbye to him and leaves, adding a stone to Dumisa's shrine on her way out, wondering as she does so if she'll ever discover the truth about what happened to him.

Regardless, it seems the fate of the Khumalo women is to forever be searching for their sons.

CHAPTER FORTY-TWO

Delilah

❂

25 December 1994
Verdriet, Magaliesburg, South Africa

It was Christmas Day as well as my fifty-seventh birthday, and I'd started it the way I'd begun every Christmas since 1955: thinking about Daniel.

When he was still a child, I'd wonder if the nuns had allowed him a tree and if they'd given him gifts. I had no idea how they celebrated Christmas in the convent, though I suspected it would be austere. I hoped that a child's energy might persuade them to be more frivolous.

And then as Daniel grew up, I wondered if he was happy and if he ever thought of me; if he was well-adjusted or if he simmered with anger over his abandonment. The older he got, the less I worried, though it should have been the other way around. Children, for the most part, are nurtured and protected. Adulthood is the point at which we're thrown to the wolves. Wasn't it just as I'd stepped over the threshold of selfhood—at the very moment when I'd expected my life to get easier—that everything had so spectacularly fallen apart?

Since I'd spent every Christmas without Daniel, I wasn't prepared for how difficult the first one after his death would be; there had always been comfort to be found in the knowledge that he was out there somewhere in the world even though he wasn't a part of mine.

When I got back from my morning hike, I was expecting to find Ruth still in bed battling her usual morning hangover.

"There you are," Ruth said as soon as Jezebel and I stepped through the door. "I was worried you'd be late and that lunch would be ruined. Go wash up! You're all sweaty."

"Look who's talking." Ruth's face was more flushed than mine, but it was clear from all the food on the kitchen counter that she'd been slaving over a stove in a beastly hot kitchen for a few hours.

"Hot flushes," Ruth said. "From menopause." She waited a beat and then said, "You know, pausing between men." She looked so desperate for a reaction that I didn't try to hide my smile. She beamed in response. "I hope you like roasted everything."

I took a quick shower before returning, my hair still wet when I sat at the table across from Ruth. We didn't have any Christmas decorations up but she'd laid out festive hats and crackers. "Here, let's pull a few."

The first bang sent Jezebel running to hide behind one of the couches, her tail between her legs. After coaxing her out, we opened the rest of the crackers by pulling the wrappers apart and then swapped the trinkets like we used to do as children. Nothing had changed since then. Ruth still went for anything sparkly or girlie, whereas I preferred the magnifying glass and tiny deck of cards.

"I almost forgot," Ruth said, standing up and going to the kitchen. "I got us the good stuff." She plucked a bottle of Moët from the fridge and brought it back, looking worriedly at

Jezebel as she did so. "Try covering her ears. I'll go open this outside."

The pop wasn't as loud as I'd been expecting but I still had to wrap my arms around Jez to calm her.

"No, thanks," I said to Ruth when she was back and trying to fill our glasses. I expected her to say, *Fine, more for me!* but instead her face fell.

"Come now," she said. "Live a little. It's your birthday and a good day for me too because you're now as old as I am!"

I was touched that she'd remembered. My birthday had always faded into insignificance when we were children, mostly because of the religious holiday and also because Ma wasn't big on celebrating them. Still, I wasn't in the mood for festivities and told her as much.

Ruth put the bottle down and then took a deep, bracing breath. "Listen, Dee. I know you've had a really shitty few months. Believe me, I know. And I have too, what with my separation and me missing Vince so damn much. I know we didn't get off to the best start, which, to be honest, is mostly your fault because you're a pain in my ass and not exactly a party to be around. But I hate seeing you this miserable and not being able to do anything about it—"

"Ruth, I—"

"Shh, let me finish. We're stuck here together and in case you haven't noticed, it's us against the world. Between Mandla and the farm, we're public enemy number one and I don't know about you, but I'd be able to handle it much better if you and I weren't waging a constant battle against each other." She looked away and then looked back at me, her eyes pleading. "We don't have to like each other, Dee, but can we just try and get along a bit better? And please just let me host this celebration for you.

I know it probably won't make you feel better, but it will make me feel less helpless, okay?"

I didn't trust myself to speak when she was finished or to look at the tears that had formed in her eyes as she spoke. Instead, I lifted up my champagne flute and held it out for her. Ruth whooped as she filled it.

"Cheers!" I took a sip and forced myself not to wince at the dryness. "You weren't joking about everything being roasted," I said, forcing a smile as I looked at the spread of chicken, potatoes, sweetended baby carrots, and creamed spinach. "I didn't know you could cook."

"I'm a woman of many talents." Ruth winked.

"I don't doubt it." We started dishing up, handing each other bowls and gravy, and remarking on how good the food looked. As we started eating, we lapsed into an awkward silence that I tried to fill by blurting out the first thing that came to mind. "Were you really a stripper?"

"Yes." Ruth laughed, clearly taken aback by the direction the conversation was going in.

"Sorry, it's none of my business."

"Not at all. I've always preferred people who speak their minds even if what's on their minds isn't always appropriate or polite. At least you always know where you stand with them. So, go ahead and ask whatever you want."

"Okay. You took your clothes off? For your profession?"
"Yes."

"And you danced with a snake?"

"Sometimes. It was a python called Frank."

"Frank? Frank the python?"

She shrugged. "What can I say? He looked like Frank Sinatra. Same beady eyes and womanizing tendencies."

I laughed, feeling some of the tension from my neck ease. "You weren't scared of it?"

"I was squeamish with it the first few times, but after you've had a python crap and pee on you, you come to think of it more as a baby and less as a potentially dangerous animal. The fact that it was so heavy that I had to wheel it around in a pram also helped make me think of it as a baby, though unsuspecting people who peered inside didn't agree."

I laughed and took another sip of the champagne, which was growing on me, before I remembered something. "I thought the law at the time prohibited stripping?"

"No, it stated that you couldn't leave the stage with less clothes than what you came on wearing. So I had to put them back on during the act without it looking like the show was over and I was just hurriedly getting dressed." She topped up our glasses. "Who told you all this, by the way?"

"Ma wrote me a few letters."

"I'm sure she had a lot to say about it, though she didn't have a problem with all the money I sent home since it helped keep the farm afloat."

And there we were after all the levity, back at the farm, which was the biggest bone of contention between us. "I thought you'd sell the farm after Ma died," I said.

"No," Ruth replied. "We wouldn't have gotten a good price for it, so I rented out the land, which paid for its upkeep. Besides, I promised Da . . ."

"What?"

"Nothing, doesn't matter." Ruth looked shifty but I didn't want to press her on it. I wasn't interested in anything to do with Da anyway.

"So you made a lot of money? From the stripping?"

"Not just the stripping. The public appearances and every-thing else that goes along with it. But yes, I did well enough that I never had to write a tell-all memoir or do a documentary, which I've been hounded to do for years."

I was about to ask her what had happened to all that money and why she was strapped for cash when Ruth suddenly jumped up.

"I almost forgot! I got you a present." She ran to her room and returned with a beautifully wrapped gift.

I immediately felt bad. "Oh, Ruth, you shouldn't have. I didn't get you anything."

"Don't worry about it." She waved it off. "It's for your birth-day, not for Christmas. Open it."

I took it from her and slowly set about unwrapping it, gently tugging at the tape so as not to tear the paper.

"Oh my God, this is painful to watch," Ruth yelped, grab-bing the package back from me and ripping it to shreds before passing back the box. "Here."

"Gee, thanks," I said wryly, lifting the lid.

"It's a silk kimono," Ruth squealed as I was still removing the tissue paper. "Like mine!"

I couldn't think of anything less suited to me. "Ah, so it is."

"I know what you're thinking," Ruth said.

I doubted it. "What?"

"That I couldn't have gotten you anything less suited to you, but that's not true. It's beige, see? Your favorite color." She looked so pleased with herself that I had to laugh.

As the afternoon wore on, Ruth and I switched over to wine and continued to tease each other while laughing and speaking of inconsequential things. We were behaving so much like I imagined normal sisters did, and I was enjoying it so much, that I felt I could broach the topic of the baby without it leading to a fight. "So, what have you decided to do about Mandla?"

Ruth's expression changed so quickly from one of contentment to anguish that I wished I hadn't brought it up. "I don't know," she said. "It's all I think about and I just keep going around and around in circles."

The fact that she hadn't dismissed taking him flat out of hand surprised me. It showed a depth of emotion and a strength of character I'd never suspected. "You found out about his prognosis on that course you went on? How unlikely he is to survive beyond his second birthday?"

"Yes, I know all that but—"

Ruth didn't get to finish her sentence. Instead, she screamed as the window behind her disintegrated, sending shards of glass shattering inward.

Jezebel, who'd been lying near it, scrambled to her feet and scampered away just in time to avoid the second rock, which took out the remaining lounge window. I reached out to grab her, pulling her toward me by the scruff of her neck.

When Ruth stood, I thought she was coming around to my side of the table to duck for cover, but instead, she turned toward the front of the house. I'd never seen such a look of fury on her face. Glass crunched under her heels as she marched toward the front door.

"Jesus, Ruth! What are you doing? Get away from there."

But she wasn't listening. She unlocked the door and yanked it open, waving her fist in the air as she screamed, "You fuckers are messing with the wrong women, do you hear me? You're going to regret the day you were fucking born!"

An hour later, when the bubble of our conviviality had truly burst and we were cleaning up the debris, I returned us firmly back to earth by saying, "Think about what you're doing, Ruth, wanting to bring an innocent child into this." I gestured at the broken glass and the rocks. "Even if he were healthy, which he isn't, it's not safe here for him."

CHAPTER FORTY-THREE

Ruth

❖

27 December 1994
New Beginnings Baby Sanctuary,
Rustenburg, South Africa

Dee's words from Christmas Day are still chasing themselves around my mind when I sit down across from the social worker two days later.

Lindiwe has to repeat my name a few times before managing to pull me back into the present. "I don't suppose you'd consider fostering another child? A healthy one?" Lindiwe asks.

"No. That's not how it works," I say. "It's not like I came here wanting to foster a child and happened to find Mandla. It's Mandla who found me and then led me here."

Lindiwe nods. "I understand."

"No, I don't think you do," I say.

I almost don't understand it myself. How can I, when there's no rational way to explain the attachment I have to Mandla? We spent less than two days together and honestly, what is that really? What's forty-two hours when measured against a lifetime?

And yet, what it comes down to is that one minute I lived a life without any knowledge of him at all and then the next, there he was like magic; as if my desperate need had conjured him from a hat—*abracadabra, sim sala bim*—and made every dream I'd ever had come true. Of all the places he could have been left, it was on my doorstep that he turned up. That had to mean something.

Actually, it means everything.

"After a lot of soul searching," I say to Lindiwe, "I realized there's no decision to be made because it was never going to be a choice. Mandla belongs with me and that is that." And it's true. "Now, let's finish the last of the paperwork so he can come home."

The call is harder to make than I thought it would be. I work my way through two cigarettes and another glass of wine before I'm able to dial the number.

He answers on the third ring. "Hello?" There's music and laughter in the background and the unexpected sound of it makes it hard to speak. "Hello?" he repeats.

"Vince, it's me."

He's having a party but then why shouldn't he? It's the festive season and he's rid of me. What's not to celebrate?

"Ruth?"

I think back to the previous Christmas, our last one together though I didn't know that at the time. We'd turned down all the usual invitations and spent Christmas Day alone together, eating gourmet toasted cheese sandwiches in bed, to hell with the crumbs. It was a damn good day.

"I can hear it isn't a good time for you," I say. "I'll call back."

"No, it's fine." He must have the portable phone because the noise starts to fade and then it's quiet. He's probably closed himself in the bedroom. "Is everything okay?"

No, it's not. You're having a party without me because you've moved on. I'm fostering a child who's going to die soon. We're under attack in our home. I miss you.

I can't help but wonder who's there. You can bet your tits that Moira Castleman has been sniffing around Vince. Bitch.

"Ruth?"

"What?"

"I asked if everything's okay?"

"Yes, it's fine. It's all fine. Couldn't be better, actually."

"I'm glad."

We lapse into silence and I swear I can hear bloody Moira's hyena laugh in the background. I wish suddenly that I hadn't shipped the framed magazine cover to myself here. Knowing it was there for her to look at would make me feel a lot better.

"Not that I don't like hearing from you, Ruthie, I do, but is there a reason why you called?"

Shit. Here goes nothing.

I take a deep breath and swallow my pride. And then I ask Vince for quite a substantial loan.

CHAPTER FORTY-FOUR

Delilah

※

28 January 1995
Verdriet, Magaliesburg, South Africa

Are you sure you won't come with me?" Ruth asked, looking so desperate for me to change my mind that I had to look away from her reflection in the bathroom mirror. "I know you don't approve, but that doesn't mean you can't join me and be disapproving there."

"You know how I feel about this. I think you're making a mistake," I said.

She rolled a curler into her hair, talking past a bobby pin in her mouth. "You said it wasn't safe to bring him home and so I fixed that. I made it safe!"

She wasn't exaggerating. The place was like Fort Knox, thanks to the loan she'd gotten from her estranged husband. If money couldn't buy happiness, then it sure could buy peace of mind.

For the past month, contractors and security experts had worked flat out to turn our home into a fortress. High electric fences were erected around the house, isolating it from the rest of the sprawling property, and the only way to access it was through an electric gate that was set up with security cameras and an intercom.

All the windows and doors had been burglar-proofed and sensors were installed along the garden perimeter so that if anyone breached the fence, we'd know about it before they reached the house. A state-of-the-art alarm system was set up inside as well.

"A bird can't fart near the house without our knowing," Ruth had said proudly once all the work was finished.

I couldn't help but think that Daniel would still be alive if the rectory where he'd lived had had this kind of security. The depressing part was that the security company hadn't even asked why we were having to go to such extreme measures to ensure our safety. Gated communities and security estates were springing up everywhere as violent crime increased.

"You can't protect yourself enough from the *kaffirs*," one of the contractors had said to Ruth.

"Actually, all of this is to protect a *kaffir* from the whites," Ruth had replied cheerfully. "And don't say *kaffir*."

The expression on his face had been priceless.

"He's going to be safe here. We all are," Ruth said now. "It's going to be fine, you'll see."

"I wish I understood," I said, shaking my head.

"What?"

"This whim of yours. Why you suddenly so desperately want this child."

"Whim?" She put the second curler down and turned around to face me. "You think this is a whim?" Before I could answer, she barreled on. "I had my first miscarriage when I was twenty-one. They said it happened all the time and that I was young, that I'd get pregnant again. And they were right, I did, when I was twenty-three. But I lost that baby as well. I fell pregnant for the third time when I was twenty-seven. Another miscarriage at twelve weeks. They ran a whole bunch of tests and still couldn't figure out what the problem was.

"The fourth and fifth miscarriages were with my second husband, Jacques, when I was twenty-nine and then thirty-one. The last one was really bad, and I almost bled to death, and so that was it. No more pregnancies." She'd been reciting the information in a dry, factual voice but then it cracked. "The thing is, I'd never felt as complete as I did for those few weeks of each of my pregnancies. It was like I'd had this gaping hole inside me my whole life that was suddenly filled."

I inhaled sharply, surprised. "That's exactly how I felt when I entered the convent. Like God completed me."

"Maybe we're all born with that piece of us missing and our life's journey is about finding it. Finding that one thing that makes us whole," Ruth said.

"It's dangerous, though. That belief that something can complete you."

"No, it's not. It's what keeps us going, don't you see that?"

"Mandla isn't going to complete you, Ruth. And I told you months ago that I wanted no part of this," I said quietly. "I told you I couldn't be around a baby, but you've given me no choice in the matter."

"And you gave me no choice but to bring him here. I'm just trying to make the best of a bad situation, Dee. Why do you always have to be so negative? If you give him a chance, you just may grow to love him."

"Exactly," I said before I could stop myself. "And what would the point of that be?"

We both knew what I meant: that Mandla was terminally ill and it was just a matter of time before he died. Why love someone who was guaranteed to break your heart?

Ruth went pale. "That's the thing about love that you never understood. It doesn't need a point." I turned and just as I left the bathroom, she called, "Tell me, did it hurt less losing Daniel because you'd never let yourself fully love him in the first place?" When I didn't reply, she said, "That's what I thought."

It took me a minute to figure out the source of the trilling noise because we hadn't had a visitor since the security system had gone up. Jezebel barked madly, running around in circles as I went to the intercom. I shushed her and then pressed the button. "Yes, hello?"

"Delilah?"

"Yes?"

"It's Riaan. I hope this isn't a bad time. I thought I'd stop by to see how you are."

I didn't need to switch the monitor on to verify that it was him. I'd know that voice anywhere. I pressed the button to let him in and then found myself in the bathroom, staring at my reflection to make sure I was presentable. I flattened my hair and then, scoffing at how ridiculous I was being, ran my hand through it again to muss it up.

I opened the door to let Riaan in and watched, amused, as Jezebel jumped all over him like he was a long-lost friend. "It's too hot for coffee," I surprised myself by saying. "Would you like a beer?" God knows, I needed one. He accepted the offer and we went outside to the patio. "How have you been? What's new?" I asked, surprised that I was really interested and not just making conversation.

Riaan started speaking about the latest developments at the Gladysvale Cave site and how they'd found fossils of an extinct giant zebra. As he spoke, I thought about how sad it was that his wonderful scientific mind had been wasted on farmwork. It would have been fine if farming was his calling, but it wasn't.

There was something to be said for duty, though. His giving up his own dreams so that he could be there for everyone else was very honorable and I wouldn't have expected anything less of him. It was another reason I would never have come back to the farm pregnant; I knew that Riaan would have done the honorable thing.

The people I'd encountered during my aid work across Africa thought I was a supremely selfless person to give up having my own life so that I could improve the lives of others. Perhaps there were other aid workers for whom this was true but it never was for me. Dedicating my life to others was a purely selfish act on my part. I'd only done it to uphold my side of the deal I'd made with God.

I'll do this for you, God, if you do that for me. I'll dedicate my life to helping others if you protect my son.

I'd told myself that in keeping up my end of the bargain, I'd have to give up my own family and their needs entirely, but really it was shame and fear rather than sacrifice that kept me away. Shame for what I'd done—both in falling pregnant and leaving my son behind, as well as dropping out of the convent and breaking my mother's heart—and fear of having to answer all their questions in the process.

When Da got sick and Ruth and Ma begged me to come home, I said that I was tied to a contract and was needed there, and since there was nothing I could do for Da, there was no point in coming home. But that wasn't the point, was it? They'd needed me and I'd let them down. I'd let Ma down too when she was dying, knowing full well that all she wanted before she died was an explanation for what I'd done and to see me one last time. Even that, I couldn't do for her. I just couldn't face up to how badly I'd let her down.

Riaan interrupted my thoughts. "Are you okay, Delilah?"

"Sorry, what?"

"You seem a million miles away again. Is everything all right?"

"Yes, sorry. It's just been a tough eight months."

"Would you like to talk about it?" Riaan asked.

Suddenly, I did. So badly.

I wanted to tell him about Daniel's death and the emotional ice-age it had brought on, freezing my feelings and making them so numb that I was only distantly aware of them. I wanted to express how I'd realized that shock is a kindness that your body grants you; how it allows you to distance yourself from the kind of heartbreak that would otherwise cleave a jagged hole down your center, one big enough for you to fall through and never claw your way out of again.

Instead, I said, "I'm fine. Really. There's nothing to tell."

"Okay," he said, looking like he didn't believe a word of it. "Did Ruth tell you I've been checking in on you?"

"Yes, she did, and I appreciate it. I'm sorry I haven't been in touch to thank you. It's been a bit crazy, what with the Coetzees and Ruth and the baby."

He was quiet for a moment and then tentatively said, "She mentioned that you lost someone? Which is also why you've been so upset?"

I nodded.

"Was it . . ." He trailed off and then looked away. "Was it the priest?"

The priest.

I froze, unsure how to answer, when Riaan said, "Look, never mind. It's none of my business. I actually came here for

210
.

a reason . . . a specific reason, I mean . . . not just to stop by for a chat."

"Oh?"

"I'm going to the site on Sunday, the one at Gladysvale, and I was wondering if you wanted to come with me for the day? It's a fun outing and you learn a lot in the process. And I'll pack a picnic basket for afterward so we can have lunch. It's very pretty there and I think you'll enjoy it—at least I do . . ." He was rambling, which is how I realized how nervous he was.

"Are you asking me out?" I teased, trying to defuse his discomfort.

"No, of course not," he stammered.

"Ah, so then you might well be married after all?"

He flushed. "No, I never married."

For some reason, the admission made me sad and I was suddenly sorry that I'd carried the joshing too far.

Riaan gazed intently at his nails before looking up again. "I'm just asking you as a friend, nothing else."

"Okay. Yes, I'd like that," I said, and found, to my surprise, that I meant it.

CHAPTER FORTY-FIVE

Ruth

❋

28 January–4 February 1995
New Beginnings Baby Sanctuary,
Rustenburg, South Africa, and Verdriet,
Magaliesburg, South Africa

This is it," I say, not quite sure if I'm more likely to throw up or burst into song.

"Yes," Lindiwe says. "Are you ready?"

"Not even close."

I wish Dee were here. Doing this together would be so much less scary than doing it alone. She can't go back in time and save her son, but we can save this child who needs us.

I follow Lindiwe down the corridor and into what looks like a classroom, and my first thought is that we've walked in on a birthday party and are in the wrong place. Toddlers, babies, and care workers stand around tables draped in green tablecloths and covered with cupcakes, sandwiches, sweets, and cold drinks. They all wear festive party hats and start cheering when we enter, which is when I see the huge cake at the center of the table.

Happy Foster Day Mandla! is written across it in blue icing.

A care worker crosses the room with my boy. He has his arms draped around her ample neck and is beaming at her. She's wearing latex gloves and gives me a pair to put on before she hands him across. Mandla, once in my arms, immediately tries to pull away.

He stretches his arms out toward the woman, calling for her in baby speak. She doesn't turn to take him back, she just keeps on walking. The parting is clearly as painful for her as it is for Mandla because she wipes at her face as he bursts into heart-broken sobs.

"Not off to the best start, are we?" I ask Lindiwe.

"Don't worry," she says. "The doctor who comes is a white lady and she looks a bit like you. She was here earlier to look him over and he didn't like it. He's worried you're going to hurt him."

"He and I both," I mutter. "He and I both."

A week passes in a sleepless blur.

It feels like an accomplishment when, in the early hours of one morning, I get Mandla to settle facedown on my chest, his head turned awkwardly to the side to accommodate two fingers in his mouth. I've heard of thumb sucking before, but he's taken it to a whole new level by sucking on his middle and index fingers simultaneously.

His room, which I went to so much effort to set up, remains empty. I hoped so much he'd like it, since I painstakingly deco-rated in a way that's "culturally sensitive" to appease Dee, but he won't sleep there. The first few nights he screamed every time I put him down in the crib until eventually I gave up. My bed is where he'll quieten down, either lying on my chest or next to me with one arm reaching out and touching me. Mandla craves constant contact and I'm so terrified that I'll smother him in my sleep that I barely manage to get any rest myself.

The insomnia hasn't helped the constant worry. The new security measures mean we feel safer in the house but they haven't stopped the threats. Some of them arrive as letters but most of them come via phone calls. The voices change and some are issued in English while others are in Afrikaans.

We're coming for you. Die kaffirtjie moet op pas. We'll show you what we do to women who don't listen.

They're all bad enough but yesterday's courier delivery was especially chilling. I signed for the package, thinking it was one of the items I'd asked Vince to ship, but the box contained a life-sized plastic doll that had been spray-painted brown. There was a hunting knife buried in its head.

The threats would be easier to deal with if Dee and I were united against them, but she continues to treat me as though I'm the enemy. True to her word, Dee hasn't been any help with Mandla at all. When she's home, she shoots me disapproving looks as though everything I'm doing is wrong, yet she won't offer any help or advice. The rest of the time, she makes herself scarce, either out hiking or with Riaan.

I know she's sulking right now but she'll come around. How can she not when Mandla is so ridiculously lovable?

I never understood why the universe deprived me of a child for so long, or why it allowed all those infertile years to carve away at me, but I know the reason now: None of the babies that I miscarried were meant to be mine. Not one of them. The universe wasn't hollowing me out, it was whittling away a Mandla-shaped space so that when he came, he'd slot right into me like a missing puzzle piece.

All those years of being barren were preparing me to recognize my soul mate when I finally met him because that's what

Mandla is. Forget all the husbands and the boyfriends who I hoped would make me feel whole. Those were all dead-end streets. The road leading me away from Vince was the only road I was ever meant to be on because it led me home.

Mandla is home. The universe was right in keeping me here.

CHAPTER FORTY-SIX

Zodwa

29 January 1995
New Beginnings Baby Sanctuary,
Rustenburg, South Africa

This is the sixth and last place on Zodwa's list. Leleti was
already very near death on the night Zodwa gave birth,
and so it's highly unlikely that she would have caught a taxi to
travel for an hour there and back to deliver her grandson to an
orphanage so far away. Still, Leleti used to work in Rustenburg
and it's possible that she knew someone at this place.

Zodwa is ushered into the social worker's office. As she
waits for her, she thinks about everything she's been doing to
make Leleti proud and wonders if it's enough: trying to finish
her studies; working a semi-respectable job as a means to an
end; having a boyfriend who, despite being a small-time gangster, is at least a man. All that Zodwa has left to do is find her
son and bring him home, proving to Leleti through her actions
that her mother was wrong and that Zodwa hasn't wasted
her life.

"Zodwa?" A woman is seated across from her saying her name.

"Sorry, *sisi*. My mind was far away."

The woman smiles. She has a cherubic face that makes
Zodwa think of someone. It takes her a few seconds to realize

216

who she bears a striking resemblance to, and then it comes to her: Desmond Tutu. "I don't suppose you're related to—"

"No," the woman says, laughing, "but I get that a lot. I'm Mrs. Nkosi. How can I help you?"

And so Zodwa begins talking, telling her everything and pulling out the photographs of herself and Dumisa as babies to show her. The woman listens intently, a small frown creasing her brow, and then reaches out for the pictures. Zodwa wonders if she's imagining the woman's intensity as she gazes at the photo of Dumisa.

Mrs. Nkosi clears her throat. "The baby disappeared from the Big Hope Informal Settlement in Magaliesburg?"

"Yes, that's right."

"And that's where you still live? In a shack?"

Zodwa bristles at the question. "Yes." She isn't homeless. Still, she feels the need to explain her situation. "I work at a *shebeen* there and am saving money to try and move somewhere better. But it's not easy, I'm still trying to finish high school. The exams and textbooks are expensive."

The woman nods like she understands and Zodwa feels a bit better until the social worker asks, "What's your health like?"

"My health?"

"Sorry, it's an occupational hazard. I noticed you have a cough and just wanted to make sure you're taking care of it."

"It's just a cold," Zodwa says. "It's almost gone."

"Good. Maybe get some Borstol for it."

"I will."

They're both silent for a moment and Zodwa wonders what the woman is thinking. Her mind seems to be racing and yet her expression is guarded.

"So," Zodwa prompts. "Can you check your files to see if there are any possible matches?"

"I don't need to," Mrs. Nkosi says. "I know all the children here and none of them fits the description." She hands the photos back to Zodwa, but doesn't meet her eyes when she says, "I'm sorry that I couldn't be more helpful."

CHAPTER FORTY-SEVEN

Delilah

❋

3 April 1995
Drimolen, Muldersdrift, South Africa

We all sat clustered around in camping chairs, our encampment of tents and vehicles spread out behind us. The moon, a waxing crescent, resembled a closing parenthesis missing its mate.

It was the fourth dig I'd joined Riaan on but the first one that required us to sleep over for a few nights. We'd started off as a boisterous group of approximately two dozen scientists, students, and volunteers sitting around the fire, but the conversation got more muted as people started drifting off to bed. Only five of us remained and after I yawned for the third time, Riaan stood and held out his hand for me. I took it and stood, trying to ignore the frisson of nerves I felt at his touch.

It was a crisp, cold night and the farther we retreated from the fire, the chillier it got.

"I'll wait here for you and then walk you to your tent," Riaan said as we split up to go to the bathrooms.

He was waiting for me when I came out, his hands tucked into his pockets and his head tilted back looking at the stars. I stood still for a moment, just watching him and thinking how he'd retained so much of his boyish charm.

"I pitched our camp over there."

When Riaan had first invited me, he'd made it clear that we'd be staying in separate tents, which had alleviated some of my anxiety. He'd arrived a few days before me along with some of the scientists, so everything was already set up, and I was grateful to have my bed ready and waiting for me.

I'd spent the day doing grunt work, and even that had required special training beforehand. My muscles were sore from spending the day crouched over buckets of sand, sifting through them to find bones or other artifacts, which had to be documented and bagged so that they could be sent for analysis. It was backbreaking but rewarding work.

"Don't worry, the tents are built for winter conditions and the sleeping bags are made for subzero temperatures, so you shouldn't be too cold," Riaan said, leading me to a tent on our site. He unzipped the flap and stepped through, and I could hear him shuffling around on the groundsheet. "Aha," he said as torchlight flooded the tent. "Here you go."

I stepped inside behind him and sat on the inflatable mattress, groaning as I stretched my legs out.

Riaan laughed. "Getting stiff?"

"Yes. I felt it when we were sitting by the fire but now it's much worse. These old bones may be too old to be sifting through ancient bones."

I expected a laugh or some kind of protest, but he was staring at me intently as he crouched in front of me. I knew that expression; I'd seen it the night before I'd left for the convent.

Then, we'd been sitting on a blanket in one of the avocado orchards after sneaking out there at midnight to say our goodbyes. Riaan had packed a picnic basket, but neither of us had touched any of the food. It was a warm night and the orchard would soon be flowering. When that happened, bees would flock to it, but right then the grove was quiet, as though it was holding its breath. I knew how it felt.

We'd been reminiscing, murmuring softly, when Riaan suddenly sat up, a look of anguish on his face. "What can I say to make you stay?" Tears filled his eyes as he reached out and tucked a strand of hair behind my ear. He did it so tenderly that I had to look away.

"Nothing," I said. "You know this is my calling. You've known for years."

He was quiet as he blinked back the tears and then he said, "No, this isn't about that. This is about the priest. I know that you're in love with him, Delilah."

"No, I'm not!" The blotches of color blooming across my neck had betrayed me. The truth was that I'd been thinking of Father Thomas even as we sat there together, knowing that he'd be fetching me the next day to take me to the convent, and feeling both excited and terrified at the prospect of being alone with him in a car for a few hours.

"I see the way you look at him. You've never looked at me that way."

"Don't be ridiculous."

"And you only decided to become a nun after you met him."

"That's only because I didn't know about converting to Catholicism until I met him!"

"Have you ever loved me?" Riaan asked, his voice raw with emotion.

"Of course I have. Of course I do. You're my best friend—"

"Not like that. Not like a friend. You know how I feel about you, Delilah, how I've always felt about you. I love you and I think you could love me too if you just tried to see me as a man. I'm not that little boy anymore, the one you became friends with all those years ago." He took my face and turned it back to his own so that I was forced to look at him.

It was uncomfortable, meeting his gaze like that, but it achieved what he'd wanted it to. I was looking at him, really focusing on him in a way that I hadn't in years. That's what happens when someone is so much a part of the fabric of your daily existence; you begin to look through them, not because they aren't important, but because they become as essential as oxygen and just as easy to take for granted.

He was right. He was no longer a boy, and if not yet a man, then he was on the very cusp of manhood. I looked at him, taking him all in, and was surprised by the changes he'd undergone without my noticing. Riaan's shoulders had broadened and his voice had deepened. His jaw was covered with stubble that in the moonlight looked like flecks of steel and fire. I wasn't prepared for how scratchy it would be, how utterly foreign, when he leaned forward and took my face in his hands and pressed his lips against mine.

At first, the kiss was gentle, and his lips felt like a butterfly alighting on mine. He smelled of soap and rain, and he tasted of strawberry jam.

"Stay and marry me, Delilah," he implored, pulling away and gazing at me, searching for some sign. "Please." He kissed me more fiercely then, pressing into me as though wanting to possess all of me, until I was lying down on the blanket with him on top of me.

I saw the same fervor in his eyes now that I had during that last night together, but then he blinked and the moment was over.

"Good night, Delilah," he said, his eyes glistening in the dark. "Good night."

CHAPTER FORTY-EIGHT

Zodwa

✳

10 May 1995
Big Hope Informal Settlement,
Magaliesburg, South Africa

Zodwa's hand trembles as it clasps the packet of tiny birth-day candles. How they can justify charging so much for them is beyond her since they're more expensive than an eight-pack of full-sized Price's candles that would burn for hours. She's slightly horrified that she spent so much on the frivolous things.

When Zodwa set out that morning to the Spar at the shopping center, she went like a sleepwalker, not knowing what she wanted until she stood in front of the cupcakes at the shop's bakery.

"I'll have one of those," Zodwa said to the black woman at the counter, who wore a net over her hair and plastic gloves on her hands even though her white counterpart didn't wear either.

"*Hhayi, sisi.* You can't just buy cupcakes one, one. You must buy them like that in a pack. Six, six, *sisonke.*" She pointed at the packages of cupcakes in their plastic wrapping. "It's not like buying cigarettes at the spaza shop." She laughed.

Zodwa felt herself flush. The desserts were expensive and Zodwa only needed one. Still, she didn't feel she could leave without them, so she spent a small fortune on six of them and a handful of multicolored candles before returning to her shack.

The pack of chocolate cupcakes is open now on the table. Zodwa considers the impossibly perfect swirl of icing on top of each little cake and wonders how they manage to get them like that. She selects one from the pack, the most perfect of all of them, and sets it down.

Today would have been her baby's first birthday. It's also a year since he disappeared. There hasn't been a day that Zodwa hasn't thought about the boy and wondered what really happened to him, if he's truly dead like everyone believes. He has to be, because what else would Leleti have done with him? Why else hasn't she found him after a year of searching?

The last conversation she had with her mother churns constantly in her mind, like a whirlpool that's in constant motion but can't go anywhere.

Where is he? Where is my son?

He . . . he . . . is gone.

Gone? Gone where, Mama? What did you do with him?

I did it for . . . you. And for him.

What? What did you do?

The candle takes seventeen minutes to burn itself down and Zodwa counts off every one of them, certain that it's longer than all the time she spent with her baby after his birth. As she sits staring at the flame, she reminds herself that her son's disappearance is her punishment.

The good Lord knows that you do not even want this child.

This was how her *gogo* had explained away a few miscarriages that had happened in the village. Zodwa had heard her say that babies could hear things from the womb, that they would leave if they suspected they were not wanted or would be born to parents they didn't deem worthy. But what about a baby that was too close to birth to miscarry? Could such a child work the same sorcery after its birth to make itself disappear? If so, it's a bitter indictment of Zodwa.

The irony, of course, is how much she wants the baby now. Zodwa would give anything to reclaim those moments after his birth, so that instead of thinking about Thembeka, she would have been focusing on him; so that instead of wishing him away, she'd have welcomed him. Perhaps if she'd paid attention and wept tears of joy instead of tears of regret, he would have stayed.

Zodwa's first lesson in motherhood is that it's a condition that cannot be reversed. A mother who has lost her child is no less of a mother; if anything, her maternal instincts are made even sharper since what she nurses is heartache and regret and, just like she would a baby, she carries them strapped to her back at all times.

CHAPTER FORTY-NINE

Ruth

☀

10 May 1995
Verdriet, Magaliesburg, South Africa

I pour a glass of wine, filling it up to the brim, before putting on my cheeriest voice and slapping on a wide smile. "Gather around, everyone!"

Everything's fine, everything's fine, everything's fine.

It isn't a large group and they're all already standing around the trays of catered snacks in the dining room, but don't think I haven't noticed everyone checking their watches and shooting looks at the door in the hopes of escaping. Jesus, it's not like I haven't wanted to do the same. Mandla has been crying steadily for the past hour. He was quiet for the two hours before that but that's only because he was napping.

My boy seems to be allergic to me, despite the fact that I'm constantly wearing latex gloves and never get to touch him skin to skin. It doesn't matter what I do, he screams his head off whenever I'm near him. To be fair, he also screams his head off when I'm not near him, so it's a no-win situation. It's been just over four months since I brought him home, and during that first tough week, I told myself things had to get better.

I tell myself the same still.

Needing to inject some enthusiasm into the goddamned event, because it looks more like a wake than a party, I bounce

Mandla on my hip and call out, "It's time to sing 'Happy Birthday'!"

Dee and Riaan shuffle closer. She leans over the cake, which I've only just unveiled. It's a triple-decker lemon sponge iced with lemon–cream cheese frosting.

"Wow," Dee says. "That's quite a creation. It looks more like a wedding cake than a child's birthday cake."

I ignore her sarcasm, reminding myself that she's here under duress and is going to find fault with everything. "That's because it is. I got a boutique confectionery shop in Sandton to make it to order. It cost a fortune getting them to drive it out here but it was worth it, don't you think?"

Riaan scratches his head. "Shouldn't the cake have 'Happy First Birthday, Mandla' written on it? And a Disney character or something cute like a teddy bear or toy train?" He eyes the mini-Mandla cake topper like he's never seen anything like it.

"Don't be ridiculous," I scoff. "It's the nineties. A cake can be anything you want it to be. And there's no rule that says just because it's a child's birthday cake it needs to be some tacky thing that looks homemade. Besides, it was ordering that cake topper that caused all the drama in the first place and I wasn't going to back down on that."

Lindiwe joins us at the table. "What drama?"

"I wanted a black baby made from fondant to be on top of the cake to complete the wedding cake motif, but all the racists in town at their *tuisnywerhuids* refused to make it." I'd approached more than five home-industry businesses, all fronted by Afrikaner *tannies* whose recipes competed for blue ribbons at the local fairs, but none of them were prepared to make the cake to order.

"Maybe they're not racist at all. Maybe they just don't know

227

what fondant is. These are women who are used to making *melktert* and *koeksisters*," Riaan says. "They're not that sophisticated." He manages to pronounce *fondant* wrong despite having heard me say it properly, making it clear that he isn't that sophisticated either.

"Oh, please. Stop being a racist apologist. If you can't recognize blatant racism when you see it, then I can't help you."

Dee snorts and says something under her breath about the pot calling the kettle black, which is why I'm gratified that Sarie and her husband, Stompie, choose that moment to join us.

"*Dankie, miesie,*" Stompie says in Afrikaans, clutching his hat as he thanks me for inviting them. They're both kitted out in their Sunday best.

"You're most welcome, Stompie. Thank you for coming."

I hope Dee has noticed the number of black guests at this party. She keeps insinuating that I'm racist but how can I be when the truth is that I don't even see Mandla as black? He's dark skinned, yes, so he's technically black but he's not like the rest of them. There's black people and then there's *blacks*. I won't say the k-word, which just proves I'm not racist. As does the fact that I have so many black friends here.

Stompie leans forward and tickles Mandla's chin. "*Hoekom die miesie vat hom die baby met die gloves?*" Why does madam wear gloves to carry the baby?

"Allergies," I say vaguely.

Of course, Stompie and Sarie don't know about Mandla's status. The stigma is just too great and they can't be trusted to keep it to themselves. If the lynch mobs are pissed off about Mandla being black, his being HIV positive will push them over the edge. As they turn away, I see Sarie nudge Stompie, nodding in the direction of my magazine cover on the wall. He follows her gaze and his eyes almost pop out of his head when he catches sight of my naked form.

"*Ek het jou mos gesê,*" she whispers. I told you so.

Stompie looks like Christmas, Easter, New Year's, and his birthday all came on the same day and I make a mental note to take the picture down. No one used to bat an eyelid in Cape Town but the farm crowd isn't quite as cosmopolitan as the Clifton crowd. I only put it up to annoy Dee anyway.

Sarie and Stompie recently announced their plans to retire, which is sad considering how long they've been a part of the family. But then, they have gotten on in years and now that we're living at the farm, we don't need caretakers anymore, though we will need to hire a maid to do housework.

I made a decent profit on the Camps Bay apartment and have some money in the bank even after paying Vince back, with interest, for the loan for all the security upgrades. I make a mental note to chat to Dee and see if we can pool our resources to give Sarie and Stompie a decent retirement gift. They'll need all the help they can get wanting to live in some godforsaken village of their birth and taking care of the entire family, and they're not going to get it anywhere else, that you can be sure of.

"Time to blow out the candle!" I slip a cream votive candle onto the cake and light it.

Everyone starts singing in that horrible stilted and hushed way people do, as though they're terrified that someone will actually hear their voice. I raise my own voice, both to drown them out and to show them how it's done. "Happy Birthday, dear Mandla. . . ." I draw out the *ahhhh* sounds. "Happy Birthday to you."

"Hip hip," Dee surprises me by calling out, and the small group replies with, "Hooray!"

"And *nog* a hip hip," Riaan shouts.

"Hooray!"

Jez barks, as though throwing in her two cents' worth.

It's time to blow out the candle. This would be the tricky part if Mandla knew how to do it. I was told to be careful about mucus, so getting it all over the cake would be a problem. I pluck the candle from the cake and then blow it out myself.

Sarie is standing by with the cake knife I had specially engraved with Mandla's name and date of birth to mark the occasion. His last name is officially Nkosi, which is Lindiwe's surname. That's how they legally name the children who come into the orphanage: by picking a first name and then assigning one of the care workers' or social workers' last names to them.

I didn't include this on the engraving.

Sarie puts some cake in a bowl for Mandla, who I've put into his high chair. By some miracle, the sight of the cake stops his crying. I give him a spoon and he uses it to attack the bowl with a few karate chops before setting it down and reaching for the cake with both hands. Everyone laughs, grateful that the screeching has stopped, and I reach for my camera to commemorate not only Mandla's first birthday, but his first taste of cake. Sugar is a no-no for HIV-positive children but you only turn one once. I'm willing to make an exception.

His fingers sink into the lowest tier of the cake and he grabs two chunks of it, one in each hand. As he brings one up to his lips, I start snapping pictures, wanting to get the expression on his face as he gets his first taste. It's not what I expected. Mandla curls his lip up in disgust and spits the cake out.

"Look at that. He isn't a big fan of sugar," I say proudly. My boy is already setting himself apart from the pack.

"I actually think he isn't a big fan of lemon–cream cheese

frosting," Dee says dryly. "What with his being a baby and not having the most discerning palate." She walks to the kitchen and pulls out a plate of chocolate cupcakes that are covered with enough blue icing to sink a battleship. "Sarie was kind enough to bake these and bring them with her. I have a feeling they'll be more to Mandla's liking."

I'm annoyed that Sarie has stolen my thunder by bringing baked goods I didn't ask for, but there's nothing to be done about it. Once the plate is in front of Mandla, he eyes it skeptically before grabbing one of the cupcakes, which he shoves straight at his face. Everything is quiet for a moment and I'm waiting for him to react the exact same way so I can say, *I told you so.*

Instead, the traitorous little bugger squeals with delight. He tries cramming even more of the cupcake in his mouth and smears so much blue icing all over his face that he looks like a Smurf. The only thing that's made him happy all day came from the efforts of a black woman.

I refuse to take that as a sign.

CHAPTER FIFTY

Delilah

·✺·

15–22 May 1995

Van Tonder Farm, Magaliesburg, South Africa

W hen I came down with the flu, Ruth banished me from the house.

"You may be contagious and we can't take the chance that Mandla might get sick. You need to leave and take your bloody germs with you!"

"Where do you want me to go?" I sniffed, feeling congested and sorry for myself.

"I could book you into a hotel or a B and B, but why don't you ask Loverboy if he can look after you?"

"No, Ruth. I couldn't impose like that."

"Oh, please." She waved me off and then marched to the phone. "What's his number?"

When I refused to give it, she looked it up in the phone book and dialed it. "Hello, Riaan? It's Ruth, here. Dee's coming down with something and I don't want her around Mandla. Do you think you could look after her for a few days at your place? You could? Oh, thank you so much. How about you come over now and pick her up. I'll make sure she's waiting for you."

"Ruth," I groaned when she put the receiver down.

"What? How many women get to play a real-life Jane Bennet

when she falls ill at Netherfield and Bingley has to take care of her?" She cupped her chin and then said, "I suppose that makes me Mrs. Bennet in this scenario."

"What are you talking about?"

"*Pride and Prejudice* by Jane Austen. And to think everyone thought you were the clever one! You really should read more books." She tutted and then headed into my room, throwing things into my rucksack. "Don't you have anything more alluring than this?" She scrunched her nose up at my old nightgown. "What happened to the silk kimono I gave you? Did you cut it up for curtains in a reverse Scarlett O'Hara move?" Before I could dig it out of the back of the wardrobe, she marched into her own room and pulled three silk nightgowns from her cupboard. "Here, take these."

"For God's sake, Ruth. I'm not wearing your ridiculous lingerie."

"Suit yourself, but—" She was interrupted by a knock. "Wow, someone is sure eager to have you over at his place," Ruth said before unceremoniously opening the door and shoving me into Riaan's arms. "Don't come back until you're a hundred percent better."

Had I been healthier, I would have been mortified. Things had been strained between Riaan and me since the camping trip at the site at Drimolen when it had become clear that he still harbored romantic feelings for me. The closer he tried to get to me, the more I withdrew. Ruth thrusting me on him like that was not only rude but it also sent mixed messages, which was the last thing I wanted to do. But, as things were, I felt terrible and was just grateful to have someone care for me while I convalesced.

Riaan's farmstead was much more modern than ours, having been rebuilt from the original thatched-roof bungalow in the '80s, and I had a large guest bedroom with an ensuite bathroom to myself. He came in to check up on me regularly, bringing me chicken soup, taking my temperature, and administering medications. The tenderness with which he performed all of his nursing duties touched me greatly. Having been the one to tend to others all my life, it was disorienting to be taken care of. In a world in which so much was constantly changing, it amazed me that something could stay exactly the same, that Riaan could be just as steadfast as he'd always been. The man who sat spooning soup into my mouth was as committed to me as the boy who'd begged me to stay.

There was a part of me that wished so much that I had.

That night, while racked with a fever that made me feel as though I'd been banished to hell, I raged against demons in my sleep. It was Daniel who came to me first, bloodied and dying. He pointed an accusing finger at me, saying he wouldn't have been at the rectory the night he died if I hadn't abandoned him in a convent. And I knew it to be true. My son would never have become a priest if I'd kept and mothered him.

After that, Father Thomas's face replaced Daniel's, and I must have cried out then because when I woke, Riaan was by my side, wiping at my tears. "Shh . . . it's fine. You're safe. You're fine," he crooned.

As my heart thumped its drumbeat of fear, I knew that what he said was true. I was safe there with him. I'd always been safe with him because he'd stopped that night forty years ago when I'd asked him to. At the sound of my panicked voice, Riaan had frozen on top of me and then looked at me like he was coming out of a daze, horror at his actions written over his face.

And then he'd stood up, begged for my forgiveness, and walked away. The same couldn't be said for other men.

"I'm here. You're safe," Riaan whispered. "I won't let anything hurt you."

As my terror passed and I lay back down, Riaan sat next to me holding my hand until I fell back to sleep.

CHAPTER FIFTY-ONE

Zodwa

⚛

22 May 1995
Big Hope Informal Settlement,
Magaliesburg, South Africa

The trip to Soweto is a waste of both time and money. The man Zodwa finally tracked down, Cyril Malema—Dumisa's comrade and supposedly the last person who saw her brother alive, the one Leleti always suspected of lying—is a raging drunk. Leleti had already crossed him off her list but Zodwa needed to speak to him for herself to try to understand her mother's skepticism.

By Zodwa's calculations, Cyril's not even thirty years old and yet he sits slumped in a darkened room like he's worn out by a lifetime of struggle. He reeks of stale beer and sweat, and his rheumy eyes battle to focus on Zodwa's face. At the mere mention of Dumisa's name, he begins rambling incoherently.

"They are coming for me. I can't hide. There's nowhere to hide. They're going to kill me. Help me, *sisi*. Help me."

Zodwa realizes that he thinks the security police are still after him. Even though she's frustrated with him, she pities him too, for living in the hell of the past even now when it's been so thoroughly vanquished.

She tries coaxing him but is still unable to get a word of

sense out of him beyond more entreaties for help, and Zodwa returns to the squatter camp defeated. She was hoping that since all inquiries about her son have led her into dead ends, she'd have more success in finding out about her brother.

Zodwa heads to get water and as she rounds the corner with her bucket, she sees Thembeka at the back of the line for the tap. It's not the first time this year that she's seen her. They've run into each other more times than she would like. The first few times, when their paths crossed while waiting in line at the latrines and then at the spaza shop, Zodwa tried to pretend that she was indifferent to her ex-friend's presence. She acted aloof, as though she was the one who'd ended the friendship and not the other way around. The problem with that tactic was that it was only effective if it evoked some kind of response, which it hadn't.

True indifference could only be achieved once you stopped caring, and Zodwa couldn't imagine that she'd ever reach that point. It angered her that Thembeka had, that she appeared to feel nothing at all toward her.

The anger spurred her on so that when she and her new *shebeen* friend, Ntombi, were walking home from work one day and she saw Thembeka, Zodwa turned to Ntombi and muttered loudly enough for Thembeka to hear, "This one thinks she's too good for the rest of us now that she's gotten a matric certificate, but what has she done with it? Nothing. She sits around all day doing nothing like her lazy boyfriend. Even *shebeen* work is too good for her."

The hostility felt good.

There was such a gossamer-thin line between love and hate; it was finer than a rifle's crosshairs. Hatred burned just as fiercely as passion, and Zodwa decided she'd take Thembeka's loathing any day rather than fade into the background of her consciousness.

And her nastiness had elicited a response from Thembeka whereas her indifference hadn't. Thembeka first looked confused and then wounded by Zodwa's comment. Her hurt buoyed Zodwa. From then on, every opportunity she got, she was sure to make similar remarks about Thembeka and her terrible taste in boyfriends, her apparent lack of ambition, and the fact that she thought she was so much better than Zodwa.

All those times, though, Zodwa had had friends with her, ones who laughed at her comments and encouraged her malice. Today, she's alone and Thembeka is by herself too. She's the last person in the line and so Zodwa has no choice but to join the queue behind her. Zodwa tries to focus on anything except Thembeka's proximity and her attention flits from one distraction to another.

Boyz II Men's "I'll Make Love to You" blares from a nearby radio and flies buzz around a rat carcass. The enticing smell of roasted *mielies* wafts over from three shacks down yet it still can't overpower the scent of baby powder and Vaseline that Zodwa knows comes from Thembeka. Just the thought of the Vaseline almost unmoors Zodwa, who considers leaving and coming back again later.

As if reading her mind, Thembeka turns around. She opens her mouth as if she's about to say something and Zodwa cringes inwardly. She's ashamed by her behavior, ashamed of her relationship with Ace, and knows she deserves whatever insult Thembeka is about to spit out at her. Still, it won't make it any easier to hear. She waits a moment and then another and when Thembeka still doesn't speak, Zodwa snaps, "What? What is it?"

Thembeka hesitates again and then shakes her head. She turns around again to face the front so Zodwa is left to study her back and neck. Her beautiful neck that will forever be out of Zodwa's reach.

CHAPTER FIFTY-TWO

Ruth

※

5 June 1995
Verdriet, Magaliesburg, South Africa

So, how did the appointment go?" Dee asks as soon as we're through the door. She's trying to sound bored, like she's only asking because she has nothing better to do, but I can see that she's been sitting there waiting for us to return.

"We won't have his blood tests back for a few days, so I don't know what his CD4 count and viral load are like, but the good news is there's no hip dysplasia or any physical problems with his legs, so there's no reason why he shouldn't be walking soon."

"Of course there isn't," she says. She'd told me that it was common for babies who'd been raised in institutions to take longer to reach all the big milestones because they didn't have that initial one-on-one time with their caregivers, which is why he'd been so slow with starting to crawl.

"I know. You were right," I concede, and then add dryly, "It's just all these new-mother hormones raging through my body making me emotional."

"I'm sure the breastfeeding must be killer too."

I snort. "Look at you, making jokes like a normal person. You're hilarious, by the way."

"Not really. You just think so because of the cabin fever and because you're a one-year-old's hostage."

"Except I'm not quite as fond of him as Stockholm syndrome suggests I should be under the circumstances."

Dee laughs. "Jokes aside, you really need to get out more. It's not healthy for either of you being cooped up like this all the time."

I eyeball her. "Seriously? And where do you suggest we go? To walk around the nursery that's owned by the right-wingers who we think called and made the last death threat, or to the teahouse run by the Coetzees' cousin? Perhaps we should go to church so the lovely *dominee* can tell me again what an abomination he thinks we are, or would you suggest—"

"Okay, okay. I get it." She's quiet for a moment and then looks at me sideways, as if nervous. "Don't take this the wrong way, but I'm just surprised."

"By what?"

"That you're allowing yourself to be bullied in this way. This isn't the Ruth I know. The Ruth I know would go out there swinging."

"Yes, well. The Ruth you're talking about is BM Ruth."

"BM?"

"Before Mandla. AM Ruth is excruciatingly aware that she's not the only one who'll be a target. Mandla will be too and I just don't want to put him in danger if I don't have to."

The thought of taking Mandla out where we'll be vulnerable and subjecting him to all that hatred just turns my stomach. I believe in energy, both good and bad. Having all that animosity directed at us, without walls to protect us, can't be good for either of us.

Dee lets out a long steadying breath and nods. "Fair enough."

"Will you hold him for a minute while I get his lunch sorted?" I don't wait for an answer. I just give her a pair of gloves and wait for her to pull them on before handing Mandla across. I can count on one hand the number of times she's held him. All of them have been in the past few weeks, though, so that's got to count for something.

"Lunch time!" I say to Mandla once his food is ready and Dee carries him over to his high chair and puts him in. "Yummy. Doesn't this look positively mouthwatering? This is all the rage in France, you know. All the best chefs are serving this to the babies with the most discerning palates."

Mandla thumps his hands on his table.

Dee puts his bib on and then picks the spoon up, dipping it into the bowl and bringing the colorful chunky mixture up to her mouth. "Hmm, this looks so good." She makes a big production out of swallowing it and then smacking her lips in appreciation. "You want to try some?"

Mandla opens his mouth and takes a bite, which he keeps in his chipmunk cheeks for a few seconds before pulling a face and spitting it all out again.

"Are you sure you don't like it? I'm going to finish it if you don't hurry up and get in here." Dee takes another bite but it goes down wrong. As she coughs and hacks the food back out in a spray across the table, Mandla lets out the first real laugh we've heard from him.

I want to cry with gratitude. "Don't take this the wrong way, but your choking was totally worth it," I say, and she nods, eyes still streaming.

When the phone rings fifteen minutes later, Dee answers it and starts to chat with what sounds like Riaan.

"Come, little man. We need to get your nappy changed." I take Mandla's bib off, wipe his face and hands down, and carry him to his room, where the changing table is.

After laying him down, I automatically put on a fresh pair of latex gloves. Undoing his nappy, I stretch for the package of baby wipes above his head, and as I pluck one out, Mandla reaches out and grabs my hand. It's always a strange sensation, seeing his fingers tightened over my mine, feeling the pressure of them, but not being able to touch the bare skin of his hand.

I remember all the nights over the past few weeks that we've lain there, chest to chest, as he's fallen asleep on top of me; all the times he's thrown up on me, wiped his snot on me, and peed on me before I could get the nappy on quickly enough. I think, too, of all my tears that have dripped down onto him during all the hours I lay awake wishing that I had a relationship with God so that I could pray to keep my boy safe. I think of the cold sweat that's broken out on my brow every time I thought Mandla might be getting a fever and I thought, *This is it, this is it, this is it.*

Despite all the bodily fluids we've exchanged, I've never once worried that I was about to become infected with the virus. I know the facts of its transmission, which happens primarily through intercourse, sharing needles, blood transfusions, and drinking infected breast milk.

So why the gloves?

I slowly strip them off, take a deep breath, and throw them away. The box full of them goes into the garbage can straight afterward. I won't be touching Mandla with a barrier between us ever again.

CHAPTER FIFTY-THREE

Zodwa

23 June 1995
Big Hope Informal Settlement,
Magaliesburg, South Africa

Z odwa."

The voice carries from behind her in the shadows but it's unmistakable.

Thembeka.

Zodwa's heartbeat is as insistent as rain drumming against a tin roof, when she turns to face the woman she loves. "What?" When Thembeka doesn't reply, just stands there biting her lip, Zodwa asks again, "What do you want?"

Thembeka still doesn't speak and Zodwa turns to go. She walks three steps before Thembeka calls out: "I heard that you've been making inquiries . . . about the baby. Trying to find out what happened to it."

Of course, nothing is ever a secret in the township. "So?"

"So." Thembeka pauses before letting out a long, steadying breath. When she speaks again, it's with surprising gravity. "I wanted to tell you that your baby didn't die at birth like everyone said."

The words are spears in Zodwa's back. She turns around again but this time she's the one who's been rendered mute.

"I saw your mother carrying it away the night it was born."

Thembeka's words tumble out in a torrent as though she's scared Zodwa will stop listening to her. "I walked past your shack earlier in the day and heard you crying out. I knew the baby was coming and I wanted to see . . . I wanted to see it for myself. To see if it looked like Mongezi in any way. To make certain. If it didn't . . . then I didn't need to keep wondering . . . then I could be sure."

"Of what? That I was a liar?" Zodwa steps toward Thembeka, who shrinks away.

"When you told me, I didn't know what to believe." Thembeka's tone is pleading, like she's desperate for Zodwa to understand. "Mongezi said he never slept with you. That you were jealous of our relationship and that you were telling lies to break us up. I didn't know who to believe."

You should have believed me, Zodwa wants to shout. *Me! Because I loved you more than anyone. I would never have hurt you.* But the words won't come.

"So, I was waiting outside the shack thinking that maybe I could talk to you," Thembeka continues, "or see the baby. It had been festering for months and I was going mad with it . . . with not knowing the truth." She looks away and then back at Zodwa. "I was standing there when your mother came outside. She was carrying plastic bags and a big kit bag. I was going to wait for her to leave and then try and see you, but as she walked past where I was standing, I heard a cry from inside the bag. A baby's cry."

Zodwa's hands go to her mouth. *Mama, what did you do?*

"I couldn't understand why Leleti would be doing that, so I followed her. It was so loud and busy that day. Everyone was celebrating Mandela. With all the noise, no one else seemed to hear the baby but I did again, ten minutes later when we were on the main road. That's when I saw Leleti set the bag down, take the baby out, and strap it to her back with a blanket. She walked off in the direction of town with the dog following behind her."

"And then what happened?"

"I couldn't follow her anymore. Mongezi was expecting me and so I turned around and came back."

"But why have you waited so long to tell me?" Zodwa wants to grab Thembeka and shake her.

"I had no idea what your mother did with the baby or if you'd even believe me. And then after Leleti died a few days later . . . I didn't know what to do. I thought . . . if Leleti knew the baby was Mongezi's . . . if she thought you were raped like you said you were . . . then she may have wanted to get rid of it so you could go back to school. I thought it was better to just keep quiet about what I saw until . . ."

"Until what?"

"Until I found out where your baby might be."

Zodwa's whole body begins to tremble. Her legs feel so weak that she has to lean against the *shebeen* fence to steady herself. "Wait . . . what?"

"There's a farm about a fifteen-minute walk from here," Thembeka is saying. "Two old white women live there. They have a black baby with them who is the exact age your baby would be. Apparently, they found it on their doorstep one night and they've kept him."

"How do you know this?"

"My mother got work at the farm next door as a migrant laborer picking avocados last week. She heard an old couple who's retiring from there talking about it."

Zodwa takes a minute to process the information. As much

as she wants to believe Thembeka, it just doesn't make any sense. Why would Leleti take Zodwa's baby and give it to strangers?

As though reading her mind, Thembeka asks, "Did Leleti know those women?"

Zodwa's about to protest that her mother would never give her baby to white people, never in a million years, when she suddenly remembers something.

Who was that you were with now?

Someone I used to work for very long ago when we were both just girls. The good Lord brought us together then and still He works His wonders today.

You were hugging her. I thought you said all white people were demons.

Not that one. That one is God's child.

Zodwa blinks a few times. Why didn't she think of that woman before? "Will you take me there? To the farm?"

To Zodwa's relief, Thembeka nods.

"Tomorrow? We'll go tomorrow?"

"Yes."

Still, something is bothering Zodwa and it takes her a moment to realize what it is. "Why are you helping me at all?" Zodwa asks. "After everything that happened? You never believed me about Mongezi, so what has changed?"

Thembeka looks away and then her eyes flit back to meet Zodwa's. "I found the letter. The one you wrote to me."

CHAPTER FIFTY-FOUR

Delilah

✴

24 June 1995
Verdriet, Magaliesburg, South Africa

Does he feel warm to you?" Ruth had her palm against Mandla's forehead, her face scrunched up in concern.

I checked. "No, which is a miracle considering how many layers you have on the child."

"We have to be careful. He's so much more susceptible to things than we are."

"Things like heatstroke?" I pulled two layers off the child.

"So he doesn't feel warm to you. Does he feel clammy?"

"Ruth!"

I wished she would stop fussing over Mandla so much. The latest blood tests showed that his CD4 count was as good as could be expected and that his viral load hadn't gone up. The encouraging prognosis should have reassured her. Instead, rather than allowing herself to enjoy it, it just made her more fretful, as though letting her guard down was inviting catastrophe.

Ruth was clearly tempted to put the layers back on Mandla but, seeing my frown, decided against it. Between the two of us, we'd finally managed to get Mandla to sleep in his own crib, though the sleep-training regime I put into place was often undermined by Ruth, who went running to pick him up every time he so much as squeaked.

"He needs me," she'd said the night I stood guard between her room and Mandla's with my arms crossed, refusing to let her pass. "He's crying out for me."

"He's babbling, Ruth, not crying. You only put him down fifteen minutes ago. He'll never learn to sleep by himself if you come running at every little noise."

She'd shot me a filthy look but went back to bed. It took another three nights of us playing that cat-and-mouse game before Mandla finally settled into a routine and slept through the night. Things were much better on all fronts but even so, Ruth kept insisting she had a feeling that something bad was going to happen.

"Life is the bad thing that's going to happen," I'd quipped back. "You can't protect him from that." It hadn't done anything to appease her.

I left Ruth to her own devices and stepped outside, quickly closing the patio sliding door behind me so as not to let a cold breeze in.

Riaan had a three-legged cast-iron pot balanced on a Cadac gas bottle out on the patio and was making an oxtail *potjie*.

"How's the food coming along?"

"Good. The meat's browned and I've already layered the veggies. It should be ready as soon as the rugby's over."

"Shouldn't you stir that?" I teased, knowing full well that a *potjie* should never be stirred. Each ingredient was added in a very particular kind of order and the pot created a pressure-cooker effect to steam everything to perfection.

"*Rooinek,*" he joked, calling me the Afrikaner insult for the English: redneck. "No clue how to make *boerekos.*"

"It's time. The match is starting!" Ruth called from inside.

It was the Rugby World Cup final between South Africa and

New Zealand, and we gathered around the television to watch the match build up. Rugby was one of the few areas where our parents' worlds had converged—rugby meaning as much to the Scots as it did to the Afrikaners—and so Ruth and I had grown up watching the sport.

Because of sanctions imposed against South Africa during apartheid, we hadn't been allowed to compete during the first two World Cups, in 1987 and 1991. It was a huge deal that South Africa was not only hosting it, but that the Springboks had also made it through to the finals to play against the Kiwis.

I'd set out bowls of *biltong* and *droëwors* to snack on during the game, because rugby just wasn't rugby without the traditional dried-meat snack. Riaan and I were drinking Castle Lagers while Ruth had wine.

On-screen, Ellis Park Stadium was packed to capacity and it was heartening to see all the new South African flags waving in the stands. Spectators had painted their faces in the black, yellow, green, red, blue, and white of the flag and the energy looked electric. The crowd was being entertained by singing and dancing, when a deafening noise suddenly ripped through the stadium.

The screen filled with a Boeing 747 passenger jet flying low over the field. *Good Luck Bokke* was painted onto the bottom of the plane and wings. Sixty-five thousand heads tilted backward to take in the spectacle playing out above them. And then Nelson Mandela was walking onto the field next to Louis Luyt, the president of the South African Rugby Union.

"Now, there are the strangest of bedfellows I've ever seen," I commented. Luyt was a staunch Afrikaner who was widely rumored to be racist.

"Desperate times call for desperate measures," Riaan commented dryly. "Look at that! He's wearing a Springbok jersey."

Indeed, Mandela was wearing not only the South African Springbok jersey and cap, but he was wearing the number six, which belonged to François Pienaar, the Afrikaner Bok captain. It was unusual to see the president looking so casual; he was normally photographed in suits or the iconic African shirts that had been nicknamed "Madiba shirts."

As Mandela shook hands with the players, saying a few words to each of them, a chant built up in the stadium and gathered momentum until it became a roar.

"Nelson! Nelson! Nelson!"

My tears rose up on the same wave as the goose bumps on my arms. "To think that he was considered such a threat to white South Africans a year ago. Look at them now. Look how much they love him."

On-screen, Nelson Mandela, looking delighted, took off his cap and waved it at the predominantly white crowd.

The first half of the game was nail-biting, and by the time the whistle blew at full-time, the score was tied 9–9.

"Extra-time is going to be interesting," Riaan said. "The guys all look buggered." He excused himself to pop outside and turn off the gas so the *potjie* wouldn't burn.

When the whistle blew again, the struggle began anew. Things were looking good until the All Blacks' fly-half scored a long-range penalty, making the score 12–9 to the New Zealanders.

"Damn it!" Ruth yelled.

I was convinced that that was it for us, and that we'd lost, when Joel Stransky leveled for the Boks. "We're back to a tie!"

"How much time is left in the game?"

"Eight minutes."

"Come on, boys! You can do it!" The words were barely out of Ruth's mouth when suddenly, from thirty meters out, Joel Stransky drop-kicked the ball. We all watched as time seemed to slow down. The ball somersaulted through the air, reaching its zenith before dropping through the poles. The crowd went ballistic.

When the whistle blew for the end of extra-time, we were all up on our feet, screaming like madmen. "We won! We actually bloody won."

"It's Madiba magic."

Later, when the intercom's buzzer squawked, Ruth looked up at it, frowning. She'd said she was expecting something bad to happen, and judging by her expression, you'd have thought it had just arrived.

CHAPTER FIFTY-FIVE

Zodwa

❖

24 June 1995
Verdriet, Magaliesburg, South Africa

Zodwa lifts her hand and presses the button before she loses her courage. She has no idea what she's going to say or how she's going to explain her presence. Her only goal is to see if the rumors are true and if so, to find out if the black child could possibly be her son.

"Yes, hello?" A disembodied voice floats up from the intercom.

"Hello," Zodwa replies, bending down to speak into the box.

"Can I help you?"

"I'm looking for . . ." She trails off, uncertain of what to say. Just then, a dog starts barking wildly in the background, drowning everything else out.

The camera, positioned on the electric fence and angled down toward the gate, moves and seems to focus in on her. Zodwa smiles up at it uncertainly.

"I'm sorry, I can't hear you with the dog barking. I'm opening the gate."

And just like that, the electric gate slides open and Zodwa is inside the huge fence walking toward the house. She turns and looks for Thembeka and catches sight of her hiding behind the wild olive trees where she left her.

Zodwa wishes that they'd spoken about the letter—that

Thembeka had told Zodwa her reaction to reading it—but after she arrived to fetch Zodwa that morning, Thembeka didn't mention it again. Even with Zodwa's mind so full of her baby, she's still desperate to know what her friend is thinking.

The house door opens up ahead and Zodwa's head snaps forward. An older white woman steps outside onto the veranda. She's slender and has gray hair that falls to just below her ears. Though her hair has grown longer since the last time Zodwa saw her, she recognizes her instantly as the woman who hugged her mother on the side of the road more than a year ago.

"Hello? Can I help you?" the woman asks.

"Hello, ma—madam," Zodwa stammers in reply.

A black dog suddenly slips out the house and runs at Zodwa, who shrinks back in fear.

"Jez!" the woman calls but the dog doesn't listen to her.

Instead, it keeps barreling toward Zodwa, its tail wagging all the while. When it reaches her, it jumps up on its hind legs as though greeting a long-lost friend.

Oh my God. It's Shadow. It's Mama's dog.

Zodwa wants to cry. She knows now that she's in the right place and this is where she will find her son because, of course, her mother left her dog behind to protect him.

"I'm so sorry about that," the woman says, chasing down the stairs after the dog. "I don't know what's gotten into her. She's usually much better behaved."

"It's fine," Zodwa says, smiling as she rubs the dog behind the ears like Leleti used to do.

"Well, she certainly seems to like you." The woman grabs the dog by the collar and marches it back inside, Zodwa trailing behind her.

Her mind reels, thinking of what she should say next, but it stubbornly remains blank. Zodwa curses herself for not coming up with a proper plan. Actually, she'd had a plan just to watch the property and see if she could catch sight of the woman or the child, but she'd abandoned that as soon as they'd arrived. Leleti had always accused her of being impulsive and she was right.

Once they reach the front door, the woman points to the back of the house. "To your basket, Jez." She claps her hands for emphasis and the dog obeys.

As it slinks off, Zodwa's able to look past it, deeper into the house, and what she sees takes her breath away.

A toddler sits on a couch and he's the spitting image of Zodwa's brother, Dumisa. More than that, it's clear from his bulging eyes and the look of distress on his face that he's chok-ing on something. Zodwa doesn't have time to think, she just acts on instinct, pushing the door inward and shouldering the woman out of the way.

"Hey!" the woman shouts, too shocked to block Zodwa's way or to come after her.

Zodwa runs through what feels like mud, taking an eternity before she reaches the child. She's dimly aware that the dog has returned, spurred to action by its owner's cry. She hears other shouts too, but they sound distorted, as though they're coming from a long way away.

When Zodwa finally reaches the boy, she bends down and picks him up, feeling the dog's teeth sinking into her hand as she does so. She ignores the sharp pain and focuses on the child's face instead. His mouth gapes open and his eyes and nose are streaming, his face a rictus of panic. He still isn't breathing. She turns him upside down and rests him on her extended fore-arm, using the heel of her hand to smack him between his shoulder blades.

More shouting erupts from somewhere nearby and then the dog is quiet.

The boy is limp in her arms.

No. No. No. No.

Someone tugs at Zodwa's jersey as they wail, but she tunes it out, focusing all of her attention on the boy. She's praying now—praying harder than she ever has.

Please, God. Please, God. Please, God.

She whacks the boy's back once more.

Don't die. Don't die. Don't die. Not now when I've finally found you.

CHAPTER FIFTY-SIX

Ruth

❉

24 June 1995
Verdriet, Magaliesburg, South Africa

I'm in the kitchen when Dee yells out and I look up to see a black girl running at Mandla. I freeze, confused as to what's happening, and then I see Mandla's face. He isn't breathing and his eyes bulge obscenely.

"Do something!" I scream at Dee. I'm rooted to the spot with my hands over my mouth, but the girl has reached him and as she picks him up, Jez lunges and bites her.

I'm expecting the girl to cry out in pain and drop Mandla, but she doesn't make a sound. She's so focused on my boy as she bends him over and starts hitting him on the back that the bite doesn't even seem to register. I wonder, madly, if she's an angel.

Riaan comes running through from the patio just then and Jez is still barking like crazy. Dee shushes her, getting her away from the girl.

Please, God. Please, God. Please, God.

Nothing happens. Mandla is still not breathing. And that's when I bolt toward them. I grab the girl's jersey, babbling at her incoherently, pleading with her to help him.

Still she smacks his back and I'm about to tear him out of her arms when something dislodges from his throat. It looks like a piece of *droëwors*, but no sooner is it out on the floor than Jez snatches it up in one gulp.

It's quiet for a moment, too quiet, and then Mandla takes a shuddering breath.

He's breathing. My boy is breathing.

"Jesus. You saved his life. You saved my boy's life. He's okay. Oh, thank God, he's okay."

I'm crying and Dee's crying and the girl is crying as I grab my boy, pulling him from her hands and planting kisses all over his face. He's screaming and I should probably give him space to breathe, but I'd graft him to my skin right now if that was possible.

I have never been that scared in all my life. I thought I was going to lose him. I thought that was it. And Jesus, wouldn't that have been the sickest joke the universe could ever have played? An HIV-positive baby dying from choking. It's such a crazy thing that I burst out laughing and everyone looks at me as if I've gone mad, which I have. I'm mad with relief.

Later, we're all sitting on the couch. Mandla is on my lap and I'm holding him with one hand while holding the girl's bandaged hand with the other. Dee cleaned the bite up and even gave her a rabies shot, which she had in that emergency first-aid kit she travels with. She's apologized over and over for leaving the *droëwors* on the table where Mandla could reach it until I finally have to shush her.

The girl looks uncomfortable to be sitting down next to me but she's staring at my boy like he's the most beautiful thing she's ever seen.

"What did you say your name was again?" She's told me

twice but I've been so focused on Mandla that I can barely concentrate.

"Zodwa," she says.

She's a very pretty girl with beautiful, glowing skin. I wish I knew how she gets it like that because it doesn't matter how much body lotion I rub onto Mandla, his skin always looks dry and gray. Her hair is tied back in two braids and the whites of her eyes glow in the gloom. She has a quiet but firm voice.

"Zodwa," I repeat. "You saved Mandla's life."

"Mandla. That's his name?"

"Yes, it means—"

"I know what it means," she says. "I'm Zulu."

All the time we're speaking, she keeps her eyes fixed on Mandla and he seems equally taken with her because he keeps reaching out to her.

"How did you know to do that?" I ask her. "Are you a nurse or something?"

She shakes her head. "I looked after all the children in my grandmother's village when I was little. I learned then what to do."

"Thank God you did."

"Did you come here looking for a job?" Dee asks. "Is that why you came?"

She stares at Dee blankly. It must be the shock.

"Did you hear we were looking for a maid?" I prompt. "Because if you want a job, you have it. You're hired!"

Zodwa looks at Mandla for a second as though making a decision, and then she smiles. "Yes," she says. "I was looking for a job."

CHAPTER FIFTY-SEVEN

Zodwa

✳

1 July 1995
Big Hope Informal Settlement,
Magaliesburg, South Africa

This is madness," Thembeka says as Zodwa packs her few possessions into the very kit bag Leleti used to ferry Mandla away. "You're really going to do it? Work for them?"

Zodwa doesn't reply. She just keeps folding her clothes and tucking them away in the bag.

"As a maid, Zodwa? What would your mother think?"

Zodwa knows exactly what her mother would think, but Leleti should have thought of that before she took Zodwa's baby away and gave him to white people.

When Thembeka doesn't get a response, she tries a different tack. "They have your child. Your son. Why didn't you just take him and bring him home?"

"And how would I do that?" Zodwa growls. "What proof do I have that he's my child besides that he looks just like my brother? Everyone here thinks my child is dead, so who are the police going to believe? A poor black girl from the squatter camp or rich white women?"

"I'll tell the police about seeing Leleti with the baby and the kit bag—"

"Even if they believe you, you didn't see where she took him.

260
·

It was only a rumor that led us there. Those people have money. They will fight with their money. What do I have? Nothing. This is the only way I can be around Mandla and see him every day."

"By working as a slave for the people who have stolen him?"

"They didn't steal him. Leleti took him there. I have to trust my mother's judgment. She must have had her reasons." Thembeka snorts and Zodwa stops packing to face her. "They don't look like bad people," she says quietly. "He lives in a nice, big house and he has lots of food and things. Can I give him that? No. This is what I can give him." She gestures at the shack and its meager contents. Zodwa can't imagine that vital boy in his beautiful clothes living here with her.

Thembeka sighs. "What did Ace say?"

"I haven't told him. He's in Hammanskraal visiting his mother this weekend. When he comes back, I'll be gone. Don't tell him where I went, okay?"

"And what about the shack? You're just going to leave it empty?"

"Mama Beauty is going to rent it out to one of the Zimbabweans or Malawians for me."

She's the only other person who knows where Zodwa is going though she doesn't know Zodwa's reasons for taking the job. Zodwa expected Mama Beauty to be judgmental about the maid's position, but she was supportive, mysteriously saying that she herself had briefly worked as something akin to a maid. She added that living in a cottage on a farm was safer than being in the township, and Zodwa had wondered then if Mama Beauty suspected the truth of her sexuality.

When Thembeka can think of no further objections, she asks in a defeated whisper, "What about . . . what about how you said you felt . . . about me?"

Finally, it's come to this. Finally, they're having the conversation that Zodwa has dreamed about and played out over and over in her mind. So why does it not feel like she thought it would? Where is the euphoria and vindication?

Instead, what she feels is a sense of loss, but a muted one that doesn't even come close to how she felt after losing her son. Romantic heartbreak is terrible but there are things more terrible than that. And though Zodwa is inexperienced when it comes to love, she's certain that it shouldn't be such a destructive force. It shouldn't rip people apart and ruin their lives, or make men want to commit violence and turn the best of friends against each other. Love should be pure and untainted, like the feeling she had for Mandla when he was reaching out for her on the couch, when she knew that she would do anything to stay with him.

"I'm sorry for everything that's happened," Thembeka says. "But I was weak and confused. That day I kissed you . . . I meant it. I wanted to kiss you but it scared me too . . . because of what that made me. And then after what happened with Mongezi, it was easier to just tell myself I hated you than have to deal with those feelings. Do you understand?"

Zodwa nods. She does. Hasn't she herself hidden away from who she is, degrading herself by sleeping with Ace to try to prove something to the world? She's the last person to judge.

"Please don't go," Thembeka says, reaching out for Zodwa. "Stay for us."

Zodwa steps out of her reach. "I'm sorry but I can't."

She will wish later that she'd kissed Thembeka goodbye.

CHAPTER FIFTY-EIGHT

Delilah

1 July 1995
Verdriet, Magaliesburg, South Africa

I'd finished packing for the next trip to the dig site at Drimolen and went in search of Ruth to say goodbye. I was about to call out for her when I heard tinkling laughter coming from Mandla's bedroom. The door was open and I peeked inside, not wanting to interrupt whatever they were up to. Ruth was on the floor resting her back against the wall, her legs stretched out in front of her with Mandla sitting on her thighs. She had one of the curtains pulled between them and was hiding behind it.

"Where's he? Where's he? Where's he?" she called in a singsong voice before pulling the curtain aside. "There he is!"

Mandla reared back with hysterical laughter as though the skit was the funniest thing he'd ever seen. He responded just as uproariously the next five times Ruth repeated it.

I wasn't prepared for the lump that rose up in my throat just then. I couldn't even name the emotion or pinpoint its cause. Was it sadness because I'd missed out on countless moments like those with Daniel during his childhood? Or was it happiness for Ruth because I'd never seen her that content? Was it possible to feel both sorrow for yourself and joy for someone else at the same time?

"Oh no. Look who it is, Mandla," Ruth shouted, changing

the game. "Look who's arrived. It's the tickle monster and he's coming to get you." Mandla squealed as Ruth lunged at him while wiggling her fingers around wildly. As he pried free of her grasp and began crawling away, huffing with exertion, Ruth pulled herself up onto her knees and went after him. Her cream linen pants were creased and dirty but if she'd noticed, she didn't seem to care, probably because she was so relieved that he was finally crawling. She made animal noises, part snorting pig and part snarling lion, which set me off laughing with how ridiculous it was.

Ruth's head snapped up and she smiled when she saw me, calling out a breathless greeting. "Sherbet, I really need to stop it with the smokes. I'm getting too old for this kind of thing."

"'Sherbet'? Who are you and what have you done with my sister?"

She laughed and got up, her knees creaking in protest. "His mind is like a sponge right now. I'd prefer him not to be soaking up all the bad words." She then sniffed the air theatrically before reaching down and picking Mandla up, planting kisses all over his face. "Someone is a little stinky. I'm not going to mention any names . . . but someone needs his nappy changed."

Ruth put Mandla down on the changing table and set about cleaning him up. "I'm getting a few things together for Zodwa's arrival tomorrow," she said, nodding at two overflowing garbage bags in the corner of the room. "Do you have anything you'd like to donate since you're more her size than I am? Oh wait, what am I saying? She probably has more clothes than you do!"

I rolled my eyes and went over to the bags, peeking inside. "Dear God, please don't tell me you're giving her stilettos and lingerie?"

"What? A girl can't have enough shoes and nice sleepwear. I'm giving her a few jerseys and blouses and pants as well."

"She won't wear the pants."

"How do you know?"

"It's a cultural thing. Zulu women don't wear trousers."

"Well, that's very backward. Maybe she's a new generation of trailblazing feminist Zulu women who'll not only wear them but start a new trend."

I couldn't help but smile. "You really like her, don't you?" It never ceased to amaze me how despite Ruth's offhand, almost casual, racism, she was able to form such strong attachments with certain black people.

"What's not to like? She saved Mandla's life."

And I realized then that that's what it boiled down to for Ruth. She thought she was blind to Mandla's blackness, but even the term *color-blind* implied that color was something, by its very nature, that had to be looked past. It's what she was doing in her connection to Zodwa: seeing past her color and embracing her in spite of it because of what the girl had done for Mandla.

There was no use in pointing that out to Ruth, who wouldn't see the subtlety of it even if I had, so I changed the subject. "Are you going to tell her?"

"Tell her what?"

"About Mandla being HIV positive?"

Ruth sighed, a long exhalation. "No, I don't think so."

"Why not?"

"There's so much stigma around the disease and I don't want her treating him differently because of it. Also, for her to be in any kind of danger, they pretty much both have to have gaping wounds that are bleeding into each other at the same time. I mean, what are the chances?"

"Minuscule," I admitted. "Still, doesn't she have a right to know?"

"I don't think so. She's here as a housekeeper primarily, not as a nanny. And I'll always be here to make sure it's a safe environment for both of them. Anyway"—Ruth sniffed—"it will be nice having a bit of company around here. Considering someone's always off gallivanting."

"You almost sound jealous."

"Please! Loverboy could at least have sprung for a nice hotel or something romantic rather than making you dig around in the dirt or whatever the hell it is you're going to do."

"He had to do a lot of convincing to get me approval on the site, I'll have you know. This is a much bigger deal than going to some hotel."

"You know what also does a lot of convincing to get you into places? Visa and MasterCard."

I laughed. "See you in a few days." And then I leaned forward and kissed Mandla goodbye.

Ruth beamed. "Have fun. Don't do anything I wouldn't do but do lots of things I would."

CHAPTER FIFTY-NINE

Zodwa

❄

2 July 1995
Verdriet, Magaliesburg, South Africa

H ere we go. This is where you'll stay," the white woman says as she opens the door.

Zodwa trails her into the maid's quarters and stops at the threshold. "Here?"

"Yes."

"By myself?"

"I should hope so, unless you have a boyfriend or a circus troupe stashed away in that kit bag?"

Zodwa flinches at the mention of a boyfriend. She hopes that Thembeka will keep her whereabouts secret from Ace.

"I was joking about the circus troupe," the woman, Ruth, says. "Sorry about the paint smell. We just had it done yesterday, which is why it's so cold in here. I've had the windows and doors open to get rid of the fumes. There's a heater over there, so it should warm up quickly enough." She looks at Zodwa's bag again. "Is that all you have?"

"Yes."

"It looks pretty heavy. What did you pack in there? Rocks?"

"Textbooks," Zodwa replies quickly.

"I've always loved books and reading but I never much cared for studying, so good for you! Okay, I'll leave you to get settled then. I'll come back a bit later with some bedding and towels and a few other necessities."

The woman sometimes lapses into speaking to Zodwa in the overly loud and slow way that you'd speak to old people or those who don't speak your language, using exaggerated gestures for emphasis. Still, she smiles a lot. Zodwa doesn't know her well enough yet to know if that's a good or a bad thing.

Without thinking, Zodwa asks what's been on her mind since she arrived. "Where's Mandla?"

"Oh, he's napping and I didn't want to wake him, which is why I have to dash back."

The woman walks out the door and down the sandy path in her high-heeled boots. Alone, Zodwa sets her bag down and turns in a circle, taking in her new home. While it has a tin roof like her shack, its walls are built from cement and bricks and there are many windows instead of just one. It's large and rectangular, almost as big as the Good Times Drinking Establishment. The floor is made of concrete with linoleum tile covering it. Two light fittings hang from the ceilings. In addition to the heater the woman indicated, there's a wood-burning stove in the corner.

Curtains hang off a cord, separating the bedroom from the rest of the space. When Zodwa pulls the curtain aside, she sees there's a proper bed and a large wardrobe in the makeshift room. She flicks the switch against the wall and the light comes on overhead. A small kitchen stands off to the side; it's made up of three cabinets as well as a table with two chairs. There's a little fridge that looks as though it was made for children and Zodwa goes to open it. It's completely empty but it's working. It's the first one she's ever had and she wishes she had something to put inside.

The only closed door beckons. When Zodwa opens it, it reveals a small bathroom with a shower, toilet, and basin. Zodwa lifts the toilet seat to check that there's water in the bowl. She presses the handle and the water flushes. It does the same thing again when she repeats the action. She turns the shower tap on and the water's hot; she stands for a few minutes with her hand in the spray, amazed at the luxury of running water and plumbing.

Zodwa can't believe this is all hers.

On the quick drive over, the woman said a whole family of farmworkers lived in it at one time, but the children all moved away and the husband and wife just retired. Zodwa doesn't know much about her mother's youth, just that she was orphaned young and fell under the care of another black woman who trained her as a housemaid on a farm. Considering the timeline of her mother's life, these quarters must be the exact place where Leleti stayed all those years ago. The knowledge makes Zodwa feel less alone.

She unpacks what little she brought with her, hanging up her four dresses and a nightgown in the wardrobe while folding her two pairs of underwear and socks into the drawers. Zodwa puts all of her books on the kitchen table and then picks out the rock from the bottom of the bag, the one she was scared the woman, Ruth, had guessed at when she commented on the weight of it.

Since she couldn't bring the whole shrine that Leleti built to Dumisa's disappearance, Zodwa brought the biggest rock from the stack. She goes outside and, under the shade of a thorn tree, lays the rock down as a base that she can add to every day, thinking how time begins anew even as we drag our past into the future.

. . .

When Ruth comes back later, Zodwa rushes to the door at the sound of the car's engine. This time Mandla is with her and Zodwa's spirits soar at the sight of her son. She didn't imagine his resemblance to Dumisa. His smile is an echo of her brother's and she wishes so much that Leleti could see it.

"We brought you some stuff," the woman calls. "Help us offload."

The back of the luxury car is filled with bulging garbage bags. Ruth carries a bag in one hand and Mandla in the other. The boy is wearing Nike *takkies* that match his Nike tracksuit and sweatshirt, as well as a woolen Nike beanie pulled low over his forehead. Just that outfit alone cost more than all of Zodwa's clothes combined. She watches as Ruth puts Mandla down on the floor of the cottage. He stares at the bare furnishings, his fingers in his mouth.

Even though Zodwa's new dwelling is so vastly superior to her old one that she may as well have moved to another planet, the boy still looks out of place there. He's the little master slumming it in the servant's quarters.

"There are sheets and duvets and linens, as well as towels and curtains and stuff for the kitchen. I also brought you some clothes." Ruth starts pulling things from a bag and Zodwa wonders if it's a joke, if the woman is making fun of her.

There are five pairs of shoes with heels that look like daggers. "I think we're the same size," the woman says. She isn't laughing, or even smiling, and so Zodwa thinks she's serious. The woman must think that Zodwa would wear prostitute shoes. "And here are some blouses and pants. This one's Versace and this one's Calvin Klein. Now, I know what you're thinking,

270

that I'm curvier than you are, but these ones are too small for me, which is why I never even wore them. They should fit."

Labels are still attached to them and when Zodwa catches sight of the prices, she feels faint. That the woman would buy clothes that cost this much but that don't fit is ridiculous enough, but the fact that she then wouldn't return them for a refund is mind-blowing.

"There's some other stuff in there as well. Sleepwear and such."

Zodwa doesn't know what to say and so she just says, "Thank you, madam."

"You'll wear a uniform in the house and I got you two of those as well. The local Spar doesn't have the best selection but they'll do for now so long as you aren't allergic to polyester." She laughs and then stands up. "Okay, I'll see you in the kitchen at eight a.m. sharp." With that, she reaches out to pick up Mandla and carries him back to the car.

As the woman puts him inside, Mandla turns back to Zodwa, smiling and waving at her. Looking at his face is like looking at the sun but Zodwa forces herself not to lower her eyes. She smiles and waves back. They're standing only a few meters apart and yet with her child in that woman's hands, it feels as if they're looking at each other from different worlds.

Zodwa's heart breaks a little then and she realizes she needs to prepare to have it broken a little more each day.

CHAPTER SIXTY

Ruth

❋

3 July 1995
Verdriet, Magaliesburg, South Africa

I t's been a long morning. Zodwa is so wet behind the ears she
may as well have just arrived from the homelands, though she
assures me she's been out of the boondocks for a few years. If it
wasn't for the fact that she saved my son's life, I would have sent
her packing and tried to find a maid with proper experience.
The thing is, despite how clueless she is, I have a good feeling
about her.

When I get impatient with her, I remind myself that skills
are something you can teach, whereas good chemistry is rare.
It's not just me who feels it, Mandla feels it too. He was throwing a gigantic hissy fit this morning because Jezebel ate a bis-
cuit out of his hand, but as soon as Zodwa came through the
door, he calmed down and gave her a huge smile. Maybe it's
because she's the only other black person in the house. He may
feel some kind of kinship with her.

So far, I've had to show Zodwa how to use the vacuum cleaner
and the microwave. Well, actually, I gave her the instruction
booklet for the vacuum because how the hell should I know how
to use it? When I show her the mop, she looks at it as if it's from
outer space.

"What? You've never cleaned a floor before?"

"Not with water," she says mysteriously, and scratches her head. What kind of floor can't be cleaned with water? "You show me how to use it," she says, and I laugh and laugh.

"Not bloody likely. We'll wait for Dee to come home. She can show you how to use all of this. For now, just vacuum and dust and then clean the kitchen and bathrooms." Once I have Zodwa sorted, I turn to Mandla. "Come, my angel boy. Let's sit over here."

Mandla looks up from his building blocks and I have to resist the temptation to pick him up. Now that he's finally started crawling, the next step is to get him walking; that won't happen if I coddle him, which is what Dee constantly accuses me of. Instead, I hold my arms out to him and he crawls over to where I'm sitting in the lounge.

With him being almost fourteen months old, I'm also focusing a lot of energy on trying to get him to talk. I know Dee says it will come with time but a child like Mandla, one who's likely to experience more pain and discomfort than healthy children, needs to be able to communicate better than those kids. Being able to explain what hurts will help a doctor understand what to treat him for, and it will also go a long way to lessening my sense of helplessness.

I pat the couch to see if Mandla will pull himself up. "You can do it, my boy. You're my own little Superman."

He gives me a rare toothy grin before his face puckers into a frown. I've never seen a child with such expressive eyebrows. It cracks me up. He's frustrated that he's down there and I'm up here, and I know I should let that motivate him to stand but I hate seeing him upset. I can't help it; I reach down and pick him up, putting him on the couch next to me.

Jez comes running over and hops up next to him. Zodwa

may be the new cleaning maid but Jez continues to be Mandla's nursemaid and most faithful companion.

"Okay, little man. Look at me." I make eye contact with him to ensure that I have his full attention, then I point to myself and say, "I am Mama."

Mandla blinks back at me.

I try it again. "Mama. Now you say it."

He shakes his head.

"Mama," I repeat, nodding and pointing to myself while smiling winningly. I feel like I'm in a beauty pageant and am trying to win over one of the harsher judges. "Mama."

Mandla smiles. *Yes, I've gotten through to him!* He opens his mouth just as Zodwa thwacks something in the bathroom. His head snaps to the side and the moment is ruined.

"Zodwa," I call. "All okay in there?"

"Yes, Madam Ruth."

"Could you keep it down a bit? I'm trying to teach Mandla how to say my name."

"Yes, Madam Ruth. Sorry." Her voice sounds strangled but it's probably because she's bending over the toilet scrubbing it.

I get Mandla to focus again. "Okay, Mandla. Say it. Say 'Mama.'"

"Kaka," he says, and then smiles widely.

"What the f—" I manage to stop myself just in time, laughing at how proud Mandla looks. "You little rascal. You can't even speak yet and you're already making jokes." I grab his chubby cheeks and squeeze them while leaning in for a nose bop. God, I love the smell of him. And now that Zodwa has shared the secret of her lovely skin—*Vaseline instead of moisturizing body cream! Who would have thought it?*—I love the silky soft texture of him too. "Come, let's try again. Say it. 'Mama.'"

"Kaka."

"Mama."

"Kaka."

There's another noise from the bathroom but this time it sounds like laughter. I must be mistaken, though, because when Zodwa comes out of the bathroom a minute later, her expression is solemn.

CHAPTER SIXTY-ONE

Delilah

✦

3 July 1995
Drimolen, Muldersdrift, South Africa

Three months after our first trip to the Drimolen site, Riaan and I were sharing sleeping quarters because one of the visiting experts needed somewhere to sleep. I'd offered up my tent, much to Riaan's surprise, but it didn't feel like too much of a sacrifice. I felt safe with him and we'd steadily been getting closer. He'd been so patient with me and I wanted to thank him by showing him that I trusted him.

When we slipped into our sleeping bags that night, each of us cocooned in our own individual one, I told myself to relax. I still had all my clothes on, plus there was a barrier of fabric between us. I had no reason at all to feel scared. Riaan flicked the switch on the camping light secured above us and the darkness rushed in to fill the void. We lay motionless for a few moments and then Riaan reached out to me, feeling for my hand. He squeezed it once and then turned on his side, propping himself up on his elbow.

"It's been a good day," he said, sighing happily.

"Yes, it has."

"I'm so glad you're here."

"Me too." And I was. I loved watching him on the site, where

276
·

he was in his element. It fascinated me the way he came alive there among all those dead things.

Riaan cleared his throat, and as I turned my head toward him, he bent down and kissed me. It was nice at first and I liked the sensation of his goatee tickling my face, but then he leaned in farther and it was the pressure of his shoulder against my chest that made my breath catch in my throat. I tensed up, my eyes wide with fright, and Riaan froze before pulling away.

"Delilah? Are you okay?"

I wasn't, but that wasn't his fault. It was because of what had happened all those years before.

Saying goodbye to my family when I left for the convent in January of 1955 had been easy. I wish it hadn't, as that would've shown some degree of feeling but all I'd felt was relief. Saying goodbye to Riaan the night before had been much harder and my eyes were still puffy and tender from the tears I'd cried throughout the night. I told myself that I was all cried out and that's why I didn't have any tears left in me.

We were all standing on the veranda. Father Thomas had already said his goodbyes, shaking my father's hand and patting my mother's shoulder, while giving a wide berth to Ruth, who'd stepped forward to hug him. He was sitting in his Plymouth Fury to give us some privacy.

The car wasn't what you'd expect a priest to drive. It was a bright candy-apple red with matching seats, dashboard, and steering wheel, but he'd explained to my father that the church had managed to get a very good price on it at an auction and they were planning to respray it once they had enough funds to do so.

Da surprised me by coming to the farmhouse to say his fare-well. It was the third day of the new year and there was much to be seen to after the Christmas break. With a productive two hours of sunlight remaining until dusk, I'd expected him to take full advantage of them.

Da was many things—a violent drunk who had absolutely no farming acumen or business savvy, a man who was not well-liked or even grudgingly respected—but I'd never considered him to be a hypocrite. I could only conclude then that his tears at my departure were genuine, and that they either came from some well of feeling he'd always managed to keep hidden, or that what he was feeling was regret.

Perhaps he looked back and saw himself for what he'd been to me: a brutish father who, though he'd shown himself capable of tenderness toward Ruth, had never shown me anything but disdain.

"Ah made ya a key," he said in his thick brogue, holding it up. Its gold contours glinted in his dirty fingers, the nails per-manently rimmed with mud. "In case ya ever change ya min' an' decide ya wan' to come home."

"I won't," I said, surprising myself with my boldness. It stung that he thought I'd fail at the one thing I wanted most in the world.

"Still, it's always good to ken tha' ya have options," Da said. "I've chiseled oot a hole in this here statue," he said, indicating one of the concrete angels Ma collected. It was the only one that didn't look somber, so I'd be able to tell it apart from all the others.

"Trust Da to pick the one that looks drunk," Ruth said, and I smiled.

"It's wedged tight in here, see?" Da said, slipping the key into the hole at the angel's base and then letting it drop with a thunk. He came over to me and I thought for a moment that he was going to embrace me, but his arms never rose higher than his ribs before he dropped them again. "It will always be there. Ah promise ya tha'." He leaned forward to give me a quick peck on the forehead. He smelled of a mixture of sweat, manure, and tobacco. "Goodbye an' good luck."

"I won't need luck," I said. "I have God. He's all I need."

"Goodbye, little sister," Ruth said loudly, stepping up to give me a hug. Her long red hair was hanging loose and a strand of it flew up and tickled my nose. She lowered her voice so our mother couldn't hear her. "Have fun with your sexy priest."

"Ruth," I said, feeling my cheeks flush. "It's not like that."

"Of course it is," she whispered. "I see how you look at him. You saucy minx." Her blue eyes were brimming with tears when she stepped back and I was touched.

"You'll come to my novitiate ceremony?"

"Of course," she said. "A room full of virgins and sacrificial wine? Sounds like a hell of a party. I wouldn't miss it for the world."

"You mean 'sacramental' wine," I corrected.

"You're absolutely right. It's the virgins who are sacrificial." She winked.

And then the only person left to say goodbye to was Ma.

And it was leaving her that I had hoped would be hardest to do because I knew how much she loved me, how much she'd pinned all of her hopes on me after she'd been forced to get married and bear children when all she'd wanted was to live a life of servitude to the Lord.

"You will have the life I never had," she'd said after sitting with Father Thomas one Sunday a year before and agreeing to let me join the convent. "You will be happy."

My mother was only thirty-six when I left and yet I remember her as an old woman. Being a farmer's wife, and a supremely unhappy one at that, had aged her prematurely, both in appearance and in spirit. Her hair was completely gray and her skin was worn and blemished. Her brown eyes looked like muddy pools as the tears gathered, ready to fall. She was wearing her usual old housedress because it was a working day, but she'd put her fancy apron on over it to mark the occasion and the special guest.

"Delilah," my mother whispered fiercely as she cupped my cheeks with both of her calloused hands.

That's all she said but I knew everything she meant by it. Ma wasn't a demonstrative woman. I couldn't recall her ever having told me that she loved me. She was the kind of woman who showed her love in scoldings and smacks against the backside because those were the things that she felt forged a person's character in the eyes of the Lord. She mostly let our father discipline Ruth (which didn't amount to much discipline at all) because she just didn't care enough to ensure that Ruth had moral fiber. To her, Ruth was always a lost cause, but I was the one thing she'd done right, and she wanted to ensure that my path to heaven was free of obstructions.

The truth was that as much as I loved my mother, I'd found her love to be stifling. It was weighted with so much expectation that it sometimes felt as though a vise had been clamped around my throat. I was her everything, her reason for living. I know people said that all the time like it was a good thing, as if they were bestowing a blessing, when in fact what they were saying was, *You are my air. Without you, I can't breathe.*

No child should have to carry the burden of being their parent's oxygen.

"I love you, Ma."

She nodded and kissed me quickly before stifling a sob and wrapping her arms around herself. I waved to Ruth, who was staring at Ma like she wanted to touch her, but also like she knew her comfort wasn't wanted. It was a hungry look. It was the way Ma looked at me.

When I got to the car and grasped the handle, I turned back for one last look. Ma's face was scrunched in misery, but it was the kind of martyred misery that makes a person feel perversely good. Like they're suffering for a worthy cause.

I blew her a kiss, thinking I'd see her again soon. The plan was that she'd come to the convent to visit me, but of course that never happened. I didn't know then that it was the last time I'd ever see her and so I suffered no guilt that leaving made me feel like I could finally breathe. Like I'd become my own oxygen.

Father Thomas and I had never been alone together, and I'd found it disorienting that our thighs were almost touching in the confines of the car. I was used to his being dressed in his vestments and standing in front of a congregation in the church. That day, though he wore his clerical collar, he was wearing trousers like any other man, and there wasn't a stained-glass window or altar boy in sight.

Forty minutes into the journey, just as I was beginning to relax, Father Thomas turned to me and asked, "Did you hear that?"

"Hear what, Father?"

"That grinding sound."

I listened carefully, not wanting to get it wrong, but I didn't hear anything.

"Something is definitely wrong," Father Thomas said just before he signaled to turn into the parking lot of what looked like a cheap motel. It was the kind of place Ma would never have allowed us to stop at.

I straightened up, alarmed. We weren't even out of Randfontein yet. I didn't want to have to turn around and go back to the farm less than an hour after we'd left. "Are you sure?"

He sounded annoyed. "Of course I'm sure. Unless you think you have more experience with automotive problems than I do?"

"No! Of course not. Sorry, Father. I just didn't hear the sound before, but now that you mention it . . ." I convinced myself I could hear it too.

He told me to sit tight as he got out of the car, lifting up the bonnet and tinkering around under it for a few minutes. I cranked my window open. I was wearing a dress and skirt that Ma had sewed using material too thick for the summer heat. Beads of sweat had begun to gather at my temples and between my breasts, and the backs of my thighs were sticking to the leather seat.

I'd just hitched the side of my skirt up to wipe at the sticky perspiration when Father Thomas dropped the bonnet and walked around to my side of the car, leaning in through the window. I yanked my skirt down but saw his eyes flit to my bare thigh.

"We'll need a replacement part," he said.

I was crushed that we'd have to turn back.

"We'll stay here for the night while we wait for it, and then we can leave tomorrow."

"Oh!" I was so relieved to hear that I wouldn't have to return to the farm that I tried not to think about what my mother would say about such arrangements. The place looked seedy and run-down, but it's not like I was there by myself. Father Thomas was there to protect me.

"Stay here and I'll go and see if they have rooms and if I can phone around for that part."

He returned five minutes later with two keys. "There's room at the inn." He smiled, reaching into the boot for my suitcase before pulling out another bag for himself. Its presence confused me. Why would he have packed a bag for the night when the plan was to return to the convent the same day he'd set out?

"This is apparently the better of the two rooms," Father Thomas said, unlocking one of the doors. "You can sleep here. I'll head out a bit later to see what I can find us for dinner."

The motel room was clean, which was a relief. A small Gideon Bible was placed next to the bed. It was the first time I'd ever stayed in a hotel room on my own, or had any kind of room to myself. I was used to sharing with Ruth and knew that I wouldn't have much privacy at the convent, so I felt intoxicated with the freedom of it.

I ran a bath, the old pipes clunking as it filled, and then soaked in the cool water, washing off the sweat of the drive. When I was done, I could see out the window that the sun had set and I wasn't sure what to get dressed into. I'd have to wear my suit again the next day and besides my convent garb, which I couldn't wear until I got there, I didn't have any other clothes with me except my nightgown and robe. I'd be taking vows of poverty and so I'd left all my worldly possessions behind.

Deciding that my flannel long-sleeved, floor-length nightgown was modest enough, I pulled it over my head and then knelt with my rosary to pray. I still remember how buoyant I felt in that moment. Despite the stuffiness of the room and the cloying heat of the nightgown, I remember feeling as though every prayer I'd ever uttered had come true.

As my lips moved, murmuring all the gratitude I was filled with, I lost track of the time. My knees were aching when a knock at the door startled me. I whipped my head to the side and felt a muscle in my neck pinch.

Checking through the peephole to make sure it was Father Thomas, I pulled on my robe over my nightgown, wincing as I moved my head too sharply, and unlatched the chain. I opened the door a fraction, hiding most of my body behind it. I expected Father Thomas to pass me my food and then to bid me good night, but instead he pushed the door open. I stepped back to let him pass, pulling the gown tighter around my neck to ensure that all my flesh was covered.

Father Thomas was carrying two parcels and the smell of deep-fried fish and *slap* chips drenched in vinegar made my stomach growl. There was a small table in the room to set everything down on. He pulled the single chair out and sat on it. I was left standing awkwardly in the middle of the room.

"Sit, Delilah."

I looked around, unsure of what the etiquette was, and he nodded at the bed. "That will have to do since there isn't another chair."

He placed two large parcels of newspaper on the table. Unwrapping each one, he set about dishing up generous portions for us both, spooning out a chunky white sauce on top of each fillet of fish.

"What's that, Father?"

"Tartar sauce. You've never had it before?"

"No, I don't think so."

"You're going to love it. Here," he said, dipping his finger in the sauce and then holding it out to me.

When it became clear that he expected me to lick the sauce from his finger, I felt the heat gather at my collarbones and flare upward across my neck and into my cheeks.

"Silly me," Father Thomas said, embarrassed. "I spend too much time with the children at the orphanage and forget how to act around adults." I laughed and then he joined in, shaking his head and looking sheepish. "Let's try again. Here," he said, dipping a spoon in the sauce and then holding it out to me.

I took it from him, relieved but also flustered. The sauce was delicious, both tart and sweet at the same time. We both set about eating though my appetite had diminished. I didn't know where to look but my eyes kept getting drawn back to his lips, which were shiny with grease. Every time he licked them, I squirmed. The room, already stiflingly hot, grew hotter with every passing moment.

When he was done, he looked at the food that remained in the newspaper on my lap. "You've barely eaten. What's wrong, Delilah? Please tell me I didn't offend you just now. I meant nothing by it."

"Not at all, Father. I just hurt my neck earlier and it's a bit painful." It was easier to blame my discomfort on that instead of admitting how small the room suddenly felt and how his body seemed to fill up so much of it.

"Oh no," he said, looking concerned as he stood up and walked toward me. My breath caught. "A neck injury can be very painful and will only get worse if not treated straight away. Before I decided to become a priest, I started studying to become a doctor. Did you know that?"

"No, Father. But honestly, I'm fine and—" I started to protest but he'd already taken my food from me and then knelt next to me on the bed. He positioned me at an angle facing away from him so that he could get a grip on my shoulders.

"Take your robe off so I can see what I'm working with here."

"Father, I don't think—"

"Oh, for goodness' sake. It's just me, Delilah. I'm a priest and you're perfectly safe with me. You don't think I mean you harm, do you?" His tone was both injured and annoyed.

"No, Father. Of course not," I said, shrugging the robe off.

He leaned in, running his fingers over the bumps of my spine that led up into the base of my skull. As Father Thomas began to massage my shoulders, I felt his warm breath against my neck and an ache rose up in my belly. The heat that had previously enveloped my face now traveled down my stomach and into my core, making it tingle in response.

"Father, I—" I tried to stand up but he pressed his hands down on my shoulders, pinning me to the bed.

"Delilah." His voice was suddenly different. More gravelly and hoarse. "My sweet Delilah. Do you have any idea how beautiful you are?"

Even as there was a part of me that knew how wrong the words were, still I couldn't help but respond to them. "I'm not the beautiful one. Ruth is."

"No. She has no light inside of her. No purity at all. But you . . . you . . . are perfect." He placed his lips against my neck and let his arms drop so that his hands were on my elbows, pinning them to my sides.

His breath seemed to come in ragged gasps and mine sped up in response. How I'd yearned to be told that just once in my life. If it had come from anyone else, I wouldn't have believed it, but I'd seen the way Ruth had looked at Father Thomas and I'd seen the way he'd spurned her. Not even Riaan, who I knew loved me, had ever told me I was more beautiful than my sister.

I felt something moist and hot travel from my neck to my ear and realized that Father Thomas was mapping a trail across my skin with his tongue. All that existed then was the heat from his body pressed against mine and the glorious thrill of it.

It was when Father Thomas cupped my breast over my night-gown that I recovered from my daze and returned to my senses. What we were doing was wrong.

Matthew 26:41 leapt to mind. *Watch and pray, that ye enter not into temptation: the spirit indeed is willing, but the flesh is weak.* The molten feeling from earlier, the delicious warmth, was gone. Instead, I felt afraid.

"No, Father, please."

"Don't play games, Delilah. Don't be coy now when you're finally getting what you wanted."

"No, I don't want—"

"Don't pretend this isn't what you and your sister were whispering about earlier, and why you were so happy when I told you we had to spend the night here. This is what you wanted. You are true to your name, Delilah. You are the destroyer of men's powers."

He stood and walked around the bed, pushing me backward as he climbed on top of me. His eyes were closed but mine were wide open, fixed on his face, which wore an expression I'd never seen before, one of such hunger and need that it made him look ferocious. It occurred to me then, and in the many sleepless nights that came afterward, that I had made him like that. I'd turned him from a devout man of God into a beast driven by animal urges. Just as I'd done the same thing to Riaan the previous night.

When it was over, Father Thomas rose and got dressed.

I couldn't move. I just lay there in shock, feeling my heart thudding against my breastbone as the bruises began to develop across my body. He went to the bathroom to fetch a towel, which he then tossed over me. "Clean yourself up and get dressed."

I did as instructed.

"Come, let us pray," he said, making me kneel down beside him. "Our Lord, Jesus Christ, Redeemer and Savior, I ask that you forgive Delilah her sins. She came here today with the express purpose of seducing a man of God. She allowed Satan to take up residence in her heart and acted like a Jezebel. In the same way that you forgave Peter's denial and those who crucified you, forgive Delilah her trespasses against one of your most faithful sons." He stood then. "We'll never speak of this again."

And he stayed true to his word. We never did.

The next morning, without any further reference to a replacement part for the car, we set off for the convent.

CHAPTER SIXTY-TWO

Zodwa

※

16 August 1995
Verdriet, Magaliesburg, South Africa

The one and a half months since Zodwa starting working at the farm have passed swiftly. When she walks from the main house to her cottage, she notices how winter has released its stingy grip, frugality giving way to abundance, mirroring her own improved circumstances.

Zodwa now earns more in a month than what she made at the *shebeen* in four. She doesn't need to spend any of her earnings on food or toiletries because the sisters are generous, ensuring most of her physical needs are met. She's sending more money home to her *gogo,* but also has enough to save toward a future that she now dares to dream about. Not that she's there for the money. Even if they didn't pay her a cent, she'd still do the job because it allows her access to her son.

Zodwa's matric exams are coming up. She fills every night with studying so that the hours after bidding Mandla farewell don't stretch out longer than they need to. Through burying herself in her coursework, Zodwa is remembering the girl she was before the rape, the one who loved learning and who excelled in her studies. If she demeans herself by laboring for these women, then surely there's dignity to be found in watching over her son. If she degrades herself by scrubbing their toilets and floors, then surely there's pride to be felt in the fact that Mandla's world is made brighter by her endeavors.

That's what she tells herself every day, which she begins by having breakfast with the family. It's a ritual that Delilah started a week or so after Zodwa's arrival when she discovered Zodwa eating by herself on the veranda while the two sisters and Mandla ate together at the dining room table.

"Why don't you come inside and join us?" she'd asked.

"I'm fine here, Madam Delilah."

"Please, call me Delilah. There's no 'madam' necessary."

Zodwa was taken aback by the offer. While she thought of the sisters as merely Ruth and Delilah, Ruth had told her to call her Madam Ruth and she'd assumed the other sister would want to be addressed similarly. The new arrangement had clearly rankled Ruth at first. She'd looked annoyed as Zodwa struggled to use a knife and fork for things she would normally have just used her hands for, but Ruth soon seemed to get used to the idea since it meant Mandla was generally in a better mood. There's something about Zodwa that engages him and he's quicker to laugh in her company.

Even if the boy didn't have the Africa-shaped birthmark on his buttock and look so much like Dumisa, Zodwa's certain she would have recognized him purely on the bond that exists between them. It's as if Mandla knows that he spent the first nine months of his journey nestled in her womb, as if he recognizes the sound of her voice from before he came into the world. He's a contemplative child who wears a frown more often than a smile, and Zodwa knows that his solemnity is her fault. She shaped her son's skeptical view of the world. She remembers the first words she ever spoke directly to him, on the day the *gogo* had been denied the opportunity to vote.

Now you know what to expect from this world.

She strives to undo the harm of that warning by trying to make him laugh every day. Silly antics usually do the trick, but when they don't, Zodwa resorts to singing Miriam Makeba's "Qongqothwane," or "The Click Song" as the whites call it. The explosive Xhosa sounds and rapid-fire lyrics hardly ever fail to elicit belly laughs from Mandla. It's gotten to the point where Ruth will sometimes pass her the fussy child and say, "For God's sake, click the child happy."

Zodwa's days pass with the same rhythms. Mondays, Wednesdays, and Fridays are cleaning days where her focus is on washing dishes, vacuuming, dusting, and mopping. Tuesdays and Thursdays are days spent washing and ironing clothes and bed linen, as well as cleaning the windows and the outside areas. She eats her lunch by herself and always takes her supper to her room. Zodwa savors the time she gets to spend alone with Mandla, which only happens when Ruth is bathing or getting dressed.

Ruth is mostly homebound. She never gets any visitors and hardly ever leaves the house, with or without the boy. She goes grocery shopping once a week and she takes Mandla with her. Ruth only leaves Mandla behind with Delilah once a month when she drives to Johannesburg to see her hairdresser.

Ruth is nothing if not mercurial. Some days, the woman is overly effusive, insisting that Zodwa sit next to her and keep her company. Especially on days when she opens a bottle of wine in the afternoon. Other days, she's so standoffish that it makes Zodwa wonder what she's done to offend her. Ruth's mood swings generally tend toward the darker side when Mandla is being especially affectionate to Zodwa or if he cries when Zodwa leaves.

Zodwa has also noticed that Ruth's general outlook is intricately tied to Mandla's well-being. The woman fusses over the child constantly, treating him like a delicate object that could shatter at any moment rather than the robust boy he is. If he shows any signs of sickening, her doting becomes smothering.

It's surprising that Mandla ever gets sick considering the amount of *umuthi* the woman gives him daily. Zodwa's tried to read the labels of all the bottles of syrups and formulas to see what they're for, but Ruth keeps the medicine cupboard locked at all times. It's the only thing she locks—she doesn't even lock her purse or her jewelry away—and Zodwa can't imagine why she feels the need to.

There are many things that the whites do that confound Zodwa. They're overly concerned with privacy and personal space yet are content to let the dog lick them in the face. Security is a big concern of theirs with bars on the windows and doors, and various panic buttons distributed throughout the house.

Zodwa isn't allowed to answer the phone or open the door; it's as if they don't deem her vigilant enough to guard against the threats that stalk them from outside the walls. Whatever it is, Zodwa is convinced it's as imaginary as the perceived threat against Mandla's health. Delilah constantly tells Ruth not to fuss over the child, but the woman doesn't listen to her own sister, and so she'd definitely not listen to Zodwa even if she built up the courage to comment on it.

The radio is constantly playing in the house because Ruth hates silence, and it's on 702 Talk Radio that Zodwa finally hears more information about the rumored Truth and Reconciliation Commission that Archbishop Desmond Tutu is spearheading. She turns the sound up to listen to what they are saying, after which Delilah approaches her.

"The commission's an important first step toward reconciliation. Are you interested in general or on a personal level?"

Zodwa surprises herself by answering honestly. "My brother went missing from Soweto in 1984."

"Was he a member of the Inkatha Freedom Party? Because he was a Zulu?"

She's impressed that Delilah would know that. "Yes, he belonged to their Youth Brigade. He disappeared while doing some work for them, but we never discovered the whole truth."

"I'm so sorry, Zodwa. I can't imagine what it must be like for you. Not knowing what happened to him."

"My mother died last year and that was the hardest for her. Never being able to bury her son. I'm going to apply to the commission to see if they have any information about him. I know it's something she would have done."

Zodwa writes away for the forms and once she submits them, there's nothing left to do but to wait. If Dumisa's name comes up in the thousands of interviews the TRC is conducting, they will notify her. She's sure that Mama Beauty will know about the commission as well and that she's done the same thing for her daughter.

The days pass quickly and while Zodwa is lonely being so far removed from her people, it's a sacrifice she's willing to make. Going back to the township to visit on her days off would invite questions that she wouldn't be able to answer. She's also nervous about running into Ace and what he might say about her disappearance. It's better for her to stay away completely so that she doesn't see Thembeka either.

She has her son and she tells herself it's more than she could ever have hoped for.

CHAPTER SIXTY-THREE

Ruth

❂

22 August 1995
Hartbeespoort Dam, Gauteng, South Africa

We're at the Spur, a restaurant that caters more to whippersnappers than their parents. While the adults sit outside under a thatched roof, sipping beers and tucking into racks of ribs as patio heaters warm them up, their children run amok on a playground in the winter sunshine.

A futuristic-looking jungle gym, swings, and a seesaw take up one end of the playground, while sandboxes and a track with plastic motorbikes for toddlers takes up the other. It's a good business model, judging by how busy the place is. There's a birthday party in full swing at one of the tables, with all the kids wearing party hats that resemble Native American Indian headdresses.

The only reason we're here is because Mandla surprised us all by starting to walk a few days ago. Without any preamble, he apparently pulled himself straight up and took a few steps, chasing after Jezebel, sure-footed as a mountain goat.

Or so I was told by Zodwa, who was the one to see it.

I came into the room a minute later and saw her with her hands clamped over her mouth, tears in her eyes. When I followed her gaze, I spotted Mandla toddling off behind the dog.

"Why didn't you call me?" Even as I clapped for Mandla,

praising him for his achievement, I was annoyed by Zodwa's reaction. She treated my son's milestone as if it was a private moment between the two of them.

"Sorry, Madam Ruth," she said, but I got the distinct impression that the apology was an empty one.

Mandla's been unstoppable ever since, and Dee talked me into taking him out so that he could walk freely without ricocheting off a wall or entering an area of the garden that's likely to be snake infested.

A woman comes up to our table now and reaches out to touch Mandla's face. I tense, ready to snatch him away if necessary.

"What a gorgeous child. Just look at those eyes." She appears to be about thirty years old and could be a fashion model. Definitely not a local then. I relax and smile back. "What's your name, cutie?" she asks him.

"Mandla," I answer because he obviously can't speak for himself.

"I have a friend who's also looking into adoption. Are you his grandmother?"

I bristle. "No, I'm his foster mother."

"Oh," she squeaks. "Cool." She clearly thinks I'm too old to be a baby's mother, foster or otherwise, but has the good sense to keep her opinion to herself. "It's my son's second birthday and we're having a little party over there. Bring Mandla over if you like. I'm Michelle, by the way."

"I'm Ruth. And thank you! That's so nice of you." I'm not normally this effusive, but I'm so relieved by her kindness that I'd happily hug her just then if she wasn't already walking away.

An all-too-familiar smell suddenly wafts up and I groan. The combination of Mandla's immune booster and the weight-gain supplement he's on makes his shit stink to high heaven.

"Come on, big guy." I pick him up and take him to the bathroom, where there's a changing table.

I'm ready to apologize to anyone unlucky enough to join us in there—seriously, the stench of it is enough to strip paint off the walls—but luck is on our side. It's only once I've thrown the nappy away in a sealed bag that a woman walks in and disappears into one of the stalls. She flushes the toilet a few minutes later and comes out again, joining us at the basins just as I'm pulling up Mandla's pants.

She looks to be in her early twenties and is a whippet of a thing with long blond hair that's about ten shades too white to be natural. Despite the gloom of the bathroom, she's wearing big sunglasses. They mostly cover up her bruised eye, but not when you look at her from the side. She has a nervous energy that I recognize. I used to have it once too when I was around her age and getting the shit kicked out of me regularly. Ma had it too, now that I think about it.

As she washes her hands, she casts quick looks at Mandla, who's smiling at her. She doesn't smile back. When she catches my gaze in the mirror, she spits out, "And what are you looking at?" She speaks in Afrikaans but I answer her in English.

"I'm looking at that shiner. Let me guess, you walked into a door?"

She seems taken aback and mutters an unconvincing, "Mind your own business."

"Fair enough. Let me just say from personal experience that doors that hurt you don't ever stop. No matter how many times they say they're sorry and they'll change. The only way to stop them is to leave."

With that, I pick up Mandla and walk out.

Once we're back at the table, the waitress returns with our order of a juice box for Mandla and a glass of wine for me. I'm aware, while unwrapping the straw and sticking it into the silver-foil circle, how we're attracting attention. People try to pretend they're not looking, but Mandla and I make an odd pair, and eyes flit over to us more often than they do to the playground.

Mandla squirms in the high chair. I pull him up out of it and set him down on the paved floor, handing him his juice in the process. He reaches for my hand with his free one and the gesture makes me smile as he leads me toward the track with the plastic motorbikes. None of them are free just then and children whiz by, legs pumping against the ground to give themselves momentum. Mandla watches, fascinated, as the kids do their laps, some of them crashing into each other, making each other shriek.

After a few minutes, a little boy who looks to be about five breaks away from the pack and comes to a halt in front of us. He has curly brown hair and is picking his nose unabashedly while staring at Mandla with fascination.

He doesn't say anything, just continues attempting to tunnel into his brain until I finally say, "Hello."

"Hello." He sounds nasal, which is to be expected considering how far up his nose his finger is.

"What's your name?"

"Kyle."

"Have you found any yet?"

"What?"

"Diamonds. Up your nose. Isn't that what you're digging for?"

He blinks and pulls his finger out, staring at the snot on the tip of it like a jeweler appraising a stone, trying to decide how many carats it's worth.

I stifle a laugh and point to Mandla. "This is Mandla."

"Is he your baby?"

"Yes, he is." I try to ignore the emotion that has unexpectedly welled up in my throat.

"Was he born like that?"

"What do you mean?"

"Was he born brown or did he change color?"

I laugh. "He was born that way."

"Oh," he says, unimpressed. "I'm thirsty." He reaches out and snatches Mandla's juice box.

Before I can react, a woman rushes at us. "Leave it, Kyle. I said leave it."

"But I want juice," the child whines, and I'm about to tell the mother it's fine, that Mandla hasn't even had a sip yet, when the woman grabs the juice from his hand. She's one of the patrons I caught staring earlier.

"It's okay," I say to his mother. "He can have some."

The woman ignores me and speaks to her child. "This one is yucky. You'll get sick if you drink from it."

Kyle starts to screech and another mother nearby plucks a juice box from her own child's hands and gives it to him. Kyle's mother doesn't say anything in protest as he takes big gulping sips from the straw even though the girl who unwillingly donated it looks like she has a cold judging by all the gunk crusted around her nose.

"I beg your pardon but what did you mean by that?" If word of Mandla's HIV status has somehow spread around town, I need to be aware of it.

She finally speaks to me directly. "You know what I mean."

"No, actually. I don't. My child isn't sick but that girl is. And yet you have no problem with your child sharing her germs."

"God alone knows what kinds of germs he has," she says, indicating Mandla. "*Kaffirs* are dirty. Everyone knows that."

The slur renders me speechless for a second. It's so utterly vicious and directed with such venom at a beautiful, innocent child that I feel sucker punched.

How dare she speak that way about my boy? How fucking dare she?

I'm about to give her a piece of my mind when the woman from earlier, Michelle, speaks from behind me. "Since you're so concerned about protecting the health of other children, you probably shouldn't have come here with a child that has impetigo. That's really contagious." She points at the scabs on Kyle's chin.

All the mothers near him suddenly reach for their children to pull them away from his infectious scabs. Kyle, startled by all the activity around him, begins to cry again and his mother swoops in to comfort him.

"Not so nice when it's your child being ostracized, is it?" I ask, picking Mandla up and walking away with Michelle. She pretends not to notice the tears that stream down my face as I kiss Mandla over and over again, telling him what a wonderful boy he is, how kind and sweet and precious.

When we're in the parking lot half an hour later and I'm strapping Mandla into his car seat, a *bakkie* that's leaving suddenly accelerates toward us, missing the open passenger door, and me behind it, by mere inches. There's glare on the windscreen, so I only see who it is as they swerve to miss us and shoot past.

The girl with the black eye and the sunglasses is in the passenger seat. She's sitting next to Klein Maynard Coetzee, the right-winger Afrikaner who's been directing threats at us for over a year. He watches me in the rearview mirror and the hate in that reflected gaze makes me shudder.

CHAPTER SIXTY-FOUR

Delilah

❉

1 October 1995
Verdriet, Magaliesburg, and Our Lady of the
Holy Trinity, Johannesburg, South Africa

The song that was playing on the radio the day I left Daniel behind at the convent was "Unchained Melody" by the Righteous Brothers. It's something I'd never forgotten because the ballad about loss and regret felt like it was being sung especially for me as Father Thomas drove me to the airport.

So when I woke up on what would have been Daniel's fortieth birthday to the sound of Ruth singing along with it on the radio, I knew it was my sign. It was time to finally claim my son. I briefly considered calling Riaan and asking him to make the drive with me, but quickly decided against it. Things had been strained between us since the night in the tent three months before when he'd kissed me and I'd reacted so strongly. Besides, how would I possibly explain Daniel's existence to him?

I was surprised and then touched by Ruth's response when I told her where I was going. "I'll come with you. You're going to need some moral support." And then she winked and smiled. "Just so you know, I offer immoral support as well, in case you ever need that too."

"What about Mandla?"

"I'll get Zodwa to come in and look after him."

"It's Sunday, Ruth."

"That's fine. I'll pay her overtime."

Zodwa kindly agreed—looking happier than I ever would have been to look after a child on my only day off—and Ruth left a long list of instructions with her for Mandla's care. Considering he was sick with a bad cold and that Ruth was so paranoid about his health, I was touched that she was prepared to leave him for the day.

We pulled up outside Daniel's church, Our Lady of the Holy Trinity, just after the second service had cleared out.

"Do you want me to come in with you?" Ruth asked, eyeing the church as though she might burst into flames if she set foot inside.

"No, I think I need to do this by myself."

She looked relieved. "Okay. There's a restaurant just across the road. I'll go sit there and have lunch while I wait for you. Join me when you're ready. Go claim that boy of yours."

Though I'd never set foot in Daniel's church before, being there felt like a homecoming. It had been a lifetime since I'd stood within the walls of a Catholic church and yet it was as familiar as breathing. My being there required no thinking, no effort at all.

Christ was nailed on the cross before me, dying for my sins. His hands and feet were bleeding, and his head, with its crown of thorns, was dipped low. The stained-glass windows depicting various biblical scenes cast yellow, blue, and red shadows onto me, making me think back to the day I first saw Father Thomas.

I knelt then in Daniel's church, the place where he'd given hundreds of sermons and blessings, where he'd married hopeful young couples and eulogized those whose days of hope had passed; where he'd blessed and forgiven and worshipped and prayed.

I looked up at the pulpit and tried to imagine my son there. I wondered what the timbre of his voice had sounded like. If it was gruff and pitched low like his grandfather's or if it was more melodious like his father's. Did he gesture when he spoke, drawing the congregation in, or did he stand still as a statue, trusting that his words would find their mark?

I hoped that he had been kind and quick to forgive. I hoped he had empathized rather than condemned. I thought he would have but I was also aware of how easy it would be to canonize him. I bent my head then and prayed for the first time in four decades. The last prayer I'd ever uttered was on that day forty years before, after Daniel was born and I handed him across to the Reverend Mother. Then, I'd prayed for God to watch over my son and protect him from harm. Now, I prayed to my son for forgiveness for ever entrusting that job to anyone but myself.

I have no idea how much time passed, but the shadows cast by the stained glass had lengthened across the room by the time I rose. When I turned to leave, I saw a nun sitting a few rows behind me. She wasn't praying. She was staring at me intently.

I smiled a greeting and she smiled back before rising and walking toward me.

"It is you," she said. "I knew you'd come, but I thought it would be sooner."

"Pardon?"

"You don't remember me?"

She looked to be in her sixties and was thickset with rounded cheeks and a florid complexion. I was about to shake my head but suddenly I was back in the convent on the day of my arrival, changing in front of a novice who looked at my bruises without uttering a word.

"Ah." She smiled. "You do."

"Yes," I replied. "I remember you from the convent. Sister Marguerite, isn't it?"

"Yes, and you're Delilah. Come," she said. "I'll show you his office and his grave."

"Whose?"

"Why, Father Daniel's of course. That's why you've come, isn't it?"

Without another word, she led me from the church and to a small building that stood to the side of it. "Another priest took over after Father Daniel's passing, but I assigned him other rooms so I could keep Father Daniel's intact in case you came. It wasn't difficult getting Father Michael to agree, considering what happened there."

I realized that she was referring to Daniel's attack and wasn't sure I was ready to see the scene of it. I stopped on the stone path, and as if reading my mind, Sister Marguerite turned and said, "There's nothing in there now that can hurt you. Come."

When we reached a room at the end of the hallway, she unhooked a chain of keys from her belt and used one to unlock the door. "This is where he spent most of his time."

The room was just as I'd imagined it, with its scarred wooden desk taking up most of the space and its walls that were covered in rows and rows of books. A large crucifix hung on the only bare wall, opposite the desk, and a threadbare carpet and couch took up the rest of the space. Dust motes twirled through the air and the scent of pinewood polish clung to everything.

The desk was bare except for a blotter made of paper, a

globe, a lamp, and a few framed photographs, which I picked up. One showed Daniel graduating from seminary school as a young man. He stood next to Sister Marguerite, who was beaming, her face half turned toward his. In another he was holding a baby at a christening, while in another, he was shaking a young black man's hand.

"That's Shaun's christening. Daniel was his godfather. And that young man is Vusi. Daniel mentored him in a youth program."

"Can you tell me what happened? The night he was shot?"

She was quiet for a while and then said, "They came in to rob the place and weren't expecting to find him here in the early hours of the morning. He must have given them a fright." She was quiet for a moment, remembering. "He was an insomniac. And when he couldn't sleep, he'd come here to work on his sermons or to read. He hadn't been sleeping those few weeks."

"You knew him well." It was a statement, not a question.

"Oh, my. Yes. I helped raised him after you left."

And all at once, I realized who she was. Father Thomas's words from the hospital came back to me.

Take a look, Delilah. That's Daniel's mother. She's been his mother ever since you left.

As I was still processing that information, she continued, oblivious to my surprise. "And then when he was ordained and was assigned here, I moved with him as a kind of secretary-slash-housekeeper. I should have been here that night as well, but he'd bought me a bus ticket to East London so I could visit with an ailing friend for a few days. He was that kind of man. Selfless and thoughtful. I didn't want to leave him, knowing what he was going through, but he insisted that he was fine."

"What he was going through?" She opened her mouth to

speak, and then paused and cleared her throat. Her eyes flicked away before they were drawn back. Something about the gesture—her obvious reluctance to say what she was about to say—made my stomach feel fluttery. "What was he going through?" I repeated, throat dry.

"He'd just recently found out, you see."

"About what?"

"Who you were."

"Who I was?" I asked, confused.

"Yes, that you were his mother."

CHAPTER SIXTY-FIVE

Zodwa

❂

1 October 1995
Verdriet, Magaliesburg, South Africa

It's the first time Zodwa has gotten to spend more than half an hour unsupervised with her son. She has no idea what the emergency was or why the sisters had to suddenly go to Johannesburg, nor does she care. The day has been an unexpected gift.

Mandla sits on the couch next to Zodwa, fighting sleep as he gulps from his sippy cup. He's exhausted from a frenetic morning spent chasing her from room to room. Each time he caught her and she lifted him up in a celebratory swoop, he squealed and then demanded to go again just as soon as his feet touched the floor. Zodwa winced when each scream of excitement was coupled with a bout of coughing that rattled Mandla's lungs, but she didn't cut the playtime short because of it.

She knows she shouldn't have let Mandla exert himself so much considering that he's had a cold for the past month, but she loves the sound of her son's laughter so much that she can't say no to him. Zodwa also can't bring herself to force the medicine he hates so much down his throat.

The pink syrup may smell like fruit but it tastes like chalk and makes him gag. Zodwa can't blame Mandla for not keeping it down or for his hysteria when he sees her coming at him with the liquid-filled syringe. She has so little quality time with him that she doesn't want to ruin it by being the one to enforce rules and make him swallow bitter medication. He also hates her constantly wiping at the mucus that runs from his nose into his mouth.

Once he's finished with the rooibos tea, Mandla passes the cup to Zodwa. He usually calls her "Dwa," since he can't pronounce her full name, but now as he reaches for her hand, he says, "Mama."

Zodwa doesn't know what prompted it, as she's never tried to get him to call her that. While she's desperate for her son's love, the last thing she wants is to confuse him. Still, it's as if he sees through the charade of what she's doing there and can see into the truth of their relationship.

"Mama," he says again, grabbing her index finger.

Zodwa doesn't realize she's crying until Mandla reaches up and wipes a tear from her cheek and then brings his hand to his face to inspect his fingers. Once he's made sure that the tears don't stain, he turns and tucks his head into Zodwa's chest so he can rest against her. That's how he falls asleep, listening to his mother's heartbeat.

For the first time since she's been there, Zodwa wonders: If she ran with him, how far would they get before Ruth came for them?

CHAPTER SIXTY-SIX

Delilah

1 October 1995
Johannesburg, South Africa

"Are you okay? You've gone terribly pale," Sister Marguerite said, her brow scrunched in concern as she steadied me.

"He knew . . . he knew I was his mother?"

"Yes, he'd gone looking for you at your last-known address. I'd helped him find your admittance records so we could track it down. It was a farm in Magaliesburg but you weren't there."

Sarie's words came back to me then.

Did your friend find you, by the way?

What friend?

The one who came here just over a month ago looking for you. I told him you hadn't lived here since you were a girl and that the family was all long gone. He was very disappointed.

Sister Marguerite was still talking. "I told him you wouldn't be there, that your last-known address was in Zaire, but he insisted on checking for himself. I think he was hoping to find some family even if he didn't find you."

He knew about me. Daniel knew about me before he died. I wasn't the stranger that I'd imagined I was as I'd stood there outside the ICU staring in. If he'd woken and seen me, he would have recognized me for who I was. The thought makes me want to both laugh and weep.

"Wait," I ask, needing her to slow down so that I can properly process everything she's saying. "How did he find out? About me, I mean."

"I told him."

"You?"

"Yes. I'd kept the secret all those years, but you know what children are like. They overhear things, don't they? So he knew a lot more than I gave him credit for. When we finally spoke about it, he said he'd suspected that the nun who'd been sent away the year he was born was his mother, though he didn't know any of your details beyond the name you'd chosen for yourself, Sister Mary Teresa. He asked me to fill in the blanks and so I did."

My skull throbbed from the pressure of all my unshed tears and as I winced at the pain of the tension headache, all at once I couldn't hold them back anymore.

He knew who I was. My boy knew.

"Oh, my dear heart. Oh, you poor, poor thing." Sister Marguerite held out her arms and swept me into them.

"Daniel, Daniel, Daniel." I had no words except my son's name. It was a prayer and an invocation, a confession and a lament; it was *please* and *thank you*; it was *forgive me* and *amen*.

Sister Marguerite held on tight, riding out the storm with me until the worst had passed. When she sensed that I was able to stand on my own again, she released me and then led me to the couch, where she instructed me to sit down while she hunted for some tissues.

"There you go. Are you feeling a bit better?"

I nodded as I dabbed at my eyes. "Yes, thank you. I'm so sorry."

"There's nothing to be sorry for."

"I'm fine now," I said. "Please continue. You were telling me about his finding out."

"I was just going to add that he didn't suspect who his father was until Father Thomas's trial. That's when Daniel worked it out for himself."

"I'm sorry? Father Thomas's trial? What trial?"

"You didn't know?"

"No."

"They wrote to you to see if you would come and be a witness but they never heard back, so I just assumed you wanted to put all that behind you."

"They? Who's they?"

"I just thought . . . well, that makes sense now, doesn't it?" She saw my look of frustration and shook her head. "Sorry. Let me start at the beginning. Three years ago, two young women from Father Thomas's congregation went to the police charging him with sexual assault. A case was opened and it went to trial a year ago. None of the nuns wanted to testify against him, even though some of them went through what you'd been through, but you were an ex-novice, you see, and had nothing to lose, so I thought you might consider it. I gave them your address but they never heard back."

"I never got their letter. The postal service wasn't very reliable." I had so many questions but the one that came out was one that had been niggling from before: "How did you know that I was in Zaire? How did you have my address there?"

"I've been keeping tabs on your whereabouts. I'm the one who's been sending you the photos of Daniel throughout the years."

"That was you?"

She nodded. "I couldn't imagine what it was like, having to

give up your child like that, especially under those circumstances. I wanted you to know that he was fine and that he was cared for even though you couldn't be with him."

"I'd always thought it was Father Thomas sending them but he denied it at the hospital."

"The hospital?"

"Yes, I saw him there when I went to try and visit Daniel."

"You were there? I kept hoping you'd come but I never saw you."

"I saw you," I said. "Twice. Once in May and then on . . . on the day Daniel died."

"But, Delilah . . . I don't understand . . . Why didn't you come in to see him or at least try to speak with me?"

"Father Thomas told me that my being there would upset you, that you were Daniel's real mother and that I had no right to see him."

She shook her head, clearly angry. "He wouldn't leave at first. He insisted on being there even though he had no right and it's not what Daniel would have wanted. I was too shocked and upset early on to put my foot down but when I'd finally had enough, and I threatened him . . . then he left."

Her fury is what betrayed her. "He did the same thing to you, didn't he?"

She bowed her head. "How do you know?"

"It was the way you looked at my bruises that day after he dropped me off at the convent. Like you knew what had caused them. And the way you were afterward when everyone found out. Like you understood."

"I did. I was just lucky enough not to get pregnant."

"So, you didn't testify?"

"No."

"Why not?"

"The church convinced me not to. They convinced all of us not to, as they like to handle their own affairs internally."

"I assume he didn't go to prison."

"No." She sighed. "He was acquitted."

I snorted. "So where is he now?"

"He was forced to retire. He's in a home not too far from here."

"And you say Daniel knew? About the . . . that Father Thomas was his real father?"

"Yes, he figured it out after all the allegations. It shook him terribly," she said. "They were close, he and Father Thomas. Daniel had even taken Father Thomas's last name, but while he saw him as a father figure, he never suspected he was his real father. It changed everything he thought he knew about the world. That's why I tried to help him find you. He was sitting up writing a letter to you on the night he was shot."

"How do you know that?"

"I found it after the attack. The letter was in an envelope addressed to you."

"But . . . why didn't you send it to me?"

"I knew nothing about you, Delilah. What state of mind you were in, or what may have been going on in your life. I wasn't even certain where in the world you were and I wasn't just prepared to send that out without knowing it would reach you . . . or if you were emotionally equipped to deal with it. I wanted you to be ready for it and I knew you'd come when you were. I've been waiting for you. I was waiting for you at the hospital."

"And Father Thomas was there standing guard, making sure we never spoke."

With that, she walked around the desk and used another key to unlock a drawer. She withdrew an airmail envelope from it and handed it across. "Here you go. Now I can be certain it's safely in your hands."

I took it with trembling fingers. "Thank you."

"You can read it later when you're ready. For now, would you like to go visit his grave? I can tell you more about him if you like."

"Yes, I'd like that very much."

We spoke for hours, Sister Marguerite and I, and speaking to the closest person Daniel ever had to a mother was the closest I'd ever felt to him. It was a gift he bestowed me on his birthday, one I would cherish until the day I died.

When I finally joined Ruth at the restaurant, I apologized for making her wait so long.

She brushed it off. "These things can't be rushed. Are you hungry?"

I shook my head. I hadn't eaten since a few nervous bites of toast at breakfast but I felt more satiated than I had in years. We set off for home and, perhaps because it was dark, or because Ruth had to face forward with her eyes on the road—I was too cowardly to look into my sister's eyes—but I started talking. I needed to drain the poison from me and tell someone exactly what had happened.

Perhaps it was knowing that I wasn't the only one it had happened to, but I felt compelled to share it then in a way I never had before.

"Ruth?"

"Yes?"

"Something happened to me that I want to tell you about."

"Okay, you know you can tell me anything."

And despite everything, how much I'd always resented her and how different we were—despite the fact that we'd never been close, and that she'd infuriated me with her self-absorption—I knew she was right.

And so I started telling her the truth about how Daniel was conceived and everything that followed. As I spoke, it all came back to me, everything that happened on that day, and afterward, when Father Thomas discovered my pregnancy. In my mind's eye, I saw him enveloping me in a hug as I stood to go, and how his expression changed so swiftly when he realized what my swollen belly pressed against him signified. He'd stood frozen for a moment, horror written on his face.

"What have you done, Delilah? What have you done?" he whispered.

Gone was the novitiate name that he'd called me a mere half an hour before. I was no longer Sister Mary Teresa to him. I'd reverted to Delilah, "the destroyer of men's powers."

"I'm—I'm sorry, Father," I stammered.

"Sorry?" He looked at me as though I was the embodiment of Satan, sent there by his enemies to annihilate him. "You've completely and utterly ruined me and yet all you can say is that you're sorry?"

"I didn't mean—"

"Be still! I don't want to hear another word out of your whorish mouth, do you hear me?"

I nodded, trying to check the terrified tears that were falling, but failing miserably.

His hands rose to his face and he began pacing, muttering to himself all the while. When he finally stilled, I could see that his expression had cleared like the sky after a storm. The shift was as sudden as the one I remembered from that day all those months ago and I marveled at how he could so swiftly move from one persona to the next like Dr. Jekyll and Mr. Hyde.

He turned to me and pinned me to the spot by the force of his stare. "You will never speak of what you did to me in that room. You will never tell a soul of how you were my undoing, do you understand?"

"Yes, Father."

"No one can know. When they ask you, you will refuse to answer because in boasting of your sin, you will taint that child with it." He nodded at my belly. "Is that what you want? To ruin your child's soul before it's even born?"

"No, Father. No, please, I—"

"If you keep our secret, I will save your child. Do you understand, Delilah? Do you agree?"

"Yes, Father."

"Promise to leave straight after his birth, never to return and never to speak of this, and I promise to always take care of him. Vow it now."

I hesitated for a moment, trying to think through the implications of what he'd said, and then his hands were upon my shoulders, shaking me. "Vow it in God's name!"

And I did.

By then, my sobbing had attracted the attention of the Reverend Mother, who knocked on the door and flew in before she'd been beckoned inside. "My goodness. What is going on in here? Sister Mary Teresa, what—"

That's when Father Thomas told her of my condition and everything was cast into turmoil. No matter how many times they asked me who the father was, I refused to answer. And with each refusal, Father Thomas grew stronger and more out-spoken in defense of my child even as he condemned me.

As I spoke, Ruth listened without once interrupting me or saying a word, lighting cigarette after cigarette with trembling fingers. When I was finally done, she spoke through clenched teeth. "I'll kill the fucking bastard. Where is he? Tell me he's still alive so I can find him and beat the living shit out of him."

"But don't you see? You were right all that time. I was madly in love with him and I was attracted to him. When he was kissing me, I responded to him. I let him kiss me because it felt good." It cost me everything to admit to that and yet I had to own up to my part in what happened.

"What the hell has that got to do with anything? You said no when he took it further. You asked him to stop."

"But I'd already seduced him by then, by sending him all those signals that I—"

"What signals? Making sure your whole body was covered by your bathrobe? Not licking his finger? Telling him you didn't want a massage and that you didn't want to take your robe off? Is that your idea of seduction?"

"No, of course not, but . . ." I trailed off. "But he said I'd tempted him—"

"Of course he did. What better way to avoid blame for your own behavior than to blame it on someone else?"

"But I responded to his kiss."

"Only for a moment before you told him to stop. Jesus, you're human, Dee! Human! We all have weaknesses and that son of a bitch was the most good-looking man I'd ever seen. It would have been impossible not to respond to him in some way. Our bodies betray us all the time, all the time. But that doesn't matter. What matters is that you wanted him to stop and you told him so."

"I did."

"He raped you. Please tell me you know that?"

And suddenly, for the very first time, I thought I did.

When we pulled up outside the farmhouse, Ruth unclipped her seat belt and turned to me. I saw then that she'd been crying steadily; her makeup was ruined and mascara trailed down her cheeks in inky rivulets. She leaned forward and clasped me toward her. We both cried until there were no tears left, and nothing to do but go inside, where Zodwa waited for us in the open doorway.

CHAPTER SIXTY-SEVEN

Ruth

❋

10 October 1995
Verdriet, Magaliesburg, South Africa

I t's been more than a week since Dee confided in me and I still can't shake the rage I feel on her behalf. It boils my blood to think that bastard priest not only raped her but then told her that she'd seduced him and, naïve girl that she was, she believed him. It shouldn't surprise me; I've seen the same thing play out in dozens of different scenarios over the years.

As women, we're told our worth and our value, and the many ways in which we fall short of others' expectations; we're told why we're whores and why society can't tolerate whores. We're reminded of the ways we dishonor the unwritten contract we didn't know we signed on the day of our birth: a contract in which we agreed to toe the line and know our place simply because we are the fairer sex.

Shit, I think I'm becoming one of those hairy, bra-burning feminists in my old age.

I always wondered why the priest had paid so much attention to Dee while ignoring me and I finally understand why. He knew the world of women is split into two types: the ones like me who'll kick a man like him in the nuts, and the ones like Dee who'll swallow the poison he feeds them, allowing it to slowly kill them. Predators like that have a sixth sense for picking out the prey that will succumb most easily, which is not the same as the weakest; if anything, Dee has proven to be the stronger of the two of us.

The intercom buzzes, interrupting my thoughts, and when I check the screen, it's a delivery van. I go cold, remembering the last delivery of the doll with the hunting knife through its head. Still, things seem to have settled down. It's even been a while since the last threatening phone call.

"Yes?" I ask through the intercom.

"I have a delivery for Ruth Richardson," a man says.

"I don't suppose you know what it is?"

"Documents," he replies, which makes me breathe a sigh of relief as I press the button to open the gate.

Mandla and Zodwa are sitting at the dining room table as he eats lunch. Jezebel sits crouched at their feet, ready to scrounge whatever Mandla drops. Considering he insists on feeding himself, she gets more than her share of scraps.

When I open the door, the man hands me a clipboard. "Please sign to confirm receipt."

He shoves a large brown envelope at me and makes a run for it when Jez decides that a visitor is more interesting than the peas and carrots raining down from above.

"Should we see what this is, Jez? Hm? Another offer for me to write my memoirs? Or a documentary request? Should we put some money on it?"

She whines in response as I reach for a knife to slit the envelope open. It takes me a minute or two to realize that it's a legal document inside, and not the kind I was imagining.

"That son of a bitch," I whisper, dropping the divorce papers on the table. "He did it. He actually did it." It's difficult to breathe past the rock of hurt that has wedged in my throat.

Wrestling off my engagement and wedding rings, I march to the front door, fling it open, and then throw them out. I mean for it to be a dramatic gesture, and for the pieces of jewelry to disappear into the long grass—where they can languish in the vipers' nests, fitting, because the man who gave them to me is a snake—but instead, they clatter onto the gravel just beyond the steps.

The diamond of my engagement ring sparkles in the sunlight, mocking me with its cheeriness.

"Damn it."

I grab the remote control and then march down the steps, pick up both rings, and then make my way out the electric gate and along the driveway to the overgrown pathway that leads to the dam. Winded by the time I get to the water, I have to take a minute to catch my breath. As I do so, I stare at the rings in my palm. The perfect rose stem profile of the engagement ring, its pinkish hue, brings back so many memories that it makes me well up again despite my fury.

I'd sworn not to marry again after my second divorce, and I'd managed to stick to that resolution for a full ten years before I met Vince and was instantly captivated by his kind eyes and gentle soul. He was a man ruled by his intellect rather than his passions, which was one of the things that attracted me.

Vince was the only one of my husbands who'd had the foresight to buy a ring before his proposal, so I knew it hadn't been a spontaneous gesture, a giddy impulse in the spur of the moment. He surprised me by taking me to dinner at an exclusive restaurant in a vineyard in Paarl. I hadn't expected such a fancy place and stuck out like a sore thumb.

"You should have told me I wasn't dressed classy enough," I whispered to Vince as we made our way through the rows of tables to our own one on the terrace overlooking the vineyards. I tugged my tight dress down as a few women glanced at my hemline. Someone recognized me too, I heard them say my name, and though I'd never been ashamed of my past, I didn't want it thrown in Vince's face all the time.

"Nonsense. You look perfect."

And that was enough for me. Suddenly, none of those behind-the-hand comments and knowing smirks mattered. What mattered was Vince and that he thought that I belonged there with him in that beautiful place with its glittering chandeliers and silver cutlery, its crystal glasses and his heart of gold. It was the best gift anyone had ever given me: to see me with such forgiving eyes.

Just before dessert was served, Vince ran his fingers through his hair and cleared his throat before reaching into his dinner jacket to pull out a small box. Inside its velvety folds sat the most utterly perfect ring I'd ever seen. It was made from rose gold and the metal took on a coppery-pink tint in the candlelight. A clear, round diamond nestled in the middle of a lush rose that was in full bloom, and the exquisitely rendered leaves extending up the side of the band looked like ivy that had grown around it.

Vince plucked it from the box, his thick fingers dwarfing the ring as he held it out to me. "Ruth, I'm not a young man anymore, so forgive me for not getting down on my knee to do this. But this old heart, scuffed as it is, wants to spend the rest of its days beating next to yours. Will you honor me by becoming my wife?"

Of course I said yes.

You promised to love me just the way I am, Vince. You even said it in your vows. Either you broke your promise or you never really knew me because I never changed.

I pull my shoulder back and then whip my arm forward with all my might, flinging the rings out over the dam. They barely make a splash before disappearing below the water's surface.

Dusting my hands off as Da used to when he'd just accomplished a necessary but difficult task, I turn to Jezebel. "It's time for Mama to have some fun," I say. Back at the house, Zodwa is waiting outside for me with Mandla in her arms. "Can you look after him for a few hours?" I ask her. "I need to go out." She looks concerned but nods without asking any questions, which is one of the many things I appreciate about her. "Don't forget to give him his antibiotics later, okay?"

I'm long overdue for blowing off some steam.

CHAPTER SIXTY-EIGHT

Zodwa

❀

10 October 1995
Verdriet, Magaliesburg, South Africa

Ruth has been away for hours. She didn't tell Zodwa where she was going but before she left, she styled her hair and reapplied her makeup, changing into a tight dress that showed off her cleavage, which she paired with those towering high heels she liked to wear. Zodwa couldn't imagine how Ruth could drive in them.

"Bye, my handsome boy," she said, cupping Mandla's face and kissing it.

There was a crazed air to Ruth, something manic in the way she moved, and Zodwa was tempted to ask her if she was okay. But she was aware that doing so would be crossing a line. She was Ruth's employee, not her friend. Mandla kicked up a fuss as Ruth was leaving, holding out his arms and calling for her. "Mama!"

"Mama will be home soon!" Ruth called as she blew a kiss and closed the door behind her.

And now it's almost 9:00 p.m. and Ruth still isn't back. Mandla's sleeping in his room and Zodwa herself is tired. She's just considering phoning Riaan to speak to Delilah when Jezebel starts barking frantically at the door. Zodwa peers outside.

Ruth's car is parked just beyond the electric gate. The driver's door is open and the headlights are on, but no one is inside.

That's when Zodwa thinks she hears a splash.

She checks on Mandla, who's still asleep despite the dog's barking, and draws his door closed before calling Jezebel and going outside. She locks the door behind her and sets off at a run for the fence, shielding her eyes against the glare of the headlights. Once through the gate, she double-checks the car to make sure Ruth isn't in it. She's not.

Has she been hijacked?

Zodwa has heard about the tactics used to steal cars and knows that people are prime targets when stopped at gates while waiting for them to open. She's just wondering if she should go inside and press the panic button on the remote control when she hears Ruth's voice coming from the dam, the water amplifying the sound. Zodwa heads toward the windmill, its blades glinting in the dark, and hears another splash as she rounds the bend.

Ruth is in the water and Jezebel paces along the water's edge, whining next to the heap of Ruth's clothes.

"Madam Ruth?" Zodwa calls, uncertain what to do.

"Oh, hello, Zodwa. Don't mind me. I'm just looking for my rings," she calls, and laughs, though it doesn't sound like amusement at all. Instead, it sounds unhinged, as though the laugh is coming from a far-off place.

"Rings? What rings are you talking about, madam?"

"My engagement and wedding rings," Ruth slurs before ducking beneath the surface.

Zodwa holds her breath, terrified that Ruth won't come back up again. Zodwa can't swim and so she won't be able to save

Ruth if it comes to that. She's just about to scream for help when Ruth's head pops out again, her hair flattened onto her skull.

"Why would your rings be in there, Madam Ruth?"

"Because that's where I threw them away after getting the divorce papers."

The divorce papers. So that's what was delivered to Ruth earlier, sending her stomping off to the dam.

"We can find them another time. Please get out so we can warm you up."

When Ruth doesn't reply, just continues treading water, Zodwa takes off her shoes. Her toes sink into the mud. Ruth begins humming something but it isn't a tune that Zodwa recognizes.

"Madam Ruth? We need to go inside. Mandla is by himself in his room and I don't want to leave him alone for too long."

Ruth doesn't even react to the boy's name. Instead, she sinks a bit lower into the water. She's no longer singing and the water is now up to her nose. Ruth seems to have retreated into some dark corner of her mind. Again, Zodwa considers pressing the panic button but doesn't want men from the security company arriving and seeing Ruth like this: naked, drunk, and acting crazy.

"I can't swim but I'm going to walk in now," Zodwa says as she hitches her housedress up. Her knees are trembling but she tries to ignore how unsteady they feel as she takes a few steps in. The water is up to her thighs and she has to concentrate not to slip on the slimy base of the dam. "I'm coming to get you. Just reach out and take my hand."

Zodwa stretches it toward Ruth but she's nowhere near deep enough. She can hear Ruth's breath against the surface of the water. Zodwa steps in deeper and fights against the rising panic as the water now slips over her waist. It doesn't matter that she can't swim. She doesn't need to. As long as she can stand, the water can't hurt her.

"Madam Ruth?" Zodwa takes another step and then another until the water laps at her breasts. She's now in grabbing distance of Ruth and is about to stretch her arm out once more when Ruth sinks below the surface again. One minute she's there and the next, she's gone.

A bubble suddenly rises up and Zodwa lunges for it, losing her footing in the process. And then she's under the surface too, water rushing into her screaming mouth. The world turns black and there is no above or below, nothing except liquid in Zodwa's mouth and ears and eyes. She screams again and swallows water, which she immediately tries to cough back out. That's when her feet connect with the bottom of the dam and Zodwa knows to push down with all her might while reaching up, up, up.

When she breaks the surface, she's coughing and spluttering but blessed air rushes back into her lungs. Ruth is floating facedown right next to her and Zodwa reaches out, grabbing her blouse and yanking Ruth toward her.

Zodwa's first reaction is one of overwhelming relief as she pulls Ruth to safety. Her second is blazing fury. This is who Leleti entrusted Mandla's care to? An alcoholic who's so pampered and spoiled by life that the mere delivery of divorce papers is enough to make her act deranged. A woman who binge drinks and almost drowns herself. This is who Leleti thought would be a better caregiver for her grandson than her own daughter?

I don't think so.

It's the same thought that plays in a loop in Zodwa's mind long after she's dragged an incoherent Ruth inside, bathed her to warm her up, and then put her to bed. It's the same thought that plays over and over as she lifts Mandla from his crib and takes him back to her cottage with her, putting him in her bed even as she wonders if she should rather be strapping him to her back and running.

CHAPTER SIXTY-NINE

Ruth

❋

11 October 1995
Verdriet, Magaliesburg, South Africa

The curtains are open and light streams in with a vengeance, boring through my retinas straight into my skull. No matter how shitty life gets, you can always count on the sun to shine like a heartless bitch.

I'm just reaching for the glass of water on the nightstand when I remember Mandla.

Fighting back nausea, I stumble to my feet and rush from the room calling to him. His bedroom door is open but as I step inside I can immediately see that he isn't in his crib. Neither is his blanket.

"Mandla! Where are you?" My breath comes in rasping gasps and it feels like I'm about to begin hyperventilating. "Dee?"

She has Mandla. Of course she does. But when I get to her room, her bed is still made. I remember then that she's away with Riaan, and the realization just makes me feel more panicked.

How did I get to bed? Where was Mandla then? I don't remember. The last thing I remember is drinking my sixth or seventh martini at the Tusk Bar & Lounge at the Palace of the Lost City. I don't remember leaving the Sun City resort or getting home, but I'm in my nightie, so at least there's that.

And then it occurs to me: Zodwa. She was looking after Mandla while I was out. I have no idea what time I arrived home, but she would have stayed with him until I got back. Where is she?

That's when I notice that the front door is wide open. Oh, Jesus, no. What comes to me then is all those voices on the phone threatening me and my boy. I see Klein Maynard Coetzee's face in the rearview mirror after he's just swerved to miss hitting me, hate reflected in his gaze. I see the *dominee* as he says, *The baby won't be safe here. Who knows what might happen to him.*

Have they taken my boy?

I have to check if Zodwa is here or if she's missing too. I wish now that I'd installed a phone in her cottage but since I didn't, I have no option but to go down there. I can't find my keys but I find the spare remote control and when I run outside, I see Vince's car parked outside the gate. I have no idea what it's doing there, why I didn't drive it inside, but that's where I head. Stones bite into the soft soles of my feet and I wish that I'd thought to put slippers on before rushing out.

The car's unlocked and my keys are still in the ignition. Thank God.

It's a short drive to the cottage but it takes an eternity.

330
•

CHAPTER SEVENTY

Zodwa

❋

11–12 October 1995
Verdriet, Magaliesburg, South Africa

Zodwa reads to Mandla under the shade of the wild fig tree. It's become her favorite place to study since there's usually a breeze and it's cooler than the cottage. The tree itself is beautiful, with its enormous roof of leaves and snaking strangler roots that are so big she's able to lean back against them for support.

She's reading *Are You My Mother?*, which makes her both indescribably sad and hopeful at the same time, and she points up at the tree above them when the baby bird in the story tumbles down, down, down from its nest. "This is a tree, Mandla."

"Tree," he repeats, and then coughs, phlegm rattling in his chest.

"Yes! Tree."

She holds her hand to his forehead. He feels hot, but then he's had a higher-than-normal temperature for a while. Zodwa forgot to give him his medication last night and didn't bring it to the cottage to give to him this morning. Ruth can do that. Why must Zodwa always be the one forcing Mandla to drink something that he hates?

What she'd like to do is something fun, like taking him to the township barber for a proper haircut. Ruth has no idea how to treat black hair and she washes Mandla's daily using white people's shampoo. His hair is dry and brittle as a result and needs proper styling as well as regular treatment with coconut oil. A boy's first haircut is an important milestone; Zodwa wants to be the one who shares that with Mandla.

She's about to start reading again when they hear pounding on the door and her name being called. It's Ruth, finally come to look for him.

"Madam Ruth, we're here," Zodwa calls.

They almost crash into each other at the side of the cottage as Ruth rounds the bend. She looks wild, with her hair having dried in disarray and her makeup streaked down her face. Her eyes burn with a crazed fear.

Good, Zodwa thinks. *I'm glad she was scared.*

"I brought him here to stay with me last night," Zodwa says, handing Mandla across.

She expects apologies and self-recrimination from Ruth. What she isn't expecting is for Ruth to slap her. As the palm of Ruth's hand connects with Zodwa's cheek, she reels back in surprise.

"Who gave you permission to bring Mandla here?" Ruth seethes. "How dare you?"

Zodwa is so taken aback that she's rendered speechless. All she can do is clutch the side of her face and stare at Ruth in shock.

"I've been out of my mind with worry. I woke up and he wasn't there. No one was there. You didn't leave a note or anything." She's shouting now and flecks of spittle land on Zodwa's face. "I thought something terrible had happened."

Zodwa blinks and steps back from both Ruth's rage and the stink of stale alcohol. It isn't just Ruth's breath. It seeps from her pores and the smell is nauseating.

Mandla starts crying as he looks between Ruth and Zodwa, and what Zodwa recalls then in that fractured moment, as her frightened son is being held by the screaming white woman, are the words from the book she was reading to Mandla just minutes before.

He did not know what his mother looked like. He did not see her.

Ruth starts walking away but calls over her shoulder, "I'm too pissed off to deal with you right now. We'll talk about this later."

Something in Zodwa snaps. "No, we'll talk about this now."

"What?" Ruth spins around.

Zodwa stands firm, trying to stop her quivering legs from buckling under her.

"What did you say?"

"I said we'll talk about this now. You're the one who has no right," Zodwa says. "You have no right to speak to me like that."

Ruth gapes at her.

"You could have died last night driving home as drunk as you were. And then you could have died again in the dam. You could have drowned but I saved you. I almost drowned saving you." Zodwa's voice is pitched dangerously low. If she raises it, she may raise her fist along with it. "I bathed you, warmed you up, put you in your pajamas, and carried you to bed, and then I brought Mandla here because you were too drunk to even stand, never mind take care of him."

"Who do you think you are?" Ruth asks, staring at Zodwa as though she's never seen her before.

"Who do I think I am?" Zodwa repeats, feeling the world spin. *I'm his mother*, Zodwa wants to roar. *I'm his mother, that's who I am.*

"Yes, who the bloody hell do you think you are talking to me like that?"

"I'm someone who cares for that little boy," Zodwa says. "I'm someone who believes he deserves better than a drunkard for a mother. And I'm someone who will report you to social services if you ever, ever get into a state like that again when you're supposed to be looking after him. Do you understand me?"

Ruth flushes and Zodwa prepares for an onslaught. Instead, Ruth puts Mandla down and then turns to vomit in the dust.

Zodwa spends a sleepless night replaying everything that happened. Of course, you can't speak to a white person that way and get away with it. It doesn't matter that it's the new South Africa; whites still hold all the power, which Ruth will prove just as soon as she fires Zodwa. And what then? Once she's not only out of a job but banished from seeing Mandla, what will she do then?

She thinks about the secret hiding spot under her mattress and the beaded purse she keeps there. She compulsively counts the notes inside it every day and knows exactly how much there is. It isn't enough to set her and Mandla up in KwaZulu, and there's no point in returning to the squatter camp. It's the first place they'll look for her.

As far as Zodwa can see, there's nothing else to be done except to apologize to Ruth and ask for her mercy. If she can just hold on to her job for another year, she'll have enough money saved to leave with Mandla and comfortably disappear into her homeland where Ruth hopefully can't find them.

Still, Zodwa wonders if she didn't make a mistake in not using the opportunity presented last night to run away with Mandla; she tells herself another one will come again and that she'll be better prepared next time.

When Zodwa goes to work early in the morning, she half

anticipates her key will refuse to yield in the lock, but she has no trouble getting inside. The house is quiet and she thinks everyone is still sleeping until she notices that the patio door is open. Ruth is never up this early, so Zodwa goes outside expecting to find Delilah and hoping to get a sense of Ruth's mood from her. She's surprised to find Ruth sitting there in her fancy robe, a cup of coffee cooling in front of her.

The two women look at each other, sizing each other up, and Zodwa is just about to launch into her apology when Ruth holds her hand up. "Let's not talk of it, okay?"

Relief washes over Zodwa. "Okay." She's on her way back inside when she thinks of something and turns back. "Mandla needs a proper haircut. Done by a barber who knows black hair. And you must stop washing his hair every day and treat it with oil instead. I'll show you what to buy."

Ruth's quiet for a few seconds before saying, "Okay."

When Zodwa starts filling the sink to wash the dishes, she spots all of Ruth's empty alcohol bottles in the garbage bin. She checks the liquor cabinet and smiles when she finds that it's completely bare.

CHAPTER SEVENTY-ONE

Delilah

❋

12 October 1995
Van Tonder Farm, Magaliesburg, South Africa

Riaan and I were at a bush pub on our way back from the site. It was his suggestion that we stop for a late lunch, but he seemed distracted during the meal and I wondered if he was in a hurry to get back to the farm.

"Is everything okay?" I asked.

He looked up at me for a moment, a long appraising stare, and then he said, "Actually, no."

"Why? What's wrong?"

He sighed. "This. This is all wrong."

My heart felt like a stone sinking into a pond.

"What I mean is . . . what are we doing, Delilah?"

I smiled and tried to make light of it. "What are we doing? We're having lunch, of course."

He put his knife and fork down, the cutlery clattering against the plate. "I'm too old for this. We're both too old to keep up with this cat-and-mouse game that we've been playing for the past year. Every time I think we're getting somewhere, you with-draw from me and I don't know why. You know how I feel about you. You know how I've always felt about you. I don't see any reason at all why we can't be together. What's stopping us?

"Do you not have feelings for me? Is that it? I know things

336
.

were complicated when you left all those years ago but things are different now. We can have a life together. What's left of our lives anyway. But obviously not if you don't feel the same way I do."

"I do care about you, Riaan, more than you know." And as I said it, I realized how true the words were.

The past sixteen months since Daniel's death had been the hardest of my life. Over the years, I'd lived through cholera and war, famine and genocide, and yet none of it had affected me like my son's death. And in the darkest depths of my despair, as I grappled with my loss and cowardice—even as Ruth made it all so much harder for me by bringing Mandla into our home— the one person who'd tried to make it better was Riaan.

He'd called and visited time and again despite my refusal to see or talk to him. He'd provided distraction with the digs, and even as I kept my distance, he'd intuited what I needed most and had tried his best to provide it for me even though I'd completely severed ties with him for almost forty years.

"I'm sensing there's a 'but,' Delilah," Riaan said, reaching for my hand and squeezing it. "I'd rather know now where I stand with you than have to live through another year of guessing and feeling like everything I do is wrong."

I squeezed his hand back and then pulled away, reaching for a tissue in my handbag. And it was while I was feeling around for one that my fingers brushed against Daniel's letter. I'd been carrying it with me since seeing Sister Marguerite. While I hadn't had the courage to open it, somehow having it with me made me feel brave. "There's something I need to tell you. About what happened when I left."

"I don't need to know about the priest," Riaan said, his jaw jutting out. "We don't need to get into all that. The past is the past. I don't know why you came back or why you've been so sad, but I want to change that. I want to make you happy and I think I can if you just give me the chance."

"The past isn't the past for me."

"Okay, but is it big enough that you'll let it stand between us now?"

"I'm trying to work through it. And I need you to know everything so that you can then make a decision having all the information. Will you grant me that? Will you listen?"

He nodded and so I began to speak, telling him everything and sparing no details.

CHAPTER SEVENTY-TWO

Ruth

✳

N o, Mama. No." Mandla's eyes are wide with terror and I want to cry seeing him in such distress.

"It's okay, baby. It's okay. Mama's here. Just one prick and then it's over. Please sit still, my boy, please."

As we sit on the bed, Mandla wriggles out of my grip and the blond technician frowns at me. "You need to keep him still, Mrs. Richardson."

"I'm trying but he's scared, which is completely understandable."

"I can't take the specimen if he can't keep still."

Mandla squirms violently as the technician comes at him with the needle again. "No, Mama. No."

"Okay," the technician says. "You're going to have to step outside and I'll call someone in to help."

"But—"

"We need this blood and we're going to hurt him if he doesn't keep still. Besides which, his HIV-positive status poses a threat to us and a needle-stick injury is the last thing any of us needs." She calls to a colleague who comes bustling in to see what the fuss is about. They make me stand up and move back so that the colleague can sit next to Mandla. I try to skirt them to hold Mandla's hand.

"Ma'am, this will be much easier without you here. If you could just step aside for a minute."

I leave, feeling like I'm failing as a mother on all fronts as Zodwa's words from two days ago come back to me.

I'm someone who believes he deserves better than a drunkard for a mother. And I'm someone who will report you to social services if you ever, ever get into a state like that again when you're supposed to be looking after him. Do you understand me?

I flush with shame just thinking about it, but luckily there's enough going on to keep me from dwelling on the memory. The room has a glass wall and I watch as a third technician joins them. All three of them struggle to hold my boy down and he shrieks for me the whole time.

"Mama! Mama! No! Mama!"

I'm trembling as much from fear and helplessness as I am from withdrawal. I'm on day three without a drink and God help me, it's tough.

I never guessed how hard it would be to have to fight back every instinct I have to protect Mandla even as I know that what they're doing is essential to monitoring the disease's impact. At seventeen months, my boy is a mere seven months away from the age most children with the virus die. I know he's not going to miraculously be cured of HIV, but I don't need him to be. I just need him to keep fighting for just a little while longer.

I've been in regular contact with Dr. Torres, the top HIV/AIDS expert at St. Vincent's Hospital in New York City, over the past few months. They've been running pharmaceutical trials for a few years and seem to be having success with a cocktail of drugs called HAART, highly active antiretroviral therapy. It's just a matter of time until they have a breakthrough, and I only need my boy to keep fighting long enough until the drugs are approved and I can get him on them.

When Mandla's cries finally die down to pathetic little sobs, it's so quiet that I can hear the clock in the reception area ticking behind me.

"Ma, jou kleintjie soek jou," the third technician says to me as she comes out of the room looking disheveled. Mom, your little one is looking for you.

I expect him to fly into my arms when I enter the room. Instead, he lies there staring at me with accusing eyes.

CHAPTER SEVENTY-THREE

Delilah

❄

25 *December 1995*

Verdriet, Magaliesburg, South Africa

Though we'd given Zodwa three weeks' leave over the festive season, she said she'd rather stick around and rest up after her exams than go anywhere. She'd passed her matric with brilliant results and we'd hosted a special celebration dinner in her honor, after which I'd pulled her aside.

"I'm so proud of you, Zodwa, and would like to give you a graduation gift to congratulate you. Why don't I get you a return bus ticket so you can spend the festive season with your family?"

"Thank you, Delilah. That's very generous of you, but since my mother died, I don't have any family left. It was just her and my brother, and now it's just me."

I knew how sprawling Zulu families could be. The likelihood of Zodwa having no remaining family at all was slim but I never commented on it. Instead, I gave her the cash value of the ticket along with books that she'd expressed an interest in as her graduation gift.

When I suggested to Ruth the week before that we include Zodwa in our Christmas-lunch plans, she'd waved it off.

"I'm sure a young girl like her would much rather spend her

vacation time with her friends than with a bunch of wrinklies and a child."

While Ruth had a point, I couldn't help but wonder if I'd missed something. "Has something happened between the two of you that I don't know about?"

"What do you mean?"

"I don't know. You've just seemed a bit . . . wary of each other lately. You didn't have a fight or anything?"

"Of course not. Don't be silly. I just think the girl needs a life outside the three of us."

"Fair enough." And so I'd left it.

Ruth and Mandla had put up a Christmas tree on December 1. It was ridiculously extravagant and looked like it was going to topple over at any moment.

"It may be the only Christmas he ever has," Ruth had said when I'd raised my eyebrows at the excess. "I want to make it a special one."

It was the first time I'd heard her acknowledge that Mandla's illness was a death sentence.

On Christmas Day and my fifty-eighth birthday, Riaan disappeared into the bathroom to dress as Father Christmas so he could hand out all the gifts that were under the tree. When he emerged a few minutes later, Mandla wanted nothing at all to do with him. The white-bearded man in a red suit who kept yelling "Ho, ho, ho" scared him.

Still, Ruth insisted on keeping up the charade of merriment. "Look who it is! It's Father Christmas. And look at all the presents he brought you!" She oohed and aahed over each gift that bore Mandla's name, waving the shiny parcels at him in an attempt to engage him.

Despite that, Mandla only opened five of his presents before losing interest. He was still coughing badly and I was beginning to worry about him as much as Ruth did. He was listless and wore a glazed expression I'd never seen before. "Do you think he's feeling okay?" I asked Ruth.

"He'll be fine. The antibiotics just need time to kick in. Let's open our gifts," she said with forced cheer.

I'd bought Riaan practical gifts that he could use at digs as well as books about paleontology and evolution. I'd also dug around in his garage until I found the saber-toothed cat's tooth he'd found in the cave on his property all those years ago when we were children. I had it mounted in a glass box and attached a plaque that was engraved with: *Riaan van Tonder, taking part in earth-shattering discoveries since 1944.*

There had been a lot of excitement recently. The Wits University paleontologists believed they'd found the most complete ape-man skull ever excavated, a 1.5-million-to-2-million-year-old skull of a female cousin of early man. It was still very hush-hush, but Riaan had been a volunteer at the Drimolen site when it was found next to the lower jaw of a male. I was proud of him and wanted him to know that I saw the potential in him that had never been allowed to be realized. He was rendered speechless by the gift and so I knew he liked it.

For Ruth, I'd made a framed collage of all the articles that had been written about her over the years, interspersing them with photos of her from magazines as well as newspaper headlines that spoke of her shocking exploits. In the center of it, I'd had the Helen Keller quote on courage written large, in calligraphy: *Never bend your head. Always hold it high. Look the world straight in the eye.*

She hooted with joy when she opened it.

Ruth, true to her nature, gave me a selection of silk and lace lingerie and sleepwear that made me blush; it also made Riaan flush until his face matched the color of his Father Christmas suit.

One of Riaan's gifts to me was a leather-bound Bible with my name embossed in gold. "In case you want to start reading the scriptures again," he told me, piercing me with his sincerity.

After a huge lunch, Riaan brought out a cake.

"Thank you for not being in charge of it," I said to Ruth, seeing the plain chocolate cake with *Happy Birthday, Delilah* written on it in gold icing. "No fondant, thank God."

"Don't thank me just yet," she replied, proceeding to cover the cake with fifty-eight miniature candles that she lit with painstaking slowness for emphasis.

When she was finally done, I pulled Mandla up on my lap, asking for his help in putting out the blazing fire. He blew once or twice, ineffectually, and grabbed at the cake halfheartedly.

"Does he feel hot to you?" I asked, trying not to inject any alarm into my voice. It was difficult to tell because his temperature ran to hot and he'd felt that way for ages.

"Little man's just tired," Ruth said. "It's been a long day." She planted a lingering kiss on his forehead and then held her arms out to him. "Besides, it would be difficult not to get hot in the reflected light of all those candles," she quipped, and I laughed gamely, though the reversal in our roles was disarming.

Who was the calm woman before me and what had she done with my sister?

I was about to blow out my own candles when Mandla suddenly leaned forward and vomited down Ruth's pants before he began having a violent seizure.

CHAPTER SEVENTY-FOUR

Ruth

⁂

27–29 December 1995
Rustenburg, Gauteng, South Africa

Two days after Christmas, I'm curled up in a chair next to Mandla's bed at a hospital in Rustenburg.

Mandla is hooked up to various drips and monitors, and he's been subjected to a huge battery of tests. The prognosis doesn't look good; he had a febrile seizure brought on by complications of pneumonia, and his CD4 count has dropped since his last test. The doctors are concerned about his viral load though they aren't talking AIDS just yet. Still, they're speaking in that somber way that worries me.

I wanted so much for my boy to have the perfect Christmas that I refused to admit how sick he was. *Stupid, selfish, Ruth.*

I've barely slept and still wear the clothes I wore on Christmas Day. Dee brought toiletries and a change of clothes, but I'm too scared to leave Mandla's side except to rush to the bathroom for a minute at a time. His temperature keeps spiking and they're concerned he'll have another seizure if they don't get it under control.

I hear a rustling from the bed and look to see Mandla struggling with his oxygen mask again. My boy is a fighter but I wish he wouldn't use so much of his strength to fight against the equipment and people that are trying to make him well. The machines, at least, are faithful in their service and do not discriminate. I wish I could say the same for the people.

When we first arrived at the hospital, it took four nurses to try to hold Mandla down so that they could draw blood and put a drip in him. As soon as I declared his status to them, two of the nurses backed away, refusing to tend to him.

"Just put gloves on, for God's sake," I shouted, trying to get them to help him.

"Pinprick accidents happen all the time," the one nurse said, "especially with flailing children. I'm not taking the risk."

The other nurse didn't say anything, she just looked at me mutinously, and I recognized her instantly. She was the woman I'd seen in the Spur bathroom that day. The one with the black eye who I saw with that racist, Klein Maynard Coetzee. I looked down at her name badge.

Mimi Coetzee. His wife.

"Get out of my way," I said. "I'll help them."

I tried to calm Mandla then as I held him down, gently shushing him and whispering his name over and over, telling him how much I loved him.

As I reach out now to try to move his hands away from the mask, I feel that his skin is hot to the touch. Before I have time to call out to the nurse that Mandla's temperature has spiked again, he starts having a seizure.

"Help! Someone help!" I shout as the machines he's hooked up to start wailing. There's movement at the door and I spin around to appeal to whatever medical personnel has come to my aid. But the person standing there, their face pale with shock, isn't a nurse or a doctor. It's Vince clutching a teddy bear.

He takes one look at us and spins around, joining me in screaming for help.

. . .

Two more days pass and still the grim expressions on the doctors' faces don't ease. Mandla is in a critical condition. My fear is a feral thing and obliterates every other emotion.

Vince stays with me the whole time, alternately holding my hand and Mandla's. He asks once if it's okay that he came. Apparently Dee told him what had happened when he called on Boxing Day. I tell him honestly that I've never been as grateful to see him in my life. Dee and Riaan are there most of the time too, bringing us food even though I can't eat a bite of it. Zodwa has tried to come see him but it's a strict family-only policy. The hospital thinks Vince and Riaan are our husbands and Dee and I don't correct them.

On my way back from the bathroom one day, someone blocks my path in the corridor. I step around them and am about to pass when I feel a hand on my arm. I look up, thinking it's one of Mandla's doctors, only to find that it's Klein Maynard Coetzee. He's wearing his AWB uniform again, and he's not the only one. Looking around, I see a whole group of AWB supporters with him. It looks like they're staging some kind of demonstration.

"We don't want that AIDS-infested *kaffir* in our hospital," Klein Maynard says.

In my exhausted state, I'm reminded of something, an echo from a conversation with Dee months ago.

It's not illegal to belong to the AWB, is it? They're perfectly within their rights to belong to whatever organization they want.

Do vile things have to personally affect you for you to give a shit?

At the time I'd considered it a stupid question because I didn't see how racism could affect me personally. How well my sister knew me, and how valid her point, because nothing is

more personal than Mandla. How extraordinarily transforma-
tive love is, how utterly it changes you so that now I can see so
clearly something I was always so blind to. When it comes to
these kinds of prejudices, you don't need to be one of the idiots
actively shouting your racism from the rooftops; silence and
inertia are collusion, and I will be complicit no longer.

"We don't want him and his disease anywhere near us,"
Klein Maynard says.

"Get the fuck out of my way, you racist bastard," I say as I
push past him. His eyes bulge with either surprise or fury.
"Come near my son, and I'll fucking kill you, do you hear me?"
I stare him down and when he blinks, shocked to be on the re-
ceiving end of a threat, I turn and march away.

After that, I begin to fight off sleep as Mandla fights off
death, superstitiously believing that as long as I stay awake,
Mandla will continue to breathe. My boy wouldn't leave me on
my watch. He won't leave me while I stand guard.

But there's only so long a human body can stay conscious
and I eventually give in to the darkness that encroaches every
time I blink. I have no idea how long I sleep but when I come to
with a start, I'm immediately aware of where I am and that I've
broken my vigil. Vince is standing over Mandla, tears streaming
down his face.

I bolt up, certain that my boy is dead.

Instead, he's awake. The fever has broken. My boy has found
his way back to me.

CHAPTER SEVENTY-FIVE

Zodwa

⚛

1 January 1996
Verdriet, Magaliesburg, South Africa

It's been eight days of absolute agony and Zodwa feels like she's going to go out of her mind.

What is wrong with my son? How can he possibly be fighting for his life when all he had was a cold?

She thinks of all the medicine Mandla spat out over the past few months and all the times she should have forced him to swallow it but didn't. Is that why he didn't get better? Is this her fault?

They wouldn't let her in to visit him at the hospital, but she could see the machines that were breathing for Mandla; all the staff who were constantly checking in on him; the medicine that was pouring into his veins. How could so much be necessary to save such a small body?

Ruth never came home at all in the first few days and Zodwa had to rely on Delilah for updates. She was grave and wouldn't say much except that the prognosis wasn't good.

"He's a very sick little boy," she said before disappearing into her room from where Zodwa would hear her weeping. The sound chilled her to her very core.

Zodwa paces constantly. Even in sleep, what little she gets, she's in constant motion, her eyelids twitching and her hands grasping for something. Her son? Hope? She starts praying to

350

•

Leleti's God, asking for His mercy, begging Him not to take Mandla from her now that she's a part of his life.

It seems that God listens because on the eighth day, Mandla is brought home from the hospital in the kind of car Zodwa thinks only presidents and famous people get driven around in. She doesn't recognize the man driving, but he's clearly someone Ruth is very close to, judging by the way they act with each other.

It's the opulence of the car that makes Zodwa hesitate when all she wants to do is run at Mandla to see for herself that he's better. Instead, she stands aside as the man opens the back door for Ruth, who gets out carrying Mandla. It's only when Mandla holds out his hand for Zodwa that she's spurred to action.

"Welcome home," Zodwa says, taking a listless Mandla from Ruth's arms. She's so shocked by his physical transformation that she dares to plant a kiss on his cheek. "You're looking thin, little man. It's time for us to fatten you up."

She leads him inside to the chocolate cake she baked for his homecoming. Zodwa was hoping for some reaction from him since it's his favorite, but he merely sticks his fingers in his mouth to suck on them and turns away from the cake, burrowing his face into her neck.

Ruth goes to put bags down in Mandla's room and the man joins Zodwa and Mandla in the kitchen.

He greets Zodwa in a distracted way and Zodwa greets him back. "Good day, sir."

When Ruth comes through from the bedroom, she introduces them formally, "This is Zodwa, our maid. Zodwa, this is Vince, my . . . soon-to-be ex-husband. He lives in Cape Town."

Ex-husband. So, he's the one who pushed Ruth over the edge that day in the dam. Zodwa smiles at him even as the mention of Cape Town sends a shiver of alarm through her.

Is that why this man is here? To take Ruth and Mandla back to Cape Town with him?

Zodwa is just thinking that she can't allow that to happen when Ruth says, "Can you watch Mandla for a second? I'm just saying goodbye to Vince. He's flying back home today."

"Of course." Relief washes over Zodwa.

The man leans forward and kisses Mandla on the forehead. "Goodbye, Mandla. Look after your mother for me."

For a split second, Zodwa thinks the man's referring to her. As Ruth and the man head outside, Zodwa watches them through the open door. The sound of their voices drifts in so that Zodwa doesn't have to make it obvious that she's eavesdropping.

"You didn't need to come," Ruth is saying. "But I do appreciate it. Thank you for the latest loan. You know I'll pay you back as soon as I can free up some cash."

"It's not a loan, Ruth. I'm just glad I could help. Is there no way to get him onto your medical aid in the future?"

"No, they declined him because of his status."

Zodwa blinks in surprise. Mandla's status? Ruth must mean his status as a foster child.

Foster children clearly can't become dependents on their guardian's health insurance. Mandla was at a private hospital, not an underfunded government one that Zodwa would have had to take him to if he was her child and his care fell to her. Zodwa had just assumed Ruth's policy was paying for Mandla's treatment. She can't begin to imagine what his stay there must have cost and yet that man paid for it like it was nothing.

Zodwa thinks of all the fancy equipment she saw at the hospital when she looked through the glass window into Mandla's private room. The only reason he had all of that was because these people have the money to pay for it. Money Zodwa doesn't have.

Zodwa thinks of her little purse under her mattress and the fantasies she's been having about running away. She flushes at how childish her dreams were.

Ruth kisses Vince on the cheek. "Thank you for coming."

"I'm always here for you, Ruth, you know that."

She shakes her head. "Not always," she says before walking away. Zodwa turns from the door back around to Mandla, burying her face in his neck for a second before Ruth returns.

CHAPTER SEVENTY-SIX

Zodwa

·❋·

6 January 1996
Verdriet, Magaliesburg, South Africa

H ere's the phone number for the club, Zodwa. Call if Mandla
gets a fever or if you're worried about anything at all,"
Ruth says, scribbling a number down by the phone.

"I will, Madam Ruth. Don't worry."

"And keep the panic-button remote control near you all the
time, okay?"

"Yes, madam." Zodwa has to stop herself from rolling her
eyes. Ruth's obsession with security borders on the ridiculous.
Typical white people, constantly thinking the black man is
coming for them.

"I'll call at eight-thirty to check on him. Listen for the phone."

"I will."

Still Ruth lingers in the doorway until Dee hoots for her,
shouting that they're going to be late for their event. Mandla is
curled up in Zodwa's lap as she reads to him from the illus-
trated Zulu alphabet book she made him for Christmas. He
doesn't even look up at Ruth's departure although she's theatrically blowing him kisses.

After Ruth finally leaves, Zodwa goes back to the book,
teaching Mandla how to say some of the Zulu words while telling him stories of their people that her *gogo* had once told her.

Her son, usually so serious, laughs and laughs when she shows him the Umzansi Dance, stamping his foot repeatedly in imitation of her now that he's feeling better.

"Again!" he calls. "Again, Dwa."

There are so many Zulu rituals Mandla will miss out on. He never had the *imbeleko* ceremony to introduce him to the ancestors and to ask for his protection after he was born. He will never attend an Umhlanga, or Reed Dance ceremony, nor will he hear the tales of the *amadlozi*, or slaughter a goat or chicken in their honor.

The whites have their own rituals and ceremonies but Mandla will be breaking with hundreds of years of tradition if he grows up with them. Zodwa wants to give him something of his true self to cling to, something that can never be taken away from him.

Once he falls asleep next to her, one hand clutching her leg, she lifts him up and takes him to his room as Jezebel pads behind them, claws ticking on the floor. Zodwa lays Mandla down in his cot and then leaves the two of them in there together before going outside to the patio to cool down.

It would have been Leleti's forty-ninth birthday today, but not even thinking about her mother's passing, and the fact that she didn't live to make this milestone, can take away from Zodwa's happiness. What she feels is more like the memory of sadness, something worn smooth from too much use.

She also feels gratitude because it was surely Leleti who gave Zodwa this gift of a night alone with her son; it wasn't easy for Delilah to convince Ruth to leave Mandla to attend their fundraising function. Still, Ruth, clearly reluctant to leave him so soon after his illness, had allowed herself to be assured.

Zodwa looks down now at one of the two letters she's taken

to carrying around with her. She applied to study social work through distance learning at the University of South Africa and almost can't believe she's been accepted. She'll be using the money she stashed away to pay for her registration next week when she goes to the campus to sign up. Saving money to run away with Mandla was a stupid fantasy whereas investing in her future is the better route. One her mother would approve of.

She folds the first letter away and opens the second one, this one from the Truth and Reconciliation Commission. It's in response to her inquiry about Dumisa, informing her that his name has come up in one of their interviews. There isn't any further information, just a notification that information about him will be disclosed in one of the upcoming hearings, and that she'll be informed of the date and venue once it's scheduled.

We'll know the truth soon, Mama. That is my birthday gift to you.

Zodwa goes inside and sits on the couch, reaching for the remote. The opening credits of the eight o'clock movie have just begun playing, with the sound turned low, when headlights sweep across the wall. It's too early for it to be the sisters, though knowing Ruth, she's probably come back just to check on Mandla. Zodwa gets up and walks to the window to see who it is. There's a *bakkie* that she doesn't recognize pulled up at the gate.

Zodwa waits for the intercom to buzz to announce their presence but nothing happens, and when she turns the volume from the TV down, she can hear the car idling.

That's when the power goes out.

The house is plunged into darkness, the picture on the television contracting to a pinpoint of blue before disappearing completely. The only light in the room now comes from the car's headlights, and Zodwa watches as a backlit figure gets out of the passenger side, reaches through the fence to flip something up, and then manually pulls the gate aside before getting back into the vehicle.

She goes cold as the car pulls inside.

The panic button? Where is the panic button?

Zodwa looks to the table but it isn't there. It's not on the couch either. When she looks back outside again, she doesn't recognize the two men who are lit up in the *bakkie*'s interior as one of them opens a door.

"We should have done this months ago. That's the only way to deal with vermin, show no mercy."

"We didn't know how bad it was then. Now we do. Now we put a stop to it."

The men are speaking in Afrikaans. What frightens Zodwa, besides the air of aggression that hangs over them, is how drunk they are. They're both slurring their words and the one staggers as he gets out of the *bakkie*. She knows from firsthand experience at the shebeen that you can't reason with angry, drunk men.

As they advance toward the house, Zodwa sees they're wearing what look like army uniforms. She shrinks back, not wanting them to see her through the window. She steps to the side and leans her back against the wall, flinching as they bang on the door.

"Open up, whore. Open the fucking door."

"We're not letting you get away with bringing that disease into our town."

Their shouting sets Jezebel off but she's still closed in the room with Mandla, so the barking is muffled. Zodwa's heart is pounding so violently that she wonders why they can't hear it.

That disease.

She doesn't know what they're talking about, but she

understands their intent. They aren't going to just turn around and leave.

"You and that AIDS-infested *kaffir* baby need to go," one of them calls as he bangs on the door again.

AIDS infested. What do they mean? It doesn't matter. She understands the "*kaffir* baby" part. They're here for Mandla, and Zodwa feels fear like it's a hand at her throat.

"Come, let's go try the back."

Zodwa spins around to look at the patio door that she came through a few minutes ago. The slam-lock security gate stands uselessly open but the sliding glass panel is closed; she can't remember if she locked it behind her. Zodwa steps toward it to check when she sees arcs of torchlight cutting through the darkness. They're coming. It's too late and so she runs for Mandla's room.

When Zodwa slips inside, Jezebel is on her feet. There's enough moonlight coming through the window for Zodwa to see that the dog's hackles are raised. Zodwa closes the door behind her, turning the key in the lock. Mandla is awake now. His eyes gleam in the dark. The dog's barking has startled him and he looks like he's on the verge of crying. She leans into the crib and picks him up, jiggling him around to soothe him. *AIDS-infested* kaffir *baby.*

She can't think about that now.

Zodwa's thoughts return to the patio door. The security system is useless if she didn't lock the sliding door behind her but she can't remember if she did. And then she remembers the remote-control panic alarms Ruth put in every room and finally understands why they were necessary.

The remote is meant to be hanging off a nail hammered into

the wall next to Mandla's changing table but she can't see it in the darkness. After reaching out for it, her fingers come away empty and she curses. Zodwa turns to the changing table and pulls out one of the drawers. As she does so, she hears voices nearby and then the sound of a chair being knocked over.

The men are inside.

For a moment or two, Zodwa stands frozen. All she can hear is her quavering breath and the whooshing of blood racing past her ears. When she starts moving again, she feels her way through the drawer with her free hand, but it doesn't contain anything but Mandla's clothes.

Zodwa pulls the next one open.

"Where's the bitch?"

"Doesn't look like anyone's home."

"The whore and the baby never go out. They must be here."

Jezebel barks in response to the voices.

Zodwa continues digging but when that drawer doesn't yield anything, she quietly opens another. She's about to give up on that one too when she feels the reassuring shape of the remote squashed into the side of it. She almost cries with relief. Instead, she pulls it out, pressing the button repeatedly. She expects an alarm to sound but nothing happens. No light blinks in response to her touch and she wonders if the battery is dead.

Please. Please. Please.

She presses it a few more times out of desperation.

"Where is that dog barking from?"

"Must be that room. It's the only one closed."

"She locks the security dog inside? What kind of idiot does that?"

They both laugh and Zodwa can hear them walking through

the house checking in every room. Mandla remains blessedly quiet. He leans his head against Zodwa's chest as though wanting to go back to sleep.

The telephone suddenly rings, startling her. It must be Ruth calling to check up on Mandla. The men ignore it. Zodwa counts seven rings before it stops. It feels like an eternity.

"Check that room."

"No way, man. The dog is in there."

The phone rings again but is silenced as it crashes to the floor. One of the men must have knocked it off the kitchen counter.

"I still can't fucking believe she brought that disease into our town. We could all get it."

"Mimi said it was the first case they've ever had at the hospital. Bad enough having to treat a filthy *kaffir*, but an AIDS-infested one at that?"

AIDS. The word is like a wasp buzzing around Zodwa's head. *AIDS. AIDS. AIDS*. She has to shake it off to concentrate.

The handle is suddenly pushed down and Zodwa's heart lurches. They're right outside the door.

CHAPTER SEVENTY-SEVEN

Ruth

✺

6 January 1996
Rustenburg Golf Club, South Africa

I'm going to go find a pay phone," I lean over and whisper to Dee as the auction bidding starts for a weekend getaway to Hermanus.

"Why?" Dee whispers back.

"I told Zodwa I'd check in at half past eight."

"She has the number to reach us here and she'll call if Mandla doesn't feel well. Besides," Dee says, checking her watch, "it's only just after eight."

I wish for the dozenth time that I'd brought my own car. I don't want to offend the fund-raisers by leaving early, especially since they're doing all of this for Mandla's orphanage, but I'm really not able to enjoy myself. Why didn't I just send a check and be done with it?

"It doesn't matter if I call a bit early," I reply, rising from the table.

Lindiwe smiles at me from the front of the room where she stands next to a table of auction items. They've raised a fortune so far and all the money is going toward expanding the HIV ward, now that it needs to house far more than just two babies. I smile back at her and motion that I'll talk to her later.

There's a pay phone near the men's room. I don't have

enough change in my purse and am just about to head back inside to ask Dee if she has any, when I find a lucky coin in the return slot of the call box. After dialing the number, I'm relieved to hear the phone ringing on the other side.

It's probably going to wake Mandla and I'm sorry about that, but hopefully Zodwa will answer quickly enough not to disturb him. After seven rings, the call cuts out. Relief sours to worry.

Maybe she's fallen asleep on the couch. Maybe she's in the bathroom. Maybe I dialed a wrong number.

The coins tumble out into the return slot and my fingers tremble as I feed them back in. I'm careful this time, dialing more slowly, and I hold my breath when the phone starts ringing again.

Dee rounds the corner just then, looking exasperated when she spots me. I hold up a hand to silence her.

Come on, Zodwa. Pick up.

And then the ringing stops as the phone is answered. "Hello? Zodwa?"

There's no reply. It sounds like static in the background.

"What is it?" Dee asks, beckoned over by the expression of concern on my face.

"It first just rang and now it sounds like it's been answered but no one is there."

"Probably just the lines acting up."

"But then how can Zodwa call if something's wrong? I think we should leave."

Dee takes the phone from my hand and puts it back in the cradle. "Riaan has made a bid on a quad bike. Can we wait half an hour to see if he's successful and then we can go?"

I sigh. "Okay, but just half an hour."

CHAPTER SEVENTY-EIGHT

Zodwa

❋

6 *January 1996*
Verdriet, Magaliesburg, South Africa

The handle turns as the door rattles and it sets Jezebel off barking again. Before Zodwa can put her hand over Mandla's mouth, he starts crying.

"The *kaffirtjie* is in there!"

"The door's locked. She must be in there with him."

"Hey, bitch," one of them calls. "We know you're in there. Open the door."

They begin banging at the door and Zodwa cries out in desperation. "Madam Ruth isn't home. It's just me here looking after the baby."

There's silence for a moment.

"Who are you?"

"I'm just the maid, *baas*." The word curdles in Zodwa's mouth but she hopes that being deferential will help defuse their anger.

"Black bitch is in there with the *kaffirtjie*."

"Good. That's even better. She can hold it so I don't have to touch it. We can take them both."

They bang on the door again and now Mandla is screaming. Jezebel barks furiously, spit flying from her muzzle. Zodwa backs away to the farthest corner of the room. She's clutching

Mandla so tightly to her chest that he cries out even louder. She tries to loosen her grip, scared that she's hurting him.

They're kicking the door, saying something she can't hear, and then it goes quiet. She hears receding footsteps and barely has time to wonder if they're leaving before she hears them coming back.

"Found the firewood ax."

There's a grunt and then the door splinters, wood chips flying everywhere. Jezebel yelps and shrinks away from the debris. Another thwack. There's now a gaping hole in the door through which torchlight shines. An arm reaches in and grapples with the lock until the door crashes open.

Zodwa turns to face the wall, putting her body between Mandla and the men. A hand grabs her and begins to tug at her but she resists. There's a snarl and then the man swears, letting go of Zodwa as he kicks out at Jezebel, who's bitten him. It's a temporary reprieve and then he's on her again, his arm wrapped around Zodwa's neck as he pulls at her from behind.

"Come, you stupid *kaffir* bitch."

He yanks so hard that Zodwa topples backward. His bicep is tight around her throat and she can't breathe. Still, she won't let go of Mandla. She cradles him against her chest to stop him from falling as his terrified screams cut through the night. From her vantage point near the floor, Zodwa can see a pair of legs that Jezebel is lunging at. They lash out at the dog, connecting with her ribs, and she yelps in pain.

Zodwa's vision closes in. The room is getting completely dark. She fights for consciousness, trying to scramble back onto her feet. As she writhes, Zodwa thinks she sees a set of legs and then another running toward the room. They're wearing blue pants and leather boots, and she can hear shouts accompanying their advance.

"Let go of her and put your hands up!"

When her head hits the ground, all Zodwa knows is that Mandla is still in her arms. They didn't take her son from her. He's safe. Mandla is safe.

CHAPTER SEVENTY-NINE

Ruth

❋

7 *January 1996*
Verdriet, Magaliesburg, South Africa

Light begins to seep through the curtains just as Mandla and Zodwa fall asleep curled up together in my room. There's an empty space at the foot of the bed where Jezebel should be. She's being kept for observation at the emergency vet but they say she should make a full recovery, thank God.

Dee hands me a mug of coffee as I join her in the kitchen. She looks terrible in her rumpled dress. What little makeup she put on for the fund-raiser is now smudged into shadows around her eyes. I'm sure I look worse. At least the power is back on. They must have fixed the substation that the Coetzees disabled.

We only returned from the hospital a little over an hour ago when Mandla and Zodwa finally got the all-clear to come home. Mandla's fine physically, though who knows what trauma now lurks in his psyche. Zodwa's neck is in a brace as a precaution-ary measure and she's covered in bruises.

My mind keeps returning to the image of her hands crossed in her lap in the emergency room. The nurse had whispered to me that victims of near strangulation almost always have flesh embedded under their fingernails, defensive wounds from when they claw at whatever is cutting off their air supply.

But instead of fighting off her attackers to save her own life, Zodwa clung to my boy, stopping them from taking him from her. That's how the police said they'd found her after the security company notified them of the panic alarm being activated: unconscious but with Mandla clutched in her arms.

Why would she do that? Risk her own life for his. It doesn't make any sense. Surely no one is that altruistic.

"I'm sorry I made you wait," Dee says. "We should have come home as soon as you wanted to."

"How could you have known? Thank God the panic alarm worked."

We're both lost in thought when a voice comes from the doorway of my room. "Does Mandla have AIDS?"

I turn around, not having heard Zodwa get up. "What?"

"Those men said Mandla has AIDS and he's going to make everyone in the town sick with it."

Damn that Mimi Coetzee! Damn her to hell. I think of the girl's fist-ruined face and shake my head. She probably gave up the information to her husband to save herself in some way. Still, when it comes down to it, everything is a choice and she chose to put an enormous target on Mandla's back.

"Zodwa, please come." I hold out my hand and she walks over looking like a little girl in Dee's nightgown. The neck brace must be uncomfortable.

Zodwa sits down next to me. "So, it's true?" she asks.

"He's HIV positive but it hasn't yet advanced to full-blown AIDS. I'm sorry we didn't tell you about his status. We were trying to protect him because there's so much stigma around the disease. I promise that you've never been at risk of contracting the virus at any point. I made certain of that. Those idiots don't know what they're talking about. There's no way Mandla could infect any of them, never mind the whole town. Ignorant bastards."

Zodwa's face is a picture of misery and I feel such a rush of affection for this girl who's saved my boy's life not once but twice. She's his guardian angel, there's no doubt about that. "We're about to get him onto a cocktail of medication that should help him. It's only just been approved but they're seeing good results—"

"There's medicine that will cure him?"

"It can't fully get rid of the HIV but it means he can live longer. It's very expensive and we're having to get it from the United States but it's worth a try. He doesn't stand a chance without it, so the timing is really lucky. If he'd been born a year before, there probably wouldn't have been any hope for him." I take her hand. "If you want to leave and work somewhere else, I'll quite honestly be devastated but I'll understand completely. You need to do what feels right for you."

"No," she says fiercely. "I'm staying with Mandla."

I wish I don't wonder why, but I do.

CHAPTER EIGHTY

Zodwa

✹

Zodwa Khumalo?" the nurse calls into the waiting room. Zodwa stands. "Here I am."

"Please come with me."

Zodwa follows her down the now-familiar hallway but the nurse turns into a different room than the one she did Zodwa's blood test in a week ago.

"Is there someone here with you?" the nurse asks, and Zodwa lies and nods.

And then the nurse tells Zodwa what she already knows. "I'm afraid that your test came back positive for HIV."

The nurse talks for half an hour, giving Zodwa brochures.

She thinks of Thembeka, who also has to be HIV positive, though she will have contracted the virus from sexual intercourse willingly entered into with Mongezi. Or, at least as willingly as Zodwa had when she'd had sex with Ace, who she will have infected because he refused to wear condoms.

The ripple effect is astonishing. In a country built on discrimination, a pandemic is breaking out because of a virus that does not discriminate. When the nurse advises Zodwa not to fall pregnant because of mother-to-child transmission, she has the strangest urge to laugh.

369

"Do you have any questions?" the nurse asks.

"How long do I have before I get sick?"

"It's different for everyone. It can happen a year after infection or as long as seven years later."

"I've heard about medication. HAART therapy," Zodwa says, testing out the words she's heard Ruth use now that Mandla is about to start taking his cocktail of drugs.

The nurse looks impressed at Zodwa's knowledge but then frowns. "It's not available here and even if it was, it costs many thousands of rands a month. It's a drug for the rich. I'm sorry."

It's as Ruth said.

Zodwa thanks her for her time and leaves. She thinks of all the times she was tempted to grab Mandla and run, the plans she had of disappearing into KwaZulu with her son so that they'd never be found. Had she done that, she would have signed Mandla's death warrant.

There's no chance for Zodwa now. She thinks back to Gertie in the squatter camp and how quickly she deteriorated. The last time Zodwa saw her she was covered in cancerous growths and you could see every one of her bones. She'd opened her mouth to cough and Zodwa had cringed at the sight of the white thrush that coated her tongue.

That's the fate that awaits Zodwa. She will die from the disease, or at least from complications that arise because of it, but her son stands a fighting chance. As long as he stays with the sisters who have the money and resources to fight for his life, he has a shot at living.

That was Leleti's gift to her grandson when she left him on those women's doorstep. She may not have known it then, but that single act took away her grandson's death sentence.

Thank you, Mama. Thank you.

CHAPTER EIGHTY-ONE

Ruth

❋

3 February 1996
Palace of the Lost City, Rustenburg, South Africa

Are you sure I can't tempt you with something sweet?" Vince asks.

We're having lunch at the sprawling Sun City resort because Vince is staying at the Palace of the Lost City hotel while he's in town for work. At least, that's what he says. I suspect he's here just for me.

"No dessert," I say. "But thank you."

"Is there anything else I can tempt you with?" He wriggles his eyebrows suggestively because it's been that kind of lunch, just like old times except I'm not three sheets to the wind.

I laugh in response. "Don't think I'm not tempted. A good old roll in the hay is probably just what the doctor ordered."

"Whoever this doctor is, I like him or her. And don't forget that the hay you'll be rolling in is an enormous bed with Egyptian-cotton sheets in the Royal Suite," he says, playing to my weakness for opulent hotel rooms and high thread counts.

"Damn you. You're not making it easy to say no."

He smiles to show he's mostly teasing and signals to the waiter for the bill.

The truth is that the old Ruth wouldn't have hesitated. The old Ruth would have had her tongue in Vince's ear during appetizers. Who am I kidding? She wouldn't even have let Vince make it out of his room to lunch. But the old Ruth is long gone and that's not necessarily a bad thing.

What the hell happened to me?

When the bill arrives, I take it and give the waiter my credit card.

"Ruth, come on, let me get lunch. It was meant to be my treat."

"Thank you, but no. I still owe you for the hospital bill."

"You don't—"

I hold my hand up to shush him. A large investment is maturing in two months' time and I'll be paying him back. With interest. No negotiations. I pull two documents from my handbag and hand them across to Vince. "This is actually a working lunch and so I'm paying you for your time."

He takes the first envelope, opens it, and flips through the pages, his eyebrows shooting up. The expression is not unlike Dee's, whose eyebrows have a tendency to do the same thing. The two of them actually weirdly remind me of each other. "A will? You wrote a will?"

"Yes."

"But you always refused to talk about estate planning whenever I broached the subject. You said it was morbid and that thinking about death was likely to attract it."

"Did I? Doesn't sound like me at all."

Vince snorts and then his expression turns to concern. "You're fine, though, aren't you? I mean, you're not—"

"For God's sake. How many times must I tell you that I wasn't actually planning to commit suicide? I was just trying to get you to stay with me."

"Okay. I suppose it makes sense to make one now. After what happened at the farm with Mandla and those thugs."

I nod, though that's not the reason I've finally drawn up a will. As scary as that ordeal was, it didn't make me aware of my own mortality. I've just come to realize more and more that if you want to make God laugh, tell him your plans. And I've never had more plans than I have now. If I'm going to be tempting fate with them, best I'm prepared for any eventuality.

"Could you please go over it and then sign as a witness? Send it to the law firm when you get back to Cape Town?" I ask.

"Of course."

"Thank you."

"What's the other one?" Vince asks as he begins to open it.

"The signed divorce papers."

He freezes, dropping the envelope like a hot potato, and then lets out a long breath as he runs both hands through his hair. "Ruth, I'm sorry that I sent you those without any warning. It just felt like it was time, you know, since—"

"Don't apologize. It absolutely was time." I nod emphatically so he'll think I mean it. I clear my throat. "Thank you for the maintenance payments you've included. I know I said before that I wouldn't accept them, but now with everything with Mandla . . . Well, you've been more than generous and I appreciate it."

"Please don't thank me." There are tears in his eyes.

There are tears in mine too.

CHAPTER EIGHTY-TWO

Zodwa

❉

3 May 1996
Rhema Bible Church, Randburg, Johannesburg

Zodwa is seated in a row with Mandla, Ruth, and Delilah on one side of her, and Mama Beauty and her white friend, Robin, on the other. Mama Beauty insisted on being there to support Zodwa despite the fact that she'd had no word yet from the commission about her own daughter.

After Zodwa introduces everyone from her side, Mama Beauty introduces Robin as her "white daughter," which makes the both of them smile.

"It's good to see the rainbow nation is alive and well," Delilah says in reply. "And that we aren't the only unusual South African family."

"There are more of us than you might suspect," Mama Beauty says but she's staring distractedly at Mandla as she speaks. She seems fixated on the boy and it makes Zodwa nervous.

Zodwa is relieved when a distinguished-looking man with gray hair, seated at a long table at the front of the room, speaks into his microphone. He asks for everyone's attention, and the buzz dies down as all heads turn to him. He identifies himself as Dr. Boraine, the deputy chair of the Truth and Reconciliation Commission, and then introduces the rest of the committee, including the chairman, Archbishop Desmond

Tutu, who sits to his left and wears the Anglican maroon skullcap and robe.

A murmur of appreciation ripples through the crowd as Desmond Tutu raises his hand in greeting and Zodwa shares everyone's collective thrill to be in such close proximity to him. The Archbishop's face is appropriately somber and he exudes a quiet power that belies his small stature.

"Chairperson, I call the first witness and ask him to please come to the witness stand."

Zodwa holds her breath as Cyril Malema makes his way over and takes a seat. He's bent over like a man four decades older and wears an ill-fitting suit, but at least he looks sober, which is a small miracle considering the state he was in when Zodwa last saw him.

"Mr. Cyril Malema, I would like to begin by welcoming you and thanking you very sincerely for your willingness to participate in the Truth and Reconciliation Commission. Would you please stand and take the oath?"

Cyril takes the oath, his hand placed on the Bible. Both his voice and his fingers tremble.

Dr. Boraine begins his questioning. "Now, Mr. Malema. In your own words, please tell us what you've come here today to share with us."

Cyril clears his throat, the sound discordant in the microphone, and begins speaking. His voice is reedy and tremulous. "I was a member of the Inkatha Freedom Party Youth Brigade in 1984, and I was sent on a mission with Dumisa Khumalo, Jakes Mogwase, and Kabetso Hlongwane that resulted in fatalities."

Zodwa's heartbeat, which has already accelerated, begins to gallop at the mention of her brother.

"What mission were you sent on?" Dr. Boraine asks while straightening his glasses.

"I was told to take Jakes and Kabetso to the border so they could cross over for military training."

"Where exactly was this? And what was the date?"

"It was at the Limpopo River border of Botswana. The date was August 23, 1984."

This is already more information than Zodwa was ever able to get out of him and she leans forward, eager to hear the rest.

Dr. Boraine consults his notes and then asks, "What about Dumisa Khumalo? Was he also supposed to cross the border?"

"No, sir. Dumisa just came with me for the mission."

"And what were your instructions?"

"To drop the two men off at a meeting point at the river to meet their contact."

"Can you tell us what happened that night, Mr. Malema?"

"Yes, sir. When we stopped at the designated spot, Jakes and Kabetso got out of the car to smoke while Dumisa and I stayed inside. As we waited for the contact who would take them across, lights were suddenly trained on us and there was screaming. It was an ambush by the security police, and they opened fire on us."

Mama Beauty takes Zodwa's hand and squeezes it as a cry suddenly erupts from an older woman seated off to the side. Judging by the way those around her console her, Zodwa assumes she must be one of the men's mother. Zodwa wishes she was sitting next to the woman so she could hold her as they both endure this ordeal.

"Did either of the men survive?" Dr. Boraine continues once the woman has quietened down to a whimper.

"No, they were both shot dead. As was Dumisa, while he was sitting in the passenger seat."

It's Zodwa's turn to cry out. Her hands fly up to her mouth, too late to stifle the sound, and Delilah reaches over and wraps her arm around Zodwa's shoulders.

"And how did the security police know that you were going to be there that night?"

Cyril Malema's head drops into his hands and there's a deathly hush in the room. He lifts his face again and says, "Because Dumisa and I told them."

Zodwa goes cold.

No. I must have heard that wrong.

But the whole room breaks out into shouts and exclamations of shock and anger.

"Please, could I please ask for quiet? Could everyone please settle down? Thank you," Dr. Boraine says after a few minutes and before addressing Cyril Malema again: "You told the security police you'd be there? You and Dumisa Khumalo informed on your own people?"

"Yes, sir." Cyril begins to cry. "We were working as double agents, you see. The security police paid us a lot of money to give them information."

Zodwa feels faint as chaos erupts around her. Voices rise in protest and condemnation, and the woman from before is wailing so loudly that Zodwa can't hear her own thoughts. She's grateful now to be seated so far away from that mother. She's dimly aware that Mama Beauty's grip on her hand has tightened like a vise.

"Please, I need to ask for silence so that Mr. Malema can continue with his testimony," Dr. Boraine says, raising his voice.

Archbishop Desmond Tutu's expression is pained. His eyebrows are knit together as he rests his chin on steepled fingers.

When the ruckus finally dies down, Dr. Boraine continues. "But why go with them that night if you had already sold your comrades out and knew what was going to happen?"

"It was Dumisa's idea, sir. He said that being out there with them would deflect suspicion so no one would guess that we were a part of it. Dumisa wasn't meant to be shot. That was a complete accident."

Zodwa listens, numb with shock, as Cyril Malema goes on to tell how he assisted the security police with burying all three of his comrades' bodies in shallow graves near the site of execution at the border. He trembles violently during his testimony—probably as much from alcohol withdrawal as from nerves—stopping repeatedly to cry and beg for forgiveness from Jakes's and Kabetso's families. He addresses the mothers by name but doesn't look at them, speaking to his lap the whole time. Of course, there's no begging for mercy from Zodwa. After all, her brother was the mastermind behind the atrocious scheme.

After the testimony is over, Zodwa wants so much to go to the two men's mothers and beg for forgiveness for what Dumisa did but shame holds her back. For there's no doubt in her mind that Cyril is telling the truth. Everything makes sense now, things Zodwa had never thought about as a child but that would have set off warning bells if she had.

Like how it was possible that Dumisa could send so much money back home on an entry-level administrator's salary, and how he could afford a secondhand car and be saving for a house mere months after starting his first job. Leleti and Zodwa's *gogo* should have realized something was amiss, but they saw only what they wanted to see.

Cyril's alcoholism makes sense now too, as does what Zodwa considered to be his incoherent ramblings when she first met him.

They are coming for me. I can't hide. There's nowhere to hide. They're going to kill me. Help me, sisi. *Help me.*

Zodwa had thought he believed the security police were still after him but, of course, he wasn't talking about them at all. He was talking about his own people and the families of the ones he betrayed. After the ANC came into power, he'd realized that his day of reckoning would come.

Dr. Boraine announces a break and loud conversations start up once again. Zodwa is grateful for the noise. It means she doesn't have to speak to Delilah, who stands and reaches out a hand for her.

"You all go ahead," Mama Beauty says. "I think Zodwa just needs a few minutes. I will sit here with her." She reassures them all that Zodwa will be fine and Zodwa nods to confirm it so that the sisters will go. As Ruth leads Mandla out of the row, it's suddenly painful for Zodwa to look at her son, who looks so much like his Judas uncle.

Once everyone has cleared out, the noise trailing behind them, Zodwa finds that she can't face Mama Beauty. Her freedom-fighter daughter might very well have been betrayed by someone like Dumisa; someone pretending to care about the struggle but who was only in it for himself.

"My child," Mama Beauty says, reaching out and taking Zodwa's hand again. "This has been a terrible blow for you, I know. One of the hardest things in life is finding out that those we love the most are the ones we know the least." She squeezes Zodwa's fingers. "Sometimes good people do terrible things. It does not make them rotten to the core; it just means that they made bad decisions. Dumisa is still Dumisa. He is still your brother. Only now he is a little less of a myth and a little more a mere mortal."

Mama Beauty is right. To think that Dumisa has been hailed a hero his whole life. To think that Zodwa forever felt like she lived in his shadow, as if she could never measure up. She thinks back to the last conversation they ever had.

You are a Khumalo, just like me. We are a great people, proudly Zulu. We meet the eyes of the world. And if we do not like what we see when we go out into it, then what do we do?

We change it.

Yes, we change it. We make it better. Now is my time but one day it will be yours. When that time comes, make me proud, little sister.

His hypocrisy makes her sick and she realizes suddenly that she no longer needs to use him as a yardstick. It's both a liberating and heartbreaking thought. "Thank you, Mama Beauty."

"The right thing is to go speak to those mothers no matter how difficult it may be, but before you go, I want to say that as you have just discovered with your brother, secrets never stay buried for long. I do not know your reasons for lying to those women about Mandla being your son, nor do I understand why Leleti lied about your son dying in birth, but I hope the time comes when you can bring your secrets into the light. As those wiser than us have said, 'The truth shall set you free.'" With that, she leans forward and kisses Zodwa's forehead before sighing and standing up.

CHAPTER EIGHTY-THREE

Ruth

❋

17 July 1996
Verdriet, Magaliesburg, South Africa

Isn't there a later semester you can sign up for so that you aren't wasting the whole year?" Dee asks Zodwa, who's at the stove cooking Mandla's lunch. Mandla is sitting on the kitchen counter squirming as Dee tries to put a bow tie on him.

I can't believe Dee's nagging the poor girl about her studies again. She was bitterly disappointed when Zodwa changed her plans at the beginning of the year and decided not to study for a social work degree at UNISA. She carried on and on about the wasted potential, especially since Zodwa did so well with her matric exams, but I don't see what the big deal is.

"We can help you with some of the fees," Dee is saying now, "if finances are the problem."

"Thank you, but no." Zodwa smiles to take the sting out of it but she's made it clear the topic isn't up for any further discussion.

I'm relieved because we have way more important things we should all be focusing on. "Off the furniture, Jez." I clap my hands and she shoots me an injured look.

"Relax," Dee says, calling Jez over for an ear rub. "The home assessment is just a formality. Lindiwe knows how we live."

"Still, I want everything to go well. Zodwa, did you make those scones I asked you to?"

"Yes, Madam Ruth."

"Please put them out with the three different jams and the clotted cream."

Why are the cushions all askew again, I wonder, *and where did the dust come from when Zodwa cleaned just this morning?* I wish I'd gotten flowers for the lounge table but it's too late now.

I've been on edge all week because the social worker from the orphanage is coming to do a home assessment as part of the adoption proceedings. It hasn't helped that Zodwa has been so distracted I've had to micromanage her, following her from room to room to make sure everything is perfect.

I don't know what's gotten into Zodwa lately. All I can think is that it's her upcoming trip home to lay her brother to rest that's worrying her, because she's been moody and a million miles away these past few days.

"There you go! All done," Dee says as she lifts Mandla from the counter and puts him down.

He's an absolute vision in his blue suit, white shirt, pink-and-blue-polka-dotted bow tie, shiny black shoes, and dapper trilby hat. My baby looks just like a little man.

"He looks like he's auditioning for a role in *The Music Man,*" Dee says dryly.

"Clothes maketh the man. And woman," I add, eyeing her up and down. "You could have made some effort yourself."

"What?" Dee looks down at her beige pants and blouse. "This is clean and ironed."

I'm about to tell her that her definition of making an effort needs reevaluating when the intercom buzzes and we all collectively jump. Zodwa's busy placing bowls of jam on a plate and drops one. Strawberry jam splatters onto Mandla's jacket.

"Damn it, Zodwa!"

"Sorry, Madam Ruth."

"Do you think you could get the door so I can wipe him down?"

Jesus, do I have to do every damn thing myself?

CHAPTER EIGHTY-FOUR

Zodwa

✳

17 July 1996
Verdriet, Magaliesburg, South Africa

Zodwa walks to the door, forcing a smile. Being here, having to cook and clean so that Ruth can make a good impression on the person who will decide if Mandla can be adopted, is excruciating.

He has a mother who loves him and would give anything to be with him. He doesn't need another one.

But, of course, that's just the thing: he does.

Zodwa opens the door, surprised when the face on the other side is one she knows. Judging by the woman's puzzled expression as she beholds Zodwa, she recognizes her too but is also struggling to place her.

"Hello," the woman says.

That's when Zodwa realizes who she is and her blood runs cold.

It's the social worker from the last orphanage she went to in her quest to find Mandla. Zodwa's first instinct is terror that the woman will recognize her and expose her as Mandla's mother. But then, when the social worker's own expression becomes fearful, their conversation from that day comes back to Zodwa, unspooling like thread in her mind.

And that's where you still live? In a shack?

What's your health like?

My health?

Sorry, it's an occupational hazard. I noticed you have a cough and just wanted to make sure you're taking care of it.

It's just a cold. It's almost gone.

Good. Maybe get some Borstol for it.

I will.

Can you check your files to see if there are any possible matches?

I don't need to. I know all the children here and none of them fits the description.

The social worker hadn't been able to meet Zodwa's eyes that day when she'd handed Dumisa's baby photo back. It had bothered Zodwa then, how fixated she'd been on the picture at first, and then how quickly that intense focus had turned to dismissal.

And then she realizes the truth: The social worker lied to her. Before Zodwa can stop herself, she blurts out, "You knew!"

CHAPTER EIGHTY-FIVE

Ruth

✳

17 July 1996
Verdriet, Magaliesburg, South Africa

The strawberry jam has left a stain on Mandla's suit lapel but there's nothing to be done for it. I'm just considering whether I should try to pick a flower from the garden to pin over it when I hear Zodwa's raised voice from the lounge.

"You knew!"

Lindiwe's voice is raised in response. "What are *you* doing here?"

I carry Mandla from the bathroom to find the two of them squaring off against each other at the front door.

"You recognized him but you lied to me," Zodwa says, clenching her fists like she's trying to stop herself from hitting someone.

"Whoa!" Dee says, rushing to the door from the kitchen. "What's the problem? Is everything okay?"

"What is *she* doing here?" Lindiwe asks Dee. She looks panicked.

"That's Zodwa, our maid that I told you about," I reply on Dee's behalf. "What on earth is going on here?"

Zodwa speaks to Lindiwe as though the rest of us aren't here. "Why did you lie to me?"

"I didn't lie," Lindiwe says but she looks shifty as all hell. "He wasn't there when you came. He'd left the day before."

"But you knew who he was! You knew! And you didn't tell me."

"Only because I knew you were sick, *sisi*!"

There's suddenly a deathly hush as the two women glare at each other, each breathing heavily with barely contained emotion, but neither speaking.

"Okay, let's all calm down." Dee is galvanized into action, taking Zodwa by the elbow and steering her away from the open door toward one of the couches. "Come in, Lindiwe," she says, beckoning for her to follow. Once they're all seated, she looks to me. "Ruth?"

I'm frozen in the bathroom doorway. The worst sense of foreboding is anchored in my stomach.

"Would anyone care to tell us what's going on? Zodwa?" Dee asks once Mandla and I sit down.

Zodwa doesn't say anything. She clamps her jaws together so tightly that the muscles at her temples bulge.

"Lindiwe?" Dee asks, turning to her for answers.

The social worker is quiet for a moment, as though deciding how much to divulge, and then she sighs. "She came to the sanctuary looking for him. She arrived the day after he went home."

"He? Who's he?" Dee asks, looking confused, but I know the answer before Lindiwe provides it.

"Mandla," Lindiwe says, and then follows up with, "Zodwa's his mother."

No. It can't be true. No. "His mother?" Dee struggles to keep up. "You're saying Zodwa is Mandla's biological mother?"

"Yes," Lindiwe says. "Ask her."

"Zodwa?" Dee's voice is a horrified whisper.

Zodwa nods and a tear falls onto her lap. She reaches up a hand to brush more away from her face. "It's true. I am his mother."

My boy chooses that moment to squirm from my lap and reach out for her. His grabby hands—those perfect ten fingers extended toward her—are the most crushing thing I've ever seen. I close my eyes and clutch him tightly to me as Zodwa begins to speak.

CHAPTER EIGHTY-SIX

Delilah

·❋·

17 July 1996
Verdriet, Magaliesburg, South Africa

I was raped," Zodwa began by way of explanation, and I felt what little grip I had on the situation get wrenched from my grasp.

How many of our stories begin that way, I wondered, with violence rather than with love? How many of our lives are ruined because some man somewhere decided he would lay claim to something that wasn't his?

"It was in August of 1993 and Mandla was born on May 10 in 1994," Zodwa continued.

"That's the same day he arrived on our doorstep," I said. "But why . . . why did you bring him here to us?" I asked while shooting a concerned glance at Ruth.

She was deathly pale. I couldn't remember ever seeing her dumbstruck and yet it seemed that Zodwa's revelation had robbed her of speech. It would be up to me to get answers.

"I didn't bring him here," Zodwa said. "My mother did."

"Your mother?"

"Yes, you knew her. Leleti Khumalo."

I had begun to shake my head no, indicating that Zodwa was mistaken, when she corrected herself.

"You knew her as Precious. She grew up here on the farm with you."

Precious! "Oh my God." I turned to Ruth. "I didn't tell you but I ran into her two years ago when I got a flat tire outside the squatter camp." It dawned on me then. "That was about two weeks before Mandla arrived. That's how she knew I was back."

Ruth looked pained but still didn't say anything as Zodwa began speaking again.

"After I gave birth that day, I feel asleep and when I woke up again, my son was gone."

I shook my head, trying to understand. "But why would Precious do that to you? Take your baby away and bring him to us?"

"She knew I didn't want the baby. I was so traumatized after . . . what happened . . . that I didn't want to be a mother. Mama knew that. And she knew about the rape. She was so upset when I told her. All I can think is that she knew she was about to die . . ."

I gasped. "She's dead?" And then I wanted to smack myself for my own stupidity. Zodwa had told me before that her mother had died. This was just the first time I was putting two and two together.

"Yes," Zodwa said. "Two days after Mandla was born. She had TB."

"I'm so, so sorry." That explained how terrible Precious had looked when I saw her.

"She knew she was about to die," Zodwa repeated. "And that she wouldn't be around to help me take care of the baby. She must have thought he would be better off without me."

Zodwa went on then, describing how she was told that her baby had died, but how she wouldn't believe it, how she'd searched for him at mortuaries and at orphanages until she met Lindiwe.

"Ruth had just taken Mandla home the day before Zodwa arrived," Lindiwe said, cutting in. "He'd tested positive for HIV and so I knew that Zodwa was positive too."

Oh, God. Zodwa was also HIV positive. Of course, she had to be since Mandla was.

Lindiwe kept talking. "Do you blame me for wanting that child to be with someone healthy who had the means to support him, rather than—"

"Lindiwe!" I was horrified by how matter-of-fact she sounded, and the degree to which she'd rationalized her deceit.

She shook her head stubbornly. "I did the right thing for Mandla. For him, I did the right thing."

I thought Zodwa would protest, but she just sat there silently, a sail emptied of wind.

"How did you know Mandla was here?" I asked Zodwa. "How did you know where to find him?"

"Someone told me there was a black baby here, and so I came that day to check if it was true."

"The day you saved Mandla from choking."

"Yes."

Ruth suddenly stood up, clutching Mandla to her. "Enough."

"Ruth—"

"No, I've heard enough." She was crying, her whole face contracted into a mask of grief. "Are you here to steal my son?" Her voice broke. "Is that why you're here because—"

Zodwa stood, eyes blazing. "He's my son, not yours. I can't steal what is rightfully mine. And I could have taken him anytime I wanted to over the past year if that's what I planned to do. Anytime!"

"So, what then?" Ruth demanded through her tears. "Why play this game and toy with us like this? What is it that you want?"

"What do I want?" Zodwa cried. "I want to live. I want to live to raise my son but that's not going to happen now. And if I can't have that, then all I want is for my son to be taken care of. I just want him to have a mother when I'm no longer here for him." The fire in her eyes dimmed then as her legs buckled beneath her. I reached out and grabbed her, steadying her.

As she began to cry, I pulled her up and I wrapped my arms around her. "It's okay," I whispered. "It's all going to be okay."

Sometimes that was all we needed to hear even if it was the biggest lie ever told.

CHAPTER EIGHTY-SEVEN

Zodwa

·

18 July 1996
Verdriet, Magaliesburg, South Africa

There's a knock at the door and Zodwa leaps to her feet, rushing to open it. It's Delilah and she's alone.

Her sad smile answers Zodwa's unasked question. "She wouldn't let me bring him, but give it time, Zodwa. It's early days still."

"Please come in," Zodwa says, stepping aside. "Would you like to sit?" She indicates the table with its two chairs.

"Thank you," Delilah says.

It would probably be more polite to skirt the issue, and the last thing Zodwa wants is to make Delilah feel uncomfortable, but she can't help blurting out, "Does Ruth want me to go? Is that what you've come to tell me?"

"No. She's upset at the moment, but it will pass. We just need to be patient with her. Give her a bit of time."

Time is the one thing Zodwa doesn't have but that's not Delilah's fault and so she doesn't say so. Instead, she says, "Thank you for helping me. I don't know why you're doing it but . . ." Zodwa trails off, trying to find the words to express her gratitude.

Delilah smiles but it's a sad smile. "I have an inkling of what you're going through." Zodwa must look skeptical because

Delilah laughs. She gets a far-off look and then says, "I was also raped, Zodwa. Probably at the same age that you were. And I too fell pregnant from that."

Zodwa's eyes widen. Whatever she might have been expecting Delilah to say, it wasn't that.

"I also had a son," Delilah continues, "but this is where our stories differ. I gave mine up whereas yours was taken from you. I wish that I'd fought as hard as you have, that I'd been as strong as you are."

Zodwa shakes her head. She's not strong. She's the weakest person she knows and she can't allow Delilah to think otherwise. "No, I—"

"Please don't sell yourself short. Do you have any idea what strength of character it's taken you this past year to live with us like this? To be a maid in your son's home, all so that you could be around him every day?" Delilah shakes her head. "I was up all last night thinking about it, how impossible this situation must have been for you."

Zodwa shrugs, uncomfortable with the praise. As difficult as it's been, being away from Mandla would have been infinitely harder.

"Anyway," Dee says, clearly sensing her discomfort and changing the subject, "I wanted to check if you need a ride to the bus terminal tomorrow?"

"I'm not going anymore."

"What?"

"How can I leave now when things are like this between me and Ruth? She could take Mandla and—"

"She won't. I promise you that. I'll be here to make sure that doesn't happen," Delilah says. "Also, Ruth is many things but she isn't stupid. She knows you could have taken Mandla by now if you'd really wanted to. She knows you aren't a threat to his safety but she's feeling backed into a corner. Your going might actually be a good thing. It will give her some space to calm down and think things through. She'll realize that there's a way for you both to be a part of his life."

Zodwa sighs and shakes her head. There's a lot at stake.

"Look, I know everything's really messed up. Precious should obviously never have taken Mandla from you and brought him here. That goes without saying. I have absolutely no idea what was going through her mind when she did that, Zodwa, but I can only imagine that she thought she was doing what was best for you after the rape. Believe me, she didn't do it because she thought you wouldn't be a good mother or to punish you."

Zodwa wipes a tear away. It's so good to hear that absolution.

"You don't need Ruth's permission to see Mandla. You realize that? He's your son. I mean you can't just take him now, for legal reasons, but after you've gone through the right channels legally, you could get him back."

Zodwa nods. "But then what? We move into our shack at the squatter camp and then? Mandla needs specialized care, which I can't afford. And I'm dying, Delilah. It's just a matter of time. I know it's selfish but I want to spend what's left of my life being a part of his life. After that, I want what's best for him."

"It's not selfish at all and if anyone will understand that, it's Ruth. Please don't cancel your trip. Go and bury your brother. Put him to rest and then come back. It will all work itself out. You'll see."

Zodwa wants so much to believe her. "Okay," she says. "I'll go."

CHAPTER EIGHTY-EIGHT

Ruth

✦

3 August 1996
Verdriet, Magaliesburg, South Africa

Dee knocks and when I answer, she comes into my room carrying a glass of water and the antibiotics that the local geriatric doctor prescribed me after doing a house call. "Are you feeling any better?"

"Not really. This pneumonia is a bitch, that's all I can say. No wonder Mandla was so sick when he had it."

She passes across the pills that are the size of bombs. "Here, swallow these."

"I'm more of a spitter than a swallower, to be honest," I retort, forcing a wink, before taking them from her. I manage to get them down but then my chest hurts again, my hand instinctively rising up to massage it.

"Still sore?"

I nod and lie back down. Jez jumps onto the bed, curling up next to me as I nestle my fingers in her fur. "How's Mandla?"

I haven't held him in two days, not since I started feeling so terrible. As much as I miss him, I don't want him near me if it means he might get sick. Dee held him up at the door earlier this morning so he could blow kisses to me.

"He's fine. He's having a nap but he should be up soon," Dee answers before changing the subject. "Vince called again to check on you."

"He's a sweet man." He's been calling a lot lately. It feels like the old days when I was being wooed.

"How did you two meet?" Dee surprises me by asking. "You never told me."

"In rehab," I say, expecting to see Dee's eyebrows go up but they don't. "I was addicted to drugs and booze. He was addicted to prescription painkillers from a car accident he'd had. They say you should never start relationships in recovery and that suited me just fine. I was done with men by then. Done, I tell you!"

Dee smiles. "Of course you were."

"Of course I wasn't." I snort, setting us both off again, and then wince at the stab of pain the laughing elicits. When it passes, I continue. "He waited a year, until after we both got clean, to call me up, and then he just kept on doing so until I agreed to go out with him."

"So, what happened?"

I shrug. "We fell in love and got married, and it was wonderful until I messed it all up."

"How?"

"I started drinking again. Popping pills."

"Why?"

"Same reason why I probably started drinking in the first place and why I always fell off the wagon. Not being able to get over wanting what I couldn't have."

"But surely he understood that?"

"He was sympathetic, but he thought we were enough, just the two of us, so he didn't understand. Not really. And he told me time and again that he couldn't be with someone who wasn't sober. Each time I apologized and promised I wouldn't do it again, he gave me a second and a third chance, but of course I kept on relapsing until I ran out of chances."

After telling Dee about it, how I'd been expecting it and yet was still surprised when the bottom finally dropped out of my world, I surprise myself by saying, "He deserves better. He always did. He's a good man who should be with someone who doesn't drag him down."

Dee sighs. I suppose there's nothing I can tell her about wanting what's best for someone else and knowing that you aren't it.

"You're sober now," she says.

"Mostly." I color with embarrassment remembering my lapse that Dee knows nothing about as well as the one that she does, and then I change the subject. "When did you last hear from Zodwa?"

"She called yesterday. Her brother's burial is going to be on Saturday."

"Good. I'm glad they'll all finally have some closure." And I find that I actually mean it.

I've been so angry these past two weeks and almost all that fury has been directed at Zodwa. Though, to be fair, I'm almost equally pissed off with the universe. It seems a cruel joke to grant me what I've always longed for most and then to snatch it away. I suspected something was strange about Zodwa's unwavering devotion to Mandla but I couldn't quite put my finger on it. Then again, who am I to talk? Didn't I fall in love with Mandla at first sight? Despite our differences? Despite everything?

My excuse was that I refused to look a gift horse in the mouth. Hers was . . . well, she didn't need an excuse, did she?

She has more claim to him than I ever will. It doesn't matter how much I love him, or how unfair this all is. She's his mother and that's what it boils down to. She's his mother and children belong with their mother. Fucking illness is making me altruistic or forgiving or some other bullshit. I hope it passes as soon as I feel better.

"Have you given any thought to Zodwa coming back on Monday?" Dee asks now, reading my thoughts.

I've thought of nothing else. Still, Dee's been so worried lately and I hate seeing that crease cleave its way into her brow again so many months after Daniel's death. "It will all be fine," I assure her. I have nothing to base this on except the fact that it has to all work itself out. It just simply has to. "You know what the crazy thing is?"

"What?"

"I always believed that Mandla ending up on our doorstep was a sign from the universe that I was meant not only to be a mother but his mother specifically. But then, after what Zodwa said, I realized that it was because of you that Mandla came to us. Because Precious saw you and wanted you to have him." Dee looks skeptical and so I continue. "Think about it, Dee. You gave up a son and regretted it every day of your life. You don't think that what I thought was my sign was actually yours?"

She smiles sadly and shakes her head. "It may have been my chance encounter with Precious that got her to bring him here, but it was you pissing me off that day that got me out of the house at that exact time so that I'd run into her. What were the chances of that? And you forget the most important thing. That I didn't want him, Ruth. I didn't want to keep him. That was all you."

Her words are salve to a wound that I've been picking open over and over again. "Perhaps he was meant to be both of ours," I say.

She nods. "Not just ours but Zodwa's too. He was hers from the beginning and he should never have been taken away from her. Can you imagine what that must have been like for her?"

I nod. Someone is trying to take my son from me now. It's excruciating.

"You're the one who believes in signs, Ruth," Dee continues. "Read the signs now. All of them point to us all being in this together."

I nod again and the pain in my chest suddenly flares up, radiating outward. I must wince because Dee stands. "I'll let you get some rest."

I don't know why but I suddenly don't want her to go, which is just silly. I want to ask her to stay but instead I say, "There's something I never told you. About Da."

"About Da?"

"Yes. Before he died, he made me promise never to sell the farm."

"Really? How strange. He hated the farm and the whole farming life. I'm surprised that what Ma wanted even factored in to his thinking."

"He didn't want it kept for her. She actually wanted to sell it and retire to the coast."

"So, why then? Just to torment her and force her to stay somewhere she didn't want to be?"

"No, because of you."

"Me?"

"He promised you on the day you left that the key would always be waiting for you if you decided to come back. He wanted to keep that promise."

"Huh."

"I'm sorry that I almost broke it. I'm glad you forced us to keep the farm and that we're here together."

"Me too. Now, try and get a good night's rest."

"I will." She just gets to the door when I call her back. "Dee?"

"Yes?"

"I love you, you know. I'm not sure when I last told you but it's true. It's important that you know that."

She comes back to the bed and grasps my hand. "You're not dying, you silly goose. You just have pneumonia. And you're going to be very embarrassed when you're feeling better and remember this moment."

"Probably, so don't remind me."

"I won't." She smiles and kisses my knuckles. "Call me if you need anything."

"I will."

Dee doesn't say she loves me back but she doesn't need to. That's the thing about family: the truest things we say to each other are never in words.

CHAPTER EIGHTY-NINE

Zodwa

·☼·

3 August 1996
KwaZulu-Natal, South Africa

Zodwa stands next to the graves, one freshly filled and the other properly settled with a gravestone at its head.

Mother and son finally rest together, and Zodwa is overcome with emotion that this is something she's been able to do for Leleti. In a life of wrong choices and wrong turns, it feels good to have achieved something that would bring her mother peace. For despite whatever the truth of Dumisa's life is, Zodwa knows her mother's love would transcend the mistakes her child made. She can't imagine Mandla ever doing anything that could make her stop loving him.

"Come, my child," Zodwa's *gogo* says to her. "Let us go now."

The news about Dumisa has aged her *gogo* dramatically. When Zodwa sat her down and gently broke it to her, she'd clutched her chest as though the truth were an arrow through her heart. She'd broken down then, rocking back and forth as she wept, mourning not only her grandson but the death of the myth that had surrounded him. Zodwa's *gogo* no longer speaks of Dumisa in awed tones. She no longer speaks of him at all.

As they walk to the village, her grandmother squeezes her arm. "You are getting too thin, my child. Is everything all right?"

"It's just been a stressful few months since finding out about Dumisa."

Her *gogo* nods but won't be drawn into commenting about him. "But you're okay otherwise?"

"Yes, *gogo*. Everything is fine."

These lies have become second nature to Zodwa. She hasn't told her *gogo* about Mandla's existence or the disease they share. While she tells herself it's better this way, to let the old woman live in ignorance rather than having her worry about things she can do nothing about—especially after the news of Dumisa's betrayal devastated her so much—the deception eats away at her.

Perhaps her reluctance is as much from self-preservation as it is from altruism. For Zodwa, truth is a gift that should be bestowed generously and wholeheartedly, not dished out grudgingly in a piecemeal fashion, and so there can be no confession about Zodwa's son that does not include an admission of her own sexuality. And once her *gogo* sees Zodwa for who she is, she'll surely turn against her just as she turned against Dumisa.

Her grandmother and the greater community will see Zodwa's sexual orientation as even more reason for shame than Dumisa's behavior. They'll believe that what came afterward— the rape and infection—are fitting punishments for her crime of loving another woman, and how could Zodwa bear living with that? Knowing that the way she was born, which she has absolutely no control over, is considered far worse than treacherous decisions her brother willingly made for self gain?

Also, even if Zodwa were able to divulge just the morsels of truth that her *gogo* would find palatable, how could she separate the meat from the gristle? What purpose could be served by delighting her grandmother with news of a grandson only to add that he could die any day from the dreaded virus that Zodwa herself passed on to him? She couldn't bear to admit that she gave her son a death sentence before she ever gave him love.

This isn't where she's meant to be. Zodwa knows that now. Her place is back at the farm with Mandla and the sisters.

Despite everything that's happened, Zodwa can't help but think how lucky Mandla is to be loved so much that two women are prepared to fight over who keeps him. It brings to mind the Bible story of King Solomon and the judgment he'd made between two mothers who both claimed the same baby to be theirs. She wonders if there's a way to stop her son from being torn in two during their struggle, and if there isn't, will she be the one to make the sacrifice to keep him whole? Or does Ruth love him enough to do the same?

Mandla is the planet around which they all orbit. They are his satellites. They couldn't wrench themselves free of the gravity he exerts even if they wanted to.

CHAPTER NINETY

Ruth

❄

5 August 1996
Verdriet, Magaliesburg, South Africa

I didn't want Zodwa and me to be squaring off like this: me in bed like an invalid and her standing over me.

I imagined myself feeling strong and better able to deal with the power imbalance because, make no mistake, I may be the one with the money but Zodwa is holding all the cards. She's Mandla's biological mother and has every legal right to him. I'm just a woman who loves another woman's son to distraction; someone who stupidly thought she could lay claim to something that wasn't hers just because she wanted it.

When I said as much to Dee earlier, she wryly quipped, "You're not the first white person to do so and you certainly won't be the last." Then she sighed and said, "Cut yourself some slack. You've come a long way in the past two years, Ruth. I'm proud of you."

"Please, take a seat," I say, and Zodwa sits in the chair Dee put there for her. "Thanks for coming to see me."

As Zodwa fidgets with her watch, I'm grateful for her preoccupation because it gives me the opportunity to look at her unabashedly. She's so young, just a little over twenty, and yet she still looks like a girl. I can't help but think back to myself at the same age, knowing nothing and thinking I knew everything, but so much more carefree than she could ever possibly be.

I'm surprised to find how protective I am of Zodwa, how much grief and anger I feel on her behalf. When did I grow to love the girl? When did she begin to feel almost like a daughter to me? Was it when she saved Mandla's life the first time? Was it the second? Was it when she saved me from drowning or was it when she stood her ground raging at me to be a better a mother? I don't know, but in that analogy Mandla becomes like my grandson and that could surely work, couldn't it? If Zodwa allowed it? Without his having a grandmother, surely there's an opening there for me, somewhere I can slot myself into.

"How did the burial go?" I ask, and Zodwa looks up.

"It was fine."

"I'm sure it was incredibly difficult. I couldn't imagine having to bury Delilah and then . . . under those circumstances too . . ." I'm purposefully vague, not wanting to be insensitive.

She nods. "Yes, it was hard."

We're both quiet and I'm wondering how to break the ice and approach the discussion of Mandla when I decide to hell with tact and diplomacy. "Please don't go, Zodwa. Please, I'm begging you to stay." And then I'm crying, which is annoying because it hurts and makes it difficult to speak, but still I struggle on, trying to get it all out. "Please don't take him away. You can both live in the cottage, which we'll have fixed up for you, or we can add on to the house . . . we can do some renovations so we can all stay here together. Whatever you want. Please just say you'll stay."

Zodwa surprises me by getting up and coming to sit next to me on the bed. She reaches for my hand and holds it, probably feeling just as overwhelmed as I do. "I don't want my son growing up seeing me as the maid. That's not how I want him to remember me."

"You won't be the maid. Stay as our guest . . . more than our guest . . . our friend." I want to say *family* but just because she feels like a daughter and Mandla feels like my son doesn't make us a family. That's something that has to be earned. "We want so much for you to be a part of our lives and for us to be a part of yours."

"It's Mandla you want. Not me."

"That's not true." But I flush as I say it. "Look, I'm not going to lie. I was devastated when I found out you were Mandla's mother. I not only felt betrayed, but also like your being here undermined the relationship Mandla and I had. It was as if I'd just been playacting at being his mother because you'd been there as a safety net all along. Does that make sense?"

Zodwa nods and I'm encouraged to go on.

"But then, when I thought about it afterward, I realized how desperately I'd needed that safety net. I'd hoped that Dee would be that for me, but she didn't want Mandla here at first and so she wasn't any help at all. I needed you, Zodwa, but I didn't realize it. You were good for me and held me to a higher standard."

"I needed you to be a better mother to him."

"And I became a better mother, didn't I?"

She nods.

"Well, that was thanks to you."

"But we can't both be his mother."

And just like that we're at the crux of it. "No."

"Mandla cannot call you Mama anymore, Ruth." It's the first time she's called me by my name without prefacing it with *madam* and she looks at me with a challenge in her eyes. "I'm his mother."

"I know." Jesus, this is going to be tough. Tougher than I thought.

"He can call you Granny," she says, as though reading my thoughts from earlier. I swear there's an evil glint in her eye as she says it.

"God, no!" I gasp. "Do I really look that old to you?" She laughs, which is what I was hoping for. "Look, we'll figure it all out, okay? I promise you that we'll find a means to make it work in a way that you're happy with. Just let me recover and get my strength back and we can take it from there. Will you do that for me? Please just stay for now?"

She thinks for a minute and then nods. "How are you feeling?"

"Like shit, but thanks for asking."

"Delilah wants to take you back to the doctor. She says the medicine isn't working."

"I know. I said we could go tomorrow."

"Okay, I'll let you sleep." She stands and turns to go.

"Zodwa?"

"Yes?"

"Thank you."

And I mean it. I've never been more grateful for anything in my life.

CHAPTER NINETY-ONE

Delilah

❂

6 August 1996

Verdriet, Magaliesburg, South Africa

I'd just made Ruth a cup of herbal tea when the phone rang. It was Vince, calling to check on how she was doing.

"Not much better, I'm afraid. These antibiotics don't seem to be having any effect. I'm taking her to see a specialist this afternoon."

"Good. I don't trust small-town doctors, no offense. How's Mandla doing?"

"He's fine. I'm having to keep him away from her, so he's a bit crabby." I didn't add that Mandla had spent the night with Zodwa at the cottage. It was too unusual an arrangement for Vince not to comment on. Zodwa being Mandla's biological mother wasn't my news to share. "I'm about to give Ruth her pills. I'll let you know what the doctor says."

"Thanks, I appreciate it. Please tell her that I send my . . . regards."

"I will. Bye, Vince."

He said *regards* but it was clear he meant *love*. Considering how animated Ruth had been after returning from their lunch at Sun City a few months before, and how her voice softened whenever she spoke about him, it was obvious that she still loved him. His concern for her while she was ill, as well as the fact that he'd rushed to her side as soon as I'd told him about Mandla's illness, made me think he hadn't gotten over her either. I was hopeful for a reconciliation and thought about planting a few seeds to get her thinking about it. Sometimes people needed a gentle nudge to get them going in the right direction.

Jezebel was at Ruth's door, whining to be let in. She was more agitated than usual and I told her to settle down as I picked up Ruth's mug of tea and her antibiotics, carrying them to her door. "Ruth?" Hearing no reply, I knocked. When she still didn't answer, I opened the door, careful not to make too much noise in case she was still sleeping.

But she wasn't sleeping.

Jezebel rushed inside and stood over Ruth, who lay face-down on the carpet, one arm stretched out toward the door. I dropped the mug then, hot liquid splashing against my shins as it shattered, and I ran through the debris to get to her.

"Ruth!"

For a second, I thought that Ruth was passed out. She'd had one bad night when she'd fallen off the wagon just after Zodwa told us the news, getting hideously drunk while Mandla slept. I'd prepared a speech and been ready to lay down the law the next morning, but she'd come through to the kitchen contrite, promising it would never happen again.

Please let it have happened again.

But even as I bent over her, gently shaking her to try to wake her, I knew that wasn't it.

My sister was cold to the touch and didn't flinch or react at all when Jezebel licked her ear. As I rolled Ruth over, she gazed vacantly up at the ceiling, her eyes having lost all their light.

CHAPTER NINETY-TWO

Zodwa

6 August 1996
Verdriet, Magaliesburg, South Africa

Z odwa is exhausted but exhilarated. Sunday's long commute back from Ulundi and yesterday's emotionally draining talk with Ruth were tiring enough, but then Mandla had also kept her up most of last night, tossing and turning in their shared bed in the cottage. Still, having him there with her is the first step in the right direction and more than she dared hope for so soon after arriving back.

She gets dressed and puts Mandla's gown and slippers on before they begin walking hand in hand to the farmhouse. The dirt road stretches out before them and the August winds whip the dust into Mandla's face. Zodwa bends to pick him up, cradling him to her breast so as to shield him.

"Mama," Mandla says, and Zodwa smiles before realizing that he's squirming away, stretching his arms out toward the house and Ruth. "Where's Mama, Dwa?"

"Ruth is sick in bed, my boy."

"I want Mama." He wriggles away from Zodwa and she puts him down again.

She has to swallow past the lump in her throat to reassure him. "We're almost there. You'll see Ruth now."

Still, he runs ahead and she watches as he disappears

through the door, which Delilah must have left open for Jez-ebel. When Zodwa steps inside, Mandla is standing at the threshold to Ruth's room. He has two fingers inside his mouth, and sucks on them.

"Lilah?" he asks around his hand.

"Stay back, Mandla. Don't come in here." Delilah speaks from inside the room. They're trying to keep Mandla away from Ruth so he doesn't get sick.

"Your foot sore?" he asks.

"No, Mandla," Delilah says. "My heart is sore." And that's when Zodwa realizes that Delilah is crying.

Before Zodwa can pick Mandla up, he runs into the room and she calls out to him, "Mandla, no! Come back here."

But he doesn't listen. He's running through shards of what looks like a broken mug, toward Delilah, who sits on the floor cradling Ruth's head in her lap. Jezebel sits whining next to them. Ruth is deathly pale and isn't moving, and Delilah weeps silently. She has a bad cut on her foot that's bleeding.

Zodwa tries to speak to ask what happened but finds that she can't, as a vision comes to her of her own mother lying im-mobile on the floor of the shack.

Mandla sits down next to Delilah and reaches out a hand to run it over Ruth's face. "Mama sleeping?"

"Yes, my boy," Delilah says. "Mama's sleeping."

He leans over then and kisses Ruth on the cheek. "Night. Sleep tight. Don't let bedbugs bite." It's what Ruth always says to him before she puts him to bed.

Delilah reaches out her hand to draw Mandla in against her, kissing the top of his head as she rocks back and forth. And then she beckons for Zodwa to join them.

CHAPTER NINETY-THREE

Delilah

※

6 August 1997
Verdriet, Magaliesburg, South Africa

I didn't know how it was possible but a whole year had somehow passed since Ruth left us. Not a day had gone by without my missing her with an ache so fierce it felt like a rock lodged beneath my breastbone.

It felt so strange at first knowing a secret about Ruth that she never even knew, one that if revealed to her would have changed her entire perception of herself. All those miscarriages were a genetic inevitability and her repeated attempts to conceive were futile. She would never have been able to carry a baby to term for the same reason that a pulmonary embolism misdiagnosed as pneumonia had killed her.

Ruth had a genetic mutation called Factor V Leiden, which was only revealed in the autopsy. It's probably what killed Da too though we never knew it then; we just thought he'd had a heart attack. The gene gave Ruth a much higher risk of developing blood clots and of having miscarriages.

Ruth could have been saved if only we'd known. A blood thinner instead of antibiotics would have broken down the clot. If only I hadn't called that ancient town doctor to see her. If only I'd insisted on putting Ruth in the car and taking her to a

413

specialist in Joburg earlier. If only she hadn't been on bed rest, which just made the clotting worse.

If only. If only. If only. Life spun on an axis of regret.

I couldn't help but wonder if Ruth had a premonition of her death or saw some sign; she was always so good at recognizing them. It couldn't be a coincidence that she made her first will a mere six months before she died. It's as if she knew what Zodwa would one day need and selflessly provided it. Didn't sound like Ruth, though, did it? Selfless, my ass.

Zodwa was surprised by the provision Ruth had made for her in her will but she shouldn't have been. After all, Zodwa saved Mandla's life more than once and Ruth was more grateful for that than she was ever able to express. Vince invested the money so that it could continue paying for Zodwa's antiretroviral therapy. She'd started it six months before and had picked up some weight, which was probably Ruth's revenge; she never liked living among such skinny women. I wish it had all been smooth sailing since then, but Zodwa had good days and bad days, with the side effects from the ARVs sometimes being worse than the disease itself. It was a waiting game but we hoped for the best. At least she wasn't alone.

Jezebel continued to pine for Ruth. She walked from room to room searching for her and it was the most pitiful sight in the world. Jez still protected Mandla fiercely and was always just a split second behind him, like his shadow. Zodwa told me that's what Jez's name had been when she still belonged to her mother. Precious named her in honor of my own childhood dog, who she must have thought of when she adopted her.

Jez had also taken up where Ruth had left off all those years ago, spying on me when I prayed. I didn't do it on my knees next to the bed anymore, which was just as well. I suspected Jez would hop up on the mattress while I was busy and lick me in the face. Now that I thought about it, I was surprised Ruth had never done the same.

Ruth would be so happy to know that her boy continued to thrive. His beauty astounded me, as did his quick mind and easy nature. He did her proud every single day, and still sometimes called her Mama when we went through the photo albums and he saw pictures of her. How lucky they were to have each other despite how fleeting their time together was. Perhaps Ruth's love for Mandla was so fierce because she always suspected how temporary their union would be.

Ruth left most of her money to Mandla in a trust and stipulated in her will that I should oversee it as Mandla's guardian in the event of her death, but she wrote it before we knew the truth about Zodwa. She had asked me to legally adopt him but I couldn't do that. Not with Zodwa being his mother and with her living with us in the farmhouse. We were all seeing a family therapist to try to figure things out. One of the last things Ruth said to me was that it would all be fine and I believed her. It would be.

There was an article in that day's paper commemorating the one-year anniversary of Ruth's death. It was a small article, but still . . . she was being remembered. All the press she got after she died would have made her insufferable. She always did like attention. I'd made another two collages from all those tributes to "South Africa's Wild Child" and they hung next to the one I made her for Christmas. Mandla was most impressed with the picture of a clothed Ruth with the snake.

Vince insisted on funding Mandla's ARVs and he visited regularly from Cape Town to check on him. I'd never seen a man more crushed or more filled with regret. However evolved Ruth had become in the last year of her life, I knew there was a small part of her that would have been happy to know that Vince was suffering. He refused to listen to any suggestion of his moving on, which was understandable. Ruth was one hell of a tough act to follow. It was harder for him because he thought she was truly gone; he didn't see her as often as I did because he wasn't looking for the signs like I was. My sister had taught me well.

She was the red butterfly matching the exact shade of her favorite Dior lipstick, that settled on Zodwa's wrist as she sat in court to testify against the Coetzee brothers before they were sentenced to twelve years in prison. She was Jezebel's wet snout against my leg when I heard that the canned-lion-hunting operation had fallen through and we no longer had to live under the constant threat of persecution. She was the voice whispering, and then yelling, that it was time to finally allow Riaan to love me. She was the anger that fueled me to drive to Johannesburg last month, and the courage that fortified me, when I finally confronted Father Thomas after all those years.

Ruth was there with me when I rang the doorbell that day, and I felt her holding my shaking legs up when I didn't back down in my condemnation of him, not even when Father Thomas started raging, and then still not when he started weeping. Ruth was there when I called it "rape" and knew it to be true, finally laying that burden down to free up my hands so I could embrace the future.

I'm going to be brave today, Ruth. For you.

I pulled my reading glasses and the envelope from my bag, inhaling deeply as I did so in order to steel my nerves. Jezebel huffed reassuringly, leaning in to my leg as though to remind me of the promise of bravery I'd just made.

Have courage, she said, and of course she was right.

I opened the envelope with trembling fingers and unfolded the pages inside, beginning to read the words that were written to me almost three and a half years before.

8 April 1994

Dearest Delilah,

This letter may come as a complete surprise to you or it may be one that you've been waiting thirty-eight years for. Regardless, I hope that its arrival is a welcome one and that I'm not imposing on you as that's the last thing I would ever want. If you choose not to reply, I will respect that completely.

Where to begin? With an introduction, I suppose. My name is Father Daniel Da Silva and I am your son. How strange it feels to write that, yet how wonderful too, to claim you: you are my mother.

I suspected for many years that the young nun, Sister Mary Teresa, who was excommunicated from the convent where I grew up was you, but it was only recently confirmed. Still, even after learning this, I may not have tried to reach out had I not discovered my father's identity and come to suspect the circumstances surrounding my conception.

Let me start by saying that I had a wonderful childhood. I was coddled and spoiled more than a child raised in a convent ever should be. Sister Marguerite, who you may remember, has served as my surrogate mother and I've wanted for absolutely nothing over the years: not love, affection, moral guidance, or material things.

While I was growing up, I viewed Father Thomas Da Silva as a father figure. I was given his last name, and I can't remember a time that he wasn't a part of my life. I worshipped him as a child

417

•

and it was his influence that led me to the seminary. Being a priest like him was all I ever wanted to be. So, you can imagine how shocked I was two years ago to hear of the allegations the young congregants made against him.

I'm ashamed to admit that I didn't believe them at first, because Father Thomas immediately went on the attack, vehemently denying their version of events. He further went on to use personal information that they'd confided in him in order to discredit them. It was only once I planned to speak out in his defense at his request that Sister Marguerite shared her own experiences with him and what she suspected your similar experience may have been.

It was devastating discovering that the man I idolized, and had tried so much to emulate, was a monster. As was finding out that I had been conceived by such a violent act of treachery. I cannot even begin to imagine how devastating it must have been for you, being a young woman on your own, wanting to dedicate your life to God and being so terribly betrayed by both Father Thomas and the church.

I want you to know that I don't blame you for leaving me. You were frightened and alone, and had all choice taken from you. I know you were threatened and that Father Thomas used his considerable influence to keep me with him while excommunicating you.

I went in search of you last month after Sister Marguerite gave me your last-known address before you left for the convent. I knew it was a long shot, but there was always a chance that you may have returned. At the very least, I hoped to find family there but as you know, they are all long gone.

My only hope now of making contact is through this letter. I hope that it somehow makes its way to you and that you would consider writing back. While it's true that I had an idyllic childhood, I always felt as though something were missing. Is it possible to miss something you never had? To yearn for and love someone you've never met?

I believe so.

It would mean so much to me if we could have a relationship. I hope you will consider it.

Your son,

Daniel

I couldn't help it then, I broke down. I'd never had the chance to know him, neither as a child nor as an adult, and I would have given everything to go back in time and change that. He'd grown into a kind man, a compassionate priest, and I could claim no responsibility for that, as I'd had no hand at all in shaping the person he'd become.

And even as I wept for Daniel, I cried, too, for all that I'd lost besides him: my girlhood, my innocence, my vocation, and my God. Looking back on my life, I had almost nothing but regrets. I finally understood that I hadn't had any control over what Father Thomas did to me or what followed with the church, but I'd chosen to excommunicate myself from my own life as a form of punishment, flagellating myself with guilt to the point where nothing else existed beyond that corrosive emotion.

It was too late for Daniel and me, but he'd given me the gift I'd sought my entire life: forgiveness and absolution. He hadn't blamed me or hated me. My son, despite everything, had somehow seen me as worthy of love. What more could any of us ever ask for?

CHAPTER NINETY-FOUR

Zodwa

❊

6 *August 1997*
Verdriet, Magaliesburg, South Africa

Zodwa wakes to find the single bed next to hers empty. She gets up and goes to the lounge, rubbing sleep from her eyes as she does so. Mandla is sitting on the couch watching television. He's too transfixed by the flickering light and colors to notice her as he drinks from a sippy cup, but Thembeka immediately rushes over to Zodwa from the kitchen, where she's been making tea.

Thembeka places her palm against Zodwa's brow. "You feel cooler."

Zodwa has been having night sweats. It necessitated bringing back the sisters' two single beds from Delilah's old room to replace the queen bed because Thembeka can't sleep when Zodwa is thrashing around. Thembeka kisses her cheek and Zodwa closes her eyes to savor the softness of it. As long as she lives, she'll never get used to the sensation of Thembeka's lips against her skin.

As long as she lives.

Who knows how long that will be? There are days when Zodwa feels like she'll live forever and then ones where the ticking of the clock feels like a countdown to her last breath, days she feels so terrible that she'd almost welcome death if it was merciful enough to come for her.

She hasn't responded to the ARVs the way Mandla has; apparently adults have a harder time on the meds than children do. Still, she's grateful that Thembeka was spared contracting the virus. The thought of having sex with a man was so distasteful to her that she'd told Mongezi she wouldn't have sex before marriage, knowing full well he had no intention of marrying her. It was this that saved her.

There are many who are not as lucky, and the news from the squatter camp is bleak. Dozens of their mutual friends have either passed away or are dying slow, painful deaths as their bodies are ravaged by opportunistic infections. The fear surrounding the disease has intensified to the point that no one dares disclose their status for fear of persecution. Those who are close to the end, and cannot hide their condition even if they tried, have been threatened by lynch mobs and even dragged from their homes.

Mama Beauty reports that she fears an entire generation is systematically being wiped out, leaving behind orphans to be raised by women like her: mothers in their golden years whose children should be taking care of them, but who are now raising their grandchildren as they helplessly watch their children die, one by one.

Zodwa pulls Thembeka even closer, grateful for her vitality. "Where's Delilah?" Zodwa asks once they part.

"It's the anniversary," Thembeka reminds her. "She took Ruth's ashes on a hike and said not to wait for her for breakfast."

A whole year.

How has it been that long since Zodwa came inside and saw

Delilah's stricken face? Then again, what's a year when so much has changed in the past four years since Zodwa was raped? She thinks back to the day she went to see the *nyanga* so that she could change her fate. How naïve she was to think that such a thing was possible.

Zodwa remembers the dream the healer asked her about, the one that had woken her from her sleep and made her decide to see the healer in the first place.

What did you dream the last time you slept?

I dreamt I was being chased.

By what?

Two white owls. Their wingspan stretched across the sky, blocking out the sun.

And then what happened?

I thought they were going to kill me, but it wasn't me they wanted.

What then?

The baby. They snatched it from me and flew away.

Zodwa knows now that the two white owls were Ruth and Delilah, and that they took Mandla not to harm him but to try to save him after Leleti left him with them. She knows too that there is no such thing as curses; they're just self-inflicted prisons that only have power over us as long as we believe in them. Our luck is what we make of it and all we can ever do is make the most of the time we have.

Zodwa can't help but think how cruel the world can be that it could give a child two women who would do anything to mother him and then take both of them away, allowing neither one the opportunity to raise him. Yet before all the loss comes all the love, and if heartbreak is the cost for loving as much as we do, then it's a price Zodwa's willing to pay.

"Mama!"

Zodwa turns to find Mandla standing on the couch waving at her. His smile is so beautiful she wants to cry. Instead, she walks over to him and picks him up. "My son. My little man," she says, kissing him all over.

He squeals and then kisses her back, blowing a raspberry against Zodwa's cheek as Delilah taught him. And in those few seconds, it doesn't matter that Zodwa is dying or that Mandla is sick. It doesn't matter that their entire lives and all their struggles amount to less than the blink of an eye in the greater scheme of things.

What matters in that brief wondrous moment is that they are there at all and that their hearts beat in proximity to each other. Each day is a blessing; each breath of air, a gift. Zodwa doesn't know how many of them she has left. All she knows is that she will fill them by trying to equip her son for a time when she'll no longer be there.

She will love him so completely that love is all he remembers even after loss is all he knows. She can only hope that it will be enough.

ACKNOWLEDGMENTS

While it's true that writing is a solitary endeavor, it takes a supremely kick-ass team to get a book published. All my time spent alone talking to (and arguing/laughing/crying with) my imaginary friends wouldn't have been possible without a wonderfully supportive tribe.

My first thanks go to the brilliant Kerri Kolen, who saw enough potential in three sample chapters to allow me to write this novel. I'm incredibly grateful to her for not only giving my first book a home, but for allowing me to continue doing what I love best. She's the best fairy godmother a writer could have.

Then, a great big thank-you goes to my amazing publisher, Putnam. I'm so proud to be a part of the Putnam family and can't believe how lucky I am to have such incredible people in my corner. Thank you to Danielle Dieterich, my wonderful editor, who took a mess of a first draft and shaped it into something I'm incredibly proud of. Her insight and guidance were invaluable and it was an absolute joy working with her.

I am forever indebted to: Ivan Held, Christine Ball, Sally Kim, Alexis Welby, Ashley Pattison McClay, Lauren Monaco, Emily Ollis, Madeline Schmitz, Brennin Cummings, as well as the Design and Production departments, my copy editor, Chandra Wohleber, all the Penguin Random House Sales consultants, the Foreign Rights division, and everyone else who had a hand in bringing this book to life and then distributing it.

Katie McKee is the best PR person an author could ever wish for. Seriously, the world would be an infinitely better and kinder place if Katie were in charge of running it. Katie for president! Jordan Aaronson is an absolute delight and I'm so grateful to her for being such an amazing champion and for all her hard work. Thanks to Kaitlin Kall for designing another fabulous cover. Thanks as well to my awesome Penguin Random House Canadian team: Bonnie Maitland, Christina Vecchiato, Sam Church (Ruinsky), and Emma Ingram just to name a few.

Booksellers, librarians, book bloggers, and bookstagrammers are some of my favorite people, and I couldn't do what I do without their amazing support. Their passion for reading ensures that books find their way into the right hands, and I can't thank them enough for that or for being such a wonderfully supportive community. Thanks especially to Scott Pardon and Courtney Calder for all their phenomenal cheerleading.

A great big thank-you goes to my phenomenal agent, Cassandra Rogers of The Rights Factory, for never giving up on me, and for all that she does to make my career possible. Thanks as well to Olga Filina for her great big heart and excellent editorial brain. I can't sing Cass's and Olga's praises loudly enough.

Thanks to Melusi Tshabalala of "Melusi's Everyday Zulu" fame for being a superb sensitivity reader and helping me get the Zulu language and culture right. Follow him on Facebook and buy his hilarious and educational book—you won't be sorry that you did! Thanks to Shayne Broomberg and Brett Uys for their technical advice with regards to farming, generators, and power stations. Thanks to Walter G. Speirs for answering questions about Scottish dialect; Tracey du Preez and Maureen Mokoena for answering medical questions; Izak Furstenburg for helping with Afrikaans translations; Liezel

Klopper and Lynne Harrison for farming-life information; and Danielle De Grooth for designing a kick-ass map. All mistakes were my own!

I'm so lucky to have the best writing groups a writer could ask for. Thank you to Lisa Rivers, Kath Jonathan, Jenny Prior, Caroline Gill, Emily Murray, Susie Whelehan, and Suzy Dugard for sharing so generously, championing so passionately, and pouring the wine when all else fails. I cannot overstate how invaluable their feedback is or what an integral part of my writing process they are. Lisa, thank you especially for all the parties you've thrown for me and for your brilliant editorial contributions. You are an angel.

I have been blessed with so many wonderful friends and such an amazing family that it's impossible to thank them all individually. Their endless support and encouragement have meant more to me than they could ever know, and I can only hope that I've expressed my gratitude to each of them for being a part of my life and for brightening my days. Leana Marais, thank you for buying enough copies of *Hum If You Don't Know the Words* to sink a battleship. To my nieces, nephews, and godchildren, thank you for not being too embarrassed by me and for constantly rearranging bookshelves so my books are always front and center. Charmaine Shepherd, you remain both my rock and my guiding light; my kindred spirit and my hero.

Thank you to everyone in my life for buying countless books and then forcing them on everyone they know, and for always coming out in support at book fairs, readings, events, and bookstores.

I am so grateful to my readers and to book clubs who have been so gracious and kind, and who have welcomed me into their homes either in person or virtually. It's such a joy to get to speak with fellow readers and to listen to their feedback and brilliant insights. I write to make sense of my world, but it's my readers who teach me the most about my work! I can be reached at bianca.bookclub@gmail.com to set up a book club Skype appointment.

Thanks to Muggle for taking me on regular walks and to Wombat for all the "acupuncture."

Finally, my biggest thanks goes to my husband, Stephen, who doesn't allow me to take anything too seriously and whose favorite joke reflects his general silliness: "You know how when you see ducks flying in a 'V,' how the one side of the 'V' is always longer than the other? Do you know why that is? It's because there are more ducks on that side."

Thanks for always making me laugh, Poodle, and for being you.

Glossary of Terms

African National Congress (ANC): a political party banned during apartheid; the ruling party of South Africa since 1994, when Nelson Mandela was elected president

Afrikaans: a language derived from the form of Dutch brought to the Cape by white settlers from Holland in the seventeenth century

Afrikaner: an Afrikaans-speaking South African with European ancestry, generally descended from the Dutch/French Huguenot settlers of the seventeenth century

Afrikaner Weerstandsbeweging (AWB): a South African neo-Nazi separatist political and paramilitary organization

Amadlozi: (Zulu) the ancestors

Babygro: an infant bodysuit, onesie

Bakkie: (Afrikaans) pickup truck, utility truck

Boer: (Afrikaans) a farmer/proud Afrikaner

Boerekos: (Afrikaans) Afrikaner/farmer food

Borehole: a deep hole bored into the ground to locate water

Bushveld: open, uncultivated land of South Africa, abundant shrubby, or thorny vegetation

Dassies: (Afrikaans) a rock hyrax (mammal) of Southern Africa

Doek: a square piece of cloth like a scarf worn by African women to cover their head

Dominee: (Afrikaans) preacher, minister

GOGO/UGOGO: (various African languages) granny

HHAYI: (Zulu) stop, no

HINJA: (Zulu) dog

IBHAYI: (Zulu) animal skin or material worn by healers

INKATHA FREEDOM PARTY (IFP): a right-wing political party in South Africa that has been led, since its founding, by Mangosuthu Buthelezi

IZINYANGA: (Zulu) plural: healers

JIRRE: (Afrikaans slang) "Jesus"; exclamation of surprise or shock

KAFFIR: an offensive and contemptuous term for a black person

KAFFIR-BOETIE: translates to "kaffir brother"; a term for a white person who fraternizes with black people or sympathizes with their cause

KAK: (Afrikaans) shit

KNOBKERRIE: (Afrikaans) walking stick

KOTA: township or street food; quarter loaf of bread hollowed out and filled mostly with chips, meat, and gravy

KWAAI: (Afrikaans slang) "cool"

KWAITO: a music genre that emerged in Johannesburg in the 1990s. Variant of house music, most popular with black South African youth.

LOBOLO: (Zulu) bride price

MAHEWU: (Zulu) fermented liquid mealie-meal porridge

MEVROU: (Afrikaans) missus

MIELIES: (Afrikaans) corn cob, sweet corn

MIESIE: (Afrikaans) missus

MLUNGU/UMLUNGU: (Xhosa, Zulu) a white person

MOROGO: wild spinach

Mpepho/impepho: (Zulu) sage

Mzukulu wami: (Zulu) "my granddaughter"

Nappy: a diaper

Ndumba/indumba: (Zulu) a healing hut

Nog: (Afrikaans) another

Nyanga/inyanga: (Zulu) a healer

Pantsula: petty gangster

Pap: a traditional South African dish made from ground maize that is then cooked with water

Polony: processed meat

Regtig: (Afrikaans) really, truly

Rooibos: translates to "red bush"; a South African tea

Sangoma/isangoma: (Zulu) a witch doctor, healer, traditional healer

Sawubona: (Zulu) "hello" or "good day"

Seshoeshoe: a printed, dyed cotton fabric widely used in traditional clothing in South Africa

Shebeen: an illicit African bar or nightclub where alcohol is served without a license

Shosholoza: a Nguni song that was sung by the mixed tribes of gold and diamond mine workers in South Africa

Sisi: (Xhosa) sister

Slap chips: South African version of French fries with bigger and thicker cut potatoes that are still soft inside after frying

Slet: (Afrikaans) slut

Takkies: (Afrikaans) sneakers

Tuisnywerhuids: (Afrikaans) home-industry business

U: IsiZulu article, similar to "the"

Umuthi: (Zulu) medicine, herbal medicine

UNDLELA ZIMHLOPHE: (Xhosa) African dream root plant used for vivid dreams

UNJANI: (Zulu) "How are you?"

VOORKAMER: (Afrikaans) translates to "front room"; a formal lounge for guests

YOH: (black South African) exclamation of surprise, shock, or sympathy

Author's Note

The canned-lion-hunting industry is unfortunately not a product of my imagination. While South Africa is a beautiful tourist destination that I wholeheartedly encourage everyone to visit, please think twice before cuddling, petting, or volunteering with lions or their cubs.

Very few of the private lion parks or predator breeding facilities in South Africa can be considered to be genuine conservation undertakings, as they breed predators for a variety of commercial purposes, like canned-lion hunting, where tame or captive-bred predators are shot in confined areas.

There is no conservation value in captive-bred lions, since none of them have ever been successfully reintroduced into the wild, and yet this industry attracts thousands of misguided volunteers from across the world who contribute in excess of $100,000 a month to it.

Very few, if any, of the lion cubs that tourists and volunteers get to pet or cuddle have been abandoned in the wild; they are simply getting the cubs used to humans so that they lose all fear, which makes them easier to shoot.

If you would like to learn more about this industry, there is an excellent documentary called *Blood Lions* that I recommend watching. The website is www.bloodlions.org. Please consider contributing to their very worthy cause.

. . .

The AIDS pandemic in South Africa in the late '90s and early 2000s was devastating. The then–South African president, Thabo Mbeki, went on record stating that "a virus cannot cause a syndrome" (implying HIV cannot cause AIDs), and his AIDs denialism had catastrophic consequences, with more than 300,000 South Africans dying.

The people worst hit by the pandemic were women and children. Besides the thousands that passed away, it fell to the women who remained (many of them grandmothers who were living in desperate poverty) to care for the HIV-positive orphans left in the wake of the crisis.

I first heard about the Stephen Lewis Foundation during my years of volunteering in Soweto. Their support of the grannies/ *gogos* of South Africa through their Grandmother to Grandmothers Campaign has been life-changing for many of these women, and I am indebted to them for what they and their volunteers have already done, and continue to do, for my countrywomen.

Please visit them at www.stephenlewisfoundation.org and consider contributing to their brilliant cause.

Mandla's story was inspired by Nkosi Johnson, a child living with AIDS in South Africa, who passed away at the age of twelve in 2001. Nkosi was legally adopted by a white woman, Gail Johnson, when his own mother, Nonthlanthla Daphne Nkosi, became too ill to care for him. Nkosi's activism inspired me to volunteer with HIV-positive children and his story is both heartbreaking and incredibly uplifting. *We Are All the Same: A Story of a Boy's Courage and A Mother's Love* by Jim Wooten is a must-read.

The character of Ruth was inspired by a real South African woman, Glenda Kemp, who began stripping in the early 1970s with her pet python, "Oupa." Her book, *Glenda Kemp: Snake Dancer*, is an interesting read.

I first became aware of Factor V Leiden when my brother-in-law, Louis Marais, passed away from a pulmonary embolism at the age of thirty-nine in 2007. It was only after Louis's death that the family became aware of the genetic mutation and had everyone tested for it. I firmly believe that Louis saved the lives of his brothers and father, who now know their risk factors and medicate accordingly, and I wanted to pay tribute to him in the writing of this story. I know that Louis would have loved Ruth just as she would have adored him.

The area where Riaan van Tonder volunteers in the novel has since been named the Cradle of Humankind. It was declared a World Heritage site by UNESCO in 1999 and is a fascinating part of the country to visit.

You can find out more information at www.thecradleof humankind.net.